"Let's see her face," Baldwin said. "Simon, come on. Help me move her."

The bailiff gave an unwilling grimace. This was the part he loathed, the first shock of seeing the corpse, of seeing the wound that killed. Sighing, he tentatively took hold of the body by the hips while Baldwin carefully moved up, taking the shoulders and rolling her over. He suddenly pulled back and exclaimed, "God!"

"What?" said Simon, nervously shooting him a glance.

Baldwin stared back, his shock slowly giving way to a quickening interest. "I'm not surprised Cottey was upset! He was right when he said the throat was cut—her head's almost off her shoulders!"

Although he tried to avert his eyes, Simon found that they kept returning to the hideous wound, and his belly began to feel like a cauldron of stew on a fire, bubbling and thickening. "I saw this woman on Saturday," he said softly. "I didn't know her name then. She was just some old woman on the road. Sad, isn't it?"

"That's not the point, though Simon," the knight replied. "Sad it may be, but there's something wrong here. Can't you see? She had her throat cut. She must have bled like a stuck pig. So where's the blood? Eh?"

Books by Michael Jecks

THE TOLLS OF DEATH
THE OUTLAWS OF ENNOR
THE TEMPLAR'S PENANCE
THE MAD MONK OF GIDLEIGH
THE DEVIL'S ACOLYTE
THE STICKLEPATH STRANGLER
THE TOURNAMENT OF BLOOD
THE BOY-BISHOP'S GLOVEMAKER
THE TRAITOR OF ST GILES
BELLADONNA AT BELSTONE
SQUIRE THROWLEIGH'S HEIR
THE LEPER'S RETURN
THE ABBOT'S GIBBET
THE CREDITON KILLINGS
A MOORLAND HANGING
THE MERCHANT'S PARTNER
THE LAST TEMPLAR

ATTENTION: ORGANIZATIONS AND CORPORATIONS
Most Avon Books paperbacks are available at special quantity discounts for bulk purchases for sales promotions, premiums, or fund-raising. For information, please call or write:

Special Markets Department, HarperCollins Publishers, Inc., 10 East 53rd Street, New York, N.Y. 10022–5299.
Telephone: (212) 207–7528. Fax: (212) 207–7222.

The Merchant's Partner

A Knights Templar Mystery

MICHAEL JECKS

AVON BOOKS

An Imprint of HarperCollinsPublishers

This is a work of fiction. Names, characters, places, and incidents are products of the author's imagination or are used fictitiously and are not to be construed as real. Any resemblance to actual events, locales, organizations, or persons, living or dead, is entirely coincidental.

AVON BOOKS
An Imprint of HarperCollins*Publishers*
10 East 53rd Street
New York, New York 10022-5299

Copyright © 1995 by Michael Jecks
ISBN: 0-06-076346-9
www.avonmystery.com

All rights reserved. No part of this book may be used or reproduced in any manner whatsoever without written permission, except in the case of brief quotations embodied in critical articles and reviews. For information address Avon Books, an Imprint of HarperCollins Publishers.

First Avon Books paperback printing: January 2005

Avon Trademark Reg. U.S. Pat. Off. and in Other Countries, Marca Registrada, Hecho en U.S.A.
HarperCollins ® is a trademark of HarperCollins Publishers Inc.

Printed in the U.S.A.

10 9 8 7 6 5 4 3 2 1

If you purchased this book without a cover, you should be aware that this book is stolen property. It was reported as "unsold and destroyed" to the publisher, and neither the author nor the publisher has received any payment for this "stripped book."

*This book is for
Peter, Sarah,
Brill and Clive.*

*Thanks for your support and loyalty,
and for always having confidence.*

—

The Merchant's Partner

- 1 -

It was not until much later, when winter had relaxed its grip and spring had touched the land with the fresh, yellow-green shades of renewal, that the feelings of horror and revulsion began to fade.

The knight knew full well that they were not gone entirely but merely superseded for a time by the pragmatic concerns of the villagers. The beginning of a new year forced the killings out of people's minds. Everyone was too busy for contemplation, preparing the fields and making use of the increasing daylight. But the murders had been committed late in the winter, and the long, cold evenings had given time for the storytellers to reflect and embellish. With their faces lighted by the angry red glow at the fireside, the families thrilled to hear about them time and again.

He could not grudge the people their fascination with the murders—it was only natural in such a quiet, rural shire. Devon was not the same as other parts of the kingdom, where people lived in continual anxiety. On the northern marches men feared more attacks from the Scottish raiders, while at the coast people were terrified of raids by the French pirates. Here the only concern was the possibility of a third failed harvest.

No, it was not surprising that the people looked to a story like that of the murdered witch to enliven their evenings, not surprising that every man had his own opinion of the truth behind the killings, or that some now lived in fear of her ghost in case she sought revenge on the village where she had been killed.

Thinking back now, he was not sure when it all began. It was surely not the day when Tanner called, the Wednesday morning when he first saw the body with his friend the bailiff. It was before, maybe on the Saturday, when he was out hunting and saw the women for the first time. The morning he spent falconing with the rector of Crediton.

"It's bitter, isn't it," said Peter Clifford again.

Without looking at him, Baldwin grinned. His concentration was focused on the slender figure clutching at his gloved fist, admiring her slate-colored back and black-barred white chest. She sat like a high-born Syrian woman, he thought. Confident, strong and elegant, not thick and heavy like a peasant, but slim and quick. Even as he gazed at her, the head under the hood turned to face him as if hearing his thoughts, the yellow, wickedly hooked beak still and controlled. It was not threatening, but she was asserting her independence, knowing she could take her freedom when she wished: she was no dog, no devoted servant—and like all falconers, he knew it.

The priest's words broke in on his meditation and, giving a wry smile, he turned back to the rector of the church at Crediton, the corners of his mouth lifting under the narrow black moustache. "Sorry, Peter. Are you cold?" he asked mildly.

"Cold?" Peter Clifford's face appeared almost blue in the chill of the early morning as he squinted at his companion. "How could I feel cold in this glorious weather? I may not be a knight, I may be used to sitting in a warm hall with a fire blazing at this time of year, I may be thin and older than you, I may be sorely in need of a pint of mulled beer, but that does not mean I feel the bitterness of this wind that cuts through my tunic like a battleaxe through butter."

Baldwin laughed and looked around at the land. They had left the forests behind and now were on open, bleak moorland. The weak winter sunshine had not yet cleared the damp mists from the ground, and their horses' hooves seemed almost to be wading in the thick dew underfoot. Bracken and heather covered the hill and shimmered under the grayness.

They had left early, almost as dawn broke, to get here. Baldwin had rescued the peregrine as a young and vicious juvenile in the previous year and Peter had not yet witnessed the bird hunting, so the knight had eagerly agreed to bring her and show off her skill. For him it was a pure delight to watch the creature climb, only to float, high and silent, almost as if she was as light as a piece of wood ash.

This was ideal land for falcons, up here on the moor, away from the woods. Shorter in the wing, hawks were better at chasing their prey and were used by their astringers to hunt among trees or other cramped areas. The falconer used his long-winged birds on open land where they could rise quickly, soaring up to their pitch and staying there, touring above their targets until they stooped down like a falling arrow, rarely missing their mark.

Shrugging himself deeper under his cloak, Peter

Clifford grimaced to himself as they rode along. Last night he had thought it would be pleasant to go hunting, after their meal and with plenty of Sir Baldwin's good Bordeaux wine inside him, heated by the great fire while they chatted of the latest Scottish attacks to the north. Then he had envisioned a warm day, the sky a perfect blue, the hawk swooping on to her targets . . . He glowered. Now he felt only cold: cold, damp and miserable. There was a fine sheen of silvery moisture all over his cloak and tunic, the wind cut through to his bones, and his face felt as though he was wearing a mask of ice. It was not as he had imagined.

His feelings of chilly discomfort were emphasized by the relative calmness of the man beside him. Baldwin sat as straight and alert as the bird on his fist, swaying and rocking with the slow walk of his horse. He was a strange man, the rector thought, this quiet, educated and self-possessed knight. Very unlike the normal warriors Peter Clifford met passing through Crediton. In build he was much the same, of course. Tall and strong, with the broad chest and shoulders of a fighter, Sir Baldwin Furnshill was the very image of the Norman knight, even down to the knife scar from temple to jaw that shone with a vivid heat in the cold, and he carried himself with a haughtiness to match his position. Only the black, neatly trimmed beard that covered the line of his jaw seemed incongruous in these days when men went clean-shaven.

With the hood of the knight's cloak lying on his back and the dark eyes roving constantly over the land, Peter could imagine him studying a battlefield, searching out the best points for an ambush, the line in the ground for the cavalry charge, the places to site the archers. His expression was curiously intense, as always, as if the knight had seen and done so much that his spirit could never be completely at ease.

But for all that the rector knew him to be a loyal friend and, more important, an honest representative of the law. Sometimes he looked as though he could only hold his temper at bay with difficulty while dealing with the local folk, but he still managed to hold it in check—unlike others the priest had known. Even the knight's predecessor, his brother Sir Reynald Furnshill, had been known to beat his men on occasion, though he was considered generally to be a fair man. In comparison, Baldwin appeared to be almost immune to anger.

There was a restlessness about him, though. It was there in his eyes and in the occasional sharpness of his tongue, as if every now and again the slow deliberations of his villeins became intolerably frustrating. Not like Simon Puttock, Peter thought. Simon never allowed his impatience to show. But Simon had gone to Lydford to be the castle's bailiff. At the thought, a vague memory stirred, and his brow creased. "Baldwin? Last night . . . Did you say Simon would be here soon?"

The question made the knight turn and raise a quizzical eyebrow. "Yes, in a couple of days—maybe three: Monday or Tuesday. He's been to Exeter, visiting the sheriff and the bishop."

"Good. I would be grateful if you could let me know when he arrives. It's been a long time since I last saw him."

The eyebrow lifted a little farther in sardonic amusement before Baldwin gave a short laugh. "Peter, you asked me that last night! I said I would send a messenger to you as soon as he arrived. Do you expect me to forget so quickly?"

Smiling, the knight studied the ground ahead, searching for prey. He had not realized how drunk Peter had been the previous night. As for him, he rarely consumed much alcohol. It was too ingrained in his nature now, even if he had turned his back on the religious life of a monk. Glancing back, he saw his quiet, restless servant Edgar close behind. Peter had once said that he appeared to be so close to Baldwin that a shadow could not squeeze between them, the knight recalled, and his smile broadened at the thought. How else should a knight and his man-at-arms be? "This should be fine. There're normally birds here. We need go no further."

On this hill they were a little above the trees, and they could look down over the woods to the occasional plumes of smoke from the cottages. In the cool morning air they looked like strings of mist trying to rise to heaven, and Peter felt strangely calmed at the sight, as if it was proof of the need of all elements to struggle ever upward to God. The thought helped to ease the pain in his head and the rumbling acid in his belly.

Sighing, he watched as a small fluttering flock of pigeons rose from the trees to their left, drifting off into the rising mist. The sun was quite high now, and the priest gazed up at it with concern. It looked watery in the pale sky, as if the heat which had once blazed would never return, and he offered up a quick prayer for a better harvest this year. From north and east he had heard of people being forced to resort to all sorts of extreme behavior to survive. In parts of the kingdom all dogs and cats had disappeared, and he had heard of people eating rats. There were even rumors of cannibalism in the east.

"Please, God!" he muttered, suddenly struck with a

sense of near panic. "Let us have a good crop this year."

"Yes," he heard Baldwin murmur in quiet agreement. "Let's hope it's better this year." But his reflective mood was broken even as he spoke. From beyond the trees, where a pool lay, there was a sudden flash of feathers as a heron rose. Drawing the hood from the peregrine, Baldwin quickly loosed her and spurred his horse, crying, "Oo-ee! Oo-ee!" to lure her on toward her prey, while Peter sat and watched and winced.

It was mid-morning when they decided to return to Furnshill for lunch. By now Peter was sure it was too late; he would never be able to warm himself again. The cold had eaten past his thick cloak, and under his two tunics and shirt, taking up permanent abode beneath his skin. Although it had been a pleasure to watch the peregrine launch herself upward, only to stoop, plummeting like an iron crossbow bolt on to her unfortunate targets, the delight in her skill was offset by his chilled dampness.

When the knight expressed himself content with their catch and suggested they should make their way back, it came as a relief to the priest, and he agreed with enthusiasm. It was short lived: soon he gave himself up to his abject, frozen misery.

Baldwin was thoughtful too. After many years of wandering and rough living he hardly felt the cold now, but he was aware that he was becoming more used to an easy life. The muscles on his shoulders still bore witness to his days of training as a swordsman, his arms were still thick and hard, his neck corded under the leathery skin, but the definition of his belly was becoming less clear, and he found himself wondering whether he was losing his fine temper, like a blade left too long unpolished and without care.

It was no false pride that led him to feel concern at the beginning of his paunch. Under the terms of his knight's tenure at Furnshill, he must be ready to go and serve the de Courtenays, the Lords of Devon, for forty days every year. It was always possible that he could be called to go to assist his lord in the north, or on the Welsh marches—or even over to France to the king's lands there.

Riding down the slope, Baldwin gave the hawk to Edgar before they passed in among the trees. The great oaks, elms and ashes towered above them here, their branches occasionally making the three men duck in their saddles as they passed along, until they came to an open area, the common land that led up to Wefford. Here they turned right, on to the main path north that led through the village itself.

Wefford was a small cluster of houses and farms that serviced the strips to the south of Furnshill, huddled squashed together like suspicious villagers watching a stranger. Baldwin knew it to be a thriving community which contributed well to his estates, providing not only money but also men to work the fields. As with all landholders, his greatest problems were caused by the areas that had insufficient menfolk to help with the manor's estate. Money coming in to his exchequer was welcome, but if there was nobody to tend his fields, his main source of income, his land, must be ruined.

Here in Wefford, though, he had never had any problems. The villeins seemed content, placidly carrying on with their lives. Even last year, in the confusion of the disastrous harvest, the people had managed to produce plenty of food: enough not just for themselves, but to share with other hamlets on the Furnshill estates, and Baldwin felt a small stirring of pride as they came into the little village.

It was laid out on either side of the north-south road from Exeter to Tiverton, a straggling huddle of cottages and outbuildings that serviced the parallel scars of the fields. All the buildings were limewashed, stolid structures with their thatching thickly covered with moss. Up to the north lay the ford which had given the place its name, and halfway along the village, opposite the building that proudly acted as inn to the local folk, was the road west to Sandford and Crediton. Baldwin glanced at it as he passed. It led in among the woods, through the dark and gloomy trunks of the ancient trees, winding as it rose and fell over the hillocks of the softly undulating land, trying to find the easiest path for the traveller.

But the track was not well kept, he could see, and his brows jerked into a quick frown. Since he had accepted the position of Keeper of the King's Peace, he had needed to take on many new responsibilities, all going back to the Statute of Winchester. There the institutions for law and order had been reorganized and new regulations set out: how the hundred, the watch and the posse should work together; how areas should train for their own defense, and how they should protect against wandering bands of outlaws. Not only must Baldwin ensure that all men in the area were armed and trained in arms, he must keep the brushwood cleared from the public highways as well, to a distance of two hundred feet. Only three weeks ago he had told the constable, Tanner, that this track must be cleared, and Tanner had agreed to arrange it. It looked as if nothing had been done.

Sighing, he turned back to the road ahead. It was not Tanner's fault, he knew. The constable would have tried to enforce the order, but how could he persuade people to do it in the middle of winter? There would be a complete lack of interest. After all, the villagers would reckon, why bother to do all this work when it was only for the protection of the king's men, who had too easy a life already, or for merchants, who deserved to be robbed when they charged more than their goods were worth? It was not for the defense of the local people that the tracks should be cleared—for the same statute demanded that all men in the land must be trained in war and armed so that they might be able to protect themselves. No, this rule was for the safety of the wealthy, and that being so, the locals reasoned, the wealthy could clear the highways themselves. The villeins of Wefford had enough work already just keeping themselves fed.

It was while he was making a mental note to speak again to Tanner that he saw someone come on to the road from a track on the right, and he stared in surprise.

Although he had ridden through this village many times on his way to Exeter or Crediton, he had never stopped, and knew no one living here. There were too many families on his lands for him to be able to know them all, but he was sure he would have known this one. Tall, covered by a heavy, gray, fur-fringed cloak that fell to the ground and was pinned with a shining metal brooch, the figure stood quietly watching, face covered by the hood as the small group approached. Though the body was covered by the draped cloak, Baldwin was sure that it must be a woman, and from the little he could see, a wealthy and elegant lady. Glancing quickly over at his companion, he saw that the rector was dozing, his head nodding gently with the steady jog of his horse, and when he looked back the lady had disappeared.

Frowning, he peered carefully, but there was no sign of her. Clearly she wanted to remain out of sight, but he was sure, as they rode up close, that he could feel her eyes on him. The sensation was unsettling, as if he was the quarry of an invisible hunter. It was this that made him turn, after they had passed, and glance back.

There, not far from the spot where he had seen the cloaked figure, was a short peasant woman with sharply suspicious features, gazing back at him round a tree before hurriedly jerking back as if to avoid being seen.

He turned back to the road with a grin lifting the corner of his mouth. Just a poor old woman trying to avoid the wealthy knight in case he demands food or drink, he thought. But then he felt a quick, cold shiver twitch his shoulders. Where did the other one go?

Agatha Kyteler watched the departing group with an expression so intense it was almost a glare. She waited until they had passed through the ford and carried on out of sight round the curve beyond. Drawing in her breath she let it out in a slow sigh, then muttered, berating herself for allowing her distrust to delay her. She still had much to do.

Pausing, she let her head fall back, then stretched her arms high overhead and yawned before rubbing slowly at the small of her back with her fists. After an afternoon of collecting herbs and roots she was exhausted, and her back was strained after so much bending. She relaxed and stooped to pick up her basket, patting the wiry head of her black and tan lurcher, which was seated beside her. As usual he responded eagerly and bounced up exuberantly before streaking off on the scent of a hare.

The basket was old, the wicker snapped and frayed, and she gave it a wry grimace as she hefted it. It was so much like her: ragged, worn and tired, too ancient to last much longer.

She knew that the local villagers were glad enough for her to be here most of the time, any small village was grateful for the help that an experienced midwife could offer, but they still looked at her askance. It was obvious why. They thought she was too clever. That was the risk, she knew. She was not a local, not brought up in the same way, trained in the same rules. While enjoying the results of her skills, the people around were scared of how she might have acquired them. And her accent was too strong as well. It set her apart from them and made them shun her. She was different. Of course, the fact that she lived a little outside the village in her own assart did not help matters. She gave a sudden grin: it was almost as if it made her stranger and even more awe-inspiring, guaranteeing her occult powers—in the eyes of her neighbors, at least.

She could not fully understand why. The people were genuinely scared of her, and yet she was no threat to anybody. There were rumors put about by the old hag Grisel Oatway, but they were hardly enough to make the people around go in terror of her.

In any case, she valued her solitude. Her life had been full enough. Peace was attractive in the evening of her life, and she was happy to be left alone with her thoughts; especially now she was in a new country. But she could not contain her annoyance when people tried to avoid her. They knew they needed her—they were always keen enough to take her advice or her medicines, like the poultice for Sam Cottey's bad arm, the mixture for Walter de la Forte's cow, and the potion for Jennie Miller to reduce her back pain.

"Hello Agatha."

The voice, low and steady, soft but assured, came from her left, between her and the road, and at the sound she stiffened, her eyes searching from bough to bough, trying to see who had spoken.

A slim figure tentatively edged away from the cover of a large chestnut tree, and Agatha saw a woman, tall and slim, face covered by the fur-lined hood. "Agatha, I need your help," she said softly.

I n the late afternoon of the Saturday, under a leaden sky in which gulls wheeled, the wind blew up from the gray sea in a series of gusts, disturbing the branches of the trees at the shore and cutting through the clothes of the man standing on the foredeck like arrows of ice. Until the old ship was secured he must stay here, but the coldness of the middle of winter made him wish he could leave this duty to another and make his way below, to his cabin and a warm pot of wine.

It was rare for him to be sailing this early in the year. As the master of the cog *Thomas,* he tried to keep the old timbers out of the sea during the freezing cold of the winter so that the clinkered hull could be retarred and sealed, but these last few years had been so hard that any cargo of food could bring high profits, and even though the *Thomas* needed maintenance, the old ship was good for a few more trips over to France and the English ports of Gascony.

From here, the master could see most of the old town. His lip curled into a disdainful sneer, twisting the podgy face into a glower of loathing under its thatch of graying brown hair, his hazel eyes flitting over the port area with near disgust. This was not what he and *Thomas* had become used to over the years.

Usually he would try to make for the wealthier Cinque ports, or for London, where the people had money and the towns were used to entertaining sailors, but not on this trip. The Cinque ports were getting too silted, making it difficult and dangerous for a cog the size of *Thomas* to maneuver into the harbor, and London was far too busy at this time of year. He sighed to himself. But this was such a miserable place!

In London there was a cheery bustle, with merchants, seamen and wharfingers shouting and swearing at each other, and the occasional fight when a curse resulted in the drawing of sword or dagger. Here was very different. Four scattered villages lay to the east of the sound, and he could just make out the Benedictine abbey that owned most of the area. Apart from that the whole place looked dead. On the docks there were a couple of men splicing heavy coils of rope, but for the most part the master could well imagine that his was the first ship seen here for months— or years. It seemed as if the place was deserted after long years of desolation.

Not, he reflected, that it would have been too surprising if it *had* been left long ago by its inhabitants. The French pirates, long competitors of the Cinque ports, had for some time spread their carnage to other southern ports. Now even the smaller places like this, Plymouth, were being attacked and fired more often and, with so many tiny villages and towns on the coast, it was easy for the murderers to attack with relative impunity. After all, there was no organized navy, so the country could hardly be defended in so many places.

The only answer was for each man to look to his own protection, and generally that meant helping the village or town.

Sighing again, he checked the cables to the front of the ship. When satisfied, he wandered along the side of the cog looking to the other hawsers, checking all was taut and safe. It was only when he had almost arrived at the rear castle that he found his passenger.

Startled, he stopped and cursed under his breath. It had been the same every time he had seen this man. He appeared when and where he wanted, but so noiselessly on his soft leather boots that it was as if he did not need to walk, he could simply drift to any point on the ship, quiet as flotsam on the water, suddenly arriving and making everyone jump in their surprise. He was standing by the rail and gazing toward the villages with a slight smile on his face. The master studied him, wondering who this taciturn man was and what he was doing here and feeling glad that he would soon be rid of him. Today, Sunday, he would lose him and hopefully never see him again.

It was not that he had threatened the master or his crew, but there was an aura of danger about him. Although he was cheerful enough, there was something about him that urged caution, something unsettling.

He was dressed well, with an embroidered blue surcoat over gray hose. His cloak was heavy, of thick, warm wool, and he wore light leather gloves. There was a harshness about the square face, an air of indifference in the set of the granite-like jaw, as if he cared nothing for the people around him. His thin, curved eyebrows exuded an arrogant haughtiness—like a new squire or a recently dubbed knight. It was as though he knew his own value, and that of others. He clearly felt sailors to be necessary but unimportant in comparison to himself, and although he treated the master with courtesy, there was an underlying contempt. It was there in the pale gray eyes. They looked through people, like a steel blade stabbing through paper, as if they could see a man's most secret thoughts.

If he had been older, his indifference toward others might have marked him out as a man of wealth. In one so young—for he was little more than six or seven and twenty years old—it merely served to warn. He was a man to be avoided.

He was obviously hardened in battle, from the width of his shoulders and strongly muscled arms. At his age, he was old enough to be dead on a battlefield or living as a wealthy lord: many men like him made their fortunes in their early twenties, becoming great by virtue of loyalty and prowess, or dying in the attempt. Constantly on the alert, always ready to reach for his sword, he did not look like a man who could be easily ambushed in a moment of thoughtlessness.

There was something strangely noble about him too, the master admitted grudgingly. It was in his posture, not slouching like an over-muscled, mindless fool, but rolling gently with the ship, looking for all the world like a new king proudly surveying his inheritance—or conquests.

To his discomfort, the man turned and fixed his light eyes on the master. "When can I go ashore?" he asked softly.

Shrugging, he glanced over the last few ropes. "We seem well enough berthed. Whenever you want. Why, are you in a hurry?" Even after the voyage he still knew little about this stranger.

"Yes," the man said, turning to face him. "I am in a

hurry." There was a suppressed eagerness in his voice, a slight thrill that hinted at keen excitement lying almost hidden under his calm-seeming exterior, like a harrier dog who has just seen his prey. Looking at him, the master could see that he appeared to have the controlled anticipation of a man-at-arms waiting for the order to go to battle.

"Do you have far to go?" he asked.

"No, not far. Just to the north of here, to a small manor." His eyes turned back to their introspective study of the land. To a place north and east of the moors. It's called Furnshill."

The master left him. Men such as he were disturbing, and all too often dangerous. It was hazardous enough just being responsible for a ship in these difficult times without courting additional troubles. He strode forward and began issuing instructions for unloading the ship.

As he left, John, Bourc de Beaumont, turned back to the view. He had other thoughts to absorb him. Not many memories, for they were too far in the past and his life had been full since the parting so many years before, with the continual training and service to the count, the Captal de Beaumont. All his life had been spent in serving him, his lord—and father. He did not regret it, it had been a good education for a man who would become a soldier, a man who would need to spend his time in training with weapons to be able to protect his master.

In that time he had hardly paused to regret his loss. Indeed, it was hard to think of it in those terms. All he now had were vague recollections, pictures seen as if through a milky haze, where faces and features were indistinct.

Was it wrong of him to come and see her, though. The Captal de Beaumont had felt so—had *said* so—not with anger, but with a slight sadness as he tried to explain that it could do her no good; it would not ease her last years. But the Bourc was sure it could not be wrong to see her just once, to see what she actually looked like. He was not going to punish her for what she had done: she had done the best she could, and without thinking of herself or her own safety. He was grateful for the opportunity she had given him, and had tried to take advantage of it.

At first it had been easy, of course. When he had been young it had all come so naturally, as if he had in truth been born to the Captal de Beaumont's wife and not to his mother, as if he had not been the Bourc, the bastard. He had known no better. But then, while he was still a squire training to be knight, the snide comments had started. It was not malicious, they were merely the cruel, pointed comments of young boys to a peer who was different. It meant little to them that he was the Captal's son. To them he had no mother and that was enough. He was marked with the worst scar possible for a child: that of not being the same as others.

But John, Bourc de Beaumont, had proud blood in his veins—from both the Captal and from Anne of Tyre—and he endured the comments, only occasionally defending his virtue and honor. As he grew into a tall man, fit and lean, the need to protect his name reduced in proportion to his size and the extent of his warrior training, until at last he had his spurs and became a knight.

He always knew that some day he would have to go and seek her. In the event he had remained much longer than he had originally planned. For a man trained in war who delighted in battle, there were few places better than the marches between French and English lands. Here there was honorable service, opportunities to prove himself a worthy man, and to earn money from ransoms and protection money. But after so many years of fighting, he wanted some peace for a few months, and a chance to find out the truth while he still could.

Slamming an open hand on to the rail in a gesture of decision, he made his way to his packs, lying on the deck by the main mast. A sudden thought made him pause. She would be old now: according to the Captal de Beaumont she should be about fifty, maybe a little more, so well into old age. She might even have died. Throwing a quick glance at the coast again, he was troubled by the thought.

With an effort he calmed himself and continued to his bags. If she had died, there was nothing he could do about it, it was God's will. And his own fault for delaying the trip for so long. Collecting his things together, he walked to the plank that would deposit him once more on solid, safe, dry land, and he felt a small smile of relief twitch at his mouth. It would be good to be able to move without the constant pitching and rolling of the round-keeled ship to make him feel continually on the brink of vomiting.

Once at the shore he hefted his packs and took stock. Spying an inn, he set off for it. A drink and some food would fill the time until his horses were offloaded.

When the innkeeper of the "Sign of the Moon" in Wefford entered his hall on the Monday, his feeling of pride was dimmed as the reek attacked his senses. It was not the ale on the floor, that acidic scent held for him the very promise of his business. The smell that assailed his nostrils was the harsh, bitter tang of vomit where young Stephen de la Forte had thrown up—again.

Even now in the early morning he felt the thrill of pride at the sight of his hall. It held the promise of comfort and pleasure, with the tables and benches laid down both sides, more at either end, and the massive hearth in the center on its bed of chalk and soil. There were no flames now, so he set to his first task, building up the fire slowly with kindling, bending low and blowing gently but persistently until the flames, small and yellow, began to lick upward enthusiastically and he could put smaller logs on top.

Sitting back on his haunches, he stared at it cautiously, satisfying himself that it had caught. Up above he could see the smoke drifting heavily, high among the blackened rafters. It would be some time before the room heated, he knew, but when it was, the smoke would disappear. Time now for the real work.

He began in the corner by the screens. At first he shoved the benches and chairs aside to be able to sweep underneath, but when he had got halfway, the novelty was wearing off. Realizing how long he had already spent, he left the furniture where it was and merely swept around it. He was keen to finish before the first customers appeared. Arriving at the discolored area, he could not help a grimace of disgust at the odor.

Fetching the big shovel he used in the stables, he carried the old rushes to the manure heap. It was fortunate that the pile was not far from his door, for there was a chill breeze coming from the south. A sudden shiver shook him, and he made haste to finish.

Once the floor was cleared, and all was as clean as he could get it, he found that there was only the hint of the vomit left on the air. The smoke from the fire hung in long streamers around the room like a mist over the moors on a windless day. Gradually eating its way into the atmosphere, it replaced the stench with its own healthy and wholesome bitterness. Nodding happily to himself, the innkeeper wandered outside to the store, and soon returned with fresh rushes, strewing them liberally over the floor. For some, laying new rushes was an irregular task only performed once a year, but for an inn it was the only way to keep the smells from becoming overpowering.

He had completed his task, and was standing with his hands on his hips when he heard the horses. Smiling, he reflected that new rushes worked for customers like cream with a cat. Whenever they were freshly laid the customers were sure to follow. Scanning the room one last time, he confirmed that all seemed well, then strode to the curtain that hid the passageway. At the end of the narrow corridor, he unlatched the front door and threw it open, peering out. Tall and imposing under his hooded cloak, with a bow on his back and sword by his side, was a man on a horse, leading a second by the reins.

The Bourc sprang down lightly. He had been forced to stop for the night at a little wayside inn, some miles from Oakhampton, and had set off again as early as possible in the morning. Now he was chilled to the bone, or so he felt. Puffing out his cheeks, he let his breath drift from compressed lips, then shook himself like a dog fresh from the water. "I think I need a pint of hot ale," he said softly.

The innkeeper nodded and smiled before turning to

fetch the drink and warm it, while the Bourc led his horses round to the stables, rubbing them down and setting out hay and water before making his way indoors. He smiled at the smell of fresh rushes, soft as the scent of hay on a summer's evening, and the promise of warmth from the burning wood at the hearth. There was a cheering tang from the beer in the pot over the flames. Sighing with pleasure, he waited silently while the innkeeper busied himself pouring the hot and spiced drink into a mug, and took it with a sigh of sheer delight. It was almost painfully lovely after the cold discomfort of the ride here. He gazed deep into the depths of the liquid before sipping, and a slow smile spread over his face.

"Am I heading the right way for Furnshill manor?"

"Yes, sir. It is only a few miles north of here."

"Good. Good," he said and sipped. Then, "Tell me, do you know the people of this area well?" The innkeeper nodded. Of course he did—who else would know the local community as well as the publican, his baffled expression implied. "Do you know where I can find a woman, an old woman called Agatha Kyteler?"

To the Bourc, it looked as though the man suddenly caught his breath, and his expression became suspicious. "Why do you want to know about her?"

Before he could answer there was a bellow, and both men's eyes went to the door. The innkeeper sighed and rose, leaving the Bourc alone, sipping at his drink and considering the innkeeper's reaction. The man had been distrustful for some reason when her name had been mentioned, he reflected, and he offered up a quick prayer that his fear of arriving too late was not going to be realized, that she had not died.

He had turned to stare at the flames as he mused and

thus did not at first notice that he was no longer alone. It was the waft of flowery scent that made him look up, and when he did he gaped in awe.

The woman who stood nearby tugging her gloves off was beautiful. She was only a little shorter than him and about the same age, with a slender body clad in a light green tunic under a gray riding cloak, and when she glanced at him, he saw that the color of her eyes almost matched her dress. High-cheeked and with pale features, she looked frail at first sight, but as he mumbled an apology and lurched to his feet he saw that it was an illusion. Her figure was strong and supple as a whip.

"Madam, please be seated," he said, and she turned to him. He found that she had a disconcertingly intense gaze. The way she stared, it was if she was concentrating her whole being on him, looking him full in the face with a strange stillness. After what felt like several minutes, she gave a faint smile and inclined her head, sitting on the bench he had moved for her, then unclasping the gray cloak from her throat and, with a short shrug, letting it fall. The Bourc had just sat with her when another man entered.

Glancing round, the Bourc saw a barrel-chested man in his late forties or early fifties. From his breadth and peculiar, rolling gait, the knight needed no flash of intuition to guess that he must have been a sailor. The life at sea had stamped itself on him too heavily. Although the face was not badly formed, the mass of wrinkles and scars made it ugly. There was no gaiety, no pleasure or joy in his eyes, only a cold brutality. Small eyes like those of a wild boar glared from the Bourc to the woman, and as he stepped forward, the fire seemed to strike sparks in his eyes as the flames were reflected.

"Angelina! Move over!" he said, standing behind them.

To the Bourc it looked as though she was reluctant to move. As if rebelling against the order, she waited a moment while the newcomer grumbled before shifting along the bench. Even then she moved farther than she needed, leaving a gap between herself and the man, and the Bourc was pleased to see a sneer of disgust twist her face when she looked at the man.

"Innkeeper!" the man bellowed. "Wine! I want wine!" Only then did he turn and peer at the Gascon. "Who are you?"

Keeping his anger under control at the rudeness, the Bourc smiled back, but his eyes were hard. "Friend, I am a traveller on my way to see the master of Furnshill manor for my lord. I am called the Bourc de Beaumont. What is your name?"

"I'm Alan Trevellyn—merchant. Who's this master of Furnshill?"

The Bourc started and peered at him on hearing the name, then stared at the woman. She clearly felt that his gaze was in response to the man's rudeness, and softened the harshness of the question by her gentle voice. Eyes on the Bourc, she said, "I think we have heard of him, Alan. He is named Sir Baldwin."

The landlord arrived with a tray of wine and handed pots to the man and woman. Other people were entering now, and he was soon busy going from one group to another.

"Sir Baldwin, eh?" said Trevellyn. "Yes, I think I remember him. He's not been there for long, has he—his brother died or something."

"I had heard," the woman said, "that Sir Baldwin came here just before the abbot was murdered last year."

"But surely you have not lived here long yourself, madam?" asked the Bourc, leaning forward and peering at her.

"She's been here long enough." The merchant put himself between them and glared wide-eyed at the Bourc, as if daring him to continue talking.

Staring back, the Bourc allowed himself a small smile and his eyebrows rose. "Do you object to me speaking to the lady?" he inquired softly.

"Yes, I do!" the merchant said, and suddenly his face contorted with fury. "She's my wife! Leave her alone, or you'll have to deal with *me*! Understand?"

The Bourc could not prevent a quick glance at her in open-eyed astonishment. That such a small, frail thing of beauty should be tied to so brutish a man seemed impossible, but even as he caught her eye, he saw the beginnings of the dampness as if she was about to weep, and she looked away quickly. When he unwillingly dragged his gaze back, the merchant's lip was curled in a disdainful sneer.

"My apologies, sir, I had not realized," the Bourc said, stiffly formal. A devil tempted him to say that he had assumed Trevellyn to be her servant he looked so poorly made, but he stopped himself. He had no wish to fight so soon after arriving here. "Anyway, I am here to see Sir Baldwin for my master, as I said, and then I have some personal business to see to. There's a lady I must see. Do you know Agatha Kyteler?"

It was not his imagination. At the name, Mrs. Trevellyn's head snapped round to stare at him and the merchant paused with his pot halfway to his mouth. Glowering at the Bourc, Trevellyn brought the mug down with slow deliberation. "Agatha Kyteler?" he said, then spat into the fire. "Why do you want to see that old bitch?"

He could feel himself bridling at this contemptuous treatment of the woman, but held his anger on a close rein. Sitting more upright, and resting his left hand on his sword, he said, "If you have something to say of her, share it with me. I know her to be an honorable lady."

"Honorable? She's a witch, that's what she is! She puts curses on people—you ask anyone around here," Trevellyn said scornfully.

Standing, his face white and taut with anger, the Bourc stared at Trevellyn. "Say that again. Say it again and defend yourself! I know her to be honorable—do you accuse *me* of lying?"

There was silence for a moment, as if every man in the hall was holding his breath. "Sirs, please!" the publican called anxiously, but the three ignored him. The Gascon was still and watchful, but his rage was boiling beneath his apparent calm. Trevellyn suddenly realized how his words had affected the stranger, and now gaped with fear while his wife looked excited, but kept silent.

At last the merchant shrank back like a whipped dog. Shooting a sullen glance at the Bourc, he shrugged. "I've said nothing that others here won't tell you, but . . . if I've offended you, I ask your pardon. Ask the innkeeper where she lives, if you want to see her. He'll know."

And that appeared to be all that he was prepared to say.

When the Bourc drained his mug, Trevellyn hardly moved. He remained sitting, staring before him and carefully ignoring the Gascon. The Bourc looked at

•

him contemptuously, then smiled at his wife. It pained him to see the sadness in her eyes, as if she was despairing at the misery of her life with her man, and the Bourc wondered again that such a lovely woman could have been manacled to such a brute. But there was no profit in thoughts like that, and he turned abruptly and went out to his horses.

For the love of God, *will* you get down, you brute! Lionors! No! *No!* I said . . . *Lionors, NO!*"

The bellow of despairing rage carried clearly from the house and far down into the valley as the servant handed the reins to the grinning hostler, and he could hear the sound of scrabbling paws slipping on the floor and pots smashing. He sighed and shook his head in vexation. Since Sir Baldwin had returned, he had been determined to maintain the great hunting pack that his father had owned, and kept a separate kennel for the hounds. But there was one bitch who refused to leave him: Lionors.

Walking inside, he sighed again when he saw the hall. One great iron candle-holder was on its side, a bench was upset, and plates and mugs lay on the floor. In the middle of the floor stood the knight, hands on hips, red-faced and glaring, while in front of him was the dog, lying on her back, belly and legs waving submissively while her massive black jowls dangled ludicrously to display her teeth. A fearful brown eye rolled as Edgar entered.

"After food again, was she?"

"No, damn it!" Baldwin kicked the submissive dog, but not hard, and strode to a chair. Flopping down, he eyed his dog sourly. "She was happy to see me."

It was always the same, the knight knew. Whenever he went out and left her behind, whether it was for an hour or a day, the result was the same: on his return she would try to bring something for him. In the beginning, when he had first come home to Furnshill, he had found it an endearing trait, a sign of the mastiff's devotion. That was almost a year ago now, though. Two pairs of boots, one rug and an expensive cloak ago. "She was trying to bring me a present."

Edgar nodded, then bent to pick up shards of broken pottery. "What was it this time?" Shaking his head, the knight motioned to the floor beside the table. When he glanced down, Edgar saw the short hunting spear, heavily chewed at the middle, which lay beside the table. "She was carrying that?" he asked, genuinely surprised.

It was only a few moments later that they heard the sound of an approaching rider. Lionors heard it first, her head snapping round as she stared at the door. Wiping his hands on his shirt, Edgar went out. After a few minutes he was back, and to Baldwin's surprise, he wore a broad smile.

"Sir Baldwin, a visitor! John, Bourc de Beaumont, son of the Captal de Beaumont."

"Of course, I knew your father well. We first met in Acre. That would be some six and twenty years ago now, of course."

Baldwin had been surprised at the demeanor of his guest. He remembered the Captal as being a cheerful, enthusiastic man, and yet the son was withdrawn, almost depressed.

The Bourc had passed on messages from his father and some small gifts, and they were sitting before the fire, which had been stoked and now roared vigorously, lighting the room with a flickering orange glow.

"He rarely talks about those times, sir."

"I'm not surprised. It was miserable. The end of Outremer. The end of the kingdom of Jerusalem. The finish of many brave and gallant men. Not, luckily, your father, though."

"He told me a little about it, but never what really happened. Could you?"

Baldwin sipped at his wine as he stared into the flames, his eyes glinting. Then they narrowed—the memory was hard. "I met your father there in the early summer, before I met Edgar. Our enemy had managed to lay siege from the land—though we still got supplies in from the sea—and were bombarding the place with catapults. I met your father early on in the siege. There were so few of us there—especially in the service of the English king—that we all knew each other. Even then he was a powerful man, or so I remember him. I was young at the time, of course. We fought together several times, and I was with him when the towers in the city wall were mined and began to crumble. We fell back together through the city as the enemy rushed in, trying to escape. It was awful."

"He told me it was vicious work in the narrow streets."

"Yes, because they were all connected, and there were so many men against us that even if we held them back for a minute, others could get round behind us. They kept leapfrogging us all the way back, all the way to the harbor. It was mayhem, hand-to-hand all the way. The harbor was to the south and we headed straight for it when we saw that the battle was lost. On the way we found Edgar here. He was wounded, and we helped him along with us. But when we got close enough to see the sea, we found our route was blocked. The enemy was before us, cutting us off. We had no choice: north, south and east were forbidden to us. We went west, to the Temple."

"You were both there during the siege of the Knights of the Temple?"

"Oh, yes!" Baldwin gave a short laugh. "Not that we were much help to them. Edgar was too ill. I myself fell on rubble on the second day and broke my ankle. Your father saved me then." He looked over at the young knight beside him. "We were at the main gate of the Temple when we were suddenly attacked by a strong force. They had a ram, and the bar that held the door gave way, snapping in the middle. Half of it landed near me, and that's what made me fall. A stone turned under my foot and broke the joint. Your father stood by me, holding off the enemy until I was dragged away and the gates fastened again. He managed to keep the men rallied.

"In the end, your father was hit by an arrow, and the wound soon festered in the heat. We were lucky. The Templars allowed all three of us to leave on one of the Templar ships. They took us away to Cyprus, where they tended our wounds and nursed us back to health." Back to Cyprus, he mused. The words hardly covered the panicked rush to the ships and the feelings of relief and elation at being removed from the immediate dangers of the ruined city.

"I have been in similar positions," said the Bourc meditatively. Drawing his dagger, he thrust it deep into the fire. When he had poured himself a fresh mug of wine, he warmed it by stirring it with the knife. "It's hard when you're surrounded and know you cannot escape."

"Aye. It's worse when your enemy has sworn to destroy you utterly and leave no survivors," said Baldwin shortly. Then he glanced up and smiled. "Anyway, that's the truth of it, for what it's worth." He threw a shrewd glance at his guest. "So did you come all the way here to hear that? The message and gifts hardly merit a knight as a messenger!"

"No," said the Bourc shortly. "No, I did not come just for that. I wanted a bed for the night as well. I will be gone early tomorrow, I came for other business, a debt which I owe from that same siege."

"How so? You can only have been a child back then."

"I was, yes. I was less than a year old. My mother, Anne of Tyre, had me by my father, but she could not escape from the city when it was taken. She gave me to my nurse, and this woman took me away."

"Oh?"

"Yes, she took me from Acre and brought me home. You see this ring?" When he lifted his left hand, Baldwin saw a gold ring which held a large red stone. The Bourc stared at it for a moment, then let his arm fall and stared into the flames. "This was given to my mother by my father. She gave it to my nurse, who gave it to my people as a token that I was my father's son. She saved my life and made sure I was safe. Now she lives near here. That's why I've come. To see her and thank her. For my life. I saw her briefly today on my way here, and will return to her tomorrow, then go home."

"Who was she? Maybe I know her."

"A lowly nurse? Maybe. She was named Agatha Kyteler."

Baldwin shook his head. "No. I don't know her. The name is unfamiliar."

It was late in the afternoon of the next day, Tuesday, when Simon Puttock and his wife arrived. By then Baldwin was sitting in his hall. John, Bourc de Beaumont had left at noon, and the knight was beginning to wonder if the bailiff and his wife had been forced to change their plans. Looking up at the sound of horses, he walked to the door and, seeing his friends, bellowed for servants.

Though it was getting dark, the day's weak sun had not managed to clear the white spatterings of frost from the dirt and grass, and Baldwin could see that behind his guests a thin gray mist was already lying in the valley. On a clear day he could see for miles from here in front of his house, and today he could make out the moors lying under their blanket of pure white snow in the far distance, looking somehow less threatening than in the summer when they loomed dark and menacing.

Baldwin's manor house was not a modern castellated property. Built in easier times, it was thatched like a farmhouse, the only concessions to safety being in the tiny windows and its position. Standing high on the side of the hill facing south, it lay in a clearing, surrounded at a safe distance by the old woods. In front there was a shallow gully in which the rainwater drained away, and it was here that the track lay, rising gradually to the flat area before his door.

The knight watched as the small party approached. In the lead was the tall, slim figure of his friend Simon

Puttock, a ruddy-faced, brown-haired man in his thirti-
eth year. Just behind him was his wife, Margaret, slim
and elegant in her fur-lined gray cloak, hood down to
show pale features glowing with the cold and exercise
under thick tresses of blond hair trapped by her net.
Bringing up the rear was their servant, Hugh, his dark
face, Baldwin saw with a widening grin, pulled into his
customary morose glower.

Spreading his arms wide, Baldwin walked forward
to meet them. "Simon, Margaret, welcome!" he
shouted as they came close, his face breaking into a
broad smile.

After the ride from Exeter, Margaret was frozen, her
fingers feeling like icicles under her gloves, but she felt
a smile tugging at her mouth on seeing his pleasure.
Before her husband could drop to the ground and help
her down, Baldwin was beside her, bowing low, then
offering her his hand with a smile, his teeth almost
startling in contrast with his black moustache. Giving
him a quick nod of gratitude, she accepted his hand
and dropped to the ground, then stood looking at the
view while she waited for the others.

She had always loved this area, with its trees and
tiny villages. The soft hills rolled gently up and down
over a landscape scored with red stripes where the rich
earth showed through the green carpet, smoke rising
where the villeins held their smallholdings. It was so
unlike the bleak, gray Devil's heathland Simon had to
look after now at Lydford. Here there were happy communities still, not like on the moors.

On the moors the weather was so cold and inclement
that nothing could survive but the heather and ferns.
Even the trees she had seen, types she knew well from
around Crediton, grew stunted and shrivelled.

Not like this lush view. Here, she felt, the land must be much as God had intended. This was how Eden must have looked: even now in the middle of winter it was green and healthy. It seemed impossible that the moors were a scant half-day's journey away.

"Come inside, both of you, out of the cold. I have food prepared. This is quite a week for entertaining!"

Baldwin led the way, chatting about his visit from Peter Clifford on the previous Friday night and the Bourc's arrival the night before, though most of what he said passed over their heads—at present they were interested only in his fire, and they hurried to the hearth.

The room was just as Margaret recalled, long and broad, with a fireplace and chimney in the north wall, and benches set around the tables. Bread and cold meats lay on platters on the table, and a pot hung from its chain over the flames, giving off a strong gamey smell. When she walked over, tugging off her gloves, and held her hands toward the flames, she saw that a thick soup was bubbling inside, and her mouth watered at the scent that slowly rose to fill the room.

As her hands gradually began to warm and struggle back to painful life, she turned to heat her back. Casting an eye over the hall, she let Simon and Baldwin's conversation float over her unheeded. They were talking about the knight's friend, the Bourc de Beaumont, and his journey to find his old nurse. She had no interest in tales of old battles, and stories of the kingdom of Jerusalem saddened her—it was depressing to think of the holy places being violated by heretics. Unfastening her cloak, she swept it off.

Baldwin stood by the table and surveyed the food, arrayed on its platters as if for inspection. Glancing down and seeing his dog, he took his knife and cut a slab of ham, tossing it to her, before turning and smiling at his guests.

To Margaret, he appeared to have changed a great deal in some ways; not at all in others. The lines on his face, the scars and weals of suffering, had almost all gone, to be replaced by a calm acceptance of life. It was as if a sheet of linen which had been wrinkled and creased had been ironed smooth again. Where the pain had sat, now there was only calm acceptance. But still he had the quick, assured manner that she recalled from last year when she had first met him.

Simon too had noticed the signs of comfort and peace, and he was pleased, knowing that it was due to his own intervention that the knight was still free. Baldwin had admitted to having been a member of the Knights Templar when they had met the year before, and Simon was sure that his decision to keep the man's secret was the right one.

It had not been easy, especially after the murder of the Abbot of Buckland. It had been a dreadful year. There had been a band of marauding outlaws, murdering and burning from Oakhampton to Crediton, and then the abbot was taken and killed as well. For a newly appointed bailiff, the series of deaths was a problem of vast proportions, but he had managed to solve them. After hearing the knight's tale, he had been forced to search his own soul, but in the end there had been little point in arresting him, and Simon had kept his secret hidden. Now he was pleased at how the knight had justified his decision.

"Do you realize, Baldwin, how well you are considered in Exeter?" he asked as they sat.

The knight raised an eyebrow and gave him a

quizzical glance, as if expecting a trap of some sort. "Oh yes?" he said suspiciously.

"Yes, even Walter Stapledon has heard good reports of you."

"Then I hope the good bishop keeps his reports to himself, my friend! I have no desire to be called away to clerk for the king or my lord de Courtenay. Edgar!" This last in a bellow. "Where's the wine?"

His servant soon arrived, bringing a pot and mugs for the sweet, heated drink, serving them all and setting the pot by the fire to keep warm as he sat with them, flashing a brief smile at Margaret and Hugh, Simon noticed, but not to him. Ah well, he thought resignedly. It was only last year I had him trussed like a chicken and called him a liar.

"So how is Lydford, Simon?"

"Lydford is cold, Baldwin."

"Cold?"

Margaret broke in. "It's freezing! It's at one side of the gorge, and the wind howls up the valley like the Devil's hounds on the scent of a lost soul."

"It sounds lovely the way you describe it," said Baldwin gravely. "I look forward to visiting you both there."

"You'll be very welcome, whenever you want to come, but the cold's not all," said Simon, grinning in apparent despair. "Since I arrived I've had visits from everyone. The landholders complaining about the tinners; the tinners complaining about the landholders. God! The king allows the tinners to take any land they want—well, it's worth a fortune in taxes to the king's wardrobe—and everyone is up in arms about them, and expect *me* to do something about it! What can *I* do? All I've been able to do so far is try to keep them all apart, but now they're starting to come to blows."

"I'm sure you'll be able to sort matters out. After all, things are never easy—you had your own troubles here last year, didn't you? Margaret, try some squirrel—or rabbit, it's fresh and young."

"Er, no, thanks," she said, wincing and taking a chicken leg. The knight glanced at her in surprise, while Simon continued:

"The trail bastons, you mean? Hah! Give me a group of outlaws any day; they're easier to deal with than free men and landowners, all you need do is catch them and see them hang. I can't even do that with the mob at Lydford."

"Anyway," said Margaret, holding up her chicken thigh and studying it as she searched for the most succulent meat. "This must all be very tedious for you, Baldwin. What's been happening here? Anything exciting?"

Laughing, the knight shrugged shamefacedly and pulled a grimace of near embarrassment. Head on one side, he said, "Not a great deal, really. Tanner hasn't cleared some of the tracks hereabouts, and my warhorse went lame some weeks ago. Apart from that . . ."

"I could learn to dislike you, you know," said Simon with mock disgust.

Baldwin laughed, but then his eyes narrowed a little. "What else is there, anyway, Simon? You must have heard more news from Exeter."

Belching softly, Simon upended his mug before rising and refilling it. When he spoke, the humor had passed, to be replaced by a sober reflection. "There's lots of news, Baldwin, but none of it's good. This must go no further, of course, but even Walter has lost all patience. He says although King Edward was irresponsible before, now his favorite, Piers Gaveston, has been killed, he's worse!"

"In what way?" asked Baldwin frowning.

"He's playing one lord off against another, ignoring the Ordinances, allowing insults to go unpunished . . . It seems that he just wants to be left alone to play about in his boats and other frivolities. He spends his time in sailing—and playing with his common friends! There are even rumors that he was not his father's son," said Simon quietly.

Nodding slowly, Baldwin reflected on the tales he had heard: that this second Edward was a supposititious child, a replacement inserted into the household like a cuckoo chick in a nest. Wherever there were troubles, Baldwin thought, there are people prepared to imagine the worst. "I cannot believe that," he said shortly. "But it's true that the state is becoming unsettled. I have heard that tenants have revolted against their lords, even that some knights have resorted to brigandage once more. And there are more outlaws— more tree companies and trail bastons—coming down from the north, displaced people who have lost their homes and villages to the Scots, who are trying to find new homes."

"That's what Walter said. He's very worried. He feels that there has to be a compromise between the king and his barons, otherwise there must be a war, and God himself can hardly know what the outcome of that would be!"

"No, and God would not want that in a Christian country."

"Of course not! That is why Walter has allied himself with Aymer de Valence, the Earl of Pembroke, to try to enlist support for the Ordinances."

"Ah!" Baldwin thought for a moment. "Yes, that would make sense. The earl could count on support from many of the barons for that. What were the Ordinances but controls to ensure good government?"

"Exactly. Walter thinks that if the king can be persuaded to agree, the troubles may be prevented from getting worse—maybe the risk of war can be averted."

"What do you think?"

Simon glanced up and into the intense dark eyes of his friend, who sat frowning in his concentration. "I think we'll be lucky to avoid war in some places," he said simply. "The Earl of Pembroke is on one side, the Earl of Lancaster on the other. Both are rich and powerful. If they fight—and they will—many men will die."

"Yes, and many women too. In any war it's always the villeins and ordinary folk who die first and last."

Shrugging, Simon nodded. "It's the way of war."

"But what of the king? You mention Pembroke and Lancaster, what about the king?"

"Does anyone worry about him? He will be with one or the other—he hasn't got enough support to make his own force without them. And would his support make any difference? After his defeat against the Scots at Bannockburn, who can trust his generalship?"

Baldwin nodded again, as if he was confirming his own thoughts and not listening to the bailiff's words. Then, as if he suddenly noticed her, he turned to Margaret. "Sorry, this must be very boring for you."

She stared back, her face suddenly drawn and tight. "Boring? How can it be when you're talking about the future of the land? *Our* future?" His eyes held hers for a moment, then dropped to her belly, and she could not prevent the smile when his gaze rose to meet hers once more with a question in their black depths.

"My apologies, Margaret. I did not mean to insult you," he said quietly. "I tend to think that matters of chivalry and warfare are only interesting to men. I forget that they affect women too." He sat still for a moment, his eyes seeming to gaze into the distance, Lionors beside him. The huge dog peered into his face, then rested her head on his lap, making him start, suddenly brought back to the world with a shock. "Blasted hound!" he muttered, but affectionately, and, taking a few slabs of meat, tossed them away from the table. As the dog softly padded to her food, he rose. "Come, let's sit by the fire."

While the knight sat in his chair, the two servants brought the benches, and soon all were sitting and gazing into the flames, the mastiff asleep, stretched long and lean before the hearth. Edgar walked out to fetch more wine while the friends chatted desultorily, Hugh sitting and nodding under the influence of the fire and alcohol.

"What else is new, Simon?" asked the knight again, and when the bailiff shrugged, turned to Margaret with a raised eyebrow.

She laughed, shaking her head. It sometimes seemed impossible to keep anything from the knight, he had a knack of noticing even the smallest signs, although how he had spotted this she could not guess: she had only begun to realize herself over the last week. Now she was sure even if Simon was not—she was too late this month. "Yes, I think I am pregnant again, but how did you . . . ?"

"It's easy, Margaret. You look too well, and you seem to dislike food that you used to love—I had the rabbits brought especially for you."

"Well, we can hope," Simon said. Then he leaned

forward and gazed fixedly at the knight. "But what about *you?* You were looking for a wife, but I can't see any sign of a woman's hand in this house. How is your search progressing?"

To the bailiff's delight, Baldwin gave a petulant shrug, like a child feigning disinterest. "Well, I . . . I . . . The thing is . . . Oh damn it!"

Six miles to the south the Bourc was glancing up through the trees as he rode, retreating into his cloak in the bitter cold. On either side the trees rose stolidly impervious to the weather, but high above he could catch occasional glimpses of the stars, shining as tiny pin-pricks of light which flared and were hidden like sparks from a fire. They glittered briefly before being smothered by the ghostly clouds rushing by, clouds that made him frown with wary anxiety. They raced by as if fearful of the weather that he knew must chase hard on their heels.

Hearing hooves, he stopped and stared ahead cautiously. It was late to be travelling. Soon he saw a man riding toward him. Showing his teeth in a short grin, he nodded. The other man, dressed warm and dark for hunting, nodded back and hurried on. The Bourc smiled ruefully to himself. He was muddy from splashing through puddles, and he knew he was hardly a sight to inspire confidence in a stranger. At a sudden thought he turned, and saw that the man was staring back with frank interest. The Bourc smiled ruefully as he kicked his horse and ambled off toward Wefford.

He had travelled far enough tonight. At the first clearing that looked hopeful, he pulled off the road. Through the trees he could see a cabin, a simple affair of rough-hewn logs. Part of the roof was gone, and it was in a sorry state, but for all that it was a refuge from the worst of the wind. He led the horses inside and saw to them before starting a fire.

Chewing at some dried meat, he considered his options. His business was finished now, so there was nothing to keep him here. The sooner he could get home the better. If he continued this way, heading to the west and retracing the route he had taken from the coast, he should arrive within a couple of days, but it would surely take a lot longer than necessary. The journey west to Oakhampton and then south was quite out of his way, working its way round the perimeter of the moors. It would be more direct and quicker to cut straight south, over the moors to the sea that way.

It was still dark the next morning, Wednesday, when, over to the south of Furnshill, Samuel Cottey harnessed his old mule to the wagon and prepared for his journey, cursing in the deep blackness before dawn as his already numbed fingers struggled with the rough brass and leather fittings, pulling hard at the thick leather straps.

"Sorry, my love," he muttered as he occasionally caught a flap of skin in the buckles, making the old animal snort and stamp. "Not long, now. We'll soon have you done."

All set, he stood back and surveyed his work, rubbing the bandage on his arm that covered the long gash. It was a week ago now that the branch had dropped from the tree he was felling and slashed the flesh of his arm like a sword, but, thanks to God, the old woman's poultices seemed to be working and it was healing. Sighing, he stretched and then walked back to the cottage, stamping his feet to get the feeling to return to cold toes. Inside the smoky room, he warmed himself by the fire in the clay hearth in the middle, smiling crookedly from the side of his mouth, the lips pale and thin in the square, ruddy face under the thatch of gray hair. Sarah, his daughter, smiled back into his light brown eyes as she handed his mug full of warmed beer to him and watched carefully as he drained it, smacking his lips and wiping his hand over his mouth, then burping appreciatively. Giving her a quick grin, he passed back the mug.

"That's good," he said, then kissed her cheek briefly. "Be back soon as I can—I'll try to be home before dark, anyway."

When she nodded, he left, stomping quickly to the wagon and clambering aboard, whistling for his dog. After a quick wave, he snapped the reins and began to make his way from Wefford to Crediton, the dog barking excitedly behind.

As he left the light from the open doorway behind, his mind turned back to their problems. This last year had been the hardest he had known, especially since his brother had been killed by the trail bastons, down far to the south on the moors. Now the family relied on him alone to keep both farms going. His sister-in-law was right when she said that the two families could not live on either holding: both were too small to support them all, and neither could be expanded without a deal of work, hacking down the trees that fringed them. No, the only way to continue was by keeping both going.

But how to do that? There was only him, his daughter Sarah, and his brother's son Paul. There was too much work for them, now that they had to try to keep both properties working. Maybe they should do as Sarah suggested, and buy more pigs. At least they could often feed themselves, they did not need grain like cows.

The sun was lighting the eastern sky as he rattled and squeaked his way down the track into the village, head down, chin on his chest and shoulders hunched in an effort to keep the bitter cold from his vulnerable neck. Samuel had been a farmer for many years, and he was used to the cruelty of the wind and the freezing snow that attacked the land every winter, but the weather got worse with each passing year. Glancing up, he saw the sky was lighted with a vivid angry red, and sighed. The sharpness of the air, the streamers of mist from his mouth, and the red sky could only mean one thing: snow was on its way at last.

Passing the inn on his left, he glanced at it with longing, already wishing he could stop and warm himself before the great fire in the hall but, shuddering and shivering, he carried on, rubbing at his arm every now and again. Beyond was the turn he needed, and he made off to the right, toward Crediton, where his brother's farm lay, between the town itself and Sandford. He had to collect their chickens and take them into the market. Paul was still too young to be allowed to go to market on his own.

It was hard, he thought, sighing again. If only poor Judith had lived longer. But his wife had succumbed to the pestilence that followed on the tail of the rain that killed off the harvest two years ago.

The trees suddenly seemed to crowd in around him, their thick trunks looming menacingly from the thin mist that still lay heavy on the ground, almost appearing to be free of the earth, as if they could move and walk if they wished. It was this feeling that made him shiver again, peering up at the branches overhead. From somewhere deep in the trees came the screech of a bird, then some rooks called overhead, sounding strange and unnatural.

All he could hear was the clattering and squeaking of the wagon, with the occasional dull, deadened thump as the iron-shod wheels struck stones or fell into holes, and it felt impossible that any noise could be heard over the row he made, but still he caught the sounds of the waking forest, and his eyes flitted here and there nervously, as if fearing what he might see.

Then, all at once, he was out of it. The track led upward here, to a small hill where the woods had been cleared, and he drew a deep breath of relief, blowing it out in a long feather of misted air. The feelings of dread left him, and he squirmed on the board that made his seat, telling himself he was a fool to be fearful of noises in the woods.

Here the trail was little more than a mud path, with stone walls and hedges on each side that were just below his level of vision, so that he could look over to the animals stockaded behind. Now he could see that the road opened out up in front as it passed the Greencliff barton, the old farm that had stood here for years, gradually growing as the family had cut down the trees for their sheep.

It was just before the farm, at a sudden thought, that he turned slightly, trying to look behind while keeping his body clenched like a tight fist of heat in the smothering chill. His dog had gone.

Calling out, he frowned, then hauled on the reins to

stop the mule and turned, cursing. The last thing he needed was for the dog to attack one of the Greencliff sheep. There was no sign of him back on the track, so Samuel dropped from the wagon and walked back, blowing on his now-frozen hands, his face stern.

It was when he was almost level with the line of the woods that he caught a snuffling sound and then a bark from the hedge to his right, and he saw a narrow path. Shaking his head impatiently, he climbed up, catching his old russet tunic on a thorn, and swearing. At the top he could see into a field full of sheep. Beneath him was a wattle fence to keep the lambs from wandering to the hedge, but a section had fallen a little. The dog must have entered here.

Precariously balanced on the summit of the wall in the hedge, he glared round. The livestock seemed untroubled. He shouted, then heard the sudden movement as the dog started, and, seeking his master, began to return, skulking as if expecting a kick.

"No more'n you deserve," Samuel muttered, scowling at him. "What were you looking at, anyway?"

There was a lump, a huddled clumping, under the hedge that led to the woods some thirty yards away. He could not see what it was in the darkness, so he stepped forward carefully, his face frowning. When he had only taken a few steps, he took a quick intake of breath and groaned. It was a body. Rushing forward and touching the hand gently, he knew there was nothing he could do. It was as cold as granite.

For a moment he stood and looked down, shaking his head. Someone who did not respect the land and its dangers, no doubt, who had trusted to their own strength and found that nature in her cruelty could destroy even the strongest. Leaning down, he gently took

a shoulder with his good arm and pulled, trying to see
if he could recognize who it was, but the body was so
cold it had frozen into its position, and it took all his
strength. He gave a haul, and at last it shifted.

It was only then, when he saw the dead, unseeing
eyes in the petrified face staring back at him above the
wicked blue lips of the gash, that he moaned in terror.
Dropping her back on her face, he stumbled back until
he tripped, and then, rising quickly and glancing at her
one last time, he ran headlong to his wagon.

The bailiff was on his horse and trotting fast, riding
down the narrow tunnel between the trees, the leaves
lighted with a bright orange glow, toward the light at
the end, branches snatching at his cloak, twigs
scratching at his face, and he had to slap them away
with his hand until he came into the clearing, and
there he found a huge fire blazing, with, in the very
center, the hottest part, the cowled figure, who slowly
turned and faced him. It was the abbot who had died
the year before, glaring at him with eyes of black cin-
der glowing red-hot at the edges, who opened a mouth
like the entrance to the void, and said in a voice deep
and contemptuous, "So you thought I was unimportant? You thought my death mattered so little? You decided to let the murderer go free? Why? Why, Simon?
Simon?"

"*Simon!* God in heaven, *will* you wake up! Simon!"

Lurching upright, his eyes wide in his shock, the
bailiff sat up on his bench, staring wide-eyed until his
heart began to slow its panicked beating. He blew out
his cheeks, ran a hand through his hair, then held both
hands to his face, shaking as the fear of the nightmare
left him. He was still at Furnshill.

"I am sorry to waken you like this, Simon, but . . . Are you all right?"

The quick concern in Baldwin's voice made Simon give a wan smile. "Yes. Yes, I was just having a dream. What is it?"

Margaret was not there. She must have gone outside. She always woke early when she was with child. Now he could only see Baldwin standing at the foot of the bench where he had made his rough bed last night, a look of wary anxiety on the knight's face.

It was not a nightmare Simon suffered from often, but he had occasionally had it over the last few months. He sighed and rubbed his eyes with the heels of his hands, trying to lose the feeling of gloom as he wiped the sleep away. "What's the matter?"

"A murder, Bailiff."

At the voice, Simon turned sharply and saw the constable, Tanner, standing behind him. "What? Who?"

Stepping forward to Simon's side, the constable glanced across to Baldwin before beginning, as if seeking approval from the Keeper of the King's Peace. "Well, Bailiff, it seems to be an old woman who lived in Wefford, down south of here. Sam Cottey—do you remember him?—he was on his way to Sandford this morning. Found the body and sent a message to me. He reckons she was murdered, says there's no way it was an accident. I thought I should come here first, see if Sir Baldwin would want to come with me."

"I do!" said the knight with conviction. "And so do you, don't you, Simon?"

The bailiff was surprised to see how seriously the knight seemed to take the matter. As far as Simon was concerned, this was surely just a local incident: probably not a murder at all, but some old woman who had met with an accident. He was happy with just his long dagger at his belt. But when he was buckling it to his waist, he caught a glimpse of the rigid set of Baldwin's face, and saw him taking his sword, pulling it out a short way and looking at it, before slipping it on over his tunic and fixing it in place.

"Anybody would think it was him who had the nightmare," Simon thought, but then they were walking out to their horses. Taking his leave quickly of Margaret, he kissed her and swung up into his saddle, smiling at her briefly before wheeling with the others and setting off to the village.

There was a light smattering of snow as they rode, the prelude to a storm from the feel of the air, and the clouds were gray and heavy. The bailiff became aware of the knight darting quick, measuring glances upward every now and again, studying the sky, and when he looked himself, his expression became pensive.

From the crowds it was clear that the hapless Cottey must be inside the inn. There could be no other explanation for so many people standing and waiting, all hoping to catch a glimpse of the cause of the excitement, or, ideally, a body. As soon as they became aware of the riders, they parted eagerly to let the three get to the door, and the babble began to increase with the people's excitement.

At the entrance Simon saw a short but thickset man, broad and strong with a pot-belly, glaring round from under sandy hair, trying to keep the people away by gesturing with a stout cudgel.

"Thank heaven you're here! These scum have nothing better to do than see someone else's misfortune. Tanner, get rid of them, will you?"

The constable slowly heaved his bulk from his old horse and patted her neck, looking round at the people. Tanner had the kind of build that inspired respect. Even without a weapon in his hand his poise was somehow threatening, with his stolid and compact body moving slowly as if to prevent two of the great muscles colliding under his skin. Usually the eyes in his square face held a kindly light, but not now: Simon had seen that expression before, on the day that they had caught the trail bastons. Mouth pursed, he looked over the faces with disgust and, under his gaze, there was suddenly a shuffling of feet and nervous coughing. A few turned and began strolling away. Others waited a little as if unconcerned, but soon followed.

The inn had a small screens area, a wooden corridor beyond the door to keep drafts from the hall itself, and beyond a curtain on their right they found a large square room, blocked at the other end by another wooden screen and hanging tapestry. Heavy logs were already crackling and spitting merrily on the hearth in the center of the room. Three large benches crowded round close, so that frozen customers could get to the heat. Though the roof was high above, the room was warm and the atmosphere heavy with the cloying odors of stale beer and wine.

Simon and Baldwin tramped in together, glad to be back in the warm after their journey, and went straight to the fire. Holding their hands to the flames, they followed the innkeeper's finger, pointing at a silent figure sitting with his back to the wall on their left. His face was in the dark, but Simon could see two wide eyes staring back at him. When the flames suddenly spluttered and flared, lighting his face, the bailiff started. The farmer's eyes were wide with terror. A black and

white sheep dog was seated between his legs, head
resting in his lap as if trying to comfort him.

"You're Cottey?" asked Baldwin gently, and the
ashen-faced farmer nodded. He looked ancient, a tired,
drooping and slumped little man.

Tanner moved away, keeping to the shadows so as
not to distract them, and pulling the innkeeper with
him. At first it seemed to the constable that the knight
and bailiff were unsure whether to question Cottey or
not, he was so upset. As if to allay any fears he might
have, Baldwin slowly seated himself, the bailiff following suit.

"We need to ask you some questions, Cottey. Is that
all right?" asked Baldwin, keeping his voice low and
soft. "You found a body?"

Nodding, the old man stared at them, then his eyes
dropped to the dog at his feet as if in fearful wonder.

"Do you know who it was?"

"Yes." It was almost a sigh.

"Who?"

"Agatha Kyteler."

Simon saw his friend start at the name and wondered why as Baldwin continued:

"Did you know her?"

"Yes."

"Did you know her well?"

The farmer gave him a curious look, as if doubting
his reasons for asking, before giving a curt shake of the
head.

"Where's her body? Did you bring it back with
you?"

"No," Cottey said, shaking his head. "I left her there.
I . . . I thought I wouldn't be able to lift her. I asked
young Greencliff to watch over her. He lives closest."

Simon sighed. "We were told you thought it was a murder. Why? What made you think that?"

The farmer looked up again and leaned forward, his haggard face moving into the firelight, so that his eyes glittered with a red and yellow madness of anger in the oval face. "Her neck," he said. "Who can cut their own throat?"

Wincing, the Bourc felt that the crick in his neck would never go away as he rose, grunting. The fire was all but gone out, and it took time to tempt it back into life, but when it was blazing, he crouched and bleakly eyed it.

Leaving the hovel, he stood outside for a moment and looked up at the sky, sniffing the air like a seaman. Plainly the cold weather was here to stay for a while, but although the clouds above were thick and heavy, he felt that they should hold off for a day or two. There was a light sprinkling of snow on the ground, but he was fairly sure there would be no more today.

When he glanced over to the south, he could see that the blue-gray moors were almost untouched with white. Except for a few hollows, there was only the merest dusting. As he frowned and considered, a finger of light seemed to gently stroke a hillock directly in front of him, as if pointing out his path.

Nodding with a gesture of decision, he went back inside. He would collect wood first, so that he would have fire in case of bad weather, but for now it was holding. He would make his way over the moors.

Refusing a jug of ale each, Baldwin and Simon led the way back to their horses. The old farmer agreed to take them to the place where he had found the old woman, and when they heard he had a wagon, they decided to take that and use it to bring the body back. The innkeeper had made sure that the mule had been fed and watered, and it was almost sprightly as it was led round to the front.

The damp chilly atmosphere outside was so sharp and bitter that it was only with a physical wrench that Simon could force himself to leave the warmth of the inn. Once out he found that snow had begun to fall, soft insubstantial flakes dropping thinly from a leaden sky making the fire seem even more appealing. The people at the front of the inn must have thought so too, because they had faded away.

Tugging on his gloves, Simon saw that there were only a few youngsters left, all of whom appeared unwilling to leave while there was a chance of seeing something interesting. He grinned at them good-naturedly as he strode to his horse and swung up, waiting for the others to mount, and while he sat there he became aware of a girl, standing a little apart and staring at him with large and serious brown eyes. She could only have been ten or eleven years of age, he thought, and gave her a quick flash of a smile. She grinned quickly, but then her eyes dropped, as if in contemplation, before she pursed her lips and turned away. It was sad, he felt, that children were introduced to death while so young, but he knew well that even here many of the children would know relatives who had starved to death in the famine. In any case, what could *he* do about it? Seeing that the other three were ready, he trotted after them toward the right-hand turn, glancing up at the sky with a frown every now and again as he wondered how bad the snow would be.

He rode along silently, watching the farmer. It was his impatience that had made the old man clam up. After he had asked his question, once Cottey had told them about the cut throat, he withdrew from them, his eyes filming over with tears as though he was in fear of something. But of what? There was something he had not told them, Simon was sure of that, and he intended to find out but, to his surprise, the farmer seemed not at all concerned by the three men, hardly even giving them a glance. His concentration was directed solely at the trees all around, eyes darting nervously from one side to the other and then upward, as if he expected to be ambushed.

When he glanced at his friend, he saw that Baldwin was deep in thought too. The name of the old woman had surprised him, Simon knew, and he wondered briefly whether he should interrupt his friend's reflective mood. He decided not to. Baldwin would explain his concerns when he was ready.

The bailiff was right. To have heard the name of the

old woman so soon after hearing it from his friend's son had worried Baldwin. It was too coincidental. If he could believe the Bourc, the main reason for the man's visit was to see and thank her for saving him. There was no reason to suppose that he was involved in her death, surely.

It was only a little over a mile to the edge of the trees, and here the farmer stopped his mule and pointed wordlessly to the gap in the hedge. The knight and the bailiff were soon clambering over it and into the field.

Tanner was surprised that the old man made no effort to drop down with the others. Staring dumbly ahead, he stayed fixed to the wooden seat, reins held ready in his hands, as if daring them to ask him to join them, not even acknowledging his dog as it jumped up onto the wagon and rested its forepaws beside him to peer around. The others were out of earshot, so the constable ambled his horse alongside the older man's, and said quietly, "What's the matter, Sam?"

When the farmer's face turned toward him, he could see the terror. "It's *her,* Stephen. *Her!* Why did it have to be me as found her?"

Looking at him, Tanner was about to ask what he meant when Simon called him from the hedge. Nodding at the bailiff, he said, "Wait here, Sam. You'll have to explain all this to us later." Swinging off his horse, the constable walked to the hedge, clambered up the steep bank and followed the other two into the field.

The snow was falling more freely now, thick clumps dropping and settling gently, making the whole area seem calm and peaceful, but the constable was not fooled, he knew only too well how dangerous the apparently soft white feathers could be to the unwary. It

was not this, though, that made him frown. He had
known the Cottey family for many years—Samuel, his
brother, their children—and knew them to be sturdy,
stolid folk. He had never known any of them to display
such fear, not even back in the past when they were all
younger, when Sam and he had fought as men-at-arms
together. Why should he be so upset at the death of an
old woman?

Simon and Baldwin were a few yards away, walking
toward a tall youth dressed in a russet tunic and
woollen hose, with a thick red blanket over his shoulders, pinned like a short cloak. A heavy-looking,
wooden handled knife was at his waist. Tanner recognized him immediately: Harold Greencliff.

The knight had not met him before. Greencliff was
a tall, fair-haired, good-looking youth in his early
twenties, broad in the shoulder with a friendly and
open face browned by the wind. Wide-set blue eyes
glowed with health from either side of the long,
straight nose. But today they were nervous and almost
shifty, not meeting the knight's gaze. From his clothes
he was not poor, but neither was he wealthy. He had
bright eyes, and looked quite sharp, but the knight did
not judge him by that alone. He knew too many fools,
who at first sight looked intelligent, to trust to his first
impression.

In his hands the boy held a shepherd's crook, and his
fingers moved along the stave as he watched them approach with a trepidation that Baldwin could not understand. It seemed odd that a corpse should create so
much fear—first with old Sam Cottey, now with this
boy. He shrugged. There must be a reason, and he was
sure to hear of it before long.

"You're Greencliff?" he asked.

"Yes," he said, peering over Baldwin's shoulder at the bailiff and constable.

"Wake up, lad!" said the knight irritably. "You're looking after the body of this old woman for Cottey, is that right? Where is she, then?"

Silently Greencliff turned and pointed to the hedge that led at right angles to the road to keep his sheep from going into the woods beyond. There, in the darkness under the plants, they could make out a small bundle. To Simon it looked like a bundle of dirty rags lying in the space made by a fox or badger path, in the gap between two stems of the hedge itself, lying half under the plants, half in the field. He and the knight walked toward it, leaving Greencliff standing, nervously fiddling with his crook, Tanner imperturbable beside him. The two walked to the body, pausing three or four yards from it.

"Did you touch her?" Simon called back to him, frowning concentration on his face.

"No, sir, no. Soon as old Sam told me she was here, I came and stood where you saw me. I didn't want to see her."

Glancing back, Baldwin nodded. He could see that the boy's footsteps had flattened a small area of grass, but no steps came from there, showing that the boy had been there when it began to snow and had not moved from there since. "Did you hear anyone this morning? See anyone?"

"No, sir."

"What about last night? Did you see or hear anything strange?"

"No, sir. Nothing."

His face was anxious, as if he was desperate to convince, and after holding his gaze for a moment, Baldwin nodded again, then cocked an eyebrow at the bailiff and pointed with his chin. "No tracks, Simon. We'll never be able to see if anyone came here last night. At least no one has been here since it began snowing."

He was right. There was no mark to upset the snow that now lay almost half an inch thick on the ground, the heavily cropped grass just poking above the surface. Shrugging, Baldwin walked the last few yards to the body.

It lay partly under the hedge, face down. The lower half projected back into the field, while the head and torso were shielded under the protection of the plants and free of snow. They could see the black of the old woman's upper garments.

"Wait," said Baldwin and stepped forward slowly to crouch, his dark eyes flitting over the ground, along either side of the body, back the way they had come, up to the hedge, then back to the inert figure itself. When he spoke, his voice was a murmur. "The weather has been so cold there's no mark on the ground: it's too hard. Even if there were, the snow would have covered them. I don't think even a hunter could see a spoor under this."

Simon nodded, dropping to a knee and peering back the way they had come, past Tanner and Greencliff to the hedge that bordered the road. Their own footsteps were distinct, flattened prints in the snow, but the snow had started while they were inside the inn. Now he could not even see Cottey's marks from when he had first seen the body. Glancing back at the knight, he asked, "Could she have come from the woods? Through the hedge?"

"No. No, I don't think so," came the pensive reply as

the knight peered up. "Look. The twigs aren't broken.
No, it looks like she fell from this side. Maybe she died
right here." He chewed his lip and considered. "Let's
see her face. Simon, come on. Help me move her."

The bailiff gave an unwilling grimace. This was the
part he loathed, the first shock of seeing the corpse, of
seeing the wound that killed. Sighing, he tentatively
took hold of the body by the hips while Baldwin carefully moved up, taking the shoulders and rolling her
over. He suddenly pulled back and exclaimed "God!"

"What?" said Simon, nervously shooting him a
glance.

Baldwin stared back, his shock slowly giving way to
a quickening interest. "I'm not surprised he was upset!
He was right when he said the throat was cut—her
head's almost off her shoulders!"

They carefully carried the figure a few yards away
from the hedge and set it down on the snow-covered
grass. Slowly shaking his head, Simon stood, hands on
hips, while Baldwin knelt and studied the body carefully. The bailiff stared down at the sad little collection
of cloth and flesh, thinking how pathetic it looked, this
sorry little mass that had been a person—if only a
villein. He was still staring when Baldwin rose.

"Whoever did this wanted to make sure. As Cottey
said, she couldn't have done this to herself."

Looking down, Simon could see what he meant. The
bones were still connected, but the flesh was cut so
deeply that the yellow cartilage of the windpipe could
be seen as a perfect tube in the sliced meat of her
throat. Wincing, the bailiff gasped and turned away,
swallowing quickly. Shutting his eyes and taking deep
breaths, he gradually soothed the oily feeling of sickness in his belly. He heard the low chuckle of the

knight and the footsteps crunching on the dry snow, but kept his eyes shut a little longer.

"Simon, come and look at this!"

His eyes snapping open, Simon turned and strode away from the body toward the hedge where the knight crouched. At his approach, Baldwin stood, and Simon was surprised to see his puzzled frown. "What is it?"

"Do you see anything strange here?"

The bailiff swallowed. His stomach was still turbulent after his shock, and he was in no mood to play games. He opened his mouth to give a sharp retort when he saw the pensive concentration in the knight's eyes. The words were stopped in his throat and he felt his gaze drop to the area where they had found the body.

Where she had lain, her image remained on the grass and earth. Snow bounded the lines of her legs. None had fallen under her, nor had the frost touched the ground. Apart from some twigs and flattened leaves, he could see nothing. Shrugging he looked up at the knight questioningly. "She was obviously lying here before it snowed," he hazarded.

"Maybe I'm . . ." Baldwin broke off, then span and stomped back to the body. Reluctantly the bailiff followed.

Although he tried to avert his eyes, Simon found that they kept returning to the hideous wound, and his belly began to feel like a cauldron of stew on a fire, bubbling and thickening, making him belch. The bile rose to sting his throat, and he winced at the rough acidic taste. The corpse seemed to hold no fears for the knight, who took the head in both hands and turned it first one way, then the other, peering into the gash and at the yellowed cartilage of the severed pipes. He stared at the blue, pinched and drawn features, into the unseeing misty eyes, before rising again and frowning down, slowly walking round the body and contemplating it with his head on one side.

"I saw this woman on Saturday," he said softly. "I didn't know her name then. She was just some old woman on the road. I've never even spoken to her, and now I must find out who murdered her." He stopped his musing and looked up at Simon. "Sad, isn't it?"

"Oh . . . yes."

The knight gave a short grin. "That's not the point, though, Simon. Sad it may be, but there's something wrong here. Can't you see? She had her throat cut. She must have bled like a stuck pig! So where's the blood? Eh?"

For all Greencliff's nervousness, Tanner was pleased to see that he was happy enough to help carry the corpse back to the wagon while Simon and Baldwin subjected the hedge to a close scrutiny. The boy even took the blanket from his shoulders and helped the constable wrap it around the thin, frail figure, setting it beside her and rolling her into it, but while the constable took the shoulders, he could not help but notice the way that Greencliff's eyes kept going back to the gap in the hedge where Agatha Kyteler had lain.

The old constable had seen many corpses in his life, brutally wounded figures after a battle, men who had bled to death after their limbs were hacked off or who suffered slow and painful deaths from stabs to the stomach, and the sad, tortured bodies of the people that tried to cross the moors in bad weather. For him, they were the worst, their hands contorted into grasping claws as they tried to drag themselves those few extra yards to safety, their faces twisted and staring with anguish, even in death. He was understanding of people who were revolted by the sights, although he bore them with equanimity, but he was faintly surprised that Greencliff should be so calm in the face of his previous apparent fear.

It was when they reached the hedge that led to the road that he realized he was wrong. Greencliff went up the incline first, stumbling backward. At the top he paused and Tanner caught sight of his face. The boy was not just nervous: he was terrified, and the constable was about to urge him on impatiently, "She's dead, boy, she won't care if you drop her now!" when he saw the boy's glance flicker over to Baldwin and Simon, and the realization hit him like a bolt from the sky: he was scared of the knight, not of the body!

From that moment, the constable kept a wary eye on him. They managed at last to heave the body down into the track, and from there it took little time to toss it unceremoniously into the back of the high wagon. Again, the constable saw that the old farmer did not move. He too seemed petrified. Even when the old woman's corpse hit the wagon and made it lurch, Cottey stayed staring resolutely ahead, shoulders hunched as if against the cold and elbows resting on his knees.

"Come on, Sam," Tanner called. "Let's get her back to Wefford." Cottey whistled and clucked to the mule, but neither spoke nor turned, and the constable shook his head in a quick flare of disgust.

Baldwin and Simon were soon back. The knight mounted his horse and watched as Simon followed suit, then glanced over at Greencliff. "We may want to see you later—when we've had a chance to find out more. You live there?" He pointed with his chin to the longhouse at the top of a small rise. When Greencliff nodded, he wheeled round, checked the others were ready, and started off back to Wefford. By the time they had entered the trees again, he found Simon had caught up with him and was riding alongside.

Smiling, the knight gave him a quick look. "Feeling better?"

"Not really, no." He was quiet for a moment, then said musingly, "It's always worst just before you see them, isn't it? It's not knowing what you're going to find that makes it more revolting. Once you've actually seen the damage, it's not so bad."

"No, I suppose not," said Baldwin, the smile fading. "Are you sure about the blood?"

The humor was wiped away like snow from armor. "Yes. She cannot have died there, not with the amount of blood she must have lost. Think about it: when you slit the throat of a pig or lamb, the blood sprays, doesn't it?"

"Well, yes . . ."

"So too with humans. If she had died there, the leaves, the ground, everything would have her gore. No, she cannot have died there."

"So where *did* she die?"

"Where?" His voice became lower and quieter, and he was musing as he continued, "That's what we must try to find out."

Yes, thought Simon. And why she was put there, too.

They clattered into Wefford at a little before lunch, and carried the wrapped figure into the inn, ignoring the protests of the owner, before calling for mulled wine.

Walking through into the dark interior, Simon strode over to the benches and sat, holding his hands out to the flames as if in a pagan ritual, feeling the numbness flee, only to leave stabs and prickles as sensation returned. Groaning, he stretched his legs toward the hearth and flexed his toes, grimacing in the exquisite pain.

After a moment he heard the curtain draw aside and the familiar stomp of his friend.

"God! Thank you for small gifts! That feels so good!" said the knight, baring his teeth as he stood close to the flames and sighed. "Innkeeper! Where's my wine?"

Simon glanced at him. "I thought you believed in moderation with your wine?'

"When it's this cold? Moderation, yes: but not to the exclusion of comfort," he said, then roared again: "Innkeeper!"

He entered scowling, a look of bitter dissatisfaction on his face, and walked to the other end of his hall, disappearing through the curtain. After a moment he was back, carrying a pair of jugs and mugs on a tray which he set down between them. Turning, he was about to leave when Simon called him back.

"This dead woman, Agatha Kyteler," the bailiff mused. "The name doesn't sound local to these parts."

"No, sir. She was quite new hereabouts. Only came here about ten years ago."

"You seemed surprised earlier when you heard who had died. When we were questioning Cottey."

"I was, sir. I heard her name only recently." The man told of the visit of the Bourc and how he had asked about the old woman. Baldwin frowned as he listened but did not say anything, and ignored Simon's questioning glance.

"What do you know about her?" asked Simon, his

eyes on his friend. He felt nervous. It was clear that the knight was worried, and from what he had said of the Bourc's visit when the Puttocks had arrived, he could guess why.

"*Know* about her? I don't . . ."

"She was murdered, you know," said Baldwin shortly, avoiding the man's eyes as he toyed with the hilt of his sword in a vaguely threatening manner. "We want to find out who did it."

"Yes, sir."

"So, answer!"

Sighing, the innkeeper poured wine for them, then sat and watched morosely as they sipped the hot, spiced liquid. "She came from far off. Some say from the Holy Land. I don't know. Took the assart down behind the Oatway place, about a mile from here, out east."

"And?" Baldwin's eyes narrowed and Simon had the impression that he was sure the publican was holding something back. "Come on, man. You're the innkeeper! You know everyone here, and you know all the gossip, too. What was said about her? Who knew her well? Who liked her, who hated her? What do you know about her?"

His eyes flitted nervously from the knight to the bailiff and back, then, as if afraid of what he might see in their faces, he stared at the flames. When he spoke again, it was in a low voice, not fearful, but slow and deliberate. "She weren't wealthy, but always had enough to survive. Very clever, she was, and that upset a lot of people. She made them feel stupid. She was arrogant too. Didn't suffer fools easily. Not without letting them know what she thought of them."

"Her friends?"

"Ask the women hereabouts. They all knew her."

"Why?"

He looked up suddenly, a small smile playing at the corners of his mouth. "She helped them with their babies. When there was a problem with the birth—any problem—she helped them. She was a good midwife." He almost mused as he spoke.

"So she'll be missed?"

"Yes," he thought, considering. "Yes, she'll be missed by some."

"Did anyone hate her? Could someone here want her dead?"

With a shrug, the innkeeper showed his indifference, but under the intensity of Baldwin's gaze, he spoke with a defensive air. "Some might've. But you can't believe what people say here! 'I hate him,' 'I'll kill him,' 'He deserves death,' you hear it every day in here. When a man gets into his cups, his mouth runs away sometimes—it's natural. You can't believe it, it's the wine talking."

"Who has said that about Kyteler?"

"Oh! I don't know. Many people have. They were scared of her. She seemed too clever, like I said. People get worried by women who're too clever."

"So who *has* said that kind of thing about her?" Baldwin pressed.

"Like I say, it means nothing. There's a few have said things. Young Greencliff, he has. And old man Oatway."

"Did they say why? Why they hated her?" asked Simon, leaning forward, his arms on his knees as he frowned.

"Why? Ha!" He gave a rich, low chuckle. "Oatway has the place between her assart and here, and he's got chickens. About a month ago, he saw one of his chickens were missing, and when he looked he found its feathers, all in a line on the way to Kyteler's place. He reckons it was her dog, but she swore it wasn't."

"If it was going out that way, it could have been a fox or anything, heading back to the wild; away from the houses and back to the forest," said Simon.

"That's what she said, too, but old Oatway wouldn't have it! He reckoned it was her dog, right enough. Anyway, he went to her and said he wanted the chicken replaced, and she refused. Since then, he's lost two more chickens, and he hates her, blames her for them."

"Hardly enough to murder for," said Baldwin mildly.

Simon glanced at him. "A chicken is enough meat for a week or more for two people. After the last couple of years, I'd say it was a very good reason to kill."

"Well," the innkeeper squirmed in his seat, "I'm not saying it's not, but I still don't think he could kill. Not old John Oatway."

"No? What about Harold Greencliff?"

"Harry? No, I don't think so. He's a good lad. No, he wouldn't kill."

"Why did he hate Kyteler?"

"I don't know. I really don't. Something happened, though. He came in here . . ."

"When?"

"Yesterday. Late afternoon, I suppose . . . Yes, it was just after dark, so it must have been about five o'clock. Anyway, he came in and took a pint of ale, and sat down over there." He pointed at the far corner, near the screen leading to the inner rooms. "A bit later, a friend of his came in, Stephen de la Forte, and they got talking, and I heard Harry say that she was a bitch and if she wasn't careful, someone would 'see to her.' "

"And?"

"Oh, they left soon after. But that's not to say he was really mad—he looked more sad to me, not really angry, just upset, so don't go thinking he went straight out to kill her. Anyway, they were back here a few hours later—before eight."

"Who? Greencliff and de la Forte?"

"Yes. They came in again and settled down for the evening with some of their friends."

"Where had they been?"

He shrugged. "How should I know? To get food or something, I don't know."

"How did they seem when they got back?"

"Oh, Stephen was noisier than usual, but I reckon they'd had drinks while they were out. It gets some people like that. Harry was quiet. He often is when he's drunk too much. He's a nice, quiet sort of a lad."

"I see," said Baldwin, but as he opened his mouth to say more, Tanner and Cottey came in from seeing to the body. Walking to the huddle of men at the fire, they sat and stared longingly at the jugs of wine until Baldwin gestured and the innkeeper rose with bad grace to fetch more, this time not forgetting himself.

"We put her out back in the outbuilding. She can wait there until the priest can come and see to her," said Tanner, watching the wine being poured as he held his hands to the fire. Sighing, he continued, "Poor old woman should be all right there. We put her up on a box. The rats should leave her alone for a day or two."

Simon nodded, then glanced over at the innkeeper, who had returned and was staring morosely at the flames once more. "Did she have any family?"

"What, here?" Looking up, he seemed disinterested now, as if he had exhausted his knowledge and would prefer to move on to talk of other things. "No, not that I've seen. Sam? You seen any family with her?"

Taking a long pull at his wine, the old farmer paused before answering. Head one side, he considered. "No. Don't think so. Mind you, you'd need to ask Oatway to know. Anyone going to see the old . . ." He hesitated. "The old woman, they'd've had to go past Oatway's place first."

"I think we need to see Oatway," said Baldwin ruminatively.

The Bourc whistled as he jogged easily southward, keeping the moors straight ahead. They looked beautiful, dark and soft with a vague hint of purple and blue, splashed with white in the shadowed areas where the low sun could not reach. Here, almost at the outskirts of Crediton, the moors took up the whole of the view, stretching from east to west as if trying to show him that they were the best route for him to take.

Soon he was out of the surrounding trees and winding down the lane that led into the town itself. Here he made his way to the market and bought bread and a little meat before carrying on. To his surprise, as he was leaving the market, he heard his voice called, and when he turned, he saw the merchant, Trevellyn, at the door to an inn.

"You leaving already?"

"Yes. My business is finished here. I am on my way back to the coast."

"I see. Going to Oakhampton, then south?"

"No," said the Bourc shortly, and explained his route. "It should be quicker."

"Yes," said the merchant. There was a strange expression in his eyes as he peered at the Bourc speculatively. "There's one easy route if you're going over the moors." Walking a short distance with the Bourc, he pointed to where the road began, and made sure that the Gascon understood the route before returning to the inn.

Mounting his horse, the Bourc stared thoughtfully after him for a moment. The merchant's helpfulness did not ring true. It was oddly out of character after their last meeting in Wefford. But his advice sounded good.

The road led between some houses, down a short hill, and out to a flat plain. Crossing a river, he found that the road was well marked and easy to follow, and soon he was whistling cheerfully as he went.

After riding for some hours the countryside began to change. In place of the thickly wooded hills near Wefford and Furnshill, the trees were becoming more sparse and the hillsides steeper and less compromising. The road straggled lazily between the hills as if clambering up them would have been too much effort, and he found himself quickening his pace. As a soldier, he disliked enclosed places: he wanted to get to the moors and openness.

Not far from them, he found the road entered a wood which stood as if bounding the moors, far from the nearest house. There had been no other travellers for over an hour, which served to heighten his sense of solitude.

Riding into the shadows, he noticed the air felt stuffy. There was a hush, as if even the wild creatures were holding their breath expectantly. The silence was intimidating. When a blackbird crashed off a branch and squawked its way along a hedge in front of him, he stopped his horse with a frown.

It had moved too early to have been upset by him.

Something else had worried it. He kicked his horse into a slow walk, and peered around with an apparent shortsighted lack of awareness. To have paused too long would have appeared suspicious, and he had no wish to avoid whoever could be ahead. But as his horse walked on, the knight was as alert as he ever had been.

Other men he had known had told him that they experienced extreme fear and a strange lassitude when they knew they were riding into a battle. He never did. To him warfare was life itself, his whole existence revolved around the fights on the marches, and without battle his life would have little meaning. No ambusher could have realized that from seeing him now.

His head moved sluggishly, as if he was dozing, and, as his horse meandered on slowly, his whole body slumped. Yet he managed to search each bush, every tree trunk, with care.

Only twenty yards into the trees he saw the first man and knew that he was about to be attacked.

The first glance merely gave him a flash of russet. If he had not already been expecting to see someone, he might have missed it, but that fleeting glimpse was enough. Considering where he would have put his own men for an ambush, he soon saw four other places where men could hide. There were too many—if he was attacked here he could be overcome too easily. With that thought in mind, he patted his horse's neck. Then, with a quick prayer, he clapped spurs to his mount and they thundered down between the trees.

Suddenly the wood was full of angry shouting. He heard the low, thrumming whistle of an arrow passing overhead, a shouted curse, cries and swearing as men realized their trap was sprung, and then he was through the woods and in the open. The moors!

Risking a look over his shoulder, he could see three men struggling with horses. One was up quickly, two others a little slower. Glancing again, the Bourc saw that the first kept ahead of the others.

In front there was no cover of any sort. A quick ambush was out of the question. He would have no chance to stop and mount an attack until he had managed to increase the distance between him and his pursuers. It would take too long to grab his bow or a lance from the packhorse. Pursing his lips, he considered as he kicked his mount again. Then, when he threw another glare back, he saw that his luck was with him. The man in front had increased his lead and was gaining while the others were falling back.

Still bent low over his horse's neck, he took the reins in his left hand and reached for his sword, checking it would pull free easily. Then he began to measure when he should turn.

It was not long. The leading man behind was a scant twenty yards away when the Bourc saw a stream ahead. Soon he felt his horse slow and pause before leaping. The Bourc just had time to drop the packhorse's leading rein before they jumped.

With his muscles coiled like huge springs, his horse bounded up and over the small stream, the packhorse following. It was then that he knew he had his opportunity. As soon as they landed, he reined in and turned, facing the man behind just as he leaped over the brook.

The Bourc immediately spurred back. While the man and his horse were still in the air, the Gascon pelted toward him, and when they landed he was only feet away. His pursuer had no chance of avoiding the swinging fist in its heavily mailed gauntlet. The blow met his chin, carrying with it the onward weight of both horses and the knight.

Seeing their friend tumble from his saddle, the other two slowed in their chase, and when they saw the Bourc draw his sword they seemed to lose enthusiasm for further battle.

"Go! Go and leave me—or accept the revenge of a knight's sword!" he shouted.

The two hesitated. Both were dark, thin-featured men, who could have been brothers, for although one was in russet and the other wore a stained blue tunic, they had the same pale skin and thick eyebrows. Their horses were cheap riding horses, not farm animals, and the men looked, although not rich, far from poverty. The Bourc's eyes narrowed as he stared at them. There was something wrong here, he felt. These men were not common footpads—or if they were, robbers in England were wealthier than in Gascony.

"Go!" he bellowed again, and the two exchanged a glance. One wheeled and started off back to the line of trees. When his companion did not move, he stopped and looked back, but before he could call, his friend had turned as well, with a last malevolent glare at the Bourc. Soon they were riding at a solid trot, back the way they had come.

Only when they had disappeared among the trees did the Bourc sheath his sword and drop from his horse. He quickly bound his prisoner's hands and feet before surveying him thoughtfully. Then, shrugging, he sat and built a fire while he waited for the man to wake.

Simon and Baldwin ate lunch at the inn, then, guided by Cottey's directions, they found their way to the dirt track that led to the Oatway holding. They rode to-

gether, with Tanner bringing up the rear, his features
set in a contemplative scowl as he lurched along.

The snow had stopped again now, but was thick
enough to cover most of the roadway, only the longer
shoots of grass just breaking through. Nearer the
trunks, the bushes and earth were untouched by the
white carpet, protected by the great branches high
overhead. It looked strange to Baldwin, as if they had
left the winter behind in the village and now had entered a warmer area where only the road itself was cold
enough to support the virgin whiteness.

While they were still out of sight of the farm, Simon
began to hear a regular noise over the steady rhythm of
the horses' hooves. Tap, tap, tap, then a pause, then two
more. It stopped, then after a moment started again,
and he cocked his head and looked over at Baldwin,
who caught his glance and shrugged.

As the tapping got louder, they arrived at a fork in
the trail. They chose the left-hand track, and the sound
became louder as they followed it. Rounding the last
bend, the forest fell back to show a large assart. In the
middle stood a weary-looking cottage with stained and
ancient thatch, which was allowing wispy tendrils of
smoke to filter out above walls that were in need of
fresh lime-wash. In front a cow stood chewing hay and
watching their approach with bored disinterest, while
between her legs chickens madly pecked at the earth
and packed dirt of the yard. Over to the left was a
strong fenced enclosure with goats, while on the right
was what looked like a coppice area, with thick stems
rising in clumps.

They slowly rode up and into the yard. It appeared
empty, but as they looked round, Simon became aware
again of the tapping. Touching his horse with his spurs,

he led the way to the back of the house. Here he found a pasture area, recently cleared. Stumps still littered the rough ground, and the snow could not hide the fact that the ground was only thinly grassed. The earth showed through in red scars.

At the far end was a tall, stooping, blue-smocked man with his back to the visitors, working at a series of heavy poles set vertically in the ground. Between each were bushes.

The knight and the bailiff exchanged a glance, then slowly rode on toward him. He was plainly unaware of their approach, and as they came closer they could hear him whistling tunelessly while he worked.

In his hand was a large-bladed bill, a short, solid curved-steel tool shaped like a stubby sickle with a wooden haft, with which he was tapping branches from the bushes around the stakes to build a woven fence of living wood which would later become a hedge—thick and strong enough to keep his animals in, and forest animals out. Suddenly he whirled, the bill raised in his hand, and stood facing them, unmoving, and they halted, considering him.

He was tall, at least five inches more than Tanner, more like Simon's own height of five feet ten, but although he appeared healthy for his age, which must surely be some five and forty years, he was quite stooped. There was a slightly unnatural color in his cheeks, as if he was on the verge of a fever. His eyes gleamed darkly from under bushy eyebrows, whose color had faded to pale grayness like his unkempt hair. It was the eyes that Simon noticed most of all. There was an odd expression in them—not fear, but a kind of suspicion.

"There's no need to fear," said Baldwin.

"No? Who are you? What do you want with me?"

"This is the Keeper of the King's Peace—and this is the Constable. I am the Bailiff of Lydford," said Simon reasonably. "Are you Oatway?"

The bill lowered a little, but the man's eyes still flitted over them in obvious doubt. "What if I am?"

"We need to ask you some questions. Did you know there's been a murder?"

"No," he said, and the surprise was plainly clear. His arm dropped down to his side, until the tool dangled, forgotten. "Who?"

"Agatha Kyteler."

"Her!" He hawked and spat, as if the name offended him. "Good!"

"Did you see her yesterday?" Simon asked.

"Yesterday?" He considered. "No. No, I don't think so . . ."

"Do you live alone?'

"No, my wife is here too." He added more softly, with a hint of sadness, "We have no children."

"Did your wife see her yesterday, do you know?" Simon persisted.

Oatway glanced down at his bill, then sighed deeply and brought it down sharply on to a log. It stayed there, gripped by its own slashing cut. "You'd better come and ask her," he said.

When he motioned, the three men dropped from their horses and followed him back to the front of the house, tying their mounts to the rail beside his log store.

Inside they found the cottage filthy, the atmosphere rancid from animal dung. Smoke hung in the rafters waiting to drift out through the thatch from the large hearth in the center of the floor. Entering, they had to step down. Like many older properties, to save the valuable animal dung, the floor of the house was built on a slope. As the winter proceeded, the level of the floor at the lower, byre end, would rise. When spring finally arrived, the manure could be taken out and spread over the fields and the floor level would drop once more.

Now, after some months of bad weather, the room stank, and Simon could see that the feces were almost at the level of the door. He tried to shut his nostrils to the stench, but found it difficult. To his satisfaction, he saw that Baldwin seemed to notice the smell more than him, although Tanner appeared impervious.

Mrs. Oatway was a broad, strong-looking woman of about her husband's age. She stood staring at them with a scowl of distrust as they trooped into her house, her hand gripping the large wooden spoon with which she had been stirring at the iron pot as if it was a weapon. Although her hair still had its native darkness, without the graying of her husband, her features were wrinkled with age and troubles. She looked as quick and sharp as a martin, shrewd and devious. And probably malicious too, from the look of her thin bloodless lips.

After quickly introducing themselves, Baldwin suggested that they should walk outside to talk, but she demurred. "I've got food to prepare. We can talk in here."

Grinning at the knight's obvious discomfort, Simon said, "We are trying to find out whether anybody saw Agatha Kyteler yesterday. Did you?"

"Her!" A sneer curled her lip. "I don't look for her. Why do I care for her, the old . . ."

"You disliked her after the affair with your chickens, didn't you?" said Simon flatly, feeling as he spoke that the words were superfluous, but wanting to cut off her flow of invective. It worked. She stopped and glowered at him.

"Well? What if I do?"

"Did. She's dead. We're trying to find out why. Why did you hate her so much?"

The shock was plain on her face, her mouth opening and shutting, and then she turned to her husband and stared at him. "Is this true? Eh?"

He shrugged as Simon said, "Answer the question, woman. Why did you hate her?"

Sighing, and after some grumbling, she told them of her suspicions about Agatha Kyteler's dog.

"Did you see her dog do it?" asked Baldwin, wincing and coughing.

"See it? No, but it was her dog, all right. We followed the feathers, didn't we?" She turned for verification to her husband, who nodded vaguely.

Simon considered. "Did you see her yesterday?"

"I . . ." She paused, her glower deepening.

"Good. When?"

"Middle of the afternoon."

"Why?" sighed Simon, and stared at her in silence.

"It was that dog again," she said at last, reluctantly.

"Her dog? What did it do?"

"It attacked my chickens again. Took another one. What was I supposed to do? Wait 'til it had killed them all? I went to tell her to keep the dog tied up. I told her if I saw it on our land again, we'd kill it."

"What did she say?"

"Her!" Her lips curled again in scorn. "Nothing, of course! She said it wasn't her dog. Said it was in the house with her all day. Well that was a lie!"

"You saw her dog, then?"

"No, but the feathers went her way again. It must have been her dog."

Shrugging, Simon glanced at Baldwin, who

coughed. "Very well," he said reasonably; "did you see anyone else there?"

Her face wrinkled with the effort of recollection. "Yes. Yes, while I was on my way there, Sarah Cottey and Jennie Miller were talking near the house. And some other woman was in the trees—I don't know who—when I left."

"What did she look like?" asked Baldwin.

"Look like? Oh, I don't know. Dressed well. Slim woman. Fairly tall and young, I'd say. Had a long cloak on, with fur on the hood."

"A gray cloak?" Baldwin's face wore a frown when Simon shot a glance at him.

"Yes, it was gray, I think."

"You saw no men?"

"No."

After checking where Jennie Miller lived, they walked out with relief to the open air. Even the extreme cold of the gathering darkness was preferable to the stench inside. The husband followed them, standing and inhaling deeply on his doorstep as he watched them mount their horses. Baldwin whirled his horse, and was about to ride off when he seemed struck by a sudden thought.

"Oatway. Why was your wife so sure that Kyteler's dog attacked your chickens?"

He stared up at the grave knight, then quickly glanced behind to the open doorway. Moving a little away from it, to stand closer to Baldwin, he said, "Because she thinks old Kyteler got her dog to come here."

"What? What do you mean?"

"Kyteler never liked my wife. My wife thinks she got the dog to come and kill our chickens, one by one."

Simon felt the hair begin to rise on his scalp as the

stooping man stared up at the knight, his voice dropping as if nervous of being overheard—not by his wife, but by someone else. "Kyteler was clever with animals. She always knew how to help hurt ones. And she could make potions for people too. She knew how to make potions, medicines and such. There's only one sort knows about that kind of thing." His eyes held Baldwin's with a fearful conviction. "She was a witch!"

It had not taken the Bourc long to light his little fire from one of the bundles on the packhorse, and he was soon sitting and warming himself. Munching on a hunk of bread, he watched the man until he saw a finger twitch and eyebrow flicker, and then he stood and contemplated the supine figure for a moment before walking over and kicking it. "Wake up! You have questions to answer!"

The man was thick-set and swarthy like a seaman. On hearing the Bourc's voice, he looked around blearily, his eyes unfocused and slowly blinking above the scuffed and bloody chin, until they caught sight of his captor and suddenly widened.

"I see you recognize me," said the Gascon affably, squatting nearby. Pulling out his long-bladed dagger, he toyed with the hilt for a moment, then studied his prisoner with a smile. When he spoke, his voice was low and reasonable. "Why were you trying to ambush me?"

Brown eyes narrowed and flitted around the landscape.

"I shouldn't bother, if I was you. They went. If they tried to come back, I would have seen them. They've left you here," said the Bourc.

"They wouldn't leave me alone." But the eyes were

uncertain as they moved over the surrounding country, and the Bourc let him search for his friends for a minute without interruption. There was no need to emphasize the fact. From here the moors fell down to the stream where he had caught the man, then rose to the trees a mile or so beyond. It was clear that no rescue was to be mounted from there. The Bourc watched as the man peered round to look up the hill, and grinned humorlessly. He knew that the country was as empty for nearly as far in that direction.

Holding the dagger delicately between finger and thumb, point dangling, the Bourc glanced at him again. "Why were you trying to ambush me? And why did your friends not shoot to kill? They had bows. I saw."

The eyes snapped back to his face and the Bourc was surprised to see no fear there. The dark face stared at him with what looked like a vague sneer. "Why do you think?"

"I have no idea. Why don't you tell me?" There was no answer. The man hawked and spat contemptuously. Sighing, the Bourc tried again. "My friend, I don't know. You don't look hard done by—you aren't starving or anything. You don't seem poor: your tunic is good quality and not worn."

Now the scornful expression grew. "We aren't footpads!"

"Ah! So why else attack someone you have never met? You have the look of a sailor, and yet I know no sailors . . ."

Seeing a quick interest, he paused. "So you *are* a sailor. But I know no sailors . . . No, I do not understand why you should have tried to rob me. So . . ."

"So maybe I just hate Gascons."

"Yes, that's possible," said the Bourc softly. With a

flick he tossed the dagger up. It turned once in the air and he caught it again by the hilt. Reaching forward, he touched the point at the top of the man's breast-bone. As the eyes widened, he smiled, then dragged the blade gently downward, so lightly he left no mark on his prisoner's skin, although it made the man squirm as it traced a mark of tickling terror down his chest. When it touched the top of his tunic, the Bourc angled it, so that it sliced through the cloth.

Speaking conversationally, he said, "You don't look worried about dying at my hands. I suppose you aren't scared of a quick death. That's fine. But it's getting close to dark, and it will be very cold tonight. I think I might just leave you here once I have cut your tunic off. After all, maybe *I* don't like sailors."

"You can't do that! I'm your prisoner, you must . . ."

"*I* must? I don't have to do anything. You attacked me. I can do as I wish with you—I'm a knight. And I have little time to take you anywhere, my lord expects me home in Bordeaux. No. I think that leaving you here to freeze slowly will be best."

Now the fear was fighting to overcome the disbelief. "You can't! What if someone finds me here and . . ."

"Finds you? Here?" The Bourc smiled at him again, his knife stilled, and he made a show of gazing round. When his eyes came back to his prisoner, he began to move the blade again. "I think it's a little unlikely, don't you? We're not close to a road here. I doubt whether anyone would come here before morning. Of course, a wolf might come along . . ."

"*Stop!*" It was a cry of panic. "I'll tell you why we were there . . . Stop! *Please!*"

The Bourc paused, his dagger poised under the man's heart. "Yes?"

"We were paid to attack you. Not to kill you, just to hurt you a bit . . ."

"Who paid you? And why?" He stared. He only knew a few people here—who could have asked for him to be ambushed?

"Trevellyn—Alan Trevellyn—he lives over north of Crediton—we work for him. He paid us to follow you today, after he pointed you out to us in the inn—told us he wanted you hurt. That's all I know."

For a minute the Bourc held the man's gaze while he considered. It was quite possible that the merchant had chosen to pay men to attack him. He had made sure of the Gascon's route by telling him which way to go. Nodding to himself, he whipped the knife down, swiftly slicing the tunic to the hem. Then he moved the blade down and cut the thongs hobbling his ankles.

"Very well. You can go now."

"But . . ."

"What?" He mounted his horse and stared down.

"My hands! And where is my horse?" the man said, struggling to his feet and dejectedly looking down at his bare chest.

"Be grateful you have hands left. As for your horse—you lost it. You know your own way home, I believe. I should begin walking."

He could still hear the man's hoarse shouting when he had left him far behind, but he soon put all thoughts of the robber out of his mind. His only concern was how to repay the merchant. Nothing else mattered.

- 7 -

Old Oatway stood and stared after the bailiff and knight as they left his holding, watching carefully as if doubting that they were truly leaving. Once out of sight of him and the house, Baldwin grimaced, glancing upward at the sky.

"It's going to freeze tonight," he muttered, and Simon nodded glumly, making the knight smile. Simon was not happy. Although he considered himself educated, and knew that rumors could easily accumulate around people in villages like Wefford with no reason, he felt nervous to have heard that the old woman was thought to be a witch. He shook himself. She was probably just a maligned old woman, that was all, surely. Glancing up, he saw the clouds were the color of old pewter, angry and heavy.

"Well, Simon? Shall we go and question this Jennie Miller? Or should we go and take a look at Kyteler's house?"

"Tanner? What do you think?"

Ambling up on his horse, Tanner looked down the lane toward Agatha Kyteler's house. "We have to see her place. We still don't know where she was killed. Maybe we'll find something there."

It was a good quarter of a mile to the little assart where the old woman had lived, and the difference between her cottage deep in the woods and the Oatway property closer to the road was startling. Here the thatch was fresh, not more than one summer old; the lime wash brilliant and white. Even the log store appeared to have been carefully maintained, the logs stacked neatly to the left of the house under an extension of the thatch.

In front were two wattle pens in which goats and chickens roamed, and there was barking and whining at the sound of their arrival. Simon and Baldwin sat on their horses while Tanner alighted and strolled to the door, banging hard on the planks with his fist. There was no reply, so after looking at Baldwin, who gave a curt nod, he lifted the wooden latch and shoved the door open.

Immediately a thin black and brown lurcher burst out, barking excitedly and capering around the horses, jumping up every now and again in an attempt to reach the riders. Laughing, Baldwin threw a quick glance at Simon. "The poor devil must have been in there since yesterday to be this happy to see a stranger!"

"Yes," said the bailiff, trying to keep his horse steady. The dog unnerved her, and she was trying to keep him in sight, reversing and turning skittishly as the black and brown streak tore round below. "Keep still, damn you!"

He was so involved he did not notice the constable come back to the door and motion to them. Grinning at his friend's discomfort, Baldwin dropped from his mount and lashed the reins to a sapling, then crouched and stroked the dog before rising, still smiling, to enter. But the smile left his face when he saw the constable's expression.

"This's where she died," he said curtly as he stood aside to let the knight in.

That was clear as soon as Baldwin's eyes accustomed themselves to the dark inside the small cottage. It was not as well built as the other houses in the village. In place of the solid timber beams, the gaps filled with cob and dirt to give a weatherproof shell, this place was a simple wooden shed, with earth and straw plastered on the outside to stop drafts.

One window high in the northern wall gave a little light into the gloomy interior. From it he could see that there was one almost square room, with a tiny attic area which had a seven-runged ladder leading up to it. Baldwin could make out the rugs and furs that made up the bed in it. Beneath, all was cluttered. In the center sat a fireplace, around which stood two small benches. To the right was a table, covered with earthenware pots and a variety of twigs, leaves and roots. A pair of large flat granite stones sat near the fire, which must have been used for grinding in place of mortar and pestle.

All over the floor were pots and vessels containing seeds and leaves, some fresh, some dry, giving the room a soft and musty odor. Around the walls and from the beams hung clumps of other branches and drying flowers, but it was to his left that his eyes were pulled. There had been a similar table to that opposite, a simple affair built of roughly hewn planks on top of a pair of trestles, but here it was fallen, as if pulled or yanked over into the room, away from the wall. The collection of herbs and other plants was scattered all over the floor, and broken pots lay underneath the toppled balks of wood.

"Wait here," said Baldwin shortly, his eyes narrowing as he stared at the floor around the table. Walking past the constable, he moved forward slowly, gazing at the wreckage while he wondered whether there had been a fight.

Turning, he looked at the other side of the room. There, he saw, the table was standing hard against the wall. The pots around it on the floor were neatly organized on both sides, as if placed in military lines. He wandered carefully toward it and picked up a pair. One contained what looked like several twigs of yew, the other held leaves and stems from a juniper. He replaced them thoughtfully and strolled back to the fallen table.

Here, it appeared, the same pots had stood at either side, with some resting on top. There were several more smashed on the ground, and leaves and roots were scattered all over the floor. Baldwin crouched down and picked up a few. Mostly they appeared to be different herbs. He smelled thyme, basil and sage. And something else. Over the heavy musk and the thick pine, he could smell the decaying sweetness. As Simon came in, darkening the room as his body shut out the light from the doorway, the knight's fingers encountered the slight stickiness, chilly and thick on the floor, directly in front of the table.

"Found anything?" Simon asked from the entrance. He saw the knight turn, his face sad and reflective.

"Yes. This is where she died. Her blood is all over the floor."

Sighing, the knight slowly traced the cloying mess from one extremity to the other. It seemed to have settled in pools on the ground, as far as he could see in the darkness. Mostly it had congealed, but here and there the thickest gobs still held viscous proof of their provenance. Tanner crouched by the fire. There was no chance of resurrecting the flames of yesterday, and he resigned himself to starting a new one so that they might have light.

Soon the flames were rising languidly from a small mass of tinder, and the constable found a small foul-smelling tallow candle which he passed to Baldwin, who waited by the table, crouching.

Taking the candle, the knight peered round, grunting occasionally to himself. To Simon, standing by the door, he looked like a hog grubbing for acorns. On hearing a muttered call, the constable strode to Baldwin, then lifted the bench while the candle was held to the top and sides, then the bottom and finally the trestles. Nodding, the knight allowed Tanner to set the table down again before continuing his study. He paused for a moment and stared fixedly, then reached down and picked up something, but Simon could not see what. At last he stood and, holding the candle high, looked hard at the wall behind the table. Snuffing the candle, he walked out, passing Simon wordlessly.

Outside once more, the dog sat, head on one side as if listening to their conversation. Tanner stood silently behind them.

"So what happened?" asked Simon. "Why would anyone kill her? It can't have been an accident."

"No, it was no accident." Baldwin dropped and snapped his fingers at the dog until it lurched to its feet and walked to them, head down and tail slowly sweeping from side to side. Ruffling the fur on the dog's head, the knight continued slowly and deliberately.

"I think someone went to her and spoke to her. She was at the table when she was killed. I think she was killed as she stood there, with her back to her killer."

The bailiff frowned as he tried to understand. "She

was standing at her table while the killer cut her throat?"

"Very likely. Blood hit the wall behind the table in a spray, so it's probable that she was facing that way when the killer struck. Blood was over the top of the table, not on the bottom, so the table was upright when the blow fell. After her throat was sliced, she fell back, and I think she pulled the table with her. No blood lay on the leg of the trestle, so I think that the table top protected it from her blood as she fell back. If she had fallen with the blow and then tried to haul herself upward, she would have left her blood on the trestle where it faced into the room. As it is, I think she was wounded and took hold of the table, then fell back to die, taking the table with her."

Both were quiet for a moment. It was Tanner who broke the silence. "Why would anyone do that to an old woman like her, though? She can't have had anything to steal. Why kill her?"

Turning to him, the knight gave him a cold smile in which the bitter anger flashed. "That's what we must find out."

While the constable went to fetch their horses, Simon contemplated his friend. "Baldwin, something's the matter. What is it?"

The knight stared at him for a moment. Then, holding out his hand, he showed what he had found on the floor. It was a gold ring, with a large red stone held in its flat face.

"That hardly seems the sort of ring for a poor old woman," mused Simon, and then he noticed the knight's expression. "Baldwin? What is it? Do you know whose ring this is?"

Baldwin stared at him dully. "Yes," he said softly. "I know whose this is."

* * *

Riding to the woods at the edge of the moors, the Bourc was frowning as he thought about the merchant. He had no desire to stay in England longer than was necessary, and could easily forget the incident, putting the attempted ambush down to outlaws. But that would be dishonorable. As a free-born Englishman, and knight, he had a chivalric duty to avenge this cowardly attack. To ignore it would leave the merchant thinking he had succeeded in scaring the Bourc, and that was not merely demeaning, it could be dangerous. If common people thought they could flout the law and attack their betters, all well-born men would be endangered.

The more he thought about it, the more he was convinced that his master would enthusiastically support him punishing the guilty man. He must go and see Trevellyn.

He was following the trail made by his horses and those of his attackers back to the copse, and slowed as he came closer. On a sudden whim, he swerved aside and rode a short way parallel to the trees, his eyes flitting over the boughs. Two men had come back this way. They could still be there.

After going east for some hundreds of yards, he abruptly cantered to the woods, crashing through the ferns and bushes at the perimeter, half expecting to feel the sting of an arrow at any moment, but he heard and saw nothing to warrant concern. When he paused, listening for any noise over the breathing of the two horses, there was nothing. He carried on.

But he kept an eye open all the way.

"Tanner? Are you all right?" Simon had watched the tall figure of the knight ride away, the small shape of the dog at his horse's heels—obviously having found another master, the dog was not willing to lose him. Now he turned, worried at the man's taciturn demeanor.

The constable was slouched on his horse as they passed the Oatway holding, chin on his breast as if asleep, but staying stiff and steady in his saddle. At Simon's question, his head snapped up, and the bailiff, to his intense annoyance, found himself being studied closely.

"What is it, Tanner?"

"I'm not sure, Bailiff."

"Come on, you've been quiet all afternoon. What is it?"

But the constable would not say more. All he had were vague suspicions: Greencliff had been nervous; the boy was more scared of the knight than of the body. That was normal for a villein, and Greencliff lived on Furnshill's land. It was only natural for him to be fearful of his master—his master held his life and livelihood in his mailed fist. That was no reason to denounce the boy.

In his youth Tanner had been a soldier for the king, as had old Samuel Cottey. They had been men-at-arms with one of the companies protecting the Welsh marches, and had witnessed all possible human cruelties at the time, or so Tanner had thought. He had seen the murders of the villagers, the rape of the women and the slow torture of men suspected of spying or fighting against the army, and it had been there, in the smoke and fury of the Welsh battles, that they had decided to leave warfare to others. They had returned home, Tanner to take up his father's profession as a farmer until he was elected to be constable. This he found a diffi-

cult responsibility to drop, but until the previous year
he had never been involved in more than the normal
routine of arresting cut-purses at Crediton market.

Last year that had all changed when the trail bastons
arrived and began to pillage the shire, killing and burning from Exeter to Oakhampton. That was when he rediscovered the joy of holding a sword. He had
rediscovered the wicked delight in fighting, when the
fighting was for a good cause. And now he had the
same feeling: that something was wrong in the area.
There was a killer loose. A killer who might strike
again.

It was hard to believe that Greencliff could be involved. He knew the boy, had known him for over ten
years, had known his father, and it seemed impossible
that he could be involved in this murder. And yet he
had been very nervous, and the body was very close to
his house . . .

"I think I'll leave you at the inn. I want to go and see
Greencliff."

The Bourc had travelled for over three miles through
the woods when he came up to the edge and gazed out
at the road. There was nothing overt to cause him
alarm, and he was about to kick his horse forward
when a sudden caution made him stop.

In front of him the lane straggled untidily down the
hill from his left, a red and muddy track cutting
through the woods. He could see how it bent, falling
down a steep incline to a rushing stream where a massive granite block acted as a simple bridge. At the other
side the road rose steeply, soon swinging right to follow the riverbank all the way to Crediton. All seemed
quiet and peaceful. There was no obvious reason for

nervousness, no indication that any other person was near, but he paused and frowned warily.

Although there was probably nothing, he felt a prickling of his scalp. Partly, he was sure, it was due to the perfect siting of the bridge. If he had wanted to attack someone on the road, this would have been the place he would have chosen. The steep sides of the two hills made a fast escape almost impossible, whether forward or back. The road narrowed at the bridge over the fast waters, funnelling the victim perfectly into a small area where it would be easy to haul a man from his horse or strike him.

Nodding to himself, he studied the trees lining the trail. They were thick, with dense bushes beneath. If someone was there, he would hardly be able to see them. But he could still feel the warning tingle of danger. Dropping from his horse, he lashed the reins to a branch and walked down the hill, along the line of the road but keeping just inside the trees. All the way he kept a wary eye on the dirt of the lane, but saw nothing alarming.

The traffic making its way from Crediton and Exeter to Moretonhampstead and beyond had chewed the path into a quagmire, and the deep ruts bore witness to the number of vehicles which had recently passed. Hoofprints scarred the red mud, leaving it cratered and pitted, looking like stew left boiling for too long.

As he walked down, pacing slowly and carefully as if hunting a deer, each step carefully measured to keep his noise to a minimum, he kept his attention on the bridge and the trees at either side. There was nothing obvious to warrant the trepidation he felt, but he had been a warrior too long to ignore his instincts. Only rarely had he known this sense of warning, but each time there had been good reason, and the feeling that this place was dangerous was not entirely due to its location. Somehow he *knew* that someone else was there.

He had covered almost half the distance when he heard a sniff and a low clearing of a throat from a few yards ahead: a man—and hidden to ambush a traveller.

Slowly, carefully, the Bourc laid his hand on his sword hilt and stepped forward softly, up to a thick oak bough with scrubby bushes at either side. Here he paused, putting out a hand to lean against the tree, listening.

"I reckon we've missed him. He's gone some other way."

He froze at the low, muttered words. They were closer than he had realized.

"Maybe. Maybe not. Maybe he's just round that bend now, just about to come down."

"Are you going to wait here all night just in case?"

"Trevellyn wanted him taught a lesson: not to insult an Englishman's wife."

"But we can't wait here all night. We'll freeze."

"We have to try to get him—do you want to lose your place on the ship?"

"It won't make much difference, will it? We never make any money on his ships now. Not since the pirates started attacking us every time we leave port."

"Just give it 'til dusk. When it's dark we'll get back to town."

The Bourc grinned mirthlessly, then began to make his painstaking way back to his horses. He led them slowly back up the hill for a distance before turning eastward and walking parallel to the stream. The men were too close to the bubbling water to hear his progress. He would leave them there. They would be occupied, and they could take a message back to Trevellyn, seemingly their ship's owner; although they had failed to teach their lesson, the Bourc did not seem to have tried to return to Crediton. Trevellyn would think himself safe.

The ride home for Baldwin and Simon was quiet. Neither was in the mood to talk. The knight rode along scowling fixedly ahead while Simon tried desperately to keep warm, taking the long fold of his old cloak and tossing it over his hunched shoulder as he rode in miserable, frozen silence. Every time the slow jogging of the horse would soon shake it free again. The trip seemed at least twice as long in the quickening darkness, with the wind slowly freezing the sweat on his back and the thickening mist ahead. Then, to his disgust, it began to snow again.

"God!" he muttered, and saw Baldwin shoot a quick glance at him.

"Cold, my friend?" he asked sardonically.

"Cold? What do you think?" responded Simon, throwing his cloak once more over his left shoulder.

"I have no idea!" The knight looked upward before taking his bearings. When he continued, there was a new note of seriousness. "We must hurry before we freeze, Simon. This snow is not going to stop."

They were back at Furnshill before six o'clock, both pleased to see the welcoming orange glow of the sconces, candles and fire through the tapestry-covered windows. Their breath was steaming in the bitter cold, and they rode straight to the stableyard, the knight bellowing for grooms, before dismounting. Even when the men had taken the horses, he stood quietly watching as their mounts were rubbed down, and when he turned to Simon, he gave a quick grin. "I always watch. It's a soldier's habit, I know, but old habits stay with you, and once you've lived in a war you learn that it's crucial that your horse is well fed and cared for. Hello! So you want food too, do you?"

This was to their visitor. As they had turned to walk to the manor house and the warm hall, they found the black and brown dog sitting inquiringly at the entrance to the stables, head on one side as if asking how much longer they must bear the cold.

The dog's tail began to sweep slowly from side to side, clearing a small fan in the snow, then he stood and waited for them. "Looks like you've a new member of your household, Baldwin," said Simon smiling. His only answer was a low grunt.

Tanner looked up sourly at the tree. His mouth twisted into a grimace of loathing as a small avalanche fell down his back and the wet trickle began its crawl toward his belt.

It was pitch black and freezing cold. The snow fell silently but inexorably. Hunching his shoulders, the constable peered ahead through slitted eyes, grunting in his misery.

After the knight and the bailiff had left, he had gone straight to the inn, drinking a couple of pints of mulled wine with the keeper. He had wanted to see if the man could add anything to his previous statement, and hoped that Greencliff might drop in, but the attempt was a failure. The landlord was happy to sell his wine, but denied knowing more than he had already told, and after morosely waiting for an hour or so, the constable decided to go and see whether he could find the youth at home. He obviously was not coming to the inn.

The track was miserable, though. Thick clumps of snow poured continually from the sky. There was nothing in his world but the cold and the snow. All creatures had fled the bitter chill, and the trees at either side were invisible. In the absolute blackness there was no track, just a small patch of clear road ahead before sight was obliterated by whiteness in the dark. Now and again Tanner would see a clump of higher snow, showing where a bush lay hidden, or the branch of a tree. Other than that there was nothing.

Shuddering, he kept his muscles clenched, trying to keep himself warm. His mouth ached, and the unprotected skin on his throat and face felt tight and crisp, as if it had become brittle and would snap if touched.

He came to the house without realizing he had left the woods, it was so still all round. It was impossible to see the edge of the woods, or the hedge where they had ridden that morning—all was hidden. But here at the house, he was aware that the road was rising, and suddenly there was the gray mass on his left. He gave a sign of relief, kicking his horse into a trot to get to the front, but then a frown darkened his face. There was no welcoming glow of fire. No smell of wood smoke.

The small windows showed as rectangles of deeper black in the darkness of the walls. He would have expected to find at the least a glimmer from behind the tapestries and curtains, but there was nothing. With a feeling of anxiety, he realized that the house must be empty. Greencliff could not be there. To make sure, he dropped heavily from his old horse and thumped at the door.

After a few minutes, he tried the latch. Inside, all was silence, the fire a faint red apology in the hearth. He looked all round, then glanced behind him. The view decided him. Leading his horse inside, he took off the saddle and bridle, then groomed her before seeing to the fire.

It was when he had just managed to coax it back into life that the knock came at the door. Instantly alert, he grabbed his old sword, a heavy-bladed falchion. Drawing the single-bladed weapon, he walked quietly to the door and opened it with a jerk.

"Thank God, Harold, I . . . Who are you?"

Tanner stared grimly at his visitor, a young man with the red blush of fear coloring his face. "I'm the Constable. Who are *you*?"

hat will you call it?" asked Simon as they entered the house, the slim figure of the dog walking ahead of them as if it had been born at Furnshill.

Throwing a quick glance at him, Baldwin said, "I'm not so sure I'll keep it. After all . . ."

"I think you'd better tell the dog that!" said Simon. "It's already decided to stay, from the look of it, whatever you think."

"It's not what *I* say that matters. I was thinking of Lionors."

"Ah! Yes, I forgot. Your wife!"

Baldwin shot him a glare of irritation, but it slowly left his features, to be replaced with a self-deprecating grin.

Lionors was apparently no difficulty. As they walked through the screens, they saw that Lionors and their companion had already met, and the two were standing and cautiously sniffing at each other in front of the fire. As they watched, the mastiff obviously decided that the newcomer was no threat, and walked away to lie before the flames, and soon the black and brown dog joined her, snuggling up against her large frame like a puppy. The mastiff lifted her head once, grumbled twice, but then flopped back down again and ignored the stranger. "I'll think of a name," said Baldwin with resignation.

Later, when he walked into his hall, Baldwin was amused to see Simon still standing and defensively warming his back before the fire, Hugh beside him and tossing more wood on, while Margaret stood by, an expression of tight-lipped exasperation straining her features. From her face, and from the look of embarrassed self-justification on Simon's, the knight knew his friend had been given sensible advice about not staying out too late in the dark when it snowed. In any case, Baldwin had heard the hissed fury in her voice—and the deference in her husband's—through the wall.

When he saw the quick toss of Margaret's head in his direction, the pained glance from Simon, and the straight back of the servant that seemed to imply that as far as he was concerned he would prefer to be anywhere other than with his master at the present, Baldwin smiled broadly.

"I suppose I could deny having heard your . . . er, talk?" he said, looking from Simon to Margaret, catching sight of a fleeting wince on the bailiff's face.

She raised a cynical eyebrow as she turned to face him with her hands on her hips. "Are you going to tell me you didn't know how dangerous it can be? How bad it is to try to travel at night? You know what the lanes can be like when the snow is heavy: are you both mad?"

"I am sorry, my lady," he said, walking to his chair in front of the fireplace. Before sitting he poured a tankard of warm wine from the jug on the hearth, then sat comfortably and sipped, his eyes fixed on her.

He looked like a bishop, sitting in his small chair as if it was a throne, she thought. Although he was not mocking her, she felt sure she could sense derision in his attitude, and drew in her breath to berate him in his turn, but before she could, he began speaking softly.

"Margaret, I'm sorry you were worried, but you must understand: there's been a murder. We could not just stop and come home as soon as it became dark. We had to see if we could discover any more."

"Of course I know that," she said sharply. "But how would it profit your investigation for you both to die on a journey home?"

"Not at all, of course, but . . ."

"Exactly!" she said, cutting him off. "Not at all! Two merchants and a monk have already died this year on the way from Tavistock. All because they carried on with their journey after dark. I will not have you two doing the same."

"But Margaret," Simon began, but she whirled, glaring, and he subsided.

"No more: I will hear no more!"

Baldwin grinned and inclined his head. "Very well, lady. I will ensure that we are back in time in future."

"Do so." She walked to a bench and sat, arms crossed. "And now, tell me about this woman who has died."

The knight and Simon exchanged a glance, then, at a brief shrug from his friend, the bailiff quickly told her of their day and what they had found about the dead woman. Tentatively sitting beside her, he told of their discovery of the body, their talk with the Oatways and their visit to the empty cottage. As he spoke, the mastiff rose and walked to Baldwin, closely followed by her black and brown shadow.

"Poor woman," Margaret mused when he finished, and Simon nodded. "And these Oatways think she was a witch?"

"Yes," said Baldwin. "They seem to believe she could make her dog do as she wished. As if a dog needed any prompting to do mischief! Anyway," he took Kyteler's dog by the head, holding it in both hands and peering into its eyes, "how could they think this one was evil?"

"That's what they do, though," said Hugh, and at his sudden interruption, they all glanced at him. Under their gaze he hunched his shoulders as if he wished he had not spoken, but then continued sulkily, "Well, it is. They get animals and make them do what they want. They can call on wild animals if they want."

Baldwin grunted, "Nonsense!"

"It's true! And if they want, some of them can change into animals, too! There've been witches all over here since men first got here," said Hugh, hotly defensive. "Ever since men came here and fought the giants away there's been witches."

"No, Hugh. There's no such thing as witches," said the knight. "There's only superstition and fear—sometimes jealousy. Never witchcraft."

"Then how did this old woman get her dog to go and eat these chickens, then?" asked the servant triumphantly.

Looking up, Baldwin smiled at him, but then his face grew somber. "Just because some old woman has a dog, and her neighbor thinks it was that dog that attacked her chickens, does not mean it really was. I think the dog deserves the chance to defend itself. Likewise, just because somebody thinks a woman is a witch does not necessarily mean she is, and she deserves the chance to defend herself."

"How can she? She's dead!"

"Yes. She is." The words came quietly.

Margaret stirred. "But, Baldwin, what if she was a witch?"

"Kyteler a witch? No, I don't think so." His face was as gentle as his voice as he looked over at her.

"Why not?"

"Because I do not believe such people exist. I cannot."

Simon leaned forward and peered at him. "But surely on your travels you must have . . ."

"No. I never found any proof of a woman having been a witch. Oh, I found plenty of examples of old women accused of being evil, of being involved in magic. I have seen many of them being killed. But there was always another reason why they were accused, it was never because anyone really believed they were guilty."

"What do you mean, 'another reason'?"

"I mean, whenever there was someone accused of being a witch, it was because the accuser wanted their money, their cattle, their house—something! Always there was something that would benefit the accuser. And, often, it would only turn up later, after the poor wretch had already died in the flames. Even the priests don't usually believe they're evil, which is why they rarely get to see the Inquisition even when they have been accused. They're usually killed by the mob. No, I do not believe in witches."

"But this old woman had all those herbs and roots," said Simon doubtfully.

The knight shot him a quick look. "Don't tell me *you* believe in witches?"

"Well," the bailiff explained apologetically, "it's not that I believe in them necessarily, or that I think

Kyteler was one, it's just that there are so many stories, and . . ."

"Oh, really!" The knight suddenly stood and strode to the fire, standing by the great lintel of the chimney, and when he spoke again his face was all in shadow, his body framed by the flames behind. "What is a witch?"

It was Margaret who answered. "Someone who uses magic to do what she wants."

"And what does she want?"

"Wealth. Love. Power. Sometimes to stay young. There are many things a witch can desire."

"Kyteler had none of these. What did *she* achieve?"

Simon stirred. "You say that, but surely witches use magic just to do evil? They don't need any benefit, they do it to please their master?"

"Their master? Who do you mean? The Devil?"

The bailiff was suddenly aware of the darkness, of the isolation of the manor as he answered, "Yes."

Filling his mug, Baldwin strolled back to his chair slowly. "Possibly. I would be happier to believe in a witch who was wealthy, though, than one who was trying to please her dark master!"

"All those herbs, though . . ." Simon began hesitantly.

"Simon, really! Do you accuse all leeches of being witches? She was probably good with them and used her skills to help others. There may come a time when even *you* are glad for the help of a wise woman who can stop the pain from a broken limb . . . Or piles!"

"What do you know of her death, anyway?" asked Margaret diplomatically after a moment.

Baldwin looked up. "Not much," he admitted. "She was seen in the afternoon by Mrs. Oatway, but from then on we have little information."

"No," mused Simon. "That's where we ought to start. We need to find out what Oatway and Greenfield were doing in the afternoon. They're the two we know who were supposed to hate her."

"Yes," said Baldwin, and stared at the fire. "There is another suspect, though, Simon. I told you of my friend's son." Glaring into the flames, he explained about the Bourc's visit to England to see the dead woman, and his ruby ring.

"Do you think he could have killed her?" Margaret asked.

Baldwin shook his head. "He was here out of gratitude. To thank her."

"If his story was true," she said quietly.

The knight did not respond, but later, when he left them to go to his room, his face still wore a troubled scowl.

When Simon at last drifted off into sleep, he had the same nightmare as before, but this time the figure in the flames was not the abbot. As it turned, to his horror he recognized the face of Agatha Kyteler, her eyes sad and accusing as they held his.

The constable arrived before nine o'clock the next morning with his companion. It had not taken them long to make the journey, though the snow had slowed them.

"Sir Baldwin, I thought you should hear this man: what he can tell about Greencliff."

The knight looked up, his jaw moving as he chewed on a crust of bread. The youth with Tanner was in his early twenties, tall, at least three inches over the constable, and with softly pale flesh. He looked fat, though his skin hung flaccid round his jowls and the hands

gripping the cap were chubby. His mousy hair was cut
well, and from his clothes he appeared well-to-do, with
a blue tunic of wool, and woollen hose of gray. On his
heavy belt he wore a small dagger.

"Who are you?"

The eyes rose and met his gaze unflinchingly.
"Stephen de la Forte."

To Simon he appeared to be a naturally haughty man
who was holding himself in with difficulty. His eyes
were a surprisingly light gray color, with glints of
amber, which made them look oddly translucent, and
they sat in a round face, where the definition of youth-
ful exercise was already fading into the rounded obe-
sity of premature middle-age. The bailiff instinctively
disliked him, and rested his elbows on the table to
study him the better.

"So, Stephen de la Forte, what can you tell us?"

The youth glanced quickly at the constable, a fleeting look, but Simon felt sure he could see a glimmer-
ing of devious intelligence there.

"I . . . I'm a friend of Harold Greencliff's—I've
known him for years. I went to his house last night to
see him, and the constable was there."

"I went there about an hour after leaving you, sir,"
interjected Tanner. "He arrived when I'd just settled
down."

"I see. Well, then. Why were you going to see him?"
asked Baldwin easily, leaning back in his chair.

"I . . ." he shot a glance over to Tanner again, suddenly nervous. "As I said, he's a friend. I saw him on
Tuesday, at the inn, and he seemed unhappy then—
troubled—so I wanted to see him again and make sure
he was all right."

"How do you mean 'troubled'?" said Simon frowning. The youth glanced at him with surprise and a certain distaste, as if he had thought the bailiff was a mere servant and should not try to become involved in the conversation of his betters. "Well?"

"I don't know. He was upset by something. I took him out to the inn and stayed with him, but he didn't tell me anything about what was worrying him."

He looked shifty, and Simon thought to himself that he appeared to be lying. Watching the boy's eyes flit away, he noted the fact for discussion with Baldwin later.

The knight was toying with a knife. Spearing a slab of meat, he studied it thoughtfully, and said, "You were so worried after Tuesday that you went back to see him late yesterday? Why not earlier?"

"I *did* go earlier!"

"And?"

His eyes dropped. "He wasn't there."

"When was that?" Simon said, leaning forward.

"I don't know. Early, not long before noon."

"I see. Tanner?"

"Yes?" The constable stepped forward.

"I assume Greencliff didn't turn up?"

"No, sir. We stayed there all night, but there was no sign of him."

"Stephen de la Forte, can you think of any reason why your friend should have run away?"

The eyes that gazed back at him were troubled, and the youth slowly shook his head, but Simon was sure that he saw certainty there. This boy obviously thought his friend was guilty.

Baldwin took a deep breath. "In that case, I think we'd better organize a search. It may have nothing to do with the death of Kyteler, but it certainly seems suspicious that on the day her body is found—especially so close to his house—he disappears. Very well." He glanced at Tanner, who nodded, and then, at the knight's dismissive wave, took the youth by the arm and led him out. It was only when they were gone and the door shut behind them that Baldwin turned back to Simon and sighed in relief.

"Let's just hope they find him, eh? I think he could help us with some points about this death, especially now he's decided to run away—that looks suspicious, doesn't it. It seems like a clear sign of guilt, thank God! It *wasn't* the Captal's son."

They spent the morning riding up over to the north on the road toward Bickleigh, the peregrine on Baldwin's arm in the hope of finding a suitable prey for their meal later, but saw nothing worth hunting. At last, when the sun had risen to its zenith, Baldwin snorted and gave a long grumbling sigh.

"This is ridiculous. I can't concentrate. Simon, Margaret, would you mind if we turned back home now?"

They exchanged a glance, then both nodded. Motioning to Edgar, Baldwin handed over the falcon, then turned his horse back home.

Up and down hills, the whole shire was smothered by the freezing blanket of white. In the distance Margaret could occasionally see the distant, grim grayness of the moors above the Dart, seeming different somehow from the rest of the countryside, gloomier and more menacing, proudly crouching on the edge of the horizon like a great cat waiting to pounce.

As they rode to the long track that wound through the ravine before the manor, Simon pointed excitedly at the path before them.

"Look at the prints! The search party must be back."

Rounding the last bend in the trail before beginning the half-mile-long straight section that pointed straight as a lance to the building itself, they could see the horses tied to the rail by the door, nuzzling at the ground or pawing the snow, trying to get to the grass that lay beneath.

"Edgar, see to the horses," Baldwin called, throwing the reins to his servant before running indoors. Pausing only to help his wife down, Simon hurried after him.

The search party was waiting in the hall, sitting at Baldwin's tables and putting the knight's men to good service fetching wine and bread. Before them sat the figure they had seen the previous morning.

Simon studied him with interest. The day before, he had looked nervous and scared of the bailiff and knight, but now he seemed dulled. He could have put it down to exhaustion, but Simon was sure he could see a glitter of defiance in the blue of the youth's eyes.

"Tanner?" the knight called, and the constable walked up from the bottom of the table.

"Hello, sir."

Motioning toward the farmer on the floor, Baldwin asked, "Where did you find him?"

Giving the boy a look of contempt, as if at his stupidity in being so predictable, the constable said, "Down south on the way to Exeter. He walked there overnight, apparently. He says he decided to leave. He wants to go to seek his fortune in Gascony." Shaking his head, Tanner glanced down at the boy.

Baldwin nodded. "Greencliff?" he said. "You know how this must make you appear to us. You're not stupid. Tell us about the day that the woman Kyteler died. What were you doing? Where did you go?"

But the youth merely stared back at him with eyes that suddenly filled with tears, and refused to answer.

After the search party had left, the constable cursing as he tried to form the ragged group of men into an escort for their prisoner, Simon stood for some minutes, gazing after them with a puzzled frown. When he turned, he saw Baldwin close by, glowering at the ground.

"I am surprised," said the knight slowly. "I find it difficult to believe that Greencliff is a murderer, and yet . . ."

"It's hard to see why he would keep silent if he was innocent. Especially when he must know he's the obvious man to suspect. And the body was right by his house."

"Yes, it was. But that's what worries me. I would have expected him to leave the body in the house or dump it somewhere else. Not there, right by his own place—it's almost as if he was trying to get us to suspect him!"

"How do you mean?"

"Come on, Simon. If you were to kill someone and wanted to avoid being found out, surely you would hide the body somewhere more imaginative, somewhere away from yourself, somewhere—even if the body *was* seen—it would not be connected to you, wouldn't you?"

Simon nodded slowly, but doubtfully. "Perhaps, Baldwin, perhaps. But equally, what if he had put Kyteler there hoping to hide her better later? He might not have expected anyone to see her there. After all, he might have thought he could get to her before anyone rose, to hide her in the trees where nobody could find her."

Scratching at his beard, his mouth drawn up into a cynical grin, the knight nodded. "I suppose so. But surely, if that was his plan, he would have been about his business early, before old Samuel Cottey would be up?"

"Don't forget the body was away from the road, hidden in the hedge. Maybe he thought he *was* going to be up before anyone else. In any case, why would anyone else have put the body there?"

"To implicate Greencliff, of course."

"But wasn't it too well hidden for that?" Simon frowned. "Away from the road, and under the hedge like that. If someone wanted to make sure that Greencliff was blamed, surely they would have made the body easier to find?"

"It was well away from the road," Baldwin admitted.

"Yes. And yet Cottey found it . . . I wonder how . . ."

"What?"

"How did he find the body over there? He would not have been able to see it from the road. I think maybe we should go and talk to old Sam and find out exactly how he *did* find Kyteler."

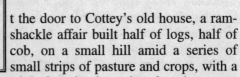At the door to Cottey's old house, a ramshackle affair built half of logs, half of cob, on a small hill amid a series of small strips of pasture and crops, with a huge wood-stack before the door, they found a young woman scattering seed for the chickens that scampered at her feet.

They had ridden from Furnshill almost as soon as they had decided to see Cottey, the black and brown dog insisting on joining them. The mastiff, taking one look at the cold snow, appeared to decide that the fire inside held more delights for a lady such as herself. Now Agatha Kyteler's dog capered along in their wake, occasionally throwing himself headlong into a thick drift when the whim took him. Arriving at the door to the house, he was a great deal more white than black or brown.

The girl stopped tossing her seeds and watched as they rode forward, and then, at the sight of the dog, she put her basket down and crouched, holding her arms widespread. The dog went into a convulsion of ecstasy, tail wagging madly, panting in apparent delight, as he danced slowly around her, allowing her to stroke and pat him.

Baldwin grinned as he swung a leg over his horse's rump. She was a reasonably attractive woman, only just out of her teens, with an agile, if sturdy, body. He could not help but notice that she appeared to be well-formed. When she glanced up at him, he saw that she had light-gray, almond-shaped eyes above a wide mouth with full and slightly pouting lips. Her hair was mousy, almost fair, and hung in a braid down her left shoulder. He drew in a breath, and let it out in a short sigh. She looked very attractive. "Calm down, fool! She's only a villein. You're just getting desperate, that's all," he told himself.

"Are you Sarah Cottey?" he asked, and she rose to her feet, wiping her hands on the front of her tunic. The innocent action pulled the cloth taut over her breasts, and Baldwin cleared his throat and averted his eyes.

"Yes, sir," she answered with a smile, seeming to notice his glance and subsequent embarrassment. She wiped her hands again as if taunting him.

"Er . . . Is your father here?"

She motioned to the road behind them. "No, he's over at my aunt's farm in Sandford. But he will be back soon, will you wait here?"

Simon exchanged a glance with Baldwin and, when he nodded, dropped from his horse, lashing the reins to a post nearby. "Thank you. Yes, we will wait."

She asked if they wanted to sit inside by the fire, but to Simon's surprise, Baldwin seemed happy enough to stand outside in the cold, talking by the door. Unknown to him, the knight remembered the smells from the Oatways' house.

"Do you know the dog? He seems happy enough to see you."

"Oh, yes. It's old Agatha's, isn't it? I always used to

make a fuss of him when I saw him. Isn't it sad about her, though? My poor father, he was so upset afterward, I thought he would never calm himself."

"Why? Was he a friend of hers?" asked Simon.

"Friend?" She looked at him with faint surprise, as if the suggestion was one she would not have expected. "No, of course not. No, he thinks she was a witch. Even just finding her, he was scared she could come back and haunt him if he treated her wrongly."

"Haunt him? Why should she want to?"

"Well, you know how these things are. People round here are worried if someone's a bit different. They feel anxious if someone new arrives in the village, and Agatha was different. He thinks she might come back as a ghost."

"How? In what way was she different?"

"In what way? She came from a land far away, so she used to say, from the kingdom of Jerusalem, and had a knowledge of herbs and roots. If someone was hurt, they'd go to her, and she could often help, even if it was only by stopping their pain for a short time."

"She was a midwife too, wasn't she?"

"Yes," she bridled slightly, as if nervous, or perhaps shy, and her cheeks' natural ruddiness deepened. "Yes, she was known for that. She was very clever."

Just then they all heard the rattle and clatter of a wagon and, looking up, they soon saw the old farmer sitting on his cart. His dog leapt from the back of the wagon and walked slow and stiff toward Baldwin's adopted friend, but they knew each other and were soon engaged in a companionable chase.

Samuel Cottey appeared unsurprised at the presence of his visitors, and he nodded at them both before springing lightly from the seat and beginning to see to the mule. While Simon and Baldwin waited, Sarah disappeared inside and soon came out again with a mug of warmed ale for her father. Taking it, he smiled at her, his face creasing into familiar wrinkles before tilting it and drinking deeply.

"So . . . What do you want, sirs?" he asked equably as he finished and wandered over to the men at his door.

"We had a few questions to ask about how you found the woman yesterday," said Baldwin by way of explanation. As he spoke, the farmer's daughter appeared again by the door, holding two pint mugs of ale for them. Smiling thankfully, Simon took both from her and passed one to Baldwin, but she hardly noticed his gratitude. She was staring at the knight as he spoke to her father, and looked pale, as if she was worried about something.

"First, can you tell us exactly how you found her? You can't have seen the body from the road."

"No, I didn't," said the farmer. His eyes were downcast, but then they rose to the knight's face, and Baldwin saw the defiance in them, as if the old man knew that he should not be scared of the dead woman, but was still not afraid to admit his fear. He quickly explained how his dog had wandered and found her body. "Daft bugger never was a sheep worrier. No, but he had found the old witch . . ."

"She wasn't a witch!" The hot defense came swiftly from the girl, surprising Baldwin.

"No, I don't think she was," he said gently, but then turned back to the farmer. "Then?"

"I . . ." His eyes became reflective as he thought. "I pulled her up a bit—she was so cold she couldn't be alive—so I lifted her a little to see who it was. I couldn't see from the way she was lying there, so I had to lift her by the shoulder. Well, when I saw who it was, I had to drop her, it was such a shock."

"Yes, yes. What then? You saw who it was, you saw how she'd died, what did you do then?"

"I buggered off! She *was* a witch." He glared at his daughter. "Everyone knows that. So I left her there and went up to the Greencliff place."

"Greencliff was there?"

"Oh, yes. He was there all right."

"How do you mean?"

"He was just out to see his sheep, he said. He was just getting ready to go."

"So he was dressed and ready? What time would that have been, do you think?"

"What time?" The farmer stared at him, then gazed at the view for a moment. Talking slowly and pensively, he said, "It was still dark, but I think the light was just starting . . . I don't know, really . . . I think it was around dawn, just before, not after . . ."

"But he was dressed and ready to go out?" Simon said, and the farmer turned to him and peered at his face.

"Yes, he was about to go out. He already had his cloak on, that bright red one. Why? Why does it matter?"

"The innkeeper said that he had made some comment about the woman on the day she died, something about her doing something. Greencliff said that if Kyteler wasn't careful, someone would do something to her. We think he might have killed her."

"That's mad!" Sarah's sudden interruption made them all turn in astonishment. "Harry wouldn't do anything like that. He's a good man, kind and gentle. He wouldn't kill like that—especially not an old woman."

"Be quiet, girl!" The old farmer's voice was harsh and thick, his face stiff in his anger at being interrupted.

"No, wait!" Baldwin's order made Sam Cottey fall back, as if the quick fury had exhausted him. "Now, Sarah," he said more quietly: "why do you think that?"

Glancing briefly at her father, she paused, but then decided that, having come so far, she should continue. "Because I know him. He's not cruel, he couldn't kill someone like that."

"The innkeeper seemed sure."

"He's wrong. Harold wouldn't kill an old woman like that, cutting her throat. He's too gentle."

Baldwin's eyes held hers for a moment, and then her gaze fell, and Simon was sure he could see the embarrassment there in the way that her face suddenly reddened.

"Perhaps," said the knight softly. Looking back at the farmer, he said, "Cottey, what would you say about that? Would you expect Greencliff to be able to kill an old woman in that way?"

"Not an old woman, no." Then his voice became bitter again. "But a witch? *I* should think he could have killed her and been glad! He might think it was a service—a Godly act—to kill the old bitch!"

Leading their horses from the house, Baldwin stopped for a moment and scratched at his head with a speculative grimace. "What do you think?"

Simon paused. "I don't know," he admitted. "I think she's as convinced it couldn't be Greencliff as her father is that Kyteler was a witch. Maybe . . ." He was cut off by running feet crunching on the soft snow.

"Sirs, sirs! Wait a minute!" It was Sarah again, rushing along the track with her skirts held high in her hands, giving Baldwin a glimpse of her legs.

"Yes?" he said.

She stopped in front of them, her face bright from her exertion, panting a little, then somewhat breathlessly leaned forward. "It can't have been Harold."

"Why?"

"He never thought Kyteler was a witch. He was sure she was clever, and she knew about plants, but he never thought she was evil or made magic. Anyway, he was a kind, gentle lad . . ." Her voice faltered as she caught sight of the knight's raised eyebrow. Baldwin smiled and said:

"So he didn't believe Kyteler sent her dog to the Oatways' chickens?"

"That!" She dismissed the idea with a curt movement of her hand, as if slapping away the suggestion. "How could anyone believe that! It was a fox or a weasel did that, not a dog. If her dog wanted to eat chickens, he would have eaten her own, not gone all the way to the Oatway holding to eat theirs."

"Hmm." Simon could see that Baldwin's eyes were looking over her shoulder, and when he followed the knight's gaze, he saw that the dog was lying in front of the door to the house, head between his forepaws and watching the huddle of humans, while the chickens strolled and pecked around him.

"But why then would Greencliff have said that about her? Why should he be so annoyed with her?" Baldwin asked after a moment.

"I don't know."

"Did he have many friends?"

"Not really, sir. Some of the other lads in the village. I suppose mainly he was friends with Stephen de la Forte."

"I see." He appeared to think for a moment. "All right, thank you for your help, anyway." He mounted his horse, then glanced back at the dog, and his voice held a hopeful note as he said, "Her dog seems happy enough here . . . I don't suppose you'd like to . . . ?"

She smiled, but shook her head. "No, I don't think father would like to have the old woman's dog here. He'd always be afraid that she might be watching over him, ready to protect him or attack the man that strikes him. No, you'd better take him back with you."

Baldwin sighed. "I suppose you're right," he said with resignation, and whistled.

Back at the road, Simon looked over at him. "Well?"

Baldwin shrugged. "It seems clear that the boy was ready to leave the house as Cottey got there, but that could mean anything! Maybe he was on his way to look after his sheep, like he said, or maybe he was going to move the body, to bury it or hide it . . . I don't know."

"What if he *was* going there to move the body? The girl seems sure that he could not have killed the old woman."

"Yes . . . It was strange, that. She was very defensive . . ."

Simon gave a short laugh. "Not that strange! She's young, so's he. He's good looking, so's she. I don't think you need look further for a reason than that."

"Possibly." Baldwin mused for a moment. "Let's see this friend of his—what was his name? Oh, yes, de la Forte. Let's see what else he can tell us."

Quickening their pace, they rode off to the inn to ask for directions. It seemed that the de la Forte house was on the way to Exeter, some three miles outside Wefford, so they turned their horses to the south and were soon there.

As they approached the property, Simon could not help letting a small whistle of approval pass his lips. "The de la Fortes seem well enough off," he said.

Baldwin nodded. The house was a large and rambling place, quite long, with a number of stables and outbuildings. In size it was bigger than his own manor, with the roof probably higher. The whitewash was fresh and clean, making the house almost seem to rise from the snowy ground in front as if it was made of the same material. Above, a thick mass of thatch was visible only from the chimney rising high overhead: around it the snow had melted, showing the graying straw beneath.

The roadway passed close to the front of the house, which itself lay in a shallow dip, while between the building and the trail was a stream, cutting a neat and precise line through the snow. As they followed the track to the house, they slowed, moving at a walk through the ford at the little stream's shallowest point before trotting up to the door.

Here the house had two stubby arms projecting forward like horns from a cow's head, and the door was in a yard formed between. There was a hitching rail, to which they tied their mounts before Simon knocked loudly at the door, while Baldwin tied up the dog with some twine he found dangling from the rail. He did not want his new dog to fight with the de la Fortes'. They did not have long to wait.

An elderly servant, a thin, gaunt man with an expression of intense trepidation, opened the door and peered out at them. Trying his most winning smile, Simon nodded to him. "Is Stephen de la Forte here?"

"I . . ." As he began to speak, there was a bellow from behind, and the servant spun round, quickly explaining to someone inside. "No, sir. No, I don't know who it is. He's asking for Master Stephen, sir."

"Out of the way!" came the voice, and the servant disappeared, his face replaced with that of an older man.

Simon felt he must be middle-aged from the thick and grizzled hair. Stout, not fat but thick in body, he stood a little shorter than the bailiff, but was almost half as wide again at the shoulder. He had a massive barrel chest, with arms that would have looked well as tree trunks, they were so massive.

His face was a maze of creases, some of them so deep that they appeared to be separate flaps of skin roughly butted together and sewn, and among them Simon could see the lighter marks, thickened with age, of old wounds from knives or swords. In the midst was a mouth, itself a colorless gash. A thick and broken nose sat between two bright and intelligent eyes, blue-gray like his son's, which stared unblinking at Simon.

"Well? Who are you and what do you want with my son?" he said, his voice harsh with distrust.

"You are de la Forte? Father to Stephen?" Simon heard the knight ask softly from behind.

"Yes. Who are you?"

Baldwin slowly paced forward until he was beside the bailiff and stared back unblinking. "I am Sir Baldwin de Furnshill," he said, announcing his title with careless pride. "I am Keeper of the King's Peace here, and my business is with your son, not with you. You will bring him here to me. Now."

Initially, Simon felt sure that de la Forte was going to explode like a child's firework. His face appeared to become suffused with blood until the veins stood out at his temples and neck. His eyes seemed to want to start from their sockets, as if they could themselves leap out and attack the knight. But as quickly as his rage appeared, it passed. After a moment's thought, he stood aside, albeit with bad grace, to let his visitors enter.

"My apologies, sir. I did not realize who you were. Please, come inside and seat yourselves by my fire while I fetch him out for you."

"Thank you," said Baldwin graciously as he swept inside.

This was no rude hovel. The screens gave into a broad and airy hall, with a huge fireplace built into one long side. Richly colored tapestries hung from the walls, with narrow-looking gaps where sconces lay to brighten the interior. Two large candle-holders in wrought-iron stood before the fire, shedding pools of light. A massive table built from thick oak timbers stood at the opposite end of the room, while a bench from it had been dragged to the heat, leaving the earth bare in two great sweeps where the rushes had been dragged apart by the bench legs. A chair and small writing table stood near the hearth, and a man, dressed like a monk in a habit, stood nearby.

"My clerk," said their host dismissively before walking to a chair and sitting, shouting at his servant to "Fetch him out!"

"You have a very pleasant house," said Simon tentatively, watching the clerk clearing his papers and hurrying from the room.

"Yes. It took many years to build, but now it is as we want it. I only hope," his face became sour, "we can make enough profit to keep it."

"To keep it? Why, what's the difficulty?"

"The Genoese, they're the problem!" he said, a sneer curling his lip. "The whore-sons want my money."

The knight turned and watched impassively as the man carried on. "I have been a successful merchant for many years, with my partner, Alan Trevellyn, and now these *Italians*"—he spat the word—"want us to pay them back the loans we have with them. It's madness! They know we can't. They just want to bankrupt us, that's all."

"Why would they want to do that?" asked Simon reasonably.

The gray eyes fixed on him. "Why? So that their own people can take over the trade from us, of course!"

"My friend has had little experience of trade. Perhaps you could explain for him," said Baldwin suavely, and Simon threw him a look of sour distaste. To his knowledge, his grasp of trade was as good as any man's.

"Alan Trevellyn and I hire ships and use them to bring wine over here from Gascony. We've been doing it for years. Going the other way we take what we can, wool mainly. When the ships arrive, they sell the cargo and use the money to buy the wine to bring back. We've been very successful over the years, but for the last two we've been unlucky. The pirates have caught our last two ships, and wiped out the profits from the previous ten. The profit is too low now, with the high costs since the harvests. So now the Italians want back the money they loaned us some time ago. What it means is, they want everything. It could mean losing our houses . . . Everything!"

They sat for some minutes in silence, and just as Simon opened his mouth to inquire about the consequences should he refuse to pay, they heard the sound of approaching feet, and through the curtain to the screens came the boy they had seen earlier, with a thin, mousy-looking woman who had enough similarity with Stephen to look like his mother. She stood just inside the doorway, darting little glances at each of the men, while her son strode in, boldly enough to Simon's eye, although his face held a curious expression. It was almost petulant annoyance, as if he were close to anger that the knight and bailiff should dare to invade his father's household.

He moved directly to a chair and sat, his pale features turned to the knight. "Well?" he asked, impatiently.

Baldwin sat quietly contemplating him. Then he sighed. "Your friend will not talk to us. It's as if he wanted to be convicted. I am not happy that he did it, though, and I want to be sure that I have the right man. So tell me, why do you think Greencliff ran away last night?"

"Last night? I've no idea," said Stephen, leaning back and crossing his legs. He appeared to have a slight smile on his face, which Baldwin felt looked a little like a sneer.

"You said to us that you went there because he was upset. In what way was he upset?"

The boy haughtily raised his hands as if in exasperation. "Oh, I don't know! Upset! Depressed! He just seemed to think that there was nothing to keep him here. He wanted to go: leave and travel. He's often said he'd like to go to Gascony."

Frowning, Baldwin peered at him doubtfully. "So although he could give no reason for his misery, you felt he was so upset that you tried to go and see him twice in one day?"

"Yes," said Stephen, and uncrossed his legs.

"How long have you known him?"

"How . . . ? Oh, almost all my life."

"You are of the same age?"

"Yes. We are both twenty."

"I suppose you must have talked about everything."

"Yes."

"So why was he upset, then? He must have told you."

To Simon it looked like a gesture such as a theatrical player might use. The boy half turned to his father, opening his mouth, then faced the knight again with a thoughtful frown on his face.

"It is difficult for me to tell you this . . . I do not know if I should, for he told me in confidence, and I swore to keep it silent for him."

"What?"

"A woman."

Baldwin sat back, his eyes still fixed on the boy, and Simon found himself immediately thinking: Sarah Cottey! It must be *her.*

"Who?" he heard Baldwin rasp.

"I cannot say."

"This is nonsense!" said Baldwin, standing abruptly. "You expect me to believe that he knew you since childhood, that you talked about everything, that you were close friends, and yet something like this, something so important, he kept from you?"

"No, sir. You don't understand." The voice was low now, almost sad. "She is well-born, not a villein. And married."

"Ah!" The knight faced him again.

"Yes. Of course I know who she is, but I swore to keep her name secret when he told me. You must understand, I cannot break my vow."

"No. No, of course not," said the knight hastily.

"But there's one thing I can tell you."

"Yes?"

"He couldn't have killed the witch?"

"How can you be so sure?"

"He was with me all afternoon on Monday, and all evening."

"So?"

"I heard from the innkeeper that old Kyteler was seen by Oatway in the early afternoon, so she was killed later in the afternoon or in the evening. I was with Harry all that time. It can't have been him."

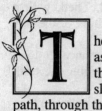he father stood at the door and watched as the two walked to their horses, untied the dog and mounted, turning and slowly making their way back down the path, through the ford, and on to the road back to Wefford.

There was a bitter wind blowing that felt as though it was licking at Simon's skin with a tongue of pointed ice. His cloak, tunic and shirt were of no use in defense.

"The weather doesn't improve, does it?" he remarked after some minutes of silence.

"Hmm? Oh! No, no it doesn't." Baldwin was jogging along with his mind completely absorbed.

Sighing, Simon said, "What part of his speech did you find confusing?"

"Only the one part that matters. Who is she?"

"This lover of Greencliff's?"

"Yes. Who could she be?"

"Unless Greencliff himself decides to tell us, I doubt whether we'll ever find out."

"No. Unless, of course, the boy de la Forte could be persuaded. I wonder . . . ?"

"What?"

"Was he lying, do you think?"

"Ah!"

Baldwin glanced across at him. "Well?"

"Well what?"

"Aren't you going to tell me not to jump to conclusions? Tell me I'm being fanciful?"

"Would you listen to me if I did?"

The knight considered. "No."

"Good!" said Simon and chuckled. Then, with a small frown, he said, "What did you think of the boy de la Forte?"

"Think of him?" Baldwin shot him a glance. "I don't know. I don't trust him. I think he is telling the truth about the woman, though."

"That Greencliff was having an affair with one?"

"Yes."

"I thought so too," said Simon, nodding. "So what do we do now?"

"I suppose we must release him. There can be no doubt that after Stephen de la Forte's evidence the boy could not have been close to the woman when she was killed."

"No, unless de la Forte was lying. I felt he was this morning, and again just now. It wasn't just a case of holding things back. I got the definite impression he was deliberately lying."

"Yes. I thought so too." Baldwin glanced up at the clouds overhead. "There's at least another hour and a half to dark. Do you think Margaret would grudge us a warming drink on our way home?"

If it had not been for the innocent expression on his face, Simon might have thought he had no ulterior motive. As it was, the bailiff knew well that the knight had a reason to want to visit the inn and his grin broadened as they increased their pace to a canter.

The innkeeper was sitting at a trestle in his hall when they arrived, both flushed from the sudden warmth after their ride. He was not alone.

This late in the afternoon, the inn was filled with people after their day's work. Farmers and laborers, local villeins and others lounged on the benches or stood near the fire. Round and portly, slight and thin, no matter what the drinker's figure, all became silent at the sight of the knight and his friend. The black and brown dog followed, slinking quietly as if he realized the impact of their entry.

"I think we've been noticed," said Baldwin quietly, almost laughing.

Simon could not find their situation amusing. His eyes were darting over the men in the room, trying to find a friendly face. There was none.

"Sirs! Please, come in and sit," said the keeper, evidently trying to put them and the others present at their ease. Walking to them, he quickly led the way to a table in a dark corner, at the back wall, near the curtain to the screen, and pulled over a pair of chairs.

"Wine," said Baldwin shortly, and the landlord nodded as he walked away. Pulling off his gloves, the knight looked around the room, and as he met the eyes of others there, they looked away. Gradually they began talking again under the firm gaze of the knight. The dog curled up under the table.

"Here, gentlemen, your wine. Warmed and spiced." The innkeeper set the tray down and poured them each a large measure.

"Good," said Baldwin, smacking his lips as he drew

the mug from his mouth. "Ah, yes. Very good, innkeeper. Will you join us? Will you take a drink?"

The expression of harassed nervousness disappeared. "Yes, sir, I'd like one. Here, let me . . ." He waved to a woman at the far end of the bar, a short and stout woman of a few years less than the landlord himself, whom Simon took to be his wife, and soon another tankard arrived.

"It seems to be a busy inn you have here, keeper," said Baldwin appreciatively.

"Yes, sir," said the publican, smiling as he looked around his empire. "Yes, we have some good customers here."

"Are they all locals?"

"Yes, all of them. We don't have many travellers at this time of year, not with the snow. That trade begins again later, when the spring begins."

"I see."

Simon leaned forward and set his pot down, resting his arms on the table, while Baldwin leaned back and gazed at the man sitting with them. The bailiff stared thoughtfully at his hot wine, then said, "We've been to see the de la Forte family. Do you know much about them?"

The innkeeper took a long pull of his drink and glanced from one to the other. "Not very much, no."

"So you do not know about their business?"

He shrugged. "Merchants. They import wine. Well . . ."

"What?"

"Oh, I was going to say, they used to, that's all. I think they've suffered more than most over the last few years. I used to buy my own stocks from them." He waved an airy hand vaguely toward the far side of the room, where he kept his barrels. "But then, when they began to lose their ships, I had to go elsewhere. Now I buy it from . . ."

"So you know the father, then?"

"Old Walter? Yes," he chuckled. "He still comes here every now and again, but not too regularly."

"What is he like?"

"How do you mean, what's he like?"

Before Simon could answer, Baldwin leaned forward conspiratorially, beckoning the landlord closer and peering round as if to make sure no one could overhear their talk. "You see, my friend," he said quietly, "Walter has suggested, in a way, that perhaps I might like to invest in some of his ideas."

"Oh yes?" The landlord's eyes were large moons, bewitched by the confidence.

"Yes." Baldwin peered over his shoulder, then beckoned again, settling farther forward on his elbows. "But . . . You will understand I'm a little suspicious, eh? I hardly know the man. What can you tell me of him?"

"Ah well." He settled, convinced of his audience by the knight's firm and steady gaze, and Simon could not help a small smile at the similarity between the innkeeper and a bird preening itself. He suddenly realized that this man spent the whole of his life having to listen to other people, and he was rarely asked to give his own opinion or express his feelings. He was enjoying the experience.

"I think he's a steady sort of businessman, in truth. He's been a merchant now for many years, and knows all the ways of the sea, and of Bordeaux in Gascony. Yes, if you want someone who knows his trade, he is good. He learned it while aboard ship as a boy, and soon managed to make enough to start to hire his own."

Frowning, Baldwin said, "But surely he would have had to make a fortune to be able to charter his own ships? How could a man who began as a crewman make that much?"

"Well, sir, I've heard tell . . ." His eyes darted nervously toward Simon and back, then his voice dropped. "I've heard tell that he was in Acre. I think he helped bring people out of the city when the Saracens took it, and he could charge as much as he wanted for that."

"Ah!"

In the dark, Simon found it difficult to read the knight's expression, but he was sure that he caught an angry glint. He recalled the knight's stories of how Acre had fallen, of how the seamen of all nations had appeared, like carrion crows to a corpse, demanding gold and jewels for taking people away to safety. After centuries of life in the Holy Land, families were ruined over a few short days, while the mariners became fabulously wealthy in hours.

"I think it was after that he managed to earn enough to hire his first ships. And build his house. But recently it seems he has suffered from the French pirates. I think he has lost several boats, and cargoes. That's probably why he wants a new partner."

"Yes, because he already does business with . . . Er . . . He told us his partner's name. Who was it?" The knight snapped his fingers as if frustratedly trying to remember.

"Alan Trevellyn, over toward Crediton. Yes, they have both been badly hurt by the troubles. You know, there have even been rumors that Trevellyn has somehow been responsible for the failures. I've heard that he was in debt to the French and told them when his ships were leaving, so he could pay back his debts with

his partner's half of the shipment as well as his own."
He sat back, his head nodding knowingly.

"Where would you have heard that from?"

Winking confidentially, the innkeeper said, "Walter de la Forte's son, sir. Stephen."

"So you think I should be careful, then?"

"Oh, yes, sir. Yes, very careful," His eyes flickered to the hilt of the sword at the knight's waist. "It's said he was quite a warrior in his youth, you know. That he was in many sea battles, not just at Acre, and that's how he got all those scars. Yes, I hear he's a bad enemy to have."

"Thank you, my friend, I am very grateful to you. You have given me a great deal to consider."

"Sir, I'm sure it's an honor to help," said the innkeeper, recognizing the dismissal and rising slowly to clear the table. When he had finished and left them, Simon glanced over at the knight.

"If he was in so many battles, that explains his scars."

Baldwin nodded. "Yes," he mused. "But there seems to be little to connect him to Agatha Kyteler apart from both of them being in Acre when the city fell—and that was over twenty years ago."

"Well surely that itself is enough of a coincidence."

"By the same token you might as well suspect me, Simon," said the knight dryly. "No, I don't see it. But who did kill the old woman?"

"I don't know. If Stephen de la Forte is telling the truth, it wasn't Harold Greencliff, though."

"No. No, his evidence shows that, doesn't it?"

Simon nodded. "Yes, we will have to let him go. Although I would like to know why he tried to run away."

"But if he refuses to tell us, we shouldn't keep him imprisoned," said Baldwin. "I will try to talk to him again tomorrow. Perhaps I can get him to tell us why he ran off."

Simon looked up sharply at the sad tone in his friend's voice, and then realized what it meant. Baldwin was sure that Greencliff was innocent, and that left him with only one suspect: his friend's son, the Bourc de Beaumont.

The next day was overcast and dreary, with a gray-black sky and a bitter wind that blew continually from the south. Gazing out from the front door, Simon and Baldwin exchanged a glance.

"We do need to speak to Greencliff," the knight reminded his friend, and then barked with laughter at the expression of doubtful misery his words brought to Simon's face. "Come on, the sooner we're moving in this, the better!"

"Simon!"

They turned to see Margaret in the doorway, her face anxious. "Take Edgar or Hugh with you. You may need to send a messenger if the weather gets worse, or if you get stuck somewhere overnight."

The bailiff glanced back at the sky, then nodded. "All right, tell Hugh to get ready."

She did better than merely sending the servant. While the two men meandered casually toward the stables and called for their horses and that of Simon's servant, Margaret went to work. When Hugh appeared, he was sulkily struggling under the weight of three packs carefully bound for protection. As he took one, Simon looked at his servant with an inquiring eye.

"She said you'd need it. There's bread and meat, and wineskins for you."

Tying the sack to his saddlebow, Simon said wonderingly, "Doesn't she know we intend being home by evening? What does she think we'll be doing today? Riding to the Scottish marches?"

Baldwin grinned, but kept silent. He was thinking how good it would be to have a wife like Margaret. He sighed, half jealous.

Meanwhile Simon was staring at his servant with exasperation. "Where's your cloak and jacket?"

"Why? Am I coming too?" His face showed his surprise.

"Of course! Come on, you'll have to do as you are. We can't wait for you to get changed."

"But I'll freeze!"

"Don't whine. You'll be fine if we ride fast. Now mount! We want to get to town as early as possible."

Smiling, Baldwin watched as Simon lifted his hands in a show of despair, only to let them drop with frustration. When Hugh was ready at last, they left the mews and stables, winding round to the front of the house where Margaret stood waiting to wave them off. The brown and black dog was there, and was about to follow, but Margaret pulled him inside. "If you're going to be travelling all over the shire, I think I'd better keep him here for now!" she said.

They waved farewell as Baldwin led the way down the narrow lane and out to the road, and once there, he spurred his mount to an easy canter.

It was soon clear that Simon's man had no great desire to be with them. Somehow he had never quite become used to the idea that a creature as tall and muscular as a horse could be trusted as a slave to his whim, and as a result he objected to trying to force it to his will. The inevitable consequence of bringing him was that the speed of the three was slowed to a more leisurely pace. Although Baldwin would occasionally urge them to move faster, he would soon discover that he and the bailiff were far in the lead and Hugh was moving along at his accustomed speed—somewhat quicker than a snail, but not a great deal.

In the end it took them a little over two hours to get to Crediton. The small market town was bustling, with wagons trailing through the slush on the roads, riders on horses trotting happily, and pedestrians groaning and complaining at the chilly mess thrown over them at the passing of each vehicle or animal. As they came closer to the church, a small herd of cattle stopped all the traffic, and the three had to pause and wait for the huge creatures to pass. They got to the church, and walked through the courtyard to the house beyond where the priest had his living quarters.

"Simon, old friend, it's good to see you again!"

The thin, older man grasped his hand enthusiastically, then stood back and studied him critically. "You're working too hard," he said at last, "and I think you aren't eating enough, but apart from that I am pleased to see you looking so well, thank God!"

"Peter, it has been a very long journey to get here, old friend. Do you not have any wine?"

Laughing, the priest led them indoors and seated them, Hugh grumpily taking a seat as close as he could to the fire. When all had a drink to hand, the priest leaned forward and peered at the knight with a serious expression on his face. "Sir Baldwin, do you have any suspect other than this miserable creature Greencliff yet?"

"I fear not, Peter, no. But why do you ask?"

Peter sat back in his chair and meditatively sipped at his wine while staring past Hugh at the flames. "It's very difficult. Sometimes a man admits to a brutal

crime in the confessional, and the confessor is bound
to keep his secret. Sometimes it likewise comes to pass
that a man is sent to the executioner when his father in
God is certain of his innocence." His eyes shot up to
stare at the knight. "I am as sure as I can be that this
boy is innocent of the woman's murder."

"But, Peter," said Simon, "does that mean he has denied it to you in confessional?"

"No! Of course not!" Peter was shocked. "If he had,
I would have to keep my peace. No, he is as yet un-
shriven, I could not have said anything otherwise."

"But you are sure?" asked Baldwin, his eyes glittering as he leaned forward.

"Yes. I am as sure as I can be that the boy is innocent of this murder. He just isn't capable."

"We think so too," said Simon.

"Why? Do you have another suspect? I thought you
said . . ."

"No, we were telling you the truth. We have no other
idea who could have done it. Do you?"

"Me?" The expression of amazement that spread
across his face was so comical that both Baldwin and
Simon began to laugh, making the priest gaze at them
reproachfully. "How could *I* know who had done it?
I . . ."

"Sorry, Peter," Simon managed at last. "No, you're
right. We didn't expect you to have any better idea than
we ourselves."

Standing, Baldwin yawned and stretched. "Since we
all agree that it was not Greencliff, I should get to the
gaol!" Sighing, he glanced at the priest and explained
about the evidence from Stephen de la Forte. "So you
see," he finished, "we are here to release him. It's not
fair to keep the boy imprisoned for no reason, and now

Stephen de la Forte says he was with Greencliff all afternoon and evening, there's little reason to keep him
locked up. No, Simon. You might as well wait. I shan't
be long."

"Bring him back here. I'll not see him go without
being fed—not in this weather," said Peter.

The town gaol stood at the entrance to the market beside the toll-booth, a small square block used mainly
for those traders found to have given short measures of
grain or bread, and only occasionally for holding
vagabonds found in the town. Strolling along the street
and trying to avoid the slush, it took the knight only a
few minutes to cover the short distance, and soon he
was at the entrance, wrinkling his nose at the smell
from the market, which had not yet been cleaned from
the last market day, and consequently was bathed in an
all-encompassing stench of animal and human ordure.
He glanced at the area, wincing, and then rapped his
knuckles on the heavy door.

Tanner had apparently been sleeping, for when he
opened the door, his hair was tousled and his eyes
bleared. At the sight of the knight, he seemed to
wake rapidly, and hauled the stiff door wide on its
hinges.

"Good morning, sir."

Stepping into the murky gloom of the gaol, the
knight sniffed with distaste. The men who were usually held here tainted the very atmosphere with the per-
vasive, metallic scent of fear. Convicts knew what
would happen to them once they were judged in court.
There were not many sentences available for a judge,
and justice usually followed swiftly after pronounce-
ment of sentence, most often involving a brief meeting

with the executioner. There was good reason to be fearful of the result of the legal process.

He shrugged. After all, that was the whole idea of justice.

"So, Tanner. How is the prisoner today?"

"Greencliff, sir? He seems well enough in body, but I wish he'd say something."

"Why? Has he stayed silent?"

"Yes, sir. Since the hour we brought him here."

Baldwin sighed. "Take me to him."

The cell was an unpleasant, square chamber dug under the floor of the main room. To get to it, Tanner had to lead the knight through the curtain at the back. Here, in the wooden floor, was a trap door with a simple latch secured by a thick wooden peg. Lifting this, the knight could peer into the dank and murky interior. "Greencliff?" he called doubtfully.

There was a sudden stir in the far corner, then a small splash as the boy stepped into a puddle, before his face suddenly appeared under the trap, and Baldwin could not help shaking his head and sighing. The boy who so recently had been a strong, tall and proud youth was a pale shadow of himself. His features were gaunt and strained, the skin appearing yellow in the half-light, his eyes vivid and unhealthy, his cheeks sunken and wan. His whole appearance was that of a man close to death, of someone who had fallen victim to an unwholesome disease.

"Tanner, get him out of there."

Fetching a ladder, the constable wandered back to the hole in the ground and slipped it down. "Come on, lad. The knight wants you up here," he called, offering his hand.

Leading the way to the front room, Baldwin stood

with his arms akimbo and looked at the boy, shaking his head. Greencliff held his gaze. There was fear there. The knight could see it deep in the boy's eyes, but he still appeared defiant. "Do you have anything else you want to say to me about the old woman's death?"

"The witch, you mean."

The knight peered at him. The boy's voice sounded as though he was caught between emotions. It was as if anger and impatience were struggling for dominance, but Baldwin was sure he could see contempt, and self-disgust as well. "Did you think she was a witch?"

"Me?" The question seemed to surprise him.

"Yes. What did you think of her?"

"I didn't *think* anything of her. I *know* what she was. *Evil!* She deserved to die!"

"Why?"

The boy held his gaze firmly and squared his shoulders with resolution, but kept silent. After a few moments Baldwin sighed.

"Very well. If you do not wish to answer, I cannot force you." Greencliff glanced across at the imperturbable Tanner, and looked as though he was sneering. Turning, he was about to return to his cell when Baldwin stopped him. "No. Your friend has told us the truth."

"What?" Greencliff spun round and stared at the knight. Strangely, Baldwin thought he was now scared. "Who?"

"Yes, we know you were with Stephen de la Forte all afternoon. He's told us."

Later, he knew that what worried him most was the fleeting glimpse of absolute surprise as the boy said, "Stephen?"

~ 11 ~

They left the youth with Peter, consuming a large bowl of stew with minced meat, the priest happily organizing more bread and ale as his guest ate.

Simon rode quietly with his chin on his chest. The three were silent, as though they were all contemplating the murder. At last, he said, "Baldwin, we must go back to Wefford and ask other people what they saw."

"Yes, you're right. We've spent two days thinking that Greencliff had to have been involved. Now we must get back to trying to find out who really was," said Baldwin and sighed.

"Calm yourself, Baldwin."

The knight threw him a puzzled glance. "Eh?"

"Just because it wasn't Greencliff, that doesn't mean it was your friend's son."

"No, but it's suspicious, isn't it? That he was here, trying to find out about her just the day before she . . ."

"Look at it this way—nobody saw him there, did they? Let's see whether someone else *was* there."

"Yes," he said, but not convinced.

"So, where do we start?"

The knight stared ahead, toward the town itself, as

if there was a clue in the scenery itself. "Jennie Miller, I suppose. Oatway said she was there with Sarah Cottey. Let's see her. She might know something that can help us."

The mill was a large sturdy building to the east of Wefford, and they found their way to it by the simple method of riding through the woods until they came to the stream, then following it north. It stood in a small, sheltered valley. Looking at it, Simon thought it looked like a safe and warm property, with thick walls and a pleasing drift of smoke rising from the tall chimney. At the eastern end lay the stream from which it gained its power, quiet and sluggish now, but wild and fast when the countryside was less frozen. They had to cross the leat to get to the buildings, and were able to use a small wooden bridge that had been thrown over to help the farmers bring their grain.

Baldwin nodded approvingly as he gazed at the mill and the stream. Mills were jealously guarded by their parishes, and although the knight had only been here once before, and then only briefly, he was proud of this one. It had been built by his brother only five years before, and he was glad to see that the walls were maintained well, their limewash shining in the light.

But then, as they approached, they heard a high scream, and they spun in the saddles to look for the source. It seemed to be a young girl's voice.

At first there was nothing, then the cry came again, shrill and urgent, from the woods to their left, on the other side of the water. Baldwin felt at once for his sword and drew it, scanning the trees with a frown while Simon fumbled for his knife and spurred his horse alongside. They exchanged a glance, then both prepared to leap the stream.

"Ignore them, they always make a lot of noise."

Turning, Baldwin saw a smiling, chubby woman in her early twenties standing in the doorway. He motioned toward the noise uncomprehendingly. "But . . . Who?"

Her smile broadening, she put a finger and thumb to her mouth and gave a piercing whistle. Immediately the sounds stopped, and were replaced by giggling and laughter, quickly approaching. After a few minutes four children appeared, two boys and two girls, the oldest being perhaps ten or eleven years old.

The knight's eyebrows rose in sardonic amusement as he carefully stowed his sword away. Simon frowned as he watched the oldest of the two girls walk sedately to her mother. It was the girl from outside the inn, the one he had seen when they had brought the witch's body back from the field. His eyes rose to take in the mother as Baldwin asked:

"You are Jennie Miller?"

Her grin broadening, she nodded as her brood accumulated around her, their eyes fixed on the strangers. "Yes. It was the children playing. I'm sorry if they troubled you."

Clearing his throat, Simon glanced at his friend as he shoved his dagger back in its sheath. "It's no trouble. We . . . Er . . . Thought someone was being attacked. That was all."

The knight dropped from his horse and glanced up at Simon, then over at Hugh, who sat glowering with a face like thunder. When he turned to the woman, Baldwin was laughing. "No, it's no trouble, apart from having a fit of the vapors!" He strode forward. "I am Baldwin Furnshill. Can we speak to you?"

At her nod, Simon leapt down, threw his reins to

Hugh and told him to wait with the horses. She led them inside, sending the children away to play.

It was sparsely furnished, but welcoming and homely. There was a large table, benches, and chairs at one end, and at the other was a huge chimney and hearth, now filled with logs and roaring. Motioning toward the flames, Jennie Miller said, "My husband isn't here right now, he's woodcutting. If you want him, you're welcome to wait by the fire . . ." Her voice trailed off inquiringly.

Taking a seat at the fire, Baldwin sat and smiled. "No, it was you we wished to see."

"Me?" Her eyes seemed huge, but not from fear, only amusement. This was no mindless peasant, Baldwin thought to himself, this was a quick-witted and intelligent woman. She was also clearly not afraid.

"It's about the death of Agatha Kyteler," said Simon as he too dragged a chair to the fire, then sat contemplatively staring at her. "Did you know her?"

She laughed as she sat. "Everyone knew old Agatha! She was always helpful to people who needed her sort of aid."

"What sort of aid?"

"Anything," she shrugged. "A salve for a burn or wound, a potion to clear the bowels, a medicine to stop pain—she could give help to almost anyone. She was very clever."

The bailiff peered at her. "You know what the people say about her? That she was a . . ."

"A witch?" She laughed. "Oh, yes, some said so. Why? Do *you* believe that?"

From his side Simon heard a low chuckle. He subsided back into his seat and left the knight to the questioning, faintly offended by his friend's amusement. It was not surprising that he should believe, after all. He was not credulous, but everyone knew that the Devil was all round, trying to win over the forces of good and subvert them. Shrugging, he watched the woman as Baldwin began to question her.

"You didn't think she was a witch?"

"No," she said dismissively. "That was only a rumor. Old Grisel wanted to blame her bad luck on someone else. Bad luck happens. When we lose a sack of corn to weevils we don't say someone put a curse on us. It just happens. When something steals chickens, there's no reason to assume that it must be because of a witch. It was probably a fox!"

"But you said she was good with herbs and making medicines. Is that why people were prepared to think it was her, do you think?"

"Yes, I think so. She was very skilled, she knew all about different plants. That doesn't mean she was a witch, though, and after all, everyone was happy to take advantage of her knowledge when they needed her."

Baldwin nodded thoughtfully, and Simon was sure he was thinking of Sam Cottey, the man who denounced the old woman as a witch but still used her poultice when he hurt his arm.

"When we spoke to Grisel Oatway, she said that she saw you there, at Kyteler's house, on the day she died. Tuesday. Why were you there?"

"Tuesday? Yes, I was there. I went to speak to her about my pains. Last time I was with child she helped with the sickness and cramps. I wanted to see her about some more herbs, like the ones she gave me before." Seeing the knight's raised eyebrows, she giggled. "Yes, I'm carrying a baby again."

"Oh . . . Fine, well . . ." To Simon's amusement, he

saw that it was the knight's turn to be embarrassed. "I see. You *did* see her?"

"Oh, yes. Yes, I was there early in the afternoon."

"Do you know when?"

"Not really. About two hours after noon, maybe."

"How was she?"

"She was fine. A bit tired, I think. She used to spend so much time out collecting plants, and I think it was getting to be a bit too much, really."

Simon cleared his throat and leaned forward. "You seem to be one of the very few people who knew her, like Sarah Cottey, but no one seems very sad that she's been killed."

"Why should we be sad? The poor old woman never tried to make friends here."

A picture came into mind of the Kyteler cottage, fresh painted, with a new roof. "The house was well-looked-after. She was surely too old to paint and thatch—who did that for her?"

Jennie Miller smiled knowingly. "She wasn't stupid," she said, and her voice seemed to imply that she was not certain that the same could be said for Simon. "Whenever someone went to her, they had to pay in some way. She was not anxious for money, she had little need for it. No, she asked for things that were useful. If someone needed her help, they had to help her."

"How long were you with her on the day she died?" asked Baldwin.

"How long? About an hour. Maybe a little more. I don't know. Sarah might be able to help, she was there just as I left."

"Do you know why she was there?"

"I think you should ask *her* that, don't you?"

Baldwin studied her with a small frown, but slowly

began to nod his head. "Perhaps we should," he agreed. "Grisel Oatway said you and Sarah were still there when she arrived?"

"Yes. I waited until Sarah had finished. She's an old friend, and I wanted to speak to her. We started to walk up the lane toward the village . . ."

"How long was she with Agatha? When roughly did you leave?"

"Oh . . . She was there maybe a half-hour. Anyway, that's when Grisel came rushing down toward the cottage. She was mad! Another of her chickens had been taken."

"She was mad? Mad enough to . . . ?"

"If you're going to ask me whether she was mad enough to kill, I'm not saying yes or no," Jennie Miller said tartly. "How could I say? She was furious, certainly, she could hardly talk without spitting. When she got to the cottage we could hear her voice clearly, shrieking at poor old Agatha while we walked back."

"You didn't go to help?"

"Help who? Would *you* have gone to separate two strong old women like them? I'd think even a knight could be nervous of doing that!"

"Yes," Baldwin said, with a sudden smile. "You may well be right."

"When you left, did you see anyone else on your way home?" asked Simon.

"Anyone else?" she paused, then spoke more quietly. "I thought I did, but Sarah didn't."

Leaning forward, both men kept silent as they waited.

"Back toward the road, I could swear that I saw a woman slipping off the track and into the trees as we came close."

"Who?" Simon felt as though they were getting closer to the details now, nearer to an understanding of what had happened.

"I don't know," she said, glancing at him with a sympathetic smile, seeing his near despair. "It was dark there under the trees like I say. It was a woman, I think, but she was wearing dark clothes. Both cloak and tunic."

"And Sarah didn't see her?" he persisted.

"Ask her, but I don't think she did. She would have said. *I* didn't mention it because I wasn't sure myself."

"Do you know of anyone who hated her enough to want to kill her?" Baldwin asked.

She screwed her face into a cynical wince. "It's hardly the sort of thing people are going to talk about in the lane, is it? No, I've never heard anyone talk about murdering her."

"Not Grisel Oatway, for example?"

"No."

He sighed and gazed into the fire for a moment. Looking up, he caught a thoughtful glance from her.

"There *is* something else."

"No," she said, but she looked troubled.

"It is very important, Jennie," the knight persisted, seeing her waver. "Whoever did this could kill again. He's like a mad wolf: once it's tasted the blood of a man, we have to kill it because it's not scared of people any more. It kills once, then it knows it *can* kill. Whoever killed Agatha Kyteler can do it again, because he *knows* he can do it."

It was then, when his friend sat back, looking like a kindly father persuading his daughter to obey for her own good, that Simon saw her expression change. She stared at Baldwin with a curious resolve, as if the decision was as difficult as agreeing to take a lover, but once her choice was made, she was committed. "Very well. But I cannot believe it was him."

"Who?"

"Harold Greencliff. When we came to the edge of the trees, where the lane meets the road, I saw him."

"With Stephen de la Forte?"

"Not that I saw. I didn't see Stephen, only Harold. I thought he was alone."

"What was he doing?"

"Nothing. Just standing there with a horse."

"His own horse?"

She gave a quick laugh. "Harold have a horse? No, he does not need a horse. Anyway, it wasn't a man's horse. It was a nice little mare, brown with a white flash on her head and little white mark on her left fore-leg like a short stocking. He was standing and holding her just off the road, almost in the trees. He looked like he was trying not to be seen."

"If it was Greencliff, did Sarah Cottey see him?"

She smiled sadly, but shook her head. "No. Sarah would have commented. She couldn't have seen him."

"Why?"

"Sarah and Harry grew up together. They were as close as brother and sister. I think she still expects him to . . ."

Baldwin gently prompted her. "Expects him to what?"

Sighing, she stared at the flames. "To ask her to marry him. She's always loved him. But he doesn't love her."

"Who is he in love with?"

"I don't know, but find the owner of the little mare and I think you'll find out."

*   *   *

Outside once more, they found Hugh lurking sulkily, still holding the three horses by their reins. He was about to make a comment when he caught sight of the two men's expressions and decided quickly not to. The look on his master's face told him that this was not a good time to mention the weather. Handing their reins to them, he watched sullenly while they mounted their horses, then climbed on to his own and, shivering slightly, trotted off after them.

There was no conversation as they went. His master and the knight were sunk deep in thought, and Hugh found himself wondering what had been said in the mill. Both seemed morose, glowering at the trail ahead as they retraced their tracks to the road. He shrugged, putting their mood out of his mind. His priority was a warm meal and drink. Drink mainly: a pint of mulled wine or ale. It was so cold out here, with the wind whistling and howling between the branches of the trees like lost souls.

At the onslaught of a fresh, bitter blast that cut through his flesh to the bones beneath, he turned his head aside and groaned with the sheer pain of it.

"Are you all right, Hugh?"

Looking up he saw Simon swivelling in his saddle to peer back. Seeing the question in his master's eyes, he tried to answer through his chattering teeth, but all he managed was a grimace. It was with relief that he heard Simon say, "Baldwin, we'll have to stop to let Hugh warm up. I think he's frozen colder than the mill leat."

"If you're sure," said Baldwin giving Hugh a sour look. "But what with him not liking horses and need-ing to sit in comfort with a fire, I honestly cannot see why you don't simply pension him and have done with him!"

"He's not that bad!" Simon laughed as they carried on. Hugh carried on in silence, but kept his ears open. "And he was outside all the time we were indoors by the fire."

There was a pause for several minutes, and then Hugh heard Baldwin mutter, "So what do you think, Simon?"

"About Greencliff? It looks suspicious, doesn't it? He was there, after the women seem to have left the witch alive, we know he was nearby."

"Yes," Baldwin mused. "But why? Why was he there? And whose horse was it? Why would Greencliff *want* to kill Agatha Kyteler?"

"Are you going to arrest him again?"

"I don't think so. Let's see if we can find out more first. Maybe it was just sheer coincidence he was there. I don't want to arrest the boy every other day! And what about the horse, and this other woman? Maybe she can help us."

"Maybe. But who is she? How can we find out *who* she is?"

By the time they clattered into Wefford, Hugh felt as if he was frozen to his saddle. His hands seemed to have taken on a will of their own and refused to obey him as he tried to force them to open and release the reins. When Baldwin sprang lightly from his horse, at first he stood impatiently and watched with his face set into an irascible grimace. Then, slowly realizing that Hugh was having difficulty, he stepped forward, peering at the servant with concern. Seeing the miserable set of Hugh's face, he quickly moved up and helped the dejected man from his horse, assisting him to the door of the inn while Simon handed the horses to the hostler.

Coming into the hall, he saw the innkeeper bustling, moving men from the fire and making space for Baldwin and the frozen servant. Simon could see that the knight had a look of perplexed concern, while Hugh merely wore his usual glower. But there was no mistaking the pain on his face as the heat began to thaw him, the warmth sinking into his flesh like stabs from needle-sharp darts of pure agony.

Sitting near his servant, the bailiff contemplated him. "How are you feeling?"

"I'll live. I've been worse," Hugh grunted.

The innkeeper returned with jugs of heated wine, setting them beside the fire to keep hot, and nodded to Hugh while pouring a mugful. To Simon he looked like a leech trying out a new quack remedy, watching intently while the servant took a gulp, then leaning forward to top up the mug before standing and walking off to see to another customer.

Baldwin took another mug, then sat with his head down, staring at the hearth, sipping every now and again at his drink like a merchant testing a new batch of wine. When Simon glanced over at him, he was surprised to see that the knight had stiffened, his eyes gazing into the distance.

"What is it?"

"I was just thinking . . ." He broke off as the innkeeper came back and stood near Hugh, watching him carefully as if to see whether his medicine would work or not. "Ah. I was about to call for you. Tell me, has Greencliff been ill recently?"

"Harry? No." His eyes flitted to Hugh, clearly comparing the strong and healthy farmer with this weak-seeming servant. "He's been fine."

"Oh. And his friend? Stephen de la Forte? Has *he* been unwell?"

The man's face was baffled as he shook his head.

"Trying to find out if Greencliff or de la Forte might have needed to go to Kyteler for something?" asked Simon with amusement as the innkeeper hurried off to serve another customer.

"It was worth a try!" said the knight. He shrugged. "But it's no help again. Greencliff was there the day Kyteler died. He was in the lane after Oatway saw the old woman. Some other woman might have been there too, after Oatway. Apparently Greencliff was very annoyed with the old woman that afternoon, so he may have seen her, though we don't know why. He may have had a chance to get to her."

"But de la Forte said . . ."

"That they were together all afternoon? That's true."

"He would, wouldn't he?" said Hugh glumly.

Simon glanced at him. "What do you mean?"

"They're close friends, aren't they? Maybe this de la Forte knows Greencliff has done it and wants to protect him. So he told you he was with Greencliff all afternoon when he wasn't."

Baldwin grunted assent. "It *would* make sense."

"I don't know," said Simon thoughtfully.

"The only other people who had a real reason to kill Kyteler were the Oatways," Hugh continued doggedly.

"But if Kyteler was still alive after she'd been there . . ." Baldwin began, and was interrupted by Simon.

"Was she? We don't know that. Grisel Oatway could have killed her. We don't know for sure that any other person saw the witch alive afterward. If they did, we haven't spoken to them!"

"Witch!" muttered the knight with a brief display of disgust, then took another sip at his drink. "All right, so we cannot be certain that Oatway did *not* kill her. Likewise we cannot be sure that Greencliff didn't. There appears to be another person involved somehow as well, this strange woman in a gray cloak. Oatway saw her, so did Jennie Miller. Sarah Cottey didn't mention her, though. Who could she be?"

"There is the other side, don't forget." Simon gulped wine, then leaned back and sighed contentedly as he felt it heat a simmering trail in his body. "Why was she carried away from her house up to Greencliff's field?"

"Maybe Grisel Oatway admitted to her husband that she had killed their neighbor and he carried the body away to hide the fact that they'd done it?" said Baldwin.

Hugh looked up. "That's daft," he said flatly. Baldwin was so surprised at the contemptuous comment he could not respond, but simply stared at the servant, who suddenly seemed to realize what he had said. Flushing an embarrassed red, he quickly carried on, "What I mean is, sir, that they're not young, the Oatways. If they were going to hide the body, why would they take it so far away? They'd dump it nearer, somewhere they knew, somewhere they knew other people wouldn't go."

"He's right," said Simon frowning. "If they had done it, they would hardly carry it so far. And, if they *were* trying to keep it all hidden, they wouldn't have left the Kyteler house with blood everywhere, would they?"

The knight mused. "That's an interesting thought. But the only conclusion must be that it's even more likely that it was Greencliff. The body was close to his house—maybe he was intending to go and hide it somewhere *he* knew, but Cottey interrupted his plans? It's possible."

"Yes. The only reason for thinking he must be innocent was the fact that Stephen de la Forte gave him an alibi, but from what Jennie Miller said, that wasn't true," Simon said. "Which means he must have been lying to protect his friend."

In the middle of the afternoon they left Wefford and began to make their way back to the manor house at Furnshill. They had to take the journey slowly, for Hugh's sake, but now even Baldwin did not grudge the servant his speed. It was too clear that the man was in pain.

They were home again by three, and when they arrived, Simon insisted that Hugh stay before the fire for the rest of the day, an order with which the man appeared to be well satisfied. It was the small grin of gratitude that showed the bailiff just how poorly his servant was feeling. Usually he would have expected a grimace and complaint even for such a welcome command.

Leaving him staring at the flames with a blanket over his shoulders, Simon took Margaret outside to where Baldwin stood contemplating his view. Turning, the knight pointed to the house with his chin. "How is he?"

Margaret shrugged. "He seems all right, but he'll need to stay indoors for a while. He got very cold."

"It was my fault," said Simon. "I should have waited while he got his clothes, but I thought he was making excuses to avoid coming with us to Crediton."

"It's easy to forget how cold it is in winter," his wife agreed. "But make sure in future that he's got his cloak and jacket if you're taking him with you."

He nodded grim-faced, feeling the implied rebuke. She was right. The winter here, so close to Dartmoor, was always brutal, as he knew well. To change the subject, he said, "Did Hugh tell you what we have learned today?"

From the look on his face she knew he felt the blame for Hugh's illness. That was only right, she thought. If they had not been quick once they realized how badly chilled Hugh was, the man could have died. Although he was the son of a moors farmer, and had himself spent much of his youth out in all weather looking after the farm's flock of sheep, he was not indestructible. The weather here was so cold as to stop a man's mind. It was foolish not to take the correct precautions when there was time. Now, though, there was no reason to make her husband feel any worse. As she gave a brief nod and listened to him explain about the conversation with Jennie Miller, she studied his features with frowning concentration.

"So you have three real suspects, then," she said at last.

"Grisel Oatway, Greencliff and his woman, you mean?" said Simon.

"No, Oatway sounds as though she only really bore the old woman a grudge," she said, frowning. "If she wanted Kyteler dead, she sounds shrewd enough to have persuaded the villagers that her neighbor was a witch, and let them do her work for her; let the mob lynch her. She doesn't sound like she's a killer herself." She shot a sharp glance at Baldwin.

The knight sighed and looked out over the hills as if seeking inspiration. "I know. There's only the one other suspect. But I find it hard to believe that my friend's son could have been involved. He was too grateful to this woman to want to kill her."

"Maybe you're right, but you'll need to speak to him."

"He's probably back in Gascony by now. He has not been seen since Tuesday. For now, I think it's the woman who is the problem. How can we find out who she is?"

"Oh, really!" her scathing tone made both men turn and stare. When she saw their puzzled expressions, she said, "The woman lives somewhere near. There can't be many for you to consider."

"But we have no idea where she might have come from, Margaret," said Baldwin, peering at her with a small frown. "It could be from miles away!"

With a small laugh, she shook her head in mock disgust. "You think so? I doubt it! She must be close by— it's surely unlikely that Greencliff would have taken a lover who lived far away. How often could he meet her if she lived far off?"

"So? How many women do you think live . . ."

"Simon, that's not the point. De la Forte said she was well-born, didn't he? And how well she was dressed! How many *wealthy* women are there round here. That's the point!"

To her relief, she saw the understanding dawn. Baldwin looked as though he had doubts, but Simon grabbed her, tugging her to him, and embraced her, hugging her tight.

"I married a philosopher," he said, gazing into her eyes and smiling.

Baldwin turned back to the hills. It was good to see his friends happy, but . . . He grinned as he accepted his jealousy.

Noticing the way he averted his gaze, Simon pulled away from his wife. He knew how much his friend wanted a wife and a son, and was sympathetic. It was impossible for him to understand how a man could live alone. But he could not stop himself patting his wife's belly affectionately, hoping again that this child would be strong and healthy, that the birth would not be difficult. He wanted a son badly, but more than that he wanted his wife to be safe and well. A passing thought struck him. Did this woman of Greencliff's have children? Then another idea leapt into his mind: was she pregnant? Had she gone to the midwife to get medicines for a birth, like Jennie Miller?

He frowned as he stared at the moors in the far distance. Who could this woman be? Was she the last person to see Agatha Kyteler before her murderer—if she herself was not the killer? Who was this mystery lover of Harold Greencliff?

But the hills gave him no inspiration.

The next morning, Jennie Miller winced, tugging her old woollen shawl tighter around her shoulders as she rattled her way toward Crediton on their little wagon. It was still freezing here on the road through the woods, even with the sun up. The ground crackled under the steel-shod wheels as ice on puddles and streams fractured under their weight.

Usually it was Thomas, her husband, who would ride into town. He would make his way in, calling cheerfully to his friends and customers, before delivering their sacks or collecting the items he needed. But this winter was hard and he must fetch more wood while it was possible in case the snow stayed.

When they had bought the wagon, it had seemed to

be a good idea. Then they had only been in the mill for two or three years. The steady flow of grain from the manor had been enough to keep them busy and provided them with a good income, even after paying the taxes to the manor. That was in Sir Reynald de Furnshill's day, of course, before his death and the arrival of Sir Baldwin. Their trade had been so good with the new mill that they had been able to bring in corn from other parts and make a good profit. That was why they had decided to purchase the wagon. It meant they could buy corn from farms far distant and sell their flour in Crediton to the bakers.

Now, though, after two years of appalling harvests, the wagon seemed less of a good idea. They could hardly afford to keep and feed the old horse, and with the prices demanded in the town for the simplest goods, Jennie felt that they were better off staying in Wefford. At least in the village most things could be bartered.

She passed the new house, where the de la Forte family lived, with little more than a cursory glower. She felt it was unfair that some were able to buy whatever they wanted when so many of her friends were starving or freezing to death for want of fuel. At the thought of death she shivered, thinking again of poor old Agatha.

The old woman was sometimes difficult to deal with, Jennie knew that. But even so, there was a strain of decency in her that was missing in others. Old Agatha was always prepared to come and see anyone in pain, always happy to help. She may not have been as subservient as some would have wished, but that was no great problem to Jennie. She was not overly humble either, except to the priest in Crediton, Peter Clifford. He was a *holy* man; he deserved respect.

Agatha Kyteler's death was very sad, she reflected. It was all round that the old woman's throat had been cut. The innkeeper had charged people a fee to look, and many had taken the opportunity, giving gory details later to the others waiting eagerly outside, and that made her feel sad, as if the old woman had been molested. Jennie was happy enough to go and watch the executions when she had a chance, but that was different. That was seeing other people who did not matter. It was quite an exciting time, usually with a small, thriving market to supply food and drink to the crowds waiting for the first hanging, waiting to see the criminals being lined up, having the ropes set around their necks until they were hauled upward, spinning slowly, twitching and jerking in their struggle for life, while the hemp tightened and stopped the breath in their throats.

If the felon was particularly strong and muscled—she had seen it a few times—one of the executioners would have to grab the swinging body, then leap up and embrace it, using his extra weight to jerk the victim down hard and fast to snap the spine. But they only did that if the felon was still alive after fifteen minutes or so, not before. After all, they had to make sure that the crowds were satisfied with their viewing first, even if there were a lot more criminals waiting for their turn. Otherwise there could be arguments over the gambling, with accusations that the executioners had intentionally killed the victim before the allotted time, that they had been bribed, and they could all do without the problems that kind of altercation produced.

At the outskirts of the town, she took a wineskin and sipped at the freezing liquid. Then, taken by a sudden urge, she halted the wagon and dropped to the ground.

Crunching through the thick layer of snow, she walked to a bush at the edge of a field strip, lifted her tunic and skirts and squatted, giving a sigh of relief. It must be the jogging of the wagon that always had this effect, she thought.

Then, over the sound of her little stream as it died to a slow trickle, she heard a merry, tinkling laugh, and the steady clopping of hooves. Lifting herself, she peered over the shrub toward the road, where she saw two riders. One, she saw, was a middle-aged man, thickset with a heavy belly, and a face like a mastiff's, all wrinkled and creased, with two small and cruel eyes. The other was a younger woman, tall, slim and dark, with long braided tresses lying over her shoulders as black as ravens' wings, framing a face as beautiful as the Madonna's. Her hood was back, but the fringe of rabbit fur showed light against the darker gray of the cloak. She glanced at the miller's wife, then through her as if she was no more important or interesting than the shrub she squatted behind. The man ignored her completely.

As Jennie stood and let her skirts fall, her hands automatically smoothing her tunic over the top, her eyes remained fixed on them.

Simon and Baldwin arrived at the de la Forte house in the middle of the morning. Both felt the cold today, as if Hugh's misery of the previous afternoon had reminded them both how chill the weather was. It had not snowed again overnight, but this morning the clouds were thick above, looking as soft as goosedown in the heavens, and promised more snow to come.

Today they were prepared. Edgar rode with them,

and each carried a sack of provisions and a wineskin. The bailiff had felt the bitterness in the air early when they left, and glancing at Baldwin, he could see that the knight was feeling the cold as well. His chest was rigid, his shoulders hunched and his mouth pursed, looking as resolutely slammed shut as an iron door. Gentle though the breeze was, it made up for its lack of speed by shearing through any protection, seeming to aim straight for the vitals.

Arriving at the house, he thought it looked very peaceful and quiet, with the smoke rising and gently swaying before dispersing in a straggling feather that trailed languidly northward. Here, between Wefford and Crediton, even the noises from the strip fields would be hidden by the thick woods all around on a clear summer's day. Now there was nothing. Not even the lowing of the oxen in their byres could be heard. The only sounds were of their hooves crunching and the occasional tinkling of their horses' harnesses, like soft bells in the pale sunlight.

With the glory of the view, with the gently rolling hills looking smothered by the tree-tops that stretched off, over to the horizon, and with the air chill and fresh in his lungs, Simon felt good: strong and healthy, alert and sharp. The ride had honed his senses, and he waited for the door to open with a keen excitement. He wanted answers from young Stephen de la Forte.

The thin, pinched face of the manservant at the door was an anticlimax, as if his temper needed immediate expression and any delay was merely frustrating. The feeling made him curt with the man, and when the old figure retreated, cowed, into the screens, he was ashamed of himself. There was no need to vent his spleen on this man.

Baldwin noticed his sharpness and smiled to himself as he followed the bailiff into the main hall. Here they were left alone for a moment while the servant disappeared through to the solar. The knight walked to the table, pulled out the bench, and sat, his eyes on his friend.

The bailiff was strolling round the room casually, his hands clasped behind his back, the very picture of suave relaxation. But Baldwin could see the suppressed excitement in the way that his head kept snapping toward the door at the faintest sound. He was clearly on edge.

They had been waiting for several minutes when they heard the clumping of feet in the solar, and shortly afterward the door opened to show Walter de la Forte. He paused, glaring from one to the other, then gave what looked like a sneer and walked to the table where Baldwin sat watching him with calm and detached interest.

To the knight it looked as if the merchant was taunting them, as though he felt they were both so insignificant as to hardly merit any respect, and Baldwin was intrigued. It was strange that a man of lowly birth should feel superior to a bailiff and a keeper of the king's peace.

It seemed to Baldwin that Simon was as interested in the man's attitude as he was, and began to question him with a soft, almost gentle voice.

"After our last meeting, we have released Harold Greencliff."

Watching closely, Baldwin saw the man's sudden doubt. Walter de la Forte glanced across at the knight, before staring back at Simon. "Released him?"

"Yes. Your son made it clear that they were together

all day, so of course Harold could not have been in-volved, could he?"

"Oh. No, I suppose not."

"Yes, but if Harold Greencliff *didn't* kill Agatha Kyteler, who did? We can find no one who can suggest any good reason so we wondered if it could be some-one from her past. We've heard that you were involved in the escape from Acre with your partner."

"So what? Anyway, who told you?"

"Did you know that Agatha Kyteler came from Acre? That she came over with a boy and saved his life?"

At first Walter de la Forte looked merely astonished, but when he spoke, his voice was as forceful as before. He asked truculently, "What's that supposed to mean? What is this? Are you accusing *me* of something? Is that it? You feel you have the right to come to my house and accuse *me* of murdering some old woman just because we were in the same place ages ago?"

"We have the right to go anywhere and ask anyone about the matter. I work for the de Courtenay family, and my friend works for the king. We have the right to question even *you*!"

Something snapped in him. The merchant half rose from his chair, his feet sliding back under him as if he was about to leap up and attack Simon, but even as he moved, Baldwin coughed and twitched his sword hilt with studied carelessness, making the steel stub at the end of the scabbard scrape over the floor with a harsh, metallic ringing. When Walter de la Forte shot him a glance, there was an expression of faint inquiry on the knight's face, as if he was merely waiting for the man's response. But Walter de la Forte saw that Baldwin's hand remained on the grip of his sword, and the mean-ing was clear.

Clearing his throat, he glanced from the knight to the bailiff with a slight nervousness. Then, slowly, he appeared to accept his position, stretching his legs out once more with what looked to Baldwin to be a physical effort, as if it was hard for him to surrender in this way. When he spoke, although he had made an effort to compose himself, Baldwin could hear the anger thickening his voice.

"What do you want to know?"

Simon walked to a chair by the fire and sat, leaning forward on his elbows. Staring at the ground at first, he said, "It's a coincidence, that's all. You are an important man in this area, do you know of anyone who could have had a motive to kill her?"

Shrugging, the merchant shook his head and folded his arms. "No."

"In that case, are you aware of anyone who had a particular grudge against her from Acre? We have heard that you made a lot of money from taking people out during the siege."

The eyes were suddenly narrow and shrewd. "If that's what you've heard, it's not true!"

"Really?" said Baldwin dubiously, and saw the merchant's eyes flit to him. "You must understand, though, that all we have to go on is what other people tell us. All we know is what they have said about you. If you want to put your own side to us, you should do so now. Otherwise we'll have to assume . . ."

"Yes, yes, yes, you've made your point!" He reflected a moment, then gave a quick shrug, as if mocking himself for unwarranted fears. "I don't see why not. I have nothing to hide." Pausing, he stared into the fire, and looked as though he was collecting his thoughts into a coherent story. When he started, his voice was low and thoughtful, almost as if he had forgotten their presence.

"Alan Trevellyn and I were in that hell-hole, Acre, during the last days of the siege—before it fell. We were shipmates on a French galley, both young and fit. We were ideal for the life. God! When we were young, a man had to stand on his own! Not like nowadays." His brows pulled into a short glower of fury, but then they cleared again and his voice became reflective once more, while his eyes moved from Simon to Baldwin. The bailiff was sure that there was a shiftiness in them, and watched him carefully as he spoke.

"When we left, it was without the ship's master. He had taken some of our men to help with the fighting near one of the city gates, and while he was gone a group of English knights with Otto de Grandison came up. They were all that were left of the English soldiers sent by the king. De Grandison took a ship, and some of his men took over ours. If we hadn't agreed to go with them, they said they would kill us. We had to agree. De Grandison slipped his lines almost immediately, but the men on our ship insisted that we must wait, and while we did they brought on men and their wives, taking all their money in exchange for organizing their escape. Gold, diamonds, rich jewels, spices: the knights took it all. But only those with a lot of money could come aboard. Others had to stay behind. If they had nothing, they had no escape. It was that easy."

Baldwin frowned. He recalled de Grandison, a strong Swiss, tall and proud. It sounded odd that he could have allowed his men to take advantage of the siege in such a way. He peered at the merchant, who now scowled back with a glower of sulky self-justification. "It wasn't our fault," he protested. "If we'd argued, what could we have done? We couldn't have fought the knights—they'd have killed us. Anyway, when the ship was full, the knights told us to make off, and we rowed out to sea.

"All was well. We got back to Cyprus and there the knights paid us off. We took the ship. They had no need for it. Alan and I shared our profits, and with them we thought we'd make our fortune. With the ship we could afford to trade, and we did for some time, all over the coasts around Outremer and back to France. After a few years, we had earned enough to be able to settle down, but we chose to carry on. We bought another ship—a cog—and sold the galley to the Genoese. With the new ship we could carry more cargo, and we took to trading between Gascony and England. We were successful, and that was where we made a good amount of money. But then things began to go downhill.

"We began to suffer from the prices," he continued, frowning moodily at his boots. "When the French king took over Aquitaine, at first we made good money from King Edward, taking men and provisions to his lands, and bought more ships. But as things began to get worse, it was hard for us to get our pay, and it was soon obvious that we'd have to get some money some other way. So we began raiding French shipping in the channel. We did well. We kept our eyes open for any kind of profit, and never turned our noses up at anything. Well, that was how Alan met his wife, Angelina. We took over a ship that was sailing from Sluys to Calais, and found we had a better prize than we had at first realized. The owner of the ship was wealthy, very wealthy. Alan caught him, and his was the prize. At first we thought the money and cargo was all that was there, but Alan realized the man himself must be valuable, and he struck a bargain, taking his daughter and half the cargo."

He stared unseeing past Simon's shoulder. "But that was the high-spot of our careers. Since then, things have gone from bad to worse. Two years ago we had a bad time when we just couldn't seem to do anything right. We even had a ship taken by the French: lost the whole cargo. That hurt us. And since then, we've had our ship attacked twice and damaged, and lost I don't know how much money. So you see it's wrong to think we made all our money from Acre."

"How did you lose so much? Just bad luck?" asked Baldwin mildly.

The eyes flashed toward the knight. "Luck? I suppose so. We made some unlucky decisions, telling the ship's master to take this course or that, and then finding a French pirate waiting, but I think most of our problems stem from misfortune of one sort or another."

"So you don't believe in witches?"

"That's rubbish," he said scornfully. "I know that's what they say, but it's not true!"

"That Agatha Kyteler was a witch, you mean?" asked Baldwin.

"Yes. She had nothing to do with us. It was just bad luck."

"But people thought you were being cursed by her?"

"Some did."

"Why should they think that?" mused Simon, then, catching a sullen glower from the merchant, his eyes suddenly widened. "She left Acre on *your* ship, didn't she!"

"She might—how can I tell? It was years ago!"

"Was it your partner who thought she might have cursed you?"

"He . . . He can be a little superstitious."

Baldwin stirred, his spurs tinkling. "She never spoke to you about her escape from Acre?"

"This has nothing to do with her death. I'll not answer stupid questions."

"Very well," said the knight. "But tell me, your partner is Trevellyn, isn't he? You told us that when we last met."

"Yes. The business is ours."

"You have no other partners, but you are in debt to the Italians?"

"Yes." He gave a sad grin which seemed to offer a glimpse of personal fears. "As I told you before, the business is sailing toward rocky shores. The Italians want their money back."

Just then they heard feet in the screens and, looking up, saw the son standing before them. Baldwin was surprised at the change in Stephen. Whereas before he had been relatively cock-sure, now he looked chastened and almost shy. Not nervous, Baldwin thought to himself, but certainly not arrogant—or as arrogant as before, anyway, he admitted to himself with a small grin.

It was only when he approached and his face was lighted by the sconces and fluttering candle flames that the knight saw the reason. One side of the youth's face was a livid bruise with painful-looking yellow and purple edging. Above it, his left eye was marked too, and as Baldwin raised an eyebrow in surprise, he felt sure that the wound must have been inflicted by the boy's father. What, the knight wondered, had Stephen done to justify a beating?

Looking at the father, he found himself thinking that it could have been anything. The brutish face glared at him, defiant and cruel, as if daring him to make any comment about how his household was organized.

Stephen walked across the room, glancing at Simon but ignoring the silent Edgar, to a low-backed chair. Whereas before he had haughtily held Baldwin's gaze, today his eyes were cast down like a shy maiden's. He did not seem to know where to put his hands, either. They rested at first in his lap, then on his knees. Soon he resolutely placed them on the chair's arms and sat still.

Baldwin smiled faintly. "When we saw you on Thursday, you said that Harold Greencliff had taken a lover. You said she was a married woman." There was a slight movement of his head, but other than that Baldwin saw no sign that he had heard. "It is difficult for you, I know, but it is possible that she might know something about the death of Agatha Kyteler. We must find out who she is."

Slowly Stephen's eyes rose to meet the knight's. "Like I said, you'd better ask Harry. I cannot betray a confidence. I swore . . ."

"Very well. I cannot force you. There is something else, though." He paused, head tilted as he considered the youth. "Why did you lie about being with him all that day, the day that Kyteler died?"

"I . . . I didn't lie! How can you suggest that? I . . ."

"We know that you lied. What I now want to know is the truth. When did you meet him and what did you do together?"

His mouth opened, but then snapped shut as if he thought the better of further blustering. He glanced away for a moment, and when he looked back, Baldwin could see some of his previous pride rising again. "We were together almost all of the time. I met him at the 'Sign of the Moon' in the afternoon, and we spent most of the rest of the day together. If you want to check, ask the innkeeper, he'll . . ."

"We *have* asked him," Baldwin said flatly. "He said you met him there at around five, late in the afternoon, and left shortly after, getting back at eight or so. Is that right?"

"I suppose so. I don't know . . ."

"Because we have someone who saw him in the road with a horse at about four, maybe just after. That means he could have gone to the house, killed the old woman, and still met you at the inn."

"But . . . He's not a murderer!" The words came softly, almost hesitantly, and Baldwin was sure he was thinking hard about his friend, wondering whether he could have been wrong about him. How hard, the knight thought, to have to doubt an old friend.

"Have you seen him since he was released?"

The question, shot out so fast, took the youth by surprise, and his head nodded before he could stop himself.

"Did he say why he decided to leave the area?"

Stephen hesitated. His eyes held a sudden fear, a hunted look that made Baldwin realize how young he still was. The knight was about to prompt him gently when his father slammed his fist on the bench beside him in rage. "Answer!"

The boy's eyes shot to his father, and his mouth framed the word "Yes." It was so soft that Baldwin could hardly hear it, but at the sound he breathed easier.

"Tell us why, Stephen."

"It was his woman. She rejected him. He felt that there was nothing here for him anymore. He just decided to go. He was trying to get to a ship, so that he could sail for Normandy or Gascony, but he hardly got anywhere when he was caught. That was all—he *swore* to me that he had nothing to do with her death! You don't really think he killed her, do you?"

Baldwin gazed at him with sympathy. There was little doubt now. Whatever else was unknown, they would be able to find out by questioning the youth again. He had little doubt of that. But in the meantime, this friend, who had been so loyal, was bound to be hurt. At the least Greencliff had lied to him, to his best friend, who had kept his secrets even when questioned by the Justice.

Sighing, he stood and motioned to Simon.

"Let's go and see Greencliff," he said.

They had only just crossed the threshold when the messenger arrived, a young lad, flushed and panting from an enthusiastic chase that had taken him all the way to Furnshill and back.

"Sir! Sir!" Riding up to them, he was close to falling from his saddle as he reined in his horse before them.

It took little time for him to tell them, gasping out the message from Peter Clifford, his eyes darting from one to another of the silent men before him. When the boy had finished, Simon and Baldwin stared at him, then at each other. Snatching their reins from the waiting hostlers, they leapt up and, setting spurs to their mounts, set off to Crediton.

At the yard before Peter Clifford's house, they turned in and dismounted quickly, their messenger taking their reins and leading the mounts to the stable area. The door was opened by Peter himself, who gave them a short nod and stood back to let them all enter. His face was serious. He did not smile at the sight of his friends, but silently led the way through to his hall.

Inside, sitting like a queen on her throne, Simon saw Jennie Miller near the fire. She looked up quickly as they came in, but although she registered a brief pleasure—or was it relief—at the sight of them, she was reserved. Looking at Peter, Simon felt sure that his reaction to her news was the cause of her seriousness.

"I understand you've already had a conversation with Jennie," the priest said. "She arrived here just over two hours ago and . . . Well I shall let her tell her own story." He walked to a seat in the shadows near the screens and sat. Glancing quickly at her, Simon saw her eyes studying the knight with a kind of suppressed excitement now that Peter was out of sight. As Baldwin sat in front of her she leaned forward to stare at him, as if he and she were alone in the room; friends meeting to gossip about old acquaintances.

"I've seen her!"

"Yes? Where? Tell us exactly what happened."

"I was on my way into town, but I had to stop for a piss just outside. Well, I just finished when I heard these horses coming. There was this pair. She was the one, though. She was wearing the same things I saw on her out in front of Agatha's place: long gray riding cloak with fur round the edge, with a blue tunic and skirts underneath, and it was the same horse. A nice little mare. Pretty little thing she was."

"Are you quite sure? You couldn't have made a mistake? It wasn't just a similar horse?" interrupted Simon dubiously. She threw him a withering look.

"It's not only knights can see the difference between a tired old hackney and a good young mare," she said, then added tartly, "and my eyes are perfectly good enough to tell colors from a couple of yards away."

Baldwin coughed discreetly, bringing her attention back to him. "That's good. Can you describe the man?"

"Oh, yes. He's short in build, not your height, sir. Very dark face, with scars and wrinkles all over. His mount was a palfrey, a gray with dappled sides. Both horses had good leather fittings with brass."

"Good!" Baldwin stood. "We should be able to find a couple like them easily enough."

"Yes, sir. I can take you there if you're worried you'll lose them."

He spun around to stare at her. "You know where they are?"

"Of course I do!" she said, seeming amused at his surprise. "I know everyone round here. I'm the miller's wife."

Simon grinned at Baldwin's dumbfounded expression, and asked: "Could you just tell us who these two people are, please, Jennie?"

"Oh, sorry, I forgot. Mr. and Mrs. Trevellyn. They're from over to the west, at South Helions."

"Trevellyn?" Baldwin glanced at Simon, who shrugged. "Now that *is* interesting!"

"Do you need anything else from this woman?" Peter's voice sounded strained, Simon thought, and as the priest stepped forward into the pool of light from a large candle-holder, the bailiff saw that his friend's face was taut and pale, and his face registered distaste when his glance fell on her.

Stirring, Baldwin shook his head quickly. "No. Thank you, Jennie. You've been very helpful."

She stood. "Suppose I'd better get on with buying what we need, then, and get on home." She smoothed her tunic and grinned at the knight before walking out enthusiastically. This was an important day for her. There was the excitement that her story would have for the people in the "Moon" later, as the only person who saw the woman in the trees and who also saw Greencliff with her horse. *That* should start some heads shaking, she thought with satisfaction. And then there was the interest there had been over the apparent breakup between Greencliff and Sarah Cottey. Was that because of Mrs. Trevellyn? She paused at the door, caught by the idea as she pensively straightened her shawl. Now *that* was a thought!

Inside, Baldwin and Simon stood and prepared to take their own leave when the priest caught them both by the arms. "Wait, I want a word with you two."

Baldwin was surprised by the urgency in his voice. "What is it, Peter?"

"What on earth have you two been saying about Greencliff? Or Mrs. Trevellyn?"

"What?" Simon was confused, but he ran through the sequence of events that so far made up their search for the killer of the witch, leading to the discovery of the identity of the woman who was involved. "What is troubling you? All we're trying to do is find Agatha Kyteler's murderer. What's wrong?"

"It was what she said. That woman will make sure that this is all over the parish within hours. And what will happen then? Everyone will assume that Mrs. Trevellyn was responsible, whether or not she was. Just as they will all think Agatha Kyteler was a witch."

"You don't think she was?"

"Agatha?" He was so amazed by the idea that his eyes opened wide at the very thought. "Good God! No, why on earth should I? She was a very pleasant woman, always ready to assist the people of the parish who hurt themselves. No, I'm sure she was no witch."

Baldwin grinned sidelong at the bailiff. "You see, Simon thinks there may be something in it because of all her roots and herbs."

"Simon?"

"I'm sorry, and I'll pray for her if that will help, but so many others think she was, I . . ."

"Agatha Kyteler was a good and kindly woman. Ignore the rumors. But you see how gossip can spread? What if news of this gets back to Alan Trevellyn?"

"Ah!" Baldwin seemed to understand this, although Simon was left looking from one to the other with growing exasperation.

"Why? Who is this man? Why should this be a problem?"

"Don't you know Alan Trevellyn?" Peter asked. "I

thought you would be sure to . . . well, he is a power-ful man, a merchant . . ."

"Partner to Walter de la Forte," murmured Baldwin softly.

"Precisely. They bring wine from Gascony. Anyway, he is known for his boldness."

Baldwin turned to Simon. "What the good priest is try-ing to say is that this man Trevellyn is a hard man, known to be cruel to his servants, and who takes the law into his own hands on occasion. I had not thought before, while we were speaking to de la Forte, but now I remember Trevellyn. He almost beat an hostler to death late last year. How will he react, I think Peter is wondering, to us asking if his wife is having an affair with a local farmer?"

Peter nodded dejectedly.

"But surely," Simon said frowning, "all we're doing is asking her about what she was doing at Agatha Kyteler's house."

Peter and the knight exchanged a glance, then the priest scratched his head while he threw a speculative frown at the bailiff. "I don't think that will help much. You see they have no children after several years of marriage. At the same time as starting rumors about the faithfulness and honor of his wife, you are asking her why she went to see the midwife—I don't *quite* see how that's going to help."

"Ah!"

It was not until they were riding on the road to Wefford from the Tiverton road that Simon threw a speculative glance ahead and suggested that they leave questioning the woman until the morning.

"Why?" asked Baldwin, swivelling in his saddle to peer at him.

"At least we'd have a better chance of thinking what we need to ask her that way. If we can frame the questions carefully, we may not need to ask her about things like . . ."

"Like whether she's been faithless to her husband, you mean?" Baldwin sighed. "I don't know. Maybe it *would* be better. But what if by the time we get there Trevellyn has already heard about the rumors? You know how fast news gets around in these parts."

"Surely they will not have heard first thing in the morning."

Baldwin gave him a sour look. "Don't bet on the fact!" he said. "I once smiled at a serving girl at an inn on the Exeter road. Next day a rumor began that I had used her that night."

Simon grinned. "And?"

"No, I had not!" he declared hotly, giving the bailiff a black scowl. At the sight of the bailiff's skeptical smile, he shrugged shamefacedly, then became pensive. "You see how it is, though? I did nothing, but the rumors still started. And there was nothing I could do to stop them—it ended up with a projected date for my bastard's birth!" He subsided, glowering gloomily ahead. A quick smile lightened his features, and he turned conspiratorially to his friend. "But the worst of it was, I would have liked to!"

He paused, scowling and shrugging himself deeper into his cloak, before continuing in a quieter, more pensive tone, "And that's why I find these rumors about an affair between Greencliff and Mrs. Trevellyn hard to believe. A wealthy merchant's wife and a villein? It hardly seems likely. Gossip is always so easily started, but stopping it is like halting a war horse in full gallop—very difficult until it has run its course."

Looking up at the sky, Simon said, "It's getting close to dark. Let's get back and sleep on it. We can get the answers we need in the morning, and if we speak to her well rested, we'll be more likely to be able to be careful and save her from embarrassment."

"Very well." Baldwin nodded. "But let's go home past her house. At least you can see the place. It's not far."

This part of the land was not an area Simon knew well, being too far to the east of his old home. He had always spent more time to the west or the north, in the country where he had grown up, and thus it was a surprise to see the great manor house of the Trevellyns at South Helions.

Baldwin's house at Furnshill could easily be mistaken for a farm, with its coziness and simplicity, while the place built by Walter de la Forte was imposing, showing the wealth of its owner. By comparison Trevellyn's was a castle. It stood in its own clearing, a massive property of gray and ochre, with granite walls topped by castellations, showing that the owner had money and influence: all kings for many years had been trying to reduce the number of fortified houses to stop the internecine warfare that still continued between lords when they had squabbles. A man who could build a place like this was wealthy and important, and the house spoke of his power.

The windows at the base were small, but those higher had been enlarged to allow more sunlight and were mullioned. The door was a small, blackened timber slab set in a tower formed of a projecting section of wall, with an overhang above in which Simon knew there would be trap doors so that defenders could drop rocks or burning oil on any attacker. Overall it gave a feeling of threatening solidity, as if it was glowering down at the humans riding past.

The land all round was set to pasture, and there were a number of sheep grazing, scraping with their hooves at the snow to get to the grass beneath. A small stream led from the house to the lane, so the bailiff correctly assumed that it had its own fresh water from a spring.

"I think I prefer your house, Baldwin," said Simon meditatively as they rode on.

"Maybe." The knight was surveying the ground around as if assessing the best point for an assault. "But if we have a new war between barons in England, and this shire is attacked, I think I'd soon get to prefer this to my own!"

The lane curved round in a great sweep after the house, avoiding the hillock it was set upon, and then began the long and steady climb up the hill west of Wefford. It took some time for them to wander up it, both deep in their thoughts, with Edgar silent, as usual, behind. At the top they could see the lane winding through the trees ahead, dark in their leafless splendor against the snow that had fallen through their branches to the ground beneath.

There, only a half mile away, stood a solitary farmhouse, and Simon regarded it with a jealous scowl. It stood so calm and quiet, a single building with a small barn nearby. The smoke drifting from the thatch promised a warm welcome.

As his eyes roved over the surrounding country, he could see that a light mist was rising from the cleared areas, making them appear gray and somehow insubstantial, as if he was looking through fogged glass. The sun was setting slowly behind them now.

It was only then he realized that the farmhouse

ahead must be Greencliff's. Pointing to it, he said, "Baldwin. We could save ourselves some time and see Greencliff now, before we see Mrs. Trevellyn. Get his side of the story before going to her."

"Do you think he'd tell us more than he already has?" Baldwin mused, staring at the house. He seemed to be talking to himself as he continued, "I suppose we could try. He doesn't know how much we've learned or guessed. The trouble is, will we learn more from her? Should we wait until we've spoken to her before we see him again?"

"You're probably right," Simon said, staring at the peaceful house again. "There's a chance we may learn something from Mrs. Trevellyn that could help us question Greencliff. Yes, let's leave it for now. We'll see him when we've been to the Trevellyn castle."

Once inside Baldwin's manor again, they were welcomed by the smell of a pair of roasting fowls, spitted on iron skewers by the fire. Hugh sat nearby, stretching occasionally to turn them.

Laughing, Simon saw that his servant appeared to have made a complete recovery. He looked as though he must have spent the whole day in front of the fire. At Baldwin's mild inquiry, Hugh nodded toward the screens, and soon Margaret appeared holding two jugs which she set on a table before greeting her husband.

Glancing at Hugh, Simon said, "Has he been making you run around all day?" with mock seriousness.

She registered surprise. "Shouldn't I have looked after him? Don't be stupid! Of course not. I've done little today, and so has he. I wasn't going to send him out when his master nearly killed him yesterday, was I? No, but at least he's cured now."

"Good," said Baldwin, sitting by the fire and pulling his boots off. "That's better! Good, so he can come with us tomorrow, then."

Hugh's face was immediately frowningly suspicious. "Why? What are we doing tomorrow?"

Sitting, Simon grabbed his wife around the waist and hauled her on to his lap. "We're going to go and see the mystery woman who was there when Kyteler died. The woman who, according to gossip, has a fancy for strong young farmers," he said, and kissed her.

Baldwin smiled at the sight of the bailiff and his struggling wife, then turned to face the fire. Yes, he thought. We'll surely find out more tomorrow.

The dark was crowding in as the Bourc settled again, squatting as he gazed at the Trevellyn house. He smiled to himself as men hurried past nearby. None could see him, hidden as he was behind the thick fringe of bracken and bramble. Two men were talking as they lopped branches from a fallen tree only a few feet away. They had been there almost from the time that he had arrived, late in the morning, and were still unaware of him.

Since he had seen the ambush, he had carefully considered what to do. The first night, he had been able to find a room in an inn in a hamlet to the south of Crediton—keeping to the woods had meant taking a great deal longer on his journey than he had expected, and he had been surprised at how far to the east he had been forced to travel before finding a bridge.

The next day, Thursday, he had risen early and crossed the stream at a small wooden bridge built by the villagers. Taking his time, he had made his way back to Wefford by quiet trails and paths, avoiding any large villages or towns. This way it had taken him until dark to get to the little hut where he had stayed before, and he had been glad to merely light a fire and tumble down to sleep.

It was the Friday when he began to plan his revenge while he spent his morning fetching wood for his fire. He knew where the man lived, so it should be easy enough to waylay him.

Any wealthy man was predictable in his habits, as the Bourc knew. Rising with the sun, he would take a light meal with his servants before dealing with whatever business his clerk wanted to bring to his attention, maybe handing out punishments to wrongdoers. The main meal would follow, and then it would be out with the dogs or hawks to see what game could be found, and back home with the carcasses.

It followed that the Bourc must try to catch him while alone to have any chance of success. There would be no likelihood of taking Trevellyn while he was out hunting—he would have too many men with him.

Late in the morning he had ridden off to the Trevellyn house. Finding a high point in front where few seemed to wander, he saw to his delight that the master of the house did not hunt. He saw the men leaving with the dogs, and stared at the group, but Trevellyn was not there. Shortly afterward he heard a bellowing, and saw a stable-lad being beaten. The hoarse shouting and pitiful crying came to his ears, making him set his jaw with distaste. It sounded as if the boy had taken too long in bringing the master's horse when it had been called for.

And now it was Saturday and he was no closer to seeing how to catch the man on his own. Whenever he had thought he had an opportunity, he had been thwarted by the proximity of others. Even now, sitting as he was high on the land behind the house, where the day before Trevellyn had wandered alone and aimlessly for the earlier part of the afternoon, he could see the workers all around, hewing wood or taking it back to the house under the watchful eyes of Trevellyn's seneschal. The master was there too, close to the house where the Bourc could not reach him.

The smile was still fixed on his face even as he decided he must leave and go back to the hut for the night before he died of cold. He placed his hands on his thighs to begin to rise, but then stilled himself as he heard the hated voice thundering at the two men before him.

"Why have you not finished? Hurry with that wood, you lazy sons-of-whores! Why should you eat when you can't even fetch the logs we need to cook on?"

There was more in the same vein, but the Bourc was surprised to see that the two men did not answer but redoubled their efforts to cut the branches away from the bough. Their faces set and troubled, they hacked and chopped with a curious silence that was at odds with their frenetic actions. Usually men would answer back if their master shouted at them, or so the Bourc had believed from what he had seen of the lower orders in this country, but these two hardly spoke. They looked terrified of the man blustering below.

"I can't finish, I'm too tired," he heard one say.

"Hisht! Save your breath! We have to, or he'll take the skin off your back. You know what he's like."

"I can't. I've got to rest, or I'll die here."

"Such talk! Just get on and . . ." He was cut off by an enraged bellow.

"What are you doing?" The Bourc saw with surprise

that the merchant had suddenly come round from the edge of the trees and now stood, hands on hips, glowering at the men. "Well? Why have you slowed? Maybe this will give you some energy!"

As he spoke, his hand reached back over his head, and the Bourc saw he held a short whip. It made a hideous whistling noise, as full of venom as a snake. Then the younger of the woodsmen cried out as it cracked. A fold of the tunic above his elbow opened and flapped, and a red flood began to stain his arm. Whimpering, the boy hefted his hatchet high overhead, but even as the axe fell, the whip slashed across his back.

The older man stoically chopped at the branches, but he was not safe. Two strokes caught him, one around his waist, one on the chest which made him stumble and forced the breath to sob in his throat.

"Pick up the branches you've already cut and carry them to the house!"

"The wagon, sir, it's not back yet, and . . ." The boy's voice faltered. His objection earned him another crack from the whip.

"Do as I order, unless you want to feel this again!"

From his vantage point the Bourc watched as the two men, one snivelling, the other silent with a kind of taut agony, collected armfuls and walked back to the house.

"And hurry. You have to finish this tonight!" the merchant shouted at their retreating backs. Then he turned and looked at their work with a sneer. "Fools!" he muttered contemptuously. He kicked at a branch, walking farther along the trunk toward the trees, and the Bourc smiled to himself.

Giving a polite cough as the merchant passed by, he

was pleased to see sudden fear in the man's face as he turned and saw the Gascon for the first time. "Mr. Trevellyn, I am so pleased to see you again. I think we have some things to talk about."

He saw the whip rise and leap back, and then it was whistling toward him.

The innkeeper at the "Sign of the Moon" was very busy that night. It seemed that everybody from the village had come to his hall to drink. There was little else to do on a cold and snow-bound night, and while it was a delight to have the room filled with people wanting his ale, it still created havoc. He only hoped that his stocks of beer would survive until the next brew was ready.

"Yes, yes," he muttered when a new hand stuck in the air or a fresh voice called to him. If it carried on like this until the spring, he would have to get someone to help. As it was, he and his wife were running witlessly like headless chickens, out to the buttery where they refilled their jugs with ale or wine, then to the hall again, where they struggled to fill the mugs and pots before they were all emptied. It was like trying to limewash a city wall, he thought. Just when you think you've finished, as you get back to the beginning, you find it's already old and worn and you have to start again.

One group he watched with a particularly sour eye. He took no delight in gossip, even if it was a stock currency here in the "Moon." He especially disliked malicious rumors that could hurt or offend, and the Miller family had an effective monopoly of them today.

Seeing a man lift his tankard in a silent plea, the innkeeper wove his way through the groups of people. As he stood pouring, he could hear the Millers.

"But how do they know it was Mrs. Trevellyn as was carryin' on with young Harry?" he heard one man ask.

Jennie leaned forward, her face serious. "Who else could it've been?" she said. "It was her who went to Greencliff and tempted him. And then they went to Agatha. You know what *that* means. And then they went back, after killing her."

"So you sayin' as it was both of them did it? They both killed Agatha?"

The innkeeper walked away sighing. It was bad hearing such talk, ruining people's characters to fill a boring evening. There was one thing for certain: it was bound to get someone into trouble. He glanced back at the little huddle, his eyes looking for empty pots, but always they were drawn back to the group. Was it worth telling them to shut up? No, they would carry on. Throw them all out? They would just hold court outside, and he would lose business at the same time. He shrugged. May as well let them continue, he thought, and went out to refill the jug again.

There was another man who was not amused by the talk. Stephen de la Forte sat near the screens, his back to the room, his face twisted as if his ale was vinegar.

His mug was empty. Turning, he tried to catch the eye of the innkeeper, but instead found himself being fixed by the gaze of the Miller girl, the oldest one, who stood and subjected him to a close scrutiny before tugging at her mother's tunic.

Jennie saw the white-faced youth staring and her

voice failed. Following the direction of her gaze, the group saw Stephen, and their chattering died, as if the sluice that fed their conversation had been shut, and suddenly all talking in the hall stopped.

Now Stephen found himself the focus of all attention. He stood and walked to the table where the Millers sat, the woman staring at him with large bold eyes. "You ought to be ashamed of yourselves," he said deliberately. "You're all saying it was those two, when there's nothing to prove it, apart from *her*," he pointed to Jennie, "saying he was in the road that day. There's nothing else says they had anything to do with it. Nothing."

"Come on, Stephen," came a voice. "Nothing wrong with wondering. That's all we're doing, just wondering who might have done it."

He spun to face the talker, an older man with round, jowled face and grizzled hair. "Nothing wrong? You've all set your mind to it that they're guilty, haven't you? Eh?" He looked around the table, staring into their eyes, until he met those of Jennie Miller. Only then did his lip curl into a sneer. Shaking his head with contempt, he spun on his heel and left, yanking so hard at the curtain as he left that he nearly pulled it from its fixings.

The wind had built again, and was whipping the snow into mad, whirling smoke before him, obliterating the view and making it hard to see the ground under his horse's feet. It was with a curse of sheer fury that the Bourc dropped from the saddle, wincing as the movement pulled the fresh scabs on his back, and led his horses on, trying to keep his head to the south. This was worse than anything he had experienced before.

Here, this far into the moors, it was hard to maintain

any course. All sense of direction had left him, and now he found it almost impossible to guess which direction was south. But he was tenacious and determined. He had never before failed to find his way, even when high in the mountains, and he was confident that he would win through, even if occasionally he would curse the thought of the easy lanes and roadways to the north which he had forsaken in favor of this bitter route.

At first he had managed to make good time. He had collected more wood, storing it as faggots on the packhorse. The sky had been clear over to the south where the moors lay. Only to the north did clouds darken the sky. But that had changed as soon as he rode on to the rolling hills. Immediately the wind had begun to gust and blow, bringing the salty taint of the sea at first, but by late morning it was full of bitter coldness.

A flurry of snow blew at him, and he tugged his cowl over his face. Here, high on the moors, the wind could change direction and dart around at will like a well-trained knife-fighter. It was impossible to find his way.

He turned and stared back the way he had come. Now he could not even see his own trail. As soon as his feet lifted, his prints were filled. Cursing again, he hauled his horse's head round and began to search for any protection: a wall, even a tree, anything that could give some relief from the elements.

Leaning on the front of his saddle, Simon stared down the hill toward the square, gray house and sighed. "I'm still not sure I'm ready for this," he admitted.

Baldwin blew out his cheeks and peered ahead. "No, neither am I," he said.

They had set off just before light, this time with Edgar again. Their packs filled, their wineskins sloshing merrily in case they became stranded, they had ridden through thick drifts to get here.

At points the drifts were so bad that they were forced to leave the lane and move into the woods at either side where the snow did not drift. Using sheep and deer trails, they had managed to continue, occasionally returning to the lane for short periods before moving aside to circumnavigate drifts. Whenever they left the shelter of the trees, they saw that the fine powder had taken possession of the land outside.

Finally they had been forced to leave the tracks completely. Where the lane opened out below Greencliff's house, the snow had completely blocked their path. They had chosen a diversion to the north, taking a path Baldwin vaguely recalled, which led them up the side of one hill under the cover of the woods until they had passed over a mile beyond the field where they had found Kyteler's body. At last, when they left the trees behind, they found themselves on a smooth and rounded hillside, and it seemed that here the snow could not drift. It had been blown away before the strong overnight winds.

At the top of the hill overlooking the house, they could see that the master and his wife must be inside. Smoke rose calmly from the chimneys. There were some tracks leaving the property by the road, but they only went a short distance, up as far as the first drift, before returning to the house.

While Baldwin stared, he could see no signs of movement. Sighing, he watched his breath dissipate on the freezing air, then glanced at Simon. "At least there should be something hot to drink down there."

"Yes, thanks to God! I'm so cold my hair will snap off at the scalp if I touch it," said the bailiff through teeth firmly clenched to prevent their chattering. "God! Come on, let's get to sit before a fire again before we die!"

At the bottom of the hill they had to ride well to their right to find a passage through another thick drift that lay deep and impassable. Once round it, they were in among the trees again and here the snow was thin. But then they could not see any route through the snow on the farther side, and after some minutes of trying, Simon heard Baldwin muttering and Edgar cursing.

In the end it was Simon who lost both temper and patience together, and with his jaw fixed, his head down, he forced a path for them, whipping his horse on. The snow was over his heavily built rounsey's chest, but the horse was strong, and barged on, whinnying slightly, taking short bounds in an effort to leap the freezing obstacle.

Once through, Simon rode for the house at a loping speed, half canter, half trot, without even glancing behind to see if the others were following. Indeed, he was not sure that they were until he drew up to the little tower that housed the main door and heard the chuckling of his friend. Even Edgar seemed amused, but when the bailiff's glowering countenance shot toward him, the servant appeared to be busily concentrating on the parcel tied behind him on the saddle. Even so, Simon was sure he caught a brief, dry chortle as he turned away.

After hammering on the door, Simon turned and glared at the white landscape. To his disgust, it began to snow again, a thin and fine drizzle of particles as fine but as dry and stolid as ash. It was like watching a rain of flour.

"We had better be quick," said Baldwin as he approached, his eyes cast upward at the leaden sky. "If this gets worse, and it looks as if it might, we could get stuck here for days."

Simon grunted, but just then he heard the latch being pulled, and they turned to see a young servant girl. "Ah, good. We're here to see your master, is he . . . ?" He paused as the girl started, a fist rising to her mouth as she stared at him from terrified eyes. "What is it, girl?"

"The master, sir. He's disappeared. We don't know where he is!"

She led the way inside. The stone-flagged screens beyond the door were long, reaching all the way to the other side of the house where another door gave out to the stable area and outbuildings. To their left were three doors, and when Simon peered in, he could see that the first led to the buttery. The others must lead to the pantry and kitchen. On the right were the two doors to the hall itself.

Entering, Simon was awed by the magnificence of the great room. It was vast for a family home, nearly as big as the hall in Tiverton castle, with a high ceiling above and stone pillars supporting it, very like the church at Crediton. Benches and tables lined the walls, leaving a central aisle to the dais. Simon could not help but study the rich-looking tapestries on the walls and the immense fireplace. It roared with massive logs that in his own house would have had to have been shortened and split. Glancing round, he saw that behind him the screens had a rail at the top, and to one side there was a staircase for musicians, so that the master and his lady could hear singing and playing while they sat to eat.

Clearly, this was a house where the old traditions still held sway. On the dais at the far end, the master's table stood, with platters and mugs spread over its surface. The family still ate in the hall with their servants and friends, then, not like so many masters and the ladies who went to eat alone in their solar behind the dais.

But as he and Baldwin marched across the floor, Edgar striding respectfully behind, it was not the hall itself that commanded their attention, but the solitary figure sitting alone on the chair just before the dais. The slim figure of a young woman dressed in blue.

This was the first time that Baldwin had met the lady, and he studied her at first with a calm and studied indifference, noting her dress and deportment. She could only be in her early twenties. Her hair was deepest black, shining blue as the light caught it, and was hung over each shoulder in braids as thick as her wrists. The heavy tunic looked as though it must be woollen, and had four decorative gilt clasps at the breast. But it was not her clothing that caught his eye, it was *her*. She was almost painfully beautiful.

The face was an oval with high and elegant cheekbones, above which her green eyes slanted slightly down to her nose. The eyebrows were matching bows of black. Her nose was thin and straight and under the delicate nostrils was a voluptuous mouth whose lips pouted invitingly. Slim and elegant, confident and proud, she sat with her hands upon the arms of the chair and appeared to be subjecting them to a close scrutiny.

She rose languorously as they walked toward her,

as if weary from lack of sleep, then turned to her servant, who hesitantly explained who they were. Baldwin watched her carefully as the maid spoke, but apart from a swift glance from her splendid green eyes, he could not see any particular reaction to the news that the Keeper of the King's Peace had arrived. Was it his imagination, or were the eyes a little red-rimmed?

"Gentlemen, you are welcome. Please be seated at the fire and accept our hospitality." Her voice was soft and low, and the gentle motion with her hand toward the flame was so graceful and ingenuous that he found himself turn to the hearth as if all will had left him. And he rather liked the sensation.

Walking slowly, he followed Simon to a trestle by the fire, and stood waiting for her to join them. Closer to her now, he could see that she had a smooth skin, tinted a warm dusky color. As she sat he could not help but float his eyes over her figure, from the slender neck to the swelling of her breasts under her tunic, and on down to the narrowness of her waist and widening of her hips. He brought his eyes back to her face as quickly as he could, but he could see in her measuring gaze that she had noticed his inspection, although not apparently with displeasure. Her mouth twitched, as if she was close to smiling at him. But then her face turned inquiringly to Simon.

He began hesitantly, staring at his lap. "Madam, I am sorry to have arrived like this, it must be difficult for you. Your maid said that your husband is missing."

"Yes," she said, and sighed. "He left the house late last night, and when we awoke this morning, he was gone."

"His horse . . . ?"

"In the stables. That is what is so surprising . . ." Her voice trailed off as she frowned at the fire.

Baldwin said, "Has he ever disappeared like this before?"

"No. Never in the five years I have been married to him, never has he done this before."

"Has anything happened recently to make him go?"

She hesitated a little, then flashed him a quick look, which he could not fathom. "No."

Simon coughed and sighed. "It may be lucky that he *has* gone for now," he said, shooting a nervous glance at Baldwin as if looking for confirmation that this was the right time to broach the subject. The knight gave a slight shrug of indifference. "Madam, we came here to speak to *you,* not your husband."

"Me?" Her surprise appeared genuine. "But why?"

"Madam . . ." He broke off again, looking to Baldwin for support. "This is very difficult . . ."

Baldwin smiled at her as he leaned forward, his eyes intense. "Mrs. Trevellyn. I am sorry to have to ask this, but we are investigating the murder of Agatha Kyteler." He was sure that she started at the name. "And we must know what you were doing at her house on the day she died."

"At her house?" She seemed to be considering whether to deny having been there, so to prevent her lying, Baldwin quickly interrupted.

"Yes, madam. You were seen at the lane going toward the old woman's house, you were seen trying to hide. You are a little too distinctive to be able to hide from the people of the village." She inclined her head to this, as if accepting it as a compliment and, to Baldwin's annoyance, he was not sure that he had not intended it to be. "Your horse was seen there too. With Harold Greencliff."

"Ah! It seems that you know I was there anyway."

"Yes, madam. But we don't yet know *why*. That is what we would like you to tell us now."

She held his gaze, and there was defiance there. "I was there to buy a potion. I had felt ill for some days. I saw her on Saturday to ask for this potion, and she told me to return when she had been able to collect the right elements to make it. That was Tuesday."

"Why did you hide?" asked Simon, his face frowning.

"Hide?"

"Yes. When people came along the lane, you hid in the trees. Why?"

It was as if she was fascinated by Baldwin. As she spoke she kept her magnificent green eyes on him, answering Simon's quick interruptions with scarcely a sidelong glance. "What would you have done? There are any number of gossips in the village. I did not want people to know I was going there. After all, she was supposed to be a witch. I wanted not to be associated with her. She was useful, but I wanted to see her privately, not with the whole village watching."

Simon looked at Baldwin and shrugged, and the knight grinned as he accepted the bailiff's defeat. He studied the beautiful face before him. Was she capable of murder? Even as he wondered, he saw her eyes seem to fill with liquid sadness, and she had to blink to clear them. But when she spoke her voice was strong and even. "It is no crime to keep such things private?"

Shrugging again, Baldwin sat back as she continued. "So, yes I hid, but only so that the village's gossips would not see me. When they had passed, I went on to the house. I saw the old woman and took the potion, then I left . . ."

"My pardon, madam," said Baldwin. "But were you alone with her the whole time?"

"Yes."

"And no one saw you enter the house?"

"No," she said, her brows wrinkled with the effort of recollection. "No, I do not think so, though . . ."

"Yes?"

"I did have a feeling I was being watched—it felt like there was a man in the trees . . . But I saw no one."

"Please continue."

"As I say, I took the potion and left. I walked back to the horse and came home."

"What time did you arrive home?"

"What time?" she appeared surprised by the question. "I do not know. After dark. Maybe half an hour after five?"

"And you were with Agatha Kyteler at about what hour?"

She shrugged indifferently. "Maybe four o'clock. I do not know."

Frowning, Simon asked, "And you only collected the potion? So you could only have been there minutes . . . ?"

"No," she said equably, "I was there long enough to take the mixture—you know, to drink it. Then I left."

"Was there anyone there when you *did* leave?" said Baldwin.

"I . . ." She hesitated.

"Yes?"

"I did not see anything, but I thought someone *was* there. It was just a feeling, you know? But I *did* think there was someone there in the trees still. I don't know why. And Agatha seemed keen to be rid of me."

"And that was all?"

"I think so, yes."

"And then you went straight back to your horse?"

She looked at him. "Yes."

"And Greencliff was there?"

"Yes. I had seen him earlier and asked him to mind my mare while I went to see Kyteler."

Simon interrupted. "But you said you didn't want the villagers to know you were there: that was why you hid in the trees on the way to her. Why didn't you mind him?"

Looking at him, her mouth opened but no sound came for a moment. Then she turned back to Baldwin as if in silent appeal. "I know the boy. He is gossiped about as much as I am. He agreed to look after my horse. That is all."

The knight nodded slowly. It would make sense, he thought. To his mind it was a great deal more likely than a high-born woman such as this having an adulterous affair with a lowly farmer.

"What about Grisel Oatway?" asked Simon. He felt he had an advantage somehow and he was determined to press it.

This time she did not even look at him. "I did not see her." The tone of her voice carried finality.

Baldwin leaned forward again, and he was about to speak when the door in the screens flew open and a manservant ran in excitedly. "Mistress! Mistress! Come quickly! Oh, please come quickly!"

They all sprang to their feet and stared at the man as he halted before her, his boots and the bottom of his tunic and hose covered in dripping snow. "What is it?" she demanded, apparently angry at the interruption.

"Mistress—it's the master—he's dead!"

Simon gaped at him, and when he looked at Baldwin, he could see that the knight was as shocked as he, but then, as the bailiff glanced at the man's widow, he stopped, his heart clutched in an icy grip. In her eyes there was no sadness. Glittering in the depths of the emerald pools was a cruel, vicious joy.

It was not there for long, and it was speedily covered by an expression of, if not grief, at least a degree of respectable regret. "Where?" she asked simply, and the man led them outside, Edgar silently bringing up the rear.

Walking quickly, the servant kept up a constant stream of apologies and pleas for pardon until she cut him off with a curt gesture, and he fell silent. Out through the door to the stable he took them, across the snow-covered yard, already trampled and flattened into a red-brown slush, to an open picket gate in the wall that gave on to the pasturage behind. Here they could easily make out footprints, leading straight to the woods. It was a place where the trees looked to Simon as though they were being cleared for a new assart, or perhaps merely to increase the lands available for the hall. Up at the treeline was another servant, moving from one foot to another in obvious agitation and wringing his hands. They made their way to him without a word.

At first the ground fell away, giving the house a solitary prominence. A small stream lay at the bottom, curling lazily round the house. The snow had not covered this rippling water. It lay with small sheer cliffs at either bank like a miniature gorge, almost, Simon thought to himself, like a tiny replica of Lydford itself.

The servant took them to a bridge built of sturdy planks, wide enough for a wagon, then they were climbing the bank to the figure waiting at the trees. He was a middle-aged man, with a face flushed from the cold. His square, stolid features showed his terror. It was as if he feared even to talk, his muscles moving as if with the ague, mouth twitching, brows wrinkling, eyelids flickering. He pointed wordlessly, then remembered his place and would have fallen to his knees if the knight had not sharply ordered him to take them to his master. With a hesitant glance at his mistress, and seeing her nod, he turned and stumbled in among the trees. It was not far.

The assart was a small semicircular clearing, with stumps cut off a few feet above the ground, and Simon realized it was a coppice. The trees were being cut to allow for regrowth. When the new long-stemmed shoots grew, they could be harvested for fencing, staves or just for burning on the fire.

At the far end, to which the servant now led them, there was a spur cut into the forest like a thin, invasive finger of land thrusting the trees apart. Inside was a recently felled oak, lying on its side waiting to be cut into planks or logs. The man led them up to it, and there, just beside the bough, was a rolled-up form. Baldwin stepped up, a hand held out to stop the others, and then crouched by the figure.

On hearing a small gasp, Simon said, "Wait here!" to the others, and went forward to join him. "Oh, God!"

All around he could see the snow was dappled and clotted with frozen black gobbets of blood.

He stood motionless, his eyes on the ground for fully a minute. Then, though waking, he took a deep breath and let it out in one long jet. Breathing slowly, he peered around the small glade. Baldwin was beside him, his eyes on the figure. Beyond was the thickest concentration of blood, as if it had jetted forward under great pressure, thick gouts lying nearby and thinner droplets farther away.

Studying it, he could see that it was almost as if the stream had all been impelled in one direction. It had not all sprayed in a circle, but started to his left, in a thinnish drizzle, then fanned round to the great thick line ahead. When he looked down he could see that the body pointed in this direction too.

Alan Trevellyn lay partially covered with snow. He was down on his knees, his torso and arms outstretched as if praying, his head on the ground between. Only one side of his body was cleared, the other was still as white as the ground. Simon paused and peered down, then crouched, hands on his knees, and stared.

Standing, he pointed at the agitated servant. "You! Did you find him here?"

"Yes, sir. I was here to collect wood for the log store when I stumbled on something. I thought it was a log . . . Or a stump . . . I had no idea it was the master . . . When I kicked at it, all the snow fell away, and I saw it was . . . was . . ." He seemed to run out of energy.

"Did you clear away the snow with your hands?"

"No, sir. I kicked, and the snow fell away, and . . ."

Simon interrupted harshly. "I know all that. Did anyone else come here to see the body after you found it? Did anyone touch the body?"

"No, sir. I stayed here with the master until you got here just now, sir. I didn't leave, sir."

Nodding, the bailiff turned back to the frowning knight.

"What is it, Simon?"

"Look!" He pointed. "There's snow over the body. But the blood's on top of the snow."

"Which doesn't make much sense," Baldwin agreed.

"No. He would hardly bury himself in the snow after dying, would he? No, someone else piled the snow around him after he was dead. And there," he indicated the rows of lines on top of the mound that covered the dead man's side, "are the finger-marks to prove it."

"Let's see what actually killed him."

Simon grunted assent, and they carefully began to clear away the snow from around the corpse.

"Do you want one of the men to help you?" asked Mrs. Trevellyn.

Looking up, Simon glanced at the two men before returning his gaze to her husband. "No," he said. "I think we can do this. Could you send one to fetch a wagon, though, to bring the body back to the house?"

"Yes, of course. I'll be inside if you want me." She shivered and wrapped her arms around herself. "It's too cold for me up here."

Simon nodded, and watched as she began to make her way back to the house, followed by her two servants, who straggled along like confused dogs expecting to be beaten. Turning back, he caught Baldwin's eye. The knight was watching her too.

*   *   *

To Simon's surprise, it did not take them long to clear the snow from Alan Trevellyn's corpse. After only a short time they had wiped it from his back and sides, and now they had a small moat around him. His stance was clear to see now, with the arms reaching up as if in supplication.

"More than likely he just fell down like that," was Baldwin's own curtly expressed view when the bailiff pointed this out to him. "Come on! Let's roll him over."

Both taking a shoulder, they pulled hard. At first he seemed to have frozen to the earth itself. Simon felt it was as if the ground knew that he would be buried soon and had no wish to give up what it knew to be its own. But then it reluctantly gave up the struggle with a sudden loosening of its grip, and Simon nearly fell back as Trevellyn's body moved, then toppled over on his side.

Simon stared at the bulging eyes, the blackened tongue, the black and red mess around the mouth where the blood had spurted and frozen or dried, at the deep wound beneath where the murderer's knife had sliced through the yellowed cartilage of the windpipe before severing the arteries, and found himself swallowing hard to keep the bitter bile at bay.

"Interesting," said Baldwin, rocking back to squat on his heels after studying the wounds. "Just like Kyteler."

The bailiff's voice was thick as he said. "Yes. Just like the witch."

The knight took a close look at the face, and Simon could see a series of scrapes where blood had been drawn. It looked as if he had been hit with a heavy weapon of some sort.

"Mace, or maybe a cudgel," he heard the knight mutter to himself. Apart from that there was little they could learn from the body.

It was not long before the men arrived to carry it back to the house, and Simon relinquished it with pleasure. As he watched the men collect it up, rolling it in a blanket and staggering with it to the cart, he stood well back, away from the gaze of those sightless, dead fish-eyes.

Even last year's killings had not been quite as bad as this. At least then it had been a series of murders caused by a group of trail bastons, wandering outlaws with no other means to earn a living. Nobody was safe from the increasing prices that made food so expensive, that made lords have to reconsider how many retainers they could afford and threw out those they felt to be a burden. It was not surprising that some resorted to violence to gain what they needed. Especially since now, by law, all men had to own weapons for their defense, and by law must practice using those weapons for the better defense of their communities and themselves. No, it was not surprising that some decided that when their world refused to give them an honest way to earn a living they should resort to violence.

That was different, an almost comprehensible reason for a life of brigandage. But now? Two deaths like this? These were made more horrible, in some strange way, by the fact that they were unique. Perhaps if there were other bodies they would not seem so shocking. Maybe it was their stark, lonely individuality that made them so hideous.

As the wagon began the slow progress back, bumping and rattling over the lumpy ground, he paused a moment. It was just the same as the witch, he thought again. And it was only then that he felt the prickle on the back of his head as the hairs began to rise erect, and he felt as if he was suddenly smothered in an ice-cold sweat.

"What is it, Simon?" he heard his friend ask as he stopped in his tracks.

"I was just thinking. How was his body? Kneeling, sort of like he was praying—or maybe begging on his knees? Could he have been pleading for his life?"

When they returned, it was obvious to Angelina Trevellyn that they were deep in thought. They walked in without talking, stepping to a bench and sitting, their servant standing behind them. As soon as they were seated, she clapped her hands, and was pleased to see how quickly the manservant came in to serve them. He gave them mugs and poured mulled wine for them, then left the jug by the fire to warm.

"Can you tell me how he died?" she asked at last.

"Madam, he was slashed. His neck." Baldwin was silent for a moment, peering into his mug, then looked up. "Do you have any idea who could have done this?"

Looking up, Simon was sure he could see a look quickly veiled—fear? Uncertainty? As soon as it appeared it was gone, and her face seemed to melt into repose as she reflected. "No, I cannot think of anyone who could do such a thing. Alan always had a temper, but to do this someone would have had to have hated him, surely?"

"Has he argued with anyone recently?"

She looked at him with a serious expression. "Sir, if you know anything about my husband, you will know that he was always strong and resolute. He was brave and never feared any man. He never hid his feelings."

"Is it true that he nearly beat a servant to death recently?"

"Oh, I do not know about that. It is true he would beat the men if they were slow or stupid, but so many of them are! You know what servants are like! They are like dogs, and must be trained. He had to beat them to keep them alert. That is not a reason to kill him."

"Did he know the witch?" Simon burst out, and she turned her face to him with sudden fear.

"The . . . the witch?" she said at last with an attempt at surprise. Under Simon's gaze, she appeared uncertain. Licking her lips with a nervous gesture, she half-shrugged, then turned once more to Baldwin.

"The bailiff wondered if there could be something . . . You see, your husband died from the same kind of wound as Agatha Kyteler."

She stared at him, and Simon felt instinctively that this was no play-acting. Her shock had every appearance of honesty. "What do you mean, the same?" she said at last.

The knight shrugged. "Exactly the same. It was just how she died, with a single cut across the throat."

"I . . . I need to think. Gentlemen, I am sorry, but this is very hard. Would you mind leaving me now? I must . . . Please go!" There was no refusing that last desperate plea. Leaving their wine, Simon and Baldwin stood, bowed, and walked out.

They found their horses in the yard and were soon mounted. At the gate, Baldwin turned back to glance at Simon. "Where to now, do you think?"

"There's only one thing I want to know right now, and that is, where was Harold Greencliff last night," said Simon shortly. When he looked up, he thought the knight was still looking back at him, but then he realized his friend was peering over his shoulder. When he glanced round, he saw that Angelina Trevellyn was standing in her doorway, watching them leave. He sighed as he turned forward again and saw Baldwin's face. It held a small, far-off smile.

As the light faded, the land was covered in a uniform dull grayness as if there was no distinction between heaven and earth. The snow took on a somber shade that seemed reflected by the sky. There was no shadow to help him, and the Bourc tripped and stumbled as he carried on, leading the horses by the reins.

At least the wind had died now, and the ground glimmered palely under the soft cloak. On all sides were gently undulating hills, and here and there he could see a craggy outcrop of stone at the highest points.

He dared not ride in case he took his horses on to dangerous ground. Better by far that he should lead them, testing his steps all the way. But soon he must stop, find a place to rest and recover from the toil of the day. Stopping, he wearily drew a hand over his brow and gazed around. His eyes flitted over a number of hillsides before they rested on one.

It stood a mile away—maybe two—a hill with what looked like a scattering of rocks on the summit, as if a house had been left to collapse there. A tall spike pointed to the sky like the jagged reminder of a corner, while there appeared to be the tumbled remains of other walls, and even the hint of an enclosure.

Sighing, he let his head drop for a moment, then dragged at the reins in his hand. He must get there before the exhaustion overtook him.

*   *   *

The snow had not dissipated in the least. As they trotted down the hillside toward the lane, it became clear to Simon that they would have as slow a struggle as they had endured earlier.

At first it looked like their worst fears were unwarranted. The lane that wound round before the house appeared relatively clear, and even as they rode farther up on to the top of the hill, it was still reasonably easy going. It was only when they began to descend once more that they found that the drifts had accumulated, and all at once they were bogged in snow which at times was over their feet as they sat on their horses. At one point Edgar showed his horsemanship, keeping his seat as his mount reared, whinnying in fear and disgust at the depth of the powder and trying to avoid the deepest drifts, and the servant was forced to tug the reins and pull the head round, to turn away from the obstacle. Standing and gentling the great creature, he glanced over at Baldwin.

"I think I'll have to walk this one."

He dropped from his saddle and, strolling ahead, spoke calmly to the horse as he led it forward, keeping a firm and steady pressure on the reins. Once it stopped and tried to refuse to carry on, shivering like a stunned rabbit, but then it accepted Edgar's soft words of encouragement and continued.

That was the worst of it. Now the land opened up and the snow was less thick. There was hardly enough to rise more than a couple of inches above their horses' hooves, and they all felt more confident, breaking into a steady, loping trot.

The house was soon visible. Simon could see it, a welcoming slab of gray in the whiteness all round, and he breathed a sigh of relief. He was about to make a

comment, turning to look at Baldwin, when he saw a
troubled frown on the knight's face. He appeared to be
staring at the ground near their feet.

"Baldwin? What's the matter?"

"Look!" When Simon followed the direction of the
pointing finger, he saw them. They were unmistakable,
and his mind swiftly returned to the hunched figure of
the dead merchant. The blood had been laid over the
top of the snow, as if a geyser had spouted it up, and
over the body the snow had been piled up into a
makeshift hide-out. There had been little fresh powder
over the body or the bloodstains. Trevellyn had died
after the snowstorm had stopped.

And here were the clear marks, slightly marred by
drifting, rounded and worn by the strong winds but still
recognizable, of a pair of feet and the hoofprints of a
horse, leading the way they were going. Back to the
door of Harold Greencliff's farm. Exchanging a look,
the two men trotted on.

There was no doubt, the marks clearly led straight to
the trodden mess in the ground before the door, the
tracks of a horse and a man. Shaking his head, Baldwin tossed his reins to Edgar and sprang down. Simon
followed, unconsciously testing the dagger at his
waist, making sure that the blade would come free if
needed. Noticing his movement, Baldwin smiled suddenly, and Simon saw that he had been doing the same
with his sword. Leaving Edgar on his horse, they
strode to the door, and Baldwin pounded heavily on
the timbers with a gloved fist.

"Harold Greencliff! I want to speak with you. Come
out!"

There was no answer. He thumped the door again,
calling, but there was still no reply, and Simon sud-

denly found himself struck with a feeling of nervousness. He felt an extreme trepidation for what they might find inside. Involuntarily he stepped backward.

"What is it?" snapped Baldwin, angry at being left outside. "God!" The sky was again starting to fill with tiny feathers of purest down, light specks of glistening beauty. But these minute granules were composed of pure coldness, and they could kill. Baldwin swore, then slammed his fist a last time on the door. *"Greencliff!"*

But there was no response. Glancing at Simon, he shrugged, then reached for the handle.

Inside it was almost as cold as out. Calling to Edgar to bring the horses in, Baldwin crossed the threshold and strode immediately for the hearth. Crouching, he studied the ash for a moment, then tugged off his glove and held his hand over it, swearing again. "Damn! We'll need to light a fresh one!'

Simon busied himself gathering tinder and straw, then set to work relighting the fire. As he blew gently but firmly at the glowing sparks, carefully adding straw and twigs as the flames started to creep upward, he was aware of Baldwin noisily clumping around the room, peering into dark corners and searching under blankets and boards. Meanwhile, Edgar unperturbedly saw to the horses, removing their saddles and bringing their packs to the fire. Tossing them down, he gave Simon a quick grin before returning to the mounts.

The fire starting to shed a little light, he carefully piled smaller pieces of wood on top, then balanced logs above, and soon the house was beginning to fill with the homely smoke, catching in their throats, making them cough and rub at their eyes to clear away unshed tears. But as the fire caught hold the smoke rose to sit heavily in thick swathes in the rafters, and the air below cleared.

"He's not here, that's for certain," Baldwin grumbled, crouching nearby.

"The footmarks seem to show that he was here last night," said Simon calmly as he watched the flames. "Maybe he's out to look after his sheep."

Baldwin jerked his chin to point at the fire. "And left his fire to go out? In this weather? Come along, Simon. Nobody would let his fire die at this time of year. It could mean death."

"Well . . ." Simon nodded slowly. "If he's gone, where has he gone to? We can't follow now, not with the snow coming again, that would be too dangerous."

"No, but I can take a look and see which direction he's going in," said the knight and stood. He walked outside, shutting the door behind him.

Already the weather had changed, and the small flakes were replaced by large petals falling at what looked like a ludicrously slow speed.

Peering, he narrowed his eyes as he tried to make out any marks in the snow. It was hard to see, the light was too diffuse behind the clouds, and with the failing light as day slipped toward night, he found that bending and looking for some differentiation in the contours was no help. All was uniformly white. There was not the relief of grays or blacks to mar the perfect apparent flatness. It was only when he stood again and stared farther away, wondering in which direction the youth would have gone, that he thought he could make out a depression left in the snow, like a shallow leat pointing arrow-straight to a mine. It led down the lane toward the trees, toward Wefford.

The wind began to build, whisking madly dancing

flakes before his eyes, occasionally knocking them into his face. This was impossible, he thought. There was no way they could find out where the boy had gone in this: it was too heavy. He turned back to the door with a mixture of despondency and anger at being foiled.

The cry started as a low rumble on the Bourc's right. He might easily have missed it, but his ears were too well attuned to sounds of danger, even after the punishment the wind had inflicted during the day, and he immediately stopped in his tracks and stared back the way he had come.

He could feel the shivering of the horses as the call began again. First low, then rising quickly to a loud howl before mournfully sliding down to a dismal wail of hunger: wolves!

Putting out his hand, he stroked his mount gently. There was no sign of them yet. They must be some distance away. He threw a quick glance at the hill ahead. The shelter it offered was a clear half-mile farther on. He gauged the remaining ground he must cover, then set his jaw and pulled at the reins, setting his face to the hill. It held the only possible cover here in this darkening land.

The howls came again, but their tone had changed. They must have found his trail, for he thought he could hear a note of fierce joy. The cries were no longer full of anguish and longing; now they were a paean of exultation. Desperation was replaced by harsh, cruel delight, as if the creatures could already taste the thick, hot blood in his veins.

When he peered at the hill again, he knew he could not survive on foot. Throwing an anxious glance behind, he could see the dog-like animals running toward him. It would be dangerous to ride, God only knew how many hazards lay just under the surface of the snow, waiting to break his horse's legs, but to walk was suicide.

Clambering on to the horse, he whirled, checking the distance once more. They were only a few hundred feet away, seven of them running at a steady lope with their eyes fixed on him. The sight of their implacable approach sent a shiver of expectant fear down his back. He knew what would happen if they were to catch him. Turning, he spurred his horse into a gallop.

The two horses ran madly with their terror. There was no need to urge them on, both knew their danger. The calls of the wolves had seen to that. All he need do was hold on, clinging for dear life as his mount bolted, ears flat back, head low, pelting forward. The Bourc let him have his head, occasionally twitching the reins a little to keep the great horse heading in the direction that would lead them, he hoped, to safety.

"Thanks be to God!"

The heartfelt prayer of gratitude sprang to his lips automatically as they stumbled into the ring, and he fell from the saddle just as the second of his horses galloped in.

Grabbing the packhorse's leading rein, he managed to haul the horse round, and then he could tug the bow free. Calling softly to the petrified animal, trying to calm him, the Bourc grabbed the arrows from the top of his pack. Only when he had them in his hand did he set the point of the bow on the ground and pull down sharply to string it. Then, arrow ready and nocked, he moved forward to the perimeter, a string of great stones that encircled his small encampment.

The howling had not stopped. Ahead the Bourc could see them approaching, not now with the mad enthusiasm of the hunting pack, but with the wary caution of dogs who have seen the boar to his lair and now watch carefully to see how to pull him down without danger.

Teeth showing in the dark, the Bourc waited while they approached, bow held firmly in hands that now felt clammy with anticipation.

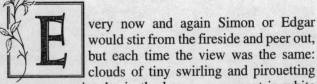

Every now and again Simon or Edgar would stir from the fireside and peer out, but each time the view was the same: clouds of tiny swirling and pirouetting motes sweeping by in the breeze, a pageant in white and gray. The knight sat and stared morosely at the fire.

It was still early when they decided they must remain for the night. The snow was here to stay for some hours and they all recognized the need to keep warm. Once the horses were fed and watered, they opened the packs that Margaret had forced them to bring and sipped at the cool wineskins, then huddled in their blankets around the fire and began to talk desultorily until sleep took them.

Simon found himself nodding soon after sitting, and his voice dropped, his words coming slower and slower, until Baldwin and Edgar were aware of a rhythmical droning as he started snoring.

"Noise like that could waken the dead," said Edgar, but not unkindly.

Baldwin nodded. It was many months since he and his servant had slept away from their new home. In the past, when they had travelled more, they had always tended to avoid other people on the road. Someone always snored, and they preferred their own sleep undisturbed.

"At least the snow's not too heavy," he said. "We should be able to get on tomorrow."

"Yes. And then we'll need to hunt for Greencliff."

Nodding, the knight sighed. "So long as the snow stays like this, we should be able to follow him."

"Yes, God forbid that it could get any worse—we could get snowed in here for ages. No one even knows we're here."

"Oh, I shouldn't worry." He peered at the bailiff's body and threw a quick smile at Edgar with a quizzically raised eyebrow. "There's a good amount of meat on *him*! We'll survive!"

His servant smiled, relaxing back and laughing silently. He was the only man Baldwin had ever met who did so, opening his mouth and letting the breath gasp out in that curious, inaudible exhalation. Baldwin had seen him laugh that way before battles, showing his teeth in a purely natural delight, taking pleasure while he might, even if he were to die shortly thereafter.

"So if we're snowed in for a while we can eat him?" Edgar said after a moment. "Ah, that would be good. There're some good joints on him! Mind, he'll be heavy to haul to the fire. How would you cook him? On a spit?"

Leaning back, the knight squinted at the recumbent figure. "I don't know," he said musingly. "He looks a bit heavy. Is there a spit strong enough in this place?"

Rolling on to an elbow, Edgar stared at him too, grinning. "I don't know. No, you're right, we'd need to paunch and joint him first. Maybe we could hang the rest of him in the open air outside? At least that way he'd keep well."

"Maybe, but he might be too tough. Perhaps we should boil him into a stew?"

"That's possible. Yes, with carrots and a thick slice of fresh bread."

There was a grunt from the bailiff, then they heard his voice. Although muffled by his blanket, the disgruntled tone was unmistakable. "When you have both finished discussing my merits as food on the hoof, perhaps you would like to go to sleep so that we can all be fresh in the morning."

Laughing, Baldwin rolled himself up in his blanket, and was soon breathing long and deep, but now Simon found sleep evaded him. He kept seeing, as if in close juxtaposition, the two gaping wounds, one which had killed the old woman, the other which had killed the merchant. And then he saw the face of Harold Greencliff next to Angelina Trevellyn.

The first attack was easy to fight off. As the Bourc watched, the pack circled, some slinking from side to side in the expanse of clear ground before the wall, others sitting and peering back, like soldiers at a siege checking on the defenses. But then he noticed one in particular, and concentrated on it.

It was a tall dog wolf, from the look of it, lean, taut and strong, with thick gray hair and eyes that stared fixedly at the Gascon. As the others in the pack walked up and down, this one slowly and deliberately inched forward like a cat, staring unblinkingly. Then, as if at his command, they hurled themselves forward.

The leader died first. John drew the string back, sighted the cruel barbs of the arrow head between the eyes of the grizzled dog, and let the arrow fly. He snatched another arrow and fixed it to the bow, drawing again. But there was no need. The wolf died instantly. The arrow sank deep into his brain, and the animal somersaulted on to his back, then lay, shuddering in his death throes. Immediately the others pulled back, withdrawing dismayed to the gloom where he could not fire with certainty. The death of their leader made them pause, as if they suddenly appreciated their prey was not defenseless. They kept just out of clear sight, silently circling his camp, a series of gray wraiths in the gloom.

The Bourc knew wolves, and now he had found a defensible area, he knew he could hold them off. Satisfied that he was safe for a moment from another attack, he investigated his camp.

He was out of the vicious wind at last. The tall walls of stone offered a barrier against the worst of the weather—the ground beneath was free even of snow. Here he tethered the horses.

Nearby, beyond the line of stone, some bushes stood, twisted and stunted as if blasted by magic into their weird shapes. He took his knife and hacked at them, wrenching branches off and tossing them into a pile. While there was firewood handy he would conserve the faggots on the packhorse. Nearer the horses he found a small hollow and set himself to lighting a fire, looking around as the flames began to curl upward.

By their light he saw that he was in a natural bowl on the top of a low hill. Its perimeter was bounded by a low wall to the south, but northward it had collapsed. Behind what he had thought was a derelict building was a rocky outcrop, three or four great slabs, one on top of the other, with a narrow, low gap like a door between the two lower ones. Peering through, he saw that there was a cavern inside. A place to sleep, safe from wind and snow.

It was while he was peering inside that the second attack began. From the corner of his eye he glimpsed a shape leaping noiselessly on to the wall. Even as the Bourc grabbed his bow and notched an arrow to the string, drawing it back and letting the shaft fly, he heard the screams of terror from the horses, and, spinning round, he saw the packhorse rearing in terror as another wolf jumped, jaws snapping, trying to reach the horse's throat.

Lurching to his feet, the Bourc tried to aim, but the wolf was too close to the horses, and he dared not risk the shot. Cursing, he ran forward shouting, and as he did, the wolf's teeth scraped a ragged tear in the horse's neck. Shrieking, the horse rose once more, but now the smell of blood appeared to enrage the Bourc's mount and made him lose his fear. Lifting his bulk up onto his hind legs as the wolf passed before him, he suddenly dropped, both hooves falling, legs stiff, the whole of his weight behind them. With a petrified screech, the wolf was crushed to the ground, forepaws scrabbling in the dirt, eyes wide in agony, as the horse rose again and again, only to bring his whole weight down on the wolf's back, not stopping until the hideous cries had ceased.

Before running to his horse's side, the Bourc stared around his camp carefully, arrow still set on the bowstring, every sense straining. There was nothing: no noise to disturb him. He slowly rose, walking along the line of the great rocks until he came to the horses. Squatting, he put aside the bow, and drew his dagger to make sure the wolf was dead. It was unnecessary. A quick look at the ruined body was enough to show that.

The horse was still shivering, eyes rolling in horror, and the Bourc stroked it for a moment. A few yards away was the packhorse, and he stared at it anxiously. He could see the blood dripping steadily from the long gash, but he gave a sigh of relief as the fire spluttered and flared. The wound was not deep enough to kill the animal. Walking to it, he made sure, then patted the horse and spoke softly to him.

It was while he was there that he heard the panting. Turning slowly, his heart beating frantically, he saw the sharp features of the wolf crouched low, eyes fixed on him as it stalked forward. He glanced at his bow, lying useless only yards away. It was close, so close, but already nearer the approaching wolf than him: he would never be able to reach it. He showed his teeth in a snarl—though whether in fear or rage, he was not himself sure—and grasped his long-bladed dagger.

When Simon awoke, it was to a sense of mild surprise, wondering where he was. At least over the night he had not suffered from the dream again. It was as if it only wanted to seek him out while he was idle, not now, while he was searching for the witch's killer. While he was employed on that task the nightmare would leave him alone, although its memory would stay with him as a spur to his commitment to the hunt.

It took them little time to saddle their horses, roll up their blankets and prepare to leave. The snow appeared not to have been so strongly blown by the wind this time, and lay evenly rather than drifting, so the three men felt that the journey to Wefford should not be too difficult. From the front of the house, they could look

over to the east where the woods began and see where
the lane made its way in among the trees, the hedges at
either side standing out as two long ramparts. The trail
itself looked like a ditch between them, like some sort
of fortification, from the way that the land rose on their
left to form the small hill.

As they mounted and turned their horses' heads to
the sun in the east, which seemed to hang larger and
redder than usual in the pale blue sky, they had to
squint from the already painful glare off the snow.
Baldwin rode alongside the trail he had seen the
evening before. In the bright sunlight the tracks still
stood out, and they led the men along the lane a short
way. But then the marks were obliterated under a fall
of snow from the branches of the trees overhead. Taking their time, they set a slow pace, between a trot and
a walk, as they went under the trees, casting about for
a continuation of the tracks, but they saw nothing.

"We'll have to get Tanner, of course," said Baldwin
after a few minutes.

Looking across at him, Simon sighed as he turned
back to the road ahead. "Yes. And raise a search party;
see if we can hunt him quickly."

Another manhunt, the knight mused sadly. He enjoyed the chase for an animal. After all, that was only
right, to hunt and kill for food and sport was natural.
But tracking a man was different, demeaning for the
man and his hunters as well.

It would be different, the knight knew, if he felt that
there had been any justifiable reason for the murders,
but there did not seem to be. He frowned and bit his lip
in his annoyance at one thought: if he had kept this boy
Greencliff in gaol, or put him back when they had
heard from Stephen de la Forte that the two of them

had *not* been together all the time when Agatha Kyteler had died, maybe Alan Trevellyn would not have died. That meant that a little of the guilt for the murder, he felt, now lay with him for making the wrong decision at the time. As his eyes rose to the road ahead, they held a frown as he swore to himself that he would catch the criminal and avenge Trevellyn's death.

Jogging along quietly beside him, Simon was not so convinced of Harold Greencliff's guilt. Why? That was the question that plagued him: *why?* Why kill the merchant? Or the witch, for that matter. The boy had made comments about her at the inn that night, but nobody could explain why he hated her. And there seemed no reason why he should kill Trevellyn either.

Then his eyes took on a more pensive look and his head sank on his shoulders. Mrs. Trevellyn was very beautiful, he admitted to himself. Was it possible that she *was* the mysterious lover? That Jennie Miller was right? Could the boy have killed her husband to win her? But if he had, why run away afterward? It made no sense!

The admission of what she had done at the witch's cottage had launched Harold Greencliff into a nightmare that would not stop. All he had ever wanted was to be able to live out his life like his father before him, a farmer. To be able to earn his living honestly. He knew he would never be rich, but that did not matter when none of his friends and neighbors were. Money and cattle were pleasant to dream of, but he felt it was more important to be satisfied and content, to work hard and earn a place in heaven, like the priests promised.

But since the death of Agatha Kyteler last Tuesday, there had been no peace for him. Maybe if he had managed to run away then, he would have left all this behind. If he had got to Gascony, perhaps then he might have been able to forget the whole affair, but it was too late now. He was marked by his guilt.

At first, when he got back home from the Trevellyns' hall, he had sat down as if in a dream, his mind empty. It felt impossible to move, and he stayed there on his bench, sitting and occasionally shivering in the lonely cold of his house, not even bothering to stoke his little fire so deep was his misery. But soon the despair returned, and the disgust, and he stood and walked around his room, sobbing. Ever since that *witch* had ruined everything, his life had been wrecked. It was all her fault: she had deserved her end.

It was like a dream, the way that he had made his decision and started taking up his meager essentials, stuffing them into his old satchel. He had picked up his ballock knife, the long dagger with the single sharp edge, from where it had fallen on the floor. He might need it, and it was good in a fight, with the two large round lobes at the base of the solid wooden grip to protect the hand.

For food, he took some fruit and dried and salted ham, which he dropped into the bag, followed by a loaf of bread as an afterthought. Then the satchel was full. He pulled a thick woollen tunic over his head, draped his blanket over his shoulders, took his staff, and left. He would never return. The shame would be too painful.

At first he had wandered in the darkness without any firm direction in mind, aimlessly following where his feet led him, and he had found himself heading south. Soon he was in among the woods. Usually he would stride through there, knowing each trunk and fallen bough like the furniture in his hall, but in the bitter cold and his despair he had meandered witlessly.

Now he knew it was a wonder that he had managed to survive and had not succumbed to the freezing temperatures. He had been lucky. The woods appeared to go on forever, leading him up gentle hills and down the other sides, through lighter snow which the winds had not been able to pile into deep drifts, heading away from his home and his past life.

Only when he had begun to smell woodsmoke did he realize he had almost arrived at Crediton, and he stopped. Almost without consciously making a choice, he had found himself starting to walk again, following the line of trees to circumnavigate the town, always keeping to the shelter of the thick boughs. When he had passed by the town, he had discovered a strange lightening of his spirit, as if he had truly left his old life behind. He had only rarely been this far from home before.

All that day he had continued, ignoring calls from other travellers, concentrating solely on the steady trudge of his feet, careless of his direction, neither knowing nor caring where he was heading, until he had realized that the snow was falling again.

It forced him to waken from his mindless, day-dreaming tramping, and he stopped dead, staring around with no idea where he was. He had arrived at a flat area, an open space fringed by trees, and now, as the first few flakes began to fall, he could see that there appeared to be no houses nearby.

Here he was quite high up, his view unimpaired, and to the left he could see over the top of some trees to a hilltop some miles away which wore a circle of trees at its summit like a crown. Before him he could see along a small cleft in the land, which appeared to forge ahead like a track, with both sides hidden under a light scattering of trees. Narrowing his eyes against the thin mist of snow, he had set his face to the valley and determinedly carried on.

But it had been no good. The snow had begun to take hold, the air becoming colder, and each fresh gust of wind felt as if it blew a little harder than the last, making the snow swoop and dive like millions of tiny, white swallows.

The random movement of the white dust held an almost hypnotic fascination, and he found himself beginning to stumble more often as he fell under the spell of the all-encompassing whiteness that now appeared to form an impermeable barrier around him. It was as if the dance of the snow motes before his eyes was an invitation to sit and sleep. He had the impression that they were soothing, calming, as if asking him to rest.

And then he had fallen.

Possibly it was a gnarled tree root hidden from sight, maybe a fallen branch, but suddenly he had discovered he was not walking any more. He had tripped, and was how lying headlong, his face resting against what had felt like a warm soft pillow of the smoothest down. Rolling, he could not help a sigh of relief. He stretched and groaned in happiness. At last he could relax: he had come far enough. Now he could sleep.

It was not until much later that he could be grateful for the interruption. At first it had seemed to be a growling, then a moaning as of pain, low and persistent. Just at the edge of his hearing, it had penetrated his thoughts and dreams like a saw cutting through bark. He had mumbled to himself and rolled, trying to sleep and lose the insistent noise, but it had continued, and as his mind grew angry at the interruption, the anger started to make him waken. It was sufficient.

The snow had strengthened, and as he lurched unwillingly back to consciousness, he realized that he was smothered in a film of light powder. Recognizing his danger, he stood quickly, his heart beating madly, while his breath sobbed in his throat, and he gazed around wildly, a feral creature recognizing the sound of a hunter. The snow had cocooned him, swaddling him under its gentle grip of death. If he had not heard that noise, he would soon surely have died, sleeping under the soothing influence of the murderous cold.

But what had made the noise? As he turned here and there looking for the source, a slow realization had come to him: it was the noise of cattle, and it came from nearby.

As soon as he had recognized the sounds, he had started off toward them. There, hidden behind a line of oaks, was an old barn. The walls were red-brown cob, not limewashed, and if he had not heard the animals inside, he would not have seen the place. After carefully looking to see that there were no people nearby, he had entered. Inside there was a store of hay, and he fashioned a rough cot from it, sitting and preparing to wait for the snow to stop.

The sudden lack of movement freed his mind from the shackles of exercise and he had found his thoughts returning to *her*. To his pain at leaving her behind. He had wept tears for her last evening as he had sat alone and miserable at his house, he could now remember. Hot, scalding tears that seared his soul. He had loved her. Inevitably, his thoughts turned to her again. To know that he could never see her again, never feel the smooth softness of her body, never hold the thick, blue-black tresses of her braids in his hands like silken ropes, never kiss her again, hold her, feel the warmth of her breasts and the flat sweep of her belly, was maddening. He had once thought that he had loved Sarah, but this was much more: this was almost a religious loss. It felt as if, after the horror of her face in the dark only two nights before, a part of him had died. When she saw him there, and spoke with such loathing, a spark of his soul had weakened and finally faded to dullness. There was nothing there any longer.

He sighed at the memory. Now, in the morning, he could accept that he could never see her again. Picking up his satchel, he swung it on to his back and made his way to the entrance, carefully peering out. There was no one there, so he walked out. He could break his fast later. For now the main thing was to get away, as far away as possible from this area. Could he get on a ship? Would it be possible to find one to take him away?

Pausing, he considered. There were docks at Exeter, he knew, but last time Tanner had found him there. It was further, but would they expect him to head down to the south? To Dartmouth or Plymouth? Weighing the satchel in his hand, he debated the two options. He would need more food on the way if he was going that far. It was a great deal further, but if he could make it, they would never think of searching for him there, would they?

Making his choice, he set his shoulders and set his face to the south. He must go to the coast, then on to Gascony and to freedom.

The village looked like a slumbering animal, as if the area had chosen hibernation in preference to the freezing misery of the winter weather, and Baldwin gazed around sourly as they rode along the street.

"God! Why aren't these people up and working yet?"

"It *is* very early, Baldwin. And I have no doubt that some are up. They will be out tending to their sheep and cattle," said Simon calmly. "Especially after the snow last night."

Baldwin grunted, and maintained a disapproving silence for the rest of their journey. It was not far. They stopped outside the inn, and at a curt nod of Baldwin's head, Edgar dropped from his horse and walked leisurely to the door. Watching, Simon saw him casually glance up at the sky, trying to assess the time. The bailiff nodded to himself. It was very early to waken the innkeeper. But then he realized his error.

After looking up to reassure himself as to the earliness of the hour, the servant grinned back at him quickly, then beat on the door in a shockingly loud tattoo before retreating a few yards.

It was a sensible precaution, from the bellow of rage that issued from inside. Simon heard rapid steps, the sound of bolts being drawn, and then the door was yanked open and the unshaven and furious features of the publication appeared, mouth wide to roar at whoever had woken him. At the sight of the knight with his servant and friend, his mouth snapped shut as if on a spring.

"Sir Baldwin," he managed at last, with a snarl that appeared to be his best approximation to a smile. "How can I serve you?"

The knight grunted. "You can fetch hot drinks for three, prepare cooked eggs and bread for our breakfast, and start to organize a search party. Then you can send word to my house that we are all well, find Tanner, and tell him to come here immediately. Prepare provisions for three days for three men."

"I . . . Er . . ."

"And you can do it all now. We must hunt a man."

It seemed to the bailiff that no sooner had they sat to watch the innkeeper's wife cooking their eggs on her old cast-iron griddle over the embers of last night's fire than the men from the village began to arrive. Farmers and peasants walked in, strolling casually as if the matter was nothing to do with them, or cautiously and reluctantly sidling through the curtain as though expecting to be arrested themselves. Each was told by Edgar to go and arm himself and return as quickly as possible, with food for at least three days.

It was not until Tanner arrived, covered in snow almost up to his knees and dripping, that Baldwin looked up and began to take an interest. The old constable walked straight to him. There was no need, he knew, for subservience with this knight. Glancing up as his bulk approached, Baldwin gave him a slow grin and waved a hand to the fire. "Have you eaten? Would you like to have some eggs?"

Glancing carelessly at the griddle, Tanner shook his head. "What's the matter, sir? The innkeeper's boy told me to come here straight away. Said we had to hunt a man."

"That's right. Greencliff has run away again."

"Harry's gone? Oh, the daft bugger!" He shook his head as if in tired annoyance, then said, "But so what? If he wasn't there for the death of the witch, because he was with de la . . ."

"It's not that easy. He was not with de la Forte," the bailiff broke in, and explained about the change in Stephen de la Forte's evidence. When he spoke of the murder of Trevellyn, there was a sudden hush in the room, as the men all around realized why they were being asked to chase Greencliff. When Simon had finished, he found he was immediately bombarded by questions from all sides, and after a moment Baldwin stood with a hand raised for silence.

"Quiet!" he thundered, and gradually the noise died down. "That's better. Now, Harold Greencliff was not at his house last night. The fire was cold, so it's likely that he left the night before. Otherwise it would at least have been warm when we got there. So, where has he gone?"

The room was quiet as the men thought, then one said, "He could've gone to Exeter, to the docks again. That's where he went after the witch was killed."

Baldwin nodded. It was certainly possible. "He could, but was there anywhere else he might go? Did he have any family or friends he could have gone to stay with? Anybody outside the area with whom he could rest?"

All round the room heads slowly shook.

"In that case, we have no choice: we must try to search for him on all of the roads." Baldwin sighed. The only result of this would be long hours in the saddle. To think that he had felt sympathy for the lad when he had been in gaol! He sat, glowering.

Simon stirred thoughtfully. "We saw the footprints in front of the house," he said. "Were they going to it or leading from it?"

"What do you mean?"

"We thought he was going home *from* Trevellyn's house, but we could have been wrong. He might have gone to Trevellyn's house, killed him, then carried on toward the west on the road. Or he could have done the murder, then headed home and carried on from there. We can't be sure which."

"Yes," Baldwin agreed. "So those are the directions we should concentrate on. Beyond Trevellyn's place, and back this way."

"He can't have come this way," said a stocky man in a tough jerkin of leather and skins.

"Why not?" asked Simon, frowning.

"I'm a hunter. Mark Rush. I was up at the lane all last night between his house and here—there's been a wolf or something attacking sheep in the pens over that way—and I was sheltered there all night. When it snowed, I went into my hut, but when it was clear enough, I was out again. He never passed me."

"Are you sure?" said Baldwin dubiously. He found that the man's eyes moved and fixed on him, curiously light and unfeeling as he spoke.

"Oh, yes. I'm sure. Nothing living passed me that night I wasn't aware of. Harry did not pass."

Simon eyed him thoughtfully, then nodded. "In that case we should look in the woods to the north and south of the lane, especially near his house." He thanked the woman, who passed him a platter with two eggs and a hunk of roughly torn bread. "I suggest we have three parties: one to ride to the west and look for signs, one to search for tracks in the woods north, the

last to look in the southern woods. Whoever finds anything should return here with a message to be left with
the innkeeper."

They talked a little longer about the details, but
agreed to this simple plan. Baldwin and Edgar would
take the western road, Simon the southern woods, and
Tanner the northern. Splitting the men into three
groups of four, Baldwin and Simon quickly finished
their breakfast, went out to their horses, and mounted.

Simon was pleased to have been able to enlist the light-
eyed hunter for his search. The man looked capable
and confident. Although quiet and soft-spoken, he
moved with an alertness and graceful ease which spoke
of his skill and strength. He was older than Simon,
probably nearer Baldwin's age of forty and odd, although whether he was older or younger than the
knight was a different matter. The bailiff could not
guess.

As they rode along to the lane leading to the Greencliff farm, Simon studied him. He wore a heavy-
looking short sword by his side. There was a bow at his
back and arrows in a quiver tied to the saddle over his
blanket in front of him, where he could reach them
quickly. Before the three groups divided, Baldwin,
Simon and Tanner had held a quick conference to confirm the main plan. Whoever was to find what could be
Greencliff's trail was immediately to send a messenger
back to Wefford so that he could guide others there. If
Simon's or Tanner's teams found no sign of the youth,
they were to carry on and join Baldwin's, for it was in
his direction that there were going to be the highest
number of roads to search, and thus he had the greatest need of men.

With the details agreed, they had separated and made their way to the areas allocated to them for searching.

Baldwin knew, as he urged his horse into an easy lope, that his would almost certainly prove to be a wild goose chase, and reviewed the road ahead. This lane led to Greencliff Barton itself, then on up the hill to the Trevellyn house, and past it to the crossroads on the Tiverton road. Where would they go from there? Into Crediton itself? Or northeast to Tiverton? Or should they carry on west? Where would the boy have gone?

In among the trees, Simon had an easier time. At the beginning of the line of trees he had called the hunter aside. "Mark Rush, I've heard of you, even if we haven't met before."

His eyes were a very pale gray, as if the rain and snow he lived in had washed the color from them. Set in the leathery, square face, it made him look as if the eyes were a reflection of his soul, which had been so worn with his outdoor life that it was weary now of continuing. But when the eyes fixed on the bailiff, he could see the glittering intelligence that lay behind.

"Yes, Bailiff?" His tone expressed polite interest, bordering on indifference.

"I have no idea where this boy has gone, or how to seek him. You do, you're a hunter. You're in charge: you can read his spoor if we find it, I won't be able to."

The hunter nodded, then glanced ahead at the waiting men. "In that case, sir, we'll come out of the woods again."

"Why?"

"It's hard going here. We'll go another half mile down the road, then go into the trees there. If he went into the trees to lose someone following him and made a big curve, we could end up following it all the way back on ourselves. If we go in further down, we can see if he left the woods south of the village or whether he went on at all. If he didn't leave them, we know he's waiting for Tanner or the knight to find him."

"So if we enter further on, we stand a better chance of finding him if he's there."

He nodded. Then, apparently taking Simon's shrug to be acknowledgment of the transfer of authority, the hunter called the other two men to them and led the way down the road to the south, with Simon taking second position behind him.

When Mark Rush stopped, it was some way past the last of the houses in the village. Here Simon knew that the woods were bordered by a grassed verge before the road, but now the grass was hidden by the layer of snow. The hunter appeared to be measuring, gazing back the way they had come for a moment, then, seemingly satisfied, he took his horse to the verge and on into the trees.

Following, Simon was again taken with the sudden hush, the stillness that existed inside. It was as if the troop had entered an inn as strangers, causing a void where there had been noise. Here it was as though the trees were intelligent beings who were suddenly aware of the invaders, and who were stunned into uncomprehending dumbness. He almost wanted to apologize to the towering boughs that loomed overhead for their noisy presence.

Smothering the feeling, he carried on, over the thin bracken and ferns that lay under the snow at the edge and into the woods. He was faintly surprised how thin the snow was even after only quite a short ride. Above, the trees were leafless, and he could see through the apparently lifeless branches to the sky above, but still the ground had little more than a thin crust of snow, a mere few inches.

On the floor he could see that several animals had passed by, their prints firm and clear on the white carpet: birds, animals running purposefully in a line—twice he saw the marks of deer, with the distinctive twin crescents of their hooves. All stood out distinctly on the thin surface, and when Simon saw the attentive gaze of the hunter, seeming to notice and catalog them all in his mind, the bailiff relaxed. There was obviously no point in trying to see the tracks before Mark Rush. The man was clearly more than capable. Sighing, Simon lapsed into a private reverie.

What was Margaret doing? Probably ordering Hugh to help her with her work! He must surely be fully recovered by now, and Margaret was good at getting him to work, using the right amount of acid and sweetness in her voice to persuade him. He smiled fondly. She always did know how to get her men to do what she wanted.

That was the kind of woman Baldwin needed, he felt sure. One who could not just excite the senses, but one who would always keep him on his toes, one who could keep his interest going. Above all, one who was intelligent. Simon was sure that the knight would need a woman who could discuss matters with him, not a pretty ornament.

The thought led him down a new and different track. What about Mrs. Trevellyn? She certainly seemed to have attracted Baldwin. Simon's lips twitched in remembered humor at the way the knight had turned in his seat to gaze back at the house as they left the day before. Yes, he had been interested!

And there was no denying her beauty, the bailiff reflected. Of course, he was more than happy with his own wife, but denying the beauty of another would be stupid and, in the light of his own devotion to Margaret, pointless. He could cheerfully confirm that he was happier with the warm and summery fair looks of his wife than he could be with the cool and wintry attraction of the brunette from France, with her calculating, green eyes, cold and deep as the sea. They were nothing like the merry, bright blue cornflower of his wife's. But still, he could appreciate her slender and willowy figure, with the long legs and tiny waist. And her flat belly, below the rich, ripe splendor of her breast, promising warmth and comfort. Yes, there was much to admire there. But was she intelligent enough for his friend?

Then suddenly the smile froze on his face as his thoughts carried on to the inevitable question: if she was clever enough, if she was capable, and if she had taken Greencliff as her lover, could she have persuaded him to kill her husband for her?

Deep in his musings, Simon nearly rode into the stationary horse of the hunter in front. Looking up, he was surprised to see that the man wore an amused grin. Thinking his humor was at his absent-mindedness, the bailiff was about to snap a quick retort when he saw that Mark Rush was pointing down at the ground.

"There he goes!"

Staring down in complete surprise—for he had not truly expected this troop to find anything—Simon saw the footprints. As the other two riders approached, he and Rush dropped down and studied them, crouching by the side of the spoor.

The hunter reached out with a tentative hand to

softly trace the nearest print, then Simon saw his eyes narrow as he glanced back to their right, the direction where the man should have come from. Seemingly satisfied, he turned and gazed the opposite way, then ruminatively down at the prints once more.

"Well?" asked Simon.

Mark Rush sniffed hard, then snorted, hawked and spat. "This is too easy. He's not trying to hide." His brow wrinkled. "I wonder why not."

Shrugging, Simon gave a gesture of indifference. "What does it matter? We'll find out when we've caught him."

"Yes," said the hunter, then grunted as he rose, a knee clicking as he moved. "Right, well I suppose we'd better get on after him. These prints're from yesterday from the look of them, they're worn. See that?" He pointed at a small round hole beside the trail. Glancing at it, Simon saw it repeated beside the footprints. "That's a walking stick. See how it hits the ground in time with his left foot, although he holds it in his right hand? He's carrying a stick, so we'd better be careful. Don't want him braining us."

They mounted, then sent one of the men back to the inn. Before he left, Simon looked up at the sky. "How long have we been in the woods, do you think, Rush?"

Squinting at the sky, the hunter seemed to consider. "Maybe two, maybe three hours?"

"I think so too. You!" This to the waiting messenger. "Get to the inn as quickly as you can, but then go on to Sir Baldwin—understand? Tell him too, and ask if he can send a couple more men, just in case we do have to fight to catch him."

"No need to worry about that, sir," said Mark Rush, indicating his bow with a jerk of his thumb.

"I'd prefer to take him alive, Rush. We'll avoid any unnecessary violence."

"Yes. I'll avoid unnecessary violence, but I'll use any that *is* necessary," he said meaningfully.

The three rode on in file now. There was no real need for a hunter to follow this trail. If the man had wanted to leave an invitation his path could not have been more easy to detect. It straggled on, winding unnecessarily round shrubs and saplings, sometimes seeming to halt, both feet placed together, and then starting out afresh. Once or twice Simon felt sure that the man must have stumbled or tripped. At one point there was a definite mark where he had fallen, and the outline of his body remained, his hands making deep prints in the snow, looking strangely sad, as if they were all that remained of him.

Simon shivered. It was curious, but he felt a kind of sympathy with this man, for no reason he could fathom. Perhaps it was merely empathy for the hunted creature? He had felt that once before, when, as a boy, he had watched a deer at bay, the hounds snapping at it, the animal's eyes rolling in his terror, knowing that he was about to die. Then, when the huntsmen had egged on the dogs, and the deer had fallen, legs flailing uselessly, beneath the pack, Simon had felt the same sadness. It was not for the hunt itself, but for the inevitability of the end. For that buck it had been death at the teeth of the hounds. For Harold Greencliff it would be the slow strangling as he was hauled up the gibbet by the rope around his neck.

With a shrug, he concentrated on the trail again. Had the boy given any compassion to the witch? Or to the man he murdered? The bailiff doubted it.

*   *   *

It was getting close to dark when the man at the back of the troop called out, and Baldwin had been getting short-tempered long before that.

Their ride had been slow and painstaking, searching carefully along the lane, with Edgar on one side and the knight on the other, both looking for tracks that could have been left by the farmer, but they found nothing. Baldwin had even insisted on going into the sheep's pasture to see whether they could find a trail there leading into the woods, but the sheep had trampled the whole area and scraped at the surface to get at the grass underneath so effectively that there was nothing that the two men could find.

Carrying on, they had slowly worked their way along the lane, up to the Trevellyn house and beyond, and Baldwin had managed to throw it only the most cursory of glances, preventing himself from staring and searching for the extraordinary beauty of Angelina Trevellyn. It was not purely his willpower that stopped him. It was the raised eyebrow and sardonic smile on Edgar's face when he happened to catch the servant's eye.

As he turned back to the road ahead, he wore an expression of vague perplexity. The look from Edgar showed more clearly than any words just how obvious his interest in the woman was. Baldwin was no fool. If it was that obvious to Edgar, it would surely be as clear to others who knew him.

His problem was, he did not know what his feelings were. Was it just sympathy for a woman recently widowed? He slumped in his saddle as he tried to analyze his emotions. Although there was a sense of lust, that was hardly enough to explain his desire to see her again. It was quite a poignant sensation, one that he had never experienced before. Was it normal to feel like this after such a brief introduction? Who could he speak to about it? Edgar?

They had almost arrived at the end of the road, and Baldwin was debating which direction to take, when the call came. Stopping his troop, they waited, and soon saw the figure of Simon's messenger.

After hearing the message, Baldwin looked at the two men in his squad. "You two go back. Find Tanner and tell him he can call off his hunt, then go back with this man and join the bailiff and the hunter."

There was a little grumbling, but they finally agreed, and Edgar and the knight sat on their horses and watched as the three disappeared round the curve in the road. Then Baldwin sighed and flicked his reins, setting off at a slow walk, his servant behind.

"Well?"

Edgar grinned at the gruff word, and at the implied question. "Sir?"

"What do you think?" Baldwin had stopped his horse and now sat frowning at Edgar with his brow wrinkled in perplexity. "Of Mrs. Trevellyn, I mean?"

"Mrs. Trevellyn? A very beautiful lady. And very marriageable, I would think, with the money she must have. Her dowry would be high, I imagine." He maintained a wooden and blank expression.

"Yes, but should I . . . ? Well, for a woman who's husband's just been killed? She's hardly begun her mourning. Should I . . . ?"

"I'm sure if you catch her husband's murderer she'll be very pleased. And grateful, sir."

As Baldwin wheeled his horse and set off, his face purposeful once more, he could not contain his glee. That the capture of Alan Trevellyn's killer would de-

light her had not occurred to him, and now he could
tell her that they had found the trail. He squared his
shoulders. He must go to her at once to tell her.

Not having to search continually for tracks made
their return along the road a great deal faster, although
the snow was thick enough to ensure that they must exercise caution. They could not risk going so fast that
their horses might slip on ice or on a hardened rut of
frozen mud.

At the turn-off to the house, they slowed and as-
cended the hill at a walk. It was strange, Baldwin
thought, that from here, outside, there was no sign of
the sadness that inevitably follows the death of the
master. Smoke still issued cheerily from chimneys,
there were sounds of shouting and woodcutting from
behind the property, and if he did not know of the
death, he would have thought that nothing had happened here.

When they had dismounted and tied up their horses,
Baldwin thumped on the door. It was soon opened by
the same young maid whom they had seen on the day
before, but now, the knight noticed, she had undergone
a transformation. Whereas before she had appeared
timid and fearful, now she seemed gay as she opened
the door, smiling as she recognized the men waiting,
and he found himself grinning in return.

She led them through to the hall again, where the fire
blazed in enthusiastic welcome. Striding in, the knight
and his man stood warming themselves by the fire
while the maid left to go into the solar at the back of the
dais. After a few moments, she returned, indicating that
they should follow her, and they soon found themselves in a warm and comfortable family room with
another roaring fire. Sitting on a bench nearby was

Mrs. Trevellyn, sewing quietly at a tapestry, and she glanced up questioningly as the two men entered.

At the sight of her cool green eyes, Baldwin felt the blood begin to thunder in his veins. She looked so soft and vulnerable, so warm and defenseless, he wanted to gather her up in his arms and gentle her. The feeling was so strong that he stood for a moment and stared, taking in her slim and languid dark beauty. It was impossible to suspect her of being involved in the murder of the old woman, let alone the killing of her own husband. He felt quite certain of that now. But when her eyes met his, he was sure that he could see a quick impatience, and at the sight he dropped into a chair, waving Edgar out to the hall. Her maid followed, so they were soon left alone.

With a sigh she set her needlework aside and subjected him to a pensive, detailed study. "So, Sir Baldwin. You wanted to see me?" Her voice was low and calm.

"Yes." Now he was here, he realized that raising the death of her husband was going to be difficult. Mentioning Alan Trevellyn must recall to her the pain of seeing his twisted body out on the hill among the trees. Taking a deep breath, he said, "Mrs. Trevellyn, I know it must be very hard for you, but we have been fortunate in our search for your husband's killer."

An eyebrow rose, and he was sure he could see a skeptical smile form. "Really? And how is this?"

"After the death of Agatha Kyteler, we found some evidence that a local man might have been involved, and when we went to see him, he had disappeared. Harold Greencliff. We went to see him yesterday, but he has gone again. Run away. But we have found his trail, and . . ."

Her eyes had widened, as if in great surprise, and a hand raised to her throat. "Harold?" Her voice quavered, suddenly weak.

"It looks like he ran away almost immediately after the killing of your husband, lady. We have sent a search party after him. The men are following his tracks in the woods. My friend the bailiff is there, and he should soon bring the boy back to be tried for the murder. Lady? Are you all right?"

She had dropped her face into her hands, as if about to weep, and the knight leaned forward a little, his hand held out tentatively, longing to touch her and try to calm her, but he let his hand fall. He dared not.

After a minute or two, she cleared her throat and looked into the flames.

"Lady? Can I fetch you anything?"

Looking at her, he was struck by the fresh sadness in her eyes, and his heart went out to her for feeling sympathy for the young farmer, even if it was misplaced. But then her eyes returned to his, and he could plainly see the fear in their emerald depths. It was that which made him stiffen with a sudden cold doubt. This was not just womanly compassion for a hunted villein. She was scared for herself.

Damn this snow!"

They had managed to follow the tracks all around the perimeter of Crediton, Mark Rush staying in among the trees, stumbling over the bracken and thin, straggling shrubs at the very edge so that he could follow the footprints while the others rode on happily in the clear area that bounded the town, listening with amusement to his muttered curses. Every time he passed too close to a tree and jogged its branches, more snow fell on him, causing another outburst.

It was not until they had passed round the town and were at the south that the trail began to turn away from the others. Rush was no fool, and he knew that if he was the fugitive he would try to confuse any pursuers. He might double back when it was not expected, or find a stream where he could travel without his prints being seen and where no hound could detect a scent, although it would be dangerous and painful to do that now with the waters frozen. What else could he do? Leave tracks and then make a trap?

These were the thoughts that kept forcing their way

into his mind as he followed the prints slowly making their way south. "Bailiff?"

At the call, Simon left his horse with the last man and wandered into the trees. "Yes?"

Pointing, the hunter glowered at the ground. "He's going south now. It's late. We can try to carry on after him if you want, but I reckon we'd be better off finding somewhere to lie up for the night and get on after him in the morning."

Simon nodded. Already the sky was darkening, and it would soon be difficult to see the prints. They had seen a farm not long before, in a new assart to the east, so they made their way to it, and were soon sitting before a fire, eating their cured meats and drinking wine. The farmer had been concerned to have three well-armed men appear at first, and had nervously fingered his dagger, until Simon explained who they were, and then he had agreed with alacrity to allow them to use his hall. As he said, if there was a killer on the loose, he would be safer with them in his house.

The house possessed a large hall, with the animals segregated by a fence, and there was plenty of space even when the constable arrived with two men. He had sent the other members of his party to their homes when he had received the message about the spoor. There seemed little point in having so many men to chase one.

They had arrived within an hour of Simon's group finishing their meal, complaining bitterly at having to track not only the outlaw but also Simon's troop to the farmhouse, and sat in front of the fire until the snow melted and steam began to rise from their clothes. The farmer bustled around enthusiastically, giving them pots of ale and cider from his buttery and providing extra blankets for those who needed them. In one corner was a table with a bench at either side, and here the constable, the hunter and the bailiff sat.

Tanner chewed meditatively at a loaf as he eyed the other two. "So you're sure we're on the right trail?"

Mark Rush and Simon exchanged a quick glance. Then the hunter nodded. "Yes, I'm sure. We picked up the tracks leading away from the lane by his house, like he was avoiding the roads. When it came to Crediton, like you saw, he avoided the town and kept going."

"It doesn't make much sense, though," the constable mused.

"What doesn't?" asked Simon.

"Well, he's heading south like he's thought it all out and decided to run away, but I didn't see any sign of a fire. Did you?"

"No," he admitted.

"So I suppose he must be trying to cover as much ground as possible before resting. We've come at least twelve miles or so already. He could have gone another seven or eight before he needed to stop."

"Yes," the hunter agreed. "He's all right. He can go at his own pace. We have to make sure we can follow his tracks, so we can only work with the sun."

Nodding, Tanner glanced at the bailiff. "Where do you think he'll be going?"

"I've no idea. I can only assume he's heading for the coast, but he's taking a great risk."

"Yes. He's heading for the moors. If he keeps going, he'll end up as feed for the crows."

Mark Rush glanced up from his pot. "Won't take long. Way he's going, he'll be dead before he gets to the moors themselves if he's not careful."

"Why do you say that?" asked Simon.

"The way he's going. His walking's all stumbling and tripping, like he's drunk. I think he'll be lucky if he makes it to the moors. I don't know, but I think tomorrow we may find his body."

Greencliff was not dead, though he was frozen to the bone. He was sitting in a small depression in the ground, a tiny natural shelter, with a little fire cheerfully throwing small shadows. But it was not enough to warm him. There was an absence of tinder, and he had been forced to make do with some green branches snapped from a tree which cast little heat. Now he sat shivering, gloomily considering a dismal future, huddled under his blanket.

There was no doubt in his mind. If he did not find somewhere warm where he could rest and eat hot food, he would freeze. His teeth chattered like a sour reminder of his predicament. There must be somewhere here for him to beg a warm place to sit. And a bowl of soup.

Here he was just inside the edge of a forest, although he was not sure where. At either side of the depression the trees marched away into the distance, while in front, to the south, the land was bare and barren: Dartmoor. He had never been this far south before—there had never been reason to come here—and the view of the rolling hills ahead was awesome. There was no definition to them. One hillock merged into another, the series of flattened peaks seeming almost to be one great, flat plain. But when he strained his eyes, he could see variations in the gray ness. There was a long patch of darker ground sweeping across from his left, leading on to the horizon, there was a series of whiter areas on the hill tops where the moon lighted them.

And between them he could just make out the shading that showed where valleys lay.

Sighing, he rubbed at his eyes with fingers that were swiftly losing all feeling. He was tired out, completely exhausted, as if his very soul was drained. It had taken the last tiny sparks of defiance to light the fire, because all he really wanted to do was lie down and sleep. It would be so good to shut his eyes and drift off for a time, to let the drowsiness steal over him and give him some peace, some real peace, such as he had not known since he put the witch's body in the hedge. If only he had immediately buried her. Why had he gone indoors to sleep and not hidden her away at once?

Just then he noticed a small star and, for some reason, his eyes were drawn to it. There was something wrong with it. Frowning and wincing, he stared, trying to focus, to see what was different about it. There were several other stars above it. They all seemed about the same size, so it was not that. What was it? There was certainly something strange about it. It looked like it was flickering, as if maybe a cloud was passing in front of it—but there were no clouds, or he would see them in the moonlight. He felt a quick, stabbing fear rise in his breast: fear of ghosts, of the demons of the moors that he had heard about. His breath caught in his throat as he thought of the stories about ghouls wandering, trying to capture men to take to hell. If Agatha had a pact with the devil, like they said at Wefford, then she would be capable of sending one for him.

Then the panic fell, as quickly as the blanket from his shoulders as he suddenly lurched to his feet, his face white in the dark as he stared, his breath catching in his throat.

It was a fire!

There was no choice to make. If he stayed still, even with his little fire, he would die. That much was obvious. The cold was too severe, the shelter too exposed and his clothes too damp from his sweat and from the occasional clumps of snow landing on him and melting. With a last, longing stare at the weak flames, he recognized that they offered no safety and no chance of survival. The fire would be sure to go out if he slept. The twigs and branches he had managed to collect were too damp to stay lighted and would need constant attention. No, he had no choice.

Leaving the fire to die, he hefted his pack and stick and began to make his way toward the flickering light ahead. He could not tell how far away it was, but it looked as though it was something over a mile. It appeared to be quite high on a hill, which was why he had mistaken it at first for a star.

There was little wind, only a slight breeze, and he made good headway at first. The snow was not deep, and the ground beneath felt solid and fairly flat with few stones or holes. But then, after only a few hundred yards, it became more difficult.

It started when he tripped and fell headlong. Gasping with horror, he rose, his face and head smothered in the white, clinging powder. That was not the worst: under the surface apparently there was a stream, and his legs were soaked with freezing water. He must keep moving, to try to keep warm; to stay alive.

With a new resolution, he set off again at a faster pace, his forehead wrinkled with the concentration of his effort, straining with determination. He would not die—he must not!

The ground now was worse. It was broken, with granite stones liberally sprinkled under the white covering, which now itself became a serious obstacle, not only hampering his movements but hiding the stones beneath. He could hardly move more than a few yards without stumbling, and he was so tired he would inevitably fall.

At one point he felt that he would never reach the fire. After yet another tumble, as he lay sobbing in frustration, he lifted his head to find that the rising land before him hid the flames, as if its promise of warmth and rest had been snatched away as he approached.

Gasping with the effort, he slowly rose to his feet and began to carry on, the breath shuddering in his throat in a continual, weeping groan, his face turned toward the fire. All his energy was gone. His boots kept striking rocks, and his toes were bruised, creating a blunted, numbed ache of pain that managed to seep over even the dulled senses of his frost-bitten feet. His stick grew heavier with each step, and the energy used to lift it and place it down, lift it and place it down, sapped his failing resources, but he kept hold of it as if it was a talisman offering some support and strength of its own.

He breasted the hill and could see the fire again more clearly. Standing still for a moment, he savored the sight as he caught his breath. It lay under an overhanging rock, at the entrance, apparently, of a cave, and the cheerful flames beckoned to him, promising peace. His breath caught in his throat, and he was not sure whether to laugh or sob. Letting his breath out in a great sighing gasp, he started off again, down the slight incline to the bottom, then up the other side to the fire, to safety and warmth.

It was when he was almost at the upward slope that he heard the howling. The voices of wolves calling to each other—and realized that *he* was their quarry.

"I think you'd better get up here a little faster," came a contemplative voice from above. "They sound a bit hungry!"

The rest of the way was a mad scramble up the hillside. He dropped his staff, his satchel fell from his shoulder, pulling his blanket with it, and it may have been this that saved him.

As he reached the top of the slope he slipped and fell, slithering face-first into a depression ringed by rocks. Behind him he heard a sudden snarling and snapping, and when he managed to rise, staring with terror, he saw four wolves tearing and ripping at his package and attacking his blanket. They had attacked his belongings rather than following and attacking him immediately.

Suddenly his legs gave way and he fell to his knees in petrified horror at the thought that the animals could have been on *him,* their teeth at his throat, their hot breath in his nostrils as they tore at him, savaging him like the bag they had just ripped apart. He gave a small cry, and was faintly surprised by how high and childish it sounded. Then he saw them turn.

"Ah, they'll be coming here now." The Bourc spoke calmly. After years of hunting wolves in Gascony, he knew how to defend himself, and now he watched carefully—he was prepared for them. Before him was a handful of arrows, their points in the ground, standing like a makeshift fence. When he gave Greencliff a quick, appraising glance, the farmer saw his dark eyes glittering in the shadow under his hood as the firelight caught them.

The Bourc gave him a nod, then pointed to the fire with his chin. "You get back. Warm yourself. Don't think you'll be any help right now." He turned back to the scene below, pulling an arrow from the ground and nocking it on his bowstring, his hands moving with the assurance of long practice.

Greencliff felt his head move in slow acceptance, and he began to walk, stumbling in his tiredness and chill. His limbs felt leaden, his head heavy, and he moved as if in a dream, his feet moving automatically like heavy metal weights in a great machine. But as he got to the fire he heard a roar, and spinning round, saw a huge animal streak forward. The bowman seemed to stand still, the wolf running straight for him, and then there was a thrumming sound and the wolf fell, an arrow in his head.

Even as he seated a fresh arrow on the bow and drew it back, two more of the evil-looking animals appeared, but they were undecided, slinking from side to side at the edge of the camp like cavalry trying to see a weakness in a line of foot-soldiers, while the Bourc's arrow-tip followed them.

With a snarl as if to boost flagging spirits, both streaked forward, and the Bourc hesitated a moment, as if unsure which to attack. Then, quickly drawing the bowstring again, he let his arrow fly at the leading animal, but perhaps in his haste, perhaps because of the darkness, his shot missed its mark.

To Greencliff's horror, the wolves rushed on, and one of them launched itself at his savior's throat. To his astonishment, he saw the man fall back, one arm held up to protect his neck, and the wolf caught his arm in its mouth, his leap carrying the man backward. But almost as soon as the man had dropped, he rolled, then sprang back to his feet. The farmer's shocked eyes shot to the figure of the wolf, which lay shuddering as it died, and when he looked back at the Bourc, he saw the short sword in his hands, now flashing and glinting as it dripped red in the firelight.

The last wolf had followed almost on the heels of the first, but had held back when it had sprung, and now hesitated, circling the man warily. Its eyes flitted from the Bourc to Greencliff with uncertainty, and while it paused, the Bourc dropped his sword, snatched up his bow, nocked an arrow to the string and fired in one smooth action. This time he made sure of his target. The wolf dropped as if felled by a pike.

When he had stood for a minute or two, the Bourc slowly lowered his bow and sighed. Holding a fresh arrow in place, he cautiously walked to each of the figures, kicked them briefly, then strode to the perimeter of the camp and peered into the darkness. Seemingly the view satisfied him, and he sauntered back to the bodies with a low but cheerful whistle. Dropping the bow, he collected his sword and went from one body to the next, slitting the animals' throats.

Looking up, he gave a quick grin. "Always best to make sure with these evil buggers!" he said contentedly. The last thing Greencliff saw as he slowly toppled sideways was his grin slowly fading in perplexed surprise. The farmer's exhaustion had won at last.

Simon and the troop were mounted and ready early the next morning just after light. He felt stiff and had a kink in his back from sleeping on a bench, but it was, as he knew, a great deal better than how he would have felt if they had tried to sleep out in the open.

They were soon back at the trail and Mark Rush began his careful perusal of the prints once more. He was convinced that today they would find a corpse at the end of the trail. It was easy to see why.

The steps were almost like a pair of long lines with deeper indentations where the boots had dropped. Between the footprints were scraping drag marks where the man had been too tired to lift his feet. Simon had no doubt that Mark Rush was right. The boy had little chance of surviving.

When they had been riding for an hour, they came across the flat area where the boy had lain. After this the steps changed direction, seeming to stagger and falter into the trees, and they found the byre. Dropping from their horses, Tanner and Mark Rush slowly drew their swords and walked in, half expecting to find Greencliff's body. While they searched, Simon glanced around at the snow nearby, then gave a cry.

"There're more prints!"

Mark Rush came out, his face expressionless, and followed the bailiff's pointing finger. To Simon he seemed to doubt what he saw. He stood staring down, his head shaking in disbelief, then he sighed and walked back, putting his sword away as he walked. "He lived to rest, then. He must have made it to the moors."

The weather was not so cold this morning, and a dampness had set in. The trees overhead occasionally dropped great clods of ice and snow, occasionally hitting one of the men. Riding along, the men were all warm enough. Even at a slow trotting pace, the exercise kept them glowing with an internal warmth, and Simon was grateful for the slight breeze.

They found that the tracks kept them going almost straight southwest, so Simon knew that they were going toward the moors. It would not be long before they were out of the trees and on the moors themselves. There they would be certain to find the boy.

*   *   *

Margaret had passed an uncomfortable night, and she rose late to find that Baldwin had already left the house. She spent an idle morning wondering what Simon was doing and where he was. She had not been overly concerned when they had not arrived on the first evening, and she was quite sure that he would be safe, but still felt an occasional twinge of concern.

She picked up her tapestry and managed almost half an hour of work before she tossed it aside impatiently, startling the old woman's dog. "Sorry, it's not your fault," she said apologetically, holding out her hand and snapping her fingers, but the dog stared at her with unblinking accusation before meaningfully standing, stretching, then lying down once more near the fire, this time with his back to her. She grinned at the obvious rejection, then rose and walked out to the front.

Here she found Edgar supervising other servants splitting logs for the fires. He looked up and gave her a welcoming smile as she emerged into the sunlight, blinking at the sudden glare.

"Morning, Edgar," she said, peering at the horizon with a hand shielding her eyes.

"Hello, my lady."

"Has Baldwin gone far?"

He shot her a quick glance, then she was sure she caught a glimpse of a grin as he turned back to the men at the logs. "I'm sure he won't be too long, madam."

This was puzzling. She had never seen any sign of the humor from the normally taciturn servant, and she suddenly wanted to know where the knight had gone. "Walk with me a while, Edgar. I'm very bored."

Looking up, he considered, but then he nodded and, after issuing instructions to the men, walked to her. "Where do you want to go?"

"Oh, just down the lane."

They set off in companionable silence, but once they were out of earshot, she gave him a quick look. "So where has he gone?"

His expression was wooden. "Just into Wefford, I think."

"Why? And why was he in such an odd mood last night when you returned?"

"Odd mood, madam?" He turned guileless eyes on her.

"You know he was. He would hardly talk to me. Every time he opened his mouth he got embarrassed. I thought he must have done something foolish."

He smiled and she suddenly stopped in amazement as a flash of intuition suddenly blazed and she caught her breath. The knight's embarrassment, his apparent shyness, his servant's amusement, all pointed to one thing in her mind.

"It's not a woman! He hasn't found a woman!"

"Madam, I didn't tell you that!" said the servant earnestly, but still with the smile transforming his features.

"But *who*?" She gasped with delight—and a little surprise.

"Ah," he turned to the view with a slight frown. "Mrs. Trevellyn."

"So you think he's gone to see her?" she asked doubtfully, and he spun to face her with horror on his face.

"No, madam, no. He wouldn't do that. Not when she's only just lost her husband. No. I think he's gone out to decide whether he ought to even think about a wife."

The servant was right. Baldwin was riding slowly, his peregrine on his wrist, but his mind several miles away.

"After all," he thought, "there are conventions. The poor woman has just lost her husband. She might not want to even think about another man until her mourning period is over."

He sighed. That was not the point, and he knew it. She was so desirable, especially now when she appeared so vulnerable. Her expression on hearing of the manhunt had made him want to hold her and comfort her, she had looked so scared. Clearly she feared for herself while her husband's killer was free, in case he might return.

For her to have heard the cruel gossip about her and a local farmer must have been painfully wounding, and to have then lost her husband seemed a vicious turn of fate. But if nothing else, Baldwin was at least now sure that she was innocent of adultery. A wanton could surely never have shown such emotion. And if the malicious rumors were untrue, she would make a wonderful wife for a knight.

It was so attractive the way that she licked her lips after sipping at a drink. So provocative, somehow.

"This is ridiculous!" he muttered viciously and glared balefully at the bird on his wrist. "Why should I even think that she'd . . . It's not as if I have huge wealth or titles . . ."

He broke off as his mind mischievously brought a picture of her to him. Of her sitting at the fireplace in the warm and comfortable solar, the long black hair falling down her back, her eyes so green and bright, staring him full in the face with her red lips parted a little, as if she was close to panting, and he smiled fondly again.

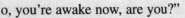

S o, you're awake now, are you?"

"Ah." No words could convey the same anguish and pain as the simple, soft and quiet groan that broke from Harold Greencliff's lips as he tried to sit up. Moaning gently, he rolled on to his side and peered through slitted eyes at the man who stood looking down at him with grave concern. When he opened his mouth, it felt as if there was a week of dried saliva encrusted around his lips, and he winced as his skin cracked.

"Keep quiet, friend. Sit back. You can't go anywhere."

As his eyes began to focus, Greencliff stared at him. He was dressed in thick and warm-looking woollen clothes, his tunic woven of heavy cloth and his cloak lined with fur. He must be a wealthy man.

His face was arresting. Swarthy and weather-beaten, square and wrinkled, it seemed as rugged as the rocks around them. Two gleaming black eyes gazed back at the farmer with interest under a thick mop of deep brown hair. Although there were lines of laughter at the eyes, now they contained only concern, and Greencliff realized what a sorry figure he must appear. Then, as the memories returned, he felt a sob rack his body in a quick shudder of self-pity.

"Calm yourself. Drink this."

The liquid was almost scalding hot, but he thought he had never tasted anything so wonderful. It was a warmed wine fit for the king himself, Greencliff thought. Though he sipped carefully, it still seared the flesh around his mouth and burned a trail down his throat, seeming to form a solid, scalding lump in his stomach. Meanwhile his host crouched and watched.

After a few moments, Greencliff took stock of his surroundings. He was in a cave of some sort. Outside, through a small doorway, he could see the fire, whose heat wafted in with the smell of burning wood. He was lying on a straw palliasse with his blanket over him, and his new friend had clearly let him sleep on his own bed because a roll and blanket on the floor showed where he had slept.

"Do you feel well enough to eat?" At the question, the farmer felt his stomach wake to turbulent life as if it had been hibernating until then, and a low rumbling started to shake his weakened frame. The man gave a short laugh. "Good. I'll have some stew ready in a little while. I have bread too, so don't worry about losing your own food."

An hour later he felt well enough to rise from the mattress and walk outside to where the man crouched by the fire, meditatively breaking twigs and branches to feed the flames. He looked up as Greencliff came out, bent double to save himself from hitting his head at the low entrance.

"How're you feeling now?" the Bourc asked.

Wincing, Greencliff sat warily on a rock near the

fire. "A lot better. I'm very grateful, if you hadn't helped me, I'd be dead."

"One day, I might need help, and I hope that I will be protected as I protected you."

"Who are you?"

"I'm called John, the Bourc de Beaumont."

"You are not from here?" It was an innocent question, and the farmer was surprised by the laugh it brought.

"No! No, I come from far away, from Gascony. I would not live *here* from choice!"

Greencliff nodded, morosely staring at the moors all round. "I can understand that!" he said. "So, why are you here?"

Grimacing, the Bourc explained about his decision to cross the moors. "The wolves chased me here, and I was attacked by one—night before last, that was. I killed it, but I got little sleep, so I chose to stay here for another day. Anyway, I thought it was easier to defend myself here. If they catch you on horseback, they'll chase you 'til your horse drops."

"Why were they trying to attack you? Are they just evil?" asked the farmer, shivering at the memory of the slavering mouths tearing at his belongings.

"No, not really. It is just the way they are. They saw me—and you—as a meal, that's all. There is not enough food for them right now. They thought we'd be easy enough to catch." He almost shuddered at the memory. The way that the beast had leaped at him had terrified him. In his mind's eye he could still see the jaws opening and smell the foul breath. In that moment he had been sure he was about to die.

The fear had almost caused his death. It slowed his reactions, so that the huge creature had almost succeeded in tearing his neck with its wickedly curved fangs, just missing and slashing his shoulder. The pain had woken him to his danger, and turning quickly, he had stabbed deep, again and again, in a fit of mad panic.

Afterward he had built the fire and waited, nursing his shoulder, but they had chosen not to attack again. The next day they were still there, and he had kept an eye on them as he sat and kept warm.

He glanced up shrewdly. "So why are you here? Who or what are you running from?"

"Me?" His start of surprise seemed to strike the Gascon as comical.

"Yes: you! Nobody who knows this place would come here to the moors in the snow unless they had a good reason. Especially at night. It's a good way to make sure of death, but nothing else. Who are you running from?"

"I . . ." He paused. There was no reason to doubt his grim-faced savior, but the truth was, he had no wish to admit to his guilt. Opening his mouth to speak, he found the breath catching in his throat again, and he had to keep silent. The sob was too close. He gave a small cough, an involuntary spasm that could have been from misery or joy, and covered his face in his hands.

"You've been through pain, I can see that," said the Bourc matter-of-factly, finishing his wine. With his eyes on his guest, his mind ran through the items he had found from the satchel. A little food the wolves had left, a flint and a knife. A long-bladed ballock knife: a single-edged blade with two globular lumps where the wooden grip met it, held in a leather sheath. When he had found it, he had been going to return it, but then he had wondered. If this boy was an outlaw, if he was escaping from justice of some sort, it might be better to keep his knife back for now. "Of course," he thought, "if he wants to tell me what made him leave, I can give it back. But not yet. Not quite yet."

It wasn't just the distrust of a man for a stranger in these difficult times. It was also the thick clots he had found on the blade, the dried brown mess of blood.

"Wait here!" Mark Rush ordered as he dropped from his horse. He wandered slowly and carefully round the little dip in the ground, following the line of staggering footprints. "Yes, he was here. He walked up here, tripped and fell. There's the mark where he lay. Looks like he got up and then began to make a fire. Not much of one, though." Kneeling, he sniffed contemplatively at the blackened twigs. "Not enough to keep him warm for more than a minute. He sat here."

Rising, he stood and stared at the ground for a minute, hands on hips as he considered. Glancing up at the bailiff's face, he shrugged. "Didn't wait long, from the look of it. Seems like he made his fire, sat by it for a bit—not for long—and went on."

"Fine. Let's get on after him, then."

Tanner ambled forward. "One minute, bailiff. Mark? How was he when he left here?"

The hunter pulled his mouth into a down-curving crescent of dubious pessimism. "Put it like this: I wouldn't gamble on his chances. I'd rather put my money on a legless, wingless cock in a fighting ring."

Nodding, Tanner glanced back at the men behind, then at the bailiff. "Sir, we may as well send the others back. The three of us are enough to catch him, even if he's well. The way things are, all we'll need is a horse to bring his body home." When Simon nodded, Tanner turned to the men, telling them to return. The bailiff instructing one to ensure that a message went to the inn, to be passed on to Simon's wife, to say that they were well. Not that it mattered much, as Tanner knew. There was little hope that they could find the boy alive now. They should be able to return home before long.

As they set off again, leaving at last the line of trees and beginning to make their way on to the moors, he found himself reflecting sadly on the last Greencliff. Tanner had known him since he was a boy.

Good-looking since he was a child, he had always been able to win apples from the women in the village while young. As he had grown, he had kept his innocent charm, and then he had taken other gifts—or so it was rumored. Why, even Sarah Cottey was supposed to have carried on with him recently, and she was only the last in a long series. The boy was lucky to have lived so long without getting a thrashing from an enraged father or brother!

Murder was a long way from enjoying a woman's embrace, though, he mused. Just because a man was popular with the local girls did not make him a killer. It was different, as the constable knew, with soldiers. He had witnessed enough rapings and people having their lives taken quickly or slowly to know the difference between the brutal and the gentle taking of a woman. Harold had only ever been kind with his women, which was why none had ever denounced him to their families. All still liked him. Even Sarah Cottey—she was infatuated with him.

But love was possessive, and perhaps that was why the boy had found the courage to kill, stabbing Trevellyn in a jealous fit so that he could have the woman he wanted. If so, that did not answer why the youth should have killed the witch, though. The reason behind *that* was still a mystery. Tanner dawdled behind the others as the thoughts drifted through his mind, making him scowl darkly as he stared with unseeing eyes at the ground.

At a sudden gasp from the hunter in front, he kicked his horse and rode forward to where Simon and Mark Rush stood pensively gazing down at a mess of confused prints.

"Looks like he walked to here, then fell," said the hunter. He peered up the shallow slope to a small group of tors huddled together as if for warmth on the top of the hill. "Wolves were about, but he managed to get up there."

"Let's see if he's still there, then," said the bailiff, and they began to make their way up the slight incline.

Tanner stayed at the back again at first, but then he shrugged and put the thoughts from his mind. If he was alive, they would be sure to find out as soon as they caught him. There was no point in speculating.

"Morning, gentlemen."

The call made them all stop and cautiously glare at the rocks before them. Then Simon tentatively rode forward a couple of yards. "Is that *you,* Greencliff?"

"No." There was a dry chuckle. Then there was a movement above them, and they saw what had appeared to be a boulder detach itself from the tor and spring lightly to the ground before them.

For a moment they contemplated him in silence, then Simon rode forward a pace or two. The man held himself alert and had the look of a fighting man, but did not look as though he was dangerous. Merely wary at the sight of three strangers out here in the wild.

Glancing to his side, Simon saw that Rush had come up alongside.

"I know this man," the hunter muttered. "I saw him trotting away from Wefford the day the witch was killed."

Simon nodded, then looked back to the Gascon. "Good morning, friend. I am a bailiff. We are hunting an outlaw, a man who is running from justice. His feet led us here—have you seen him?" He gave a brief description.

"He is not here now," said the Bourc.

"What do you mean? Have you seen him?" Simon asked eagerly.

The Bourc put his head to one side thoughtfully as he peered up at the bailiff. "I have, but he did not seem to be an outlaw. I gave him a place to sleep last night. He was here with me, but he left some time ago. Come to my camp, I will show you the path he took and you can warm yourselves by my fire for a while," he said quietly, and, turning, led the way to the ring of old stones that stood at the summit, just under the tor.

To Simon it looked like an enclosure. It was about fifteen paces across and roughly circular, lined with boulders of the local gray granite, with here and there a patch of orange or brown lichen peeping out from under a thatch of snow. At one side was a pile of the Gascon's tools and belongings, with, beside them, his pony and a small packhorse. To the right, beyond a fire of fresh kindling, was a low gap in the rocks of the tor. Near the fire were the carcasses of two wolves, freshly skinned, the flesh clean and glistening with silver where the membranes held the muscles. The pelts were stretched on wooden frames nearby. Simon walked to them and kicked one corpse thoughtfully while their host strode to the fire and crouched contemplatively in front of it.

"So he was here. Where did he go?" he asked.

Looking up, he saw the Bourc grin. "Oh, yes. He was here." With a jerk of his chin, he pointed toward the middle of the moors. "He left about an hour ago, just as you all appeared through the trees. Made an excuse and ran for it. He won't have gone far."

"Right!" Mark Rush tugged his horse's reins, pulling it over to the far side of the enclosure, Tanner following, while Simon stood and looked out in the direction John had shown. There, clear against the white background, were the footsteps. Now they were more purposeful, each step defined as an individual print without the dragging lines where the feet seemed too heavy to lift above the crust of snow. As he looked, he became aware of the man at his side.

"What are you after him for?"

"Murder. He's killed two people."

"Really?" The note of sadness made Simon turn to him with an eyebrow raised. "I'm sorry, Bailiff. It just seems so unlikely, he is a pleasant enough lad."

"It seems he's killed a man and a woman. Both over the last week."

There was a brief pause, then the black eyes met Simon's in a frown. "How did he kill them?"

"He cut their throats."

The Bourc sighed, then told him of the blood-stained ballock dagger. When he had finished, the bailiff stared after the men on their horses, now riding slowly away after the fugitive. "That more or less proves it, doesn't it?" he said musingly.

*   *   *

These were the steps of a rested man. His prints showed deep at the toe, light at the heel, and Tanner saw that the boy had been running. He sighed. It was sad to think of the youth, only just an adult, bolting in fear of his life, trying to escape his death.

Because that was what the outcome would be if he was found guilty of the murders, and the boy must know that. There was only one penalty to avenge the murder of a man or woman: hanging.

There was a small gasp of excitement at his side, and when he looked over, Mark Rush's eyes were fixed on the horizon. Following his gaze, Tanner saw a tiny figure in the distance, a slender, stick-like shape, seeming to pelt across the snow.

"Come on!" cried the hunter, and both whipped their mounts.

Tanner stuck rigidly to the footprints. It was possible that the boy had thought of taking any pursuers over rough or broken ground to try to throw them off. If he had led them toward a mire, they could get stuck. The constable kept his eyes down, but saw no sign of any obstacles. Jolting and lurching, they rode up one slope, then down the other side. Now they could see him, some distance off making for a copse in a valley. "Bugger!" he thought. "Must stop him before that, it'll take hours to find him if he reaches it." But he need not have feared.

As they pelted forward, he saw the shape take a tumble, tripping and falling, rolling, to lie for a moment as if winded. Then he got up again, and set off once more, but this time he was slower, and looked as though he was limping. His speed was gone, and the two men chasing felt confident enough to slow to an easy canter, taking the pursuit more carefully to protect their horses.

They rode up in front, swinging round in a curve, to come to a halt facing him, sitting on their horses between him and the protection of the trees. As he sat and watched the wretched figure of the man staggering toward them, Tanner felt the sadness again. It looked as if he had been ruined. His hair was matted and slicked down over his head, damp from falling in the snow. His tunic and jacket were covered in white as well, making him look like a weird monster of the winter. But his eyes were full of his grief. Even from a distance Tanner could see that.

"We hunted *that*?" He heard the hunter say in wonder, as if he too was feeling compassion for a destroyed life. The constable nodded and let out his breath in a long drifting feather on the frozen air.

A few yards from them, Greencliff stopped and stood surveying them with a frowning face that seemed close to breaking into tears. When they both kicked their horses forward, he took a half-pace back, then twitched the front of his tunic aside, and pulled his dagger out. "Leave me alone!"

"Come on, Harold. You can't stab *me*." Tanner felt that the words sounded ridiculous even as he said them.

"I can't go back. I *won't*! There's nothing for me. Just let me go. Please . . ." His eyes filled with tears. "Just let me go."

"You know we can't do that, Harold. We have to take you back."

"Why? Sir Baldwin doesn't need me . . ."

"Bugger Sir Baldwin," said Mark Rush from Tanner's side. "We can't let you go after you murdered

Alan Trevellyn. What's it to be? Alive or dead?" As he spoke he pulled his bow over his head and checked the string.

"Alan Trevellyn?" Tanner was sure that he saw absolute horror in the boy's eyes. "Dead?"

The bow was ready. Mark Rush took his time over selecting an arrow, then tugged one free and fitted it. "I suppose you wanted to just scare him? That's why you cut his throat, like you did with the old witch too. Never mind. You can apologize to them both when you get to hell."

Tanner watched as the boy gaped, but then, as if with a sudden resolution, he pulled his dagger's sheath free and put the blade away, tossing it toward the men. "You can put up your bow. I surrender to you. Yes, I killed them both." The words were said calmly, but with what looked to Tanner like a kind of tired but firm defiance. He stood patiently while the constable swung from his horse and strolled over to the prisoner, tied his hands with a thong, then picked up his dagger and pointed back the way they had come.

"Come on, Harold. Let's get back."

Simon watched the slow approach of the three men, two on horseback, one staggering slightly on foot, with a feeling of relief. At least there was no one else hurt. Greencliff had not managed to stab one of the men when they captured him.

He heard the crunch of snow as the Bourc strolled over to stand beside him. At the sound of a sigh, Simon turned with surprise. It seemed out of place for the man. From what he had seen of the stranger, he had appeared to be strong and self-sufficient, not the sort to express sympathy for a murderer and outlaw.

Catching the bailiff's eye, the Bourc shrugged, ashamed. "I know. He's a killer. But he's a likeable sort of lad. I wouldn't have thought he was capable of murder. He seems too quiet. And he seems more sad than cruel."

"But you said you found blood on his dagger!"

"So I did. So I did. Could it have been in defense?" Simon paused and considered. "Defense? No, I don't think so. Both murders were from behind, both of them had their throats cut. I don't think they could have been killed except by a man who wanted to murder them. I can't see it was defense. In any case, what defense would he need from an old woman?"

"Old woman?"

"Yes, he killed an old woman in Wefford."

Simon became aware of a sudden tenseness as the man leaned forward and said, "What was this woman's name, Bailiff?"

"Her name?" The three men were almost with them now, the lone walker struggling in the deeper snow that lay beneath the hillside, moving slowly and swinging his arms as if trying to maintain his balance. "She was called Agatha Kyteler."

There was a sudden intake of breath from the man, and Simon turned to see that his eyes were filled with horror as he stared at the figure laboring toward them. "Agatha? You killed Agatha Kyteler?"

The bailiff gasped. "Of course! You must be the Bourc de Beaumont!"

"Yes, I am, but how . . . ?"

"I am friend to Sir Baldwin. He mentioned you had been staying with him. He would like to see you again, I am sure. Would you ride back with us?"

The Bourc stared past the bailiff toward the center of

the moors, and when he glanced back, he smiled ruefully. "My friend, I think it would be a very good idea
for me to return with you, and when I next leave for the
coast, I think I shall take the roadways like others do,
and avoid my own short cuts! Ah! Here they are."

Turning back, Simon saw the men entering the ring
of stones.

Now he could see the youth close to again, Simon
felt that he was unwell. He had the feverish red and apparently sweating face of a convalescent. Was it that or
was it just his guilt? Was it illness from his nights out
in the cold or a deeper sickness at the knowledge of
what he had done, of what his price must be now he
was captured? His hands looked blue, as though the
blood was cut off, and the bailiff made a note to get the
thong tying him loosened.

His eyes were bright and steady, not ashamed or
worried. They almost looked relaxed, as if he had
tested himself and found himself to be stronger than he
had expected. Although he appeared dirty and unkempt, he still stood tall—a bit like Baldwin, Simon
thought. Proud and arrogant in his confidence.

The boy stood staring at him for a moment, then
peered over his shoulder. Throwing a quick glance behind him, Simon saw that the Bourc was crouching by
the fire and feeding it with fresh branches. The bailiff
saw that the boy was struggling to control a shiver, and
wordlessly led the way to the heat, Greencliff squatting
and holding his bound hands to the flames with a small
grunt of pain. After a moment Simon pulled his dagger
free and, reaching over, sliced through the thong. The
boy gave him a nod of gratitude before returning his
gaze to the fire.

Tanner hobbled his horse before walking to the three

by the fire. He stood and watched his prisoner for a moment, then pulled the ballock knife from his belt and tossed it to the ground beside the bailiff.

Looking up, Simon saw his serious—sad?—gaze and picked it up. Pulling the blade from the sheath, he saw the stains and picked at them with his fingernail. There was no way to tell for certain, but it looked a dirty brown, like dried blood.

"Whose blood is this, Harold?" he asked.

The light eyes glanced at him, then down at the knife for a moment with apparent disinterest before he shrugged and faced the flames. "Trevellyn's, probably."

"He admitted the murders," said Tanner, and dropped down beside the bailiff.

"Why did you do it, Harold? Why kill them?" Simon said, frowning at the gasp from the Bourc.

The boy did not even bother to turn to face them. "I wanted to get away. I wanted money. They refused to give me any."

"But you must have known that Agatha Kyteler had nothing! I suppose Alan Trevellyn was wealthy, but she had nothing! Why kill her?"

But they could get nothing more from him. He ignored their questions, sitting silently, his face set, with his hands to the fire, and his shoulders hunched as if they could act as a barrier to their questions.

It was nearly dark when Jennie Miller walked into the inn and sat at a bench near the door with her pot of cider. It was too early for most of the people to have arrived, but there were already some men standing and talking in hushed voices. She knew why. Her husband had been told earlier that some of the men had returned from the hunt. They had found where Harold Greencliff was. He would be brought back soon.

In a small village like Wefford, this was news of the first order. Unused to the excitements normal in more populous or busier places, where the number of travellers passing through led to their own difficulties, Wefford had experienced its first taste of real crime in decades, and found that it had a sour flavor.

But where there were problems, there were also compensations, and this affair was no different. After all, nobody would miss old Agatha too much. She had scared too many people after the rumors put about by that old hag Oatway. Her death had caused more interest than anything she had done while living.

When the curtain opened to show a slightly nervous, scowling and dark-haired man, she looked up with interest. The face was familiar, but she could not remember where she had seen him. Thin featured, with weather-beaten skin and thick dark hair that straggled at the sides. Appearing shy, he hung back at the screens as if nervous of crossing the floor. Not tall, he looked quite thickset, but quick and lithe, a bit like her husband's horse. Where had she seen him before? Surely he had been *on* a horse? It was then that she recognized him—it was the bailiff's servant . . . What was his name? The one who had waited outside with the horses when the knight and bailiff arrived to ask her about the day that Agatha died.

Shifting quickly on her bench, she smiled at him, and saw a minimal relaxing of his glower. Patting the bench seat beside her, she beckoned to him, then waved at the innkeeper.

"What would you like to drink?" she asked innocently, and he asked for a strong ale, sitting ungraciously beside her.

"Aren't you the man that came to see me with Sir Baldwin Furnshill and the bailiff the other day?" she said when his beer had arrived and he had taken a deep draft.

He nodded, wiping his mouth with the back of his hand, and now his face had lost some of its black dejection. The flavor of the beer restored some, if not all, of his equanimity.

Hugh was annoyed. So far today he had been told to help two serving women (either old enough to be his mother) with moving barrels in the buttery, then Margaret had asked him to help an hostler in the stables area, and finally, he had been instructed by a haughty man-servant that Hugh had been assigned to *him* to help with the mews, the sheds behind the stables where the falcons were left to mew, or moult.

When he had gone to Margaret to demand some sympathy, she had been short with him. Of course he understood that she was upset at the continuing absence of her husband, but that was no reason to take things out on him. On seeing him, she had made it very clear that he was expected to help wherever he was needed while they stayed under Baldwin's roof, and that meant doing whatever the servants felt was useful. After being peremptorily ordered to go out and help with the mews, he had obeyed, but had then made sure that he could not be seen afterward, and had quickly saddled his horse to come into the village for an evening of peace before he could be asked to do anything else.

Now, as he sat and glared moodily at his pot, he was struck with a sense of the unfairness of it all. After all, he was the servant of a bailiff. He should not have to mess about helping hostlers—the knight should have enough men to look after his horses and those of his guests!

Looking at him, Jennie could see that he was feeling gloomy, and quickly ordered him another pot of ale. After all, if the bailiff's man knew nothing, especially when he had been living with the knight, the Keeper of the King's Peace, then no one could know anything.

"I hear they're bringing back young Greencliff," she said tentatively, as if musing. "Shame that. He's such a nice lad, too."

"Yes. They should be back later, or first thing tomorrow."

"Your master? He's with them?"

"He's *leading* them," said Hugh tetchily, then resumed his gloomy stare at his pot. "They all seem to think Greencliff must be dead, though. He was out in all that snow, so it's unlikely he'll survive."

"Oh." She was quiet for a minute, then said, "What about *her*? That French wife of Trevellyn?"

Hugh stared at her uncomprehendingly, wondering what she was talking about. "Eh? What, the widow? What about her?"

"Didn't you know? She was having an affair with Greencliff. That's why he was with her horse when she went to see the witch. He was helping his lover, looking after the horse of the woman he was having an affair with. I think *she* killed old Agatha while he held her horse!"

When the little group rode into town the following morning, Simon was pleased to see Baldwin, Edgar and Hugh standing outside the inn opposite the gaol. Saying, "You see to him, Tanner," he dismounted and led his horse to the group of men standing on the patch of brushed earth, which showed red where the snow had been swept away.

"So, Bailiff. You were successful," the knight said smiling, nodding toward the man being led into the little gaol, then, with surprise, he said, "John! I thought you left for Gascony days ago."

He was about to question them about the hunt and where they had met, when he noticed the pinched look on Simon's face and called out for the innkeeper. Soon, mulled wine was brought, the steam rising steadily from the liquid, and the smell from the sweetened mixture with its strong spices made the bailiff's mouth water. Taking a mug gratefully, he cupped it in his hands and blew on the surface to cool it a little, then took a sip of the scalding drink as the Bourc accepted another pot from the innkeeper.

"And, surprisingly enough, he's alive, too!" Simon

said, voicing the knight's thoughts as he stared after the figures entering the gaol. "Yes, and it feels like I nearly died of the cold myself on the way."

Mark Rush soon joined them, and they walked indoors out of the cold.

After his initial pleasure at seeing the men returning, Simon saw that Baldwin had sunk into a pensive reverie. The Keeper of the Peace was wondering whether he would shortly see the boy, his villein, hanged in the market square for the murders. It was surely not pleasant, Simon thought, to have to see the last remaining member of an old family on the estate coming to this kind of ignominious end. Far better that the boy had died on the moors or in the woods. To an extent, perhaps, it would have been better for all concerned if Greencliff had put up a defense and had died with an arrow in his head. At least that way there would have been an end to the matter. Now there would have to be a trial, with the lad perhaps attempting to defend himself—though how he could try to was beyond Simon's imagination. The evidence all pointed to him.

As the knight called for more drinks, an eyebrow delicately rising at the speed with which the men finished off their first pots, Simon leaned forward on his elbows and jerked his head toward the Gascon. "Your friend knows a little more about the day Trevellyn died, and the day Agatha Kyteler was killed."

"Really?" said Baldwin, glancing across the Bourc, who looked up inquiringly. "John? Simon says you can help us with the death of your old nurse and the merchant. Is that right?"

Before the Gascon could answer, Simon fixed him with a gleaming eye. "Be very careful how you respond, John. Your father's friend thought you might be the killer."

The Bourc stared at him, then at the sheepish knight. "You thought *I* did it?"

Shifting uneasily, Baldwin grimaced. "It did seem odd that you were with the old woman when . . ."

Laughing, Simon enjoyed the sight of his friend's embarrassment. "Don't worry, Baldwin. Anyway, he has an alibi, even if we didn't already have Greencliff. Rush saw the Bourc on the road at dusk that day, far south of Wefford."

"So what do you know of these killings, John?" the knight asked.

"I saw them both before they died."

"Both?"

"Yes. When I left you on Tuesday morning, I went to see Agatha, as I said. I told you about the escape from Acre, but not the last detail. Agatha told me that herself. My mother wanted to save me, so she went to the boats to ask for a passage. You know more about it than I do, of course, but apparently it was mayhem. Boats everywhere, and all of the sailors demanding huge fees to save people. My mother carried me along the harbor, begging for help, but no one would help. Then she thought she had found one. Trevellyn's ship.

"The master was happy to take her, he said. Pleased to, he said. But then he named his fee. Not money, not her jewels, just her. He wanted *her!*" He sipped his drink sullenly, but then grinned lopsidedly. "My mother apparently refused his kind offer, and asked that he accept a more sensible fee, but he insisted, and she came away empty-handed. Anne of Tyre, my mother, was of an important family, and I suppose she could not comprehend how low things had sunk by then. Anyway, she gave me to my nurse, and pleaded with her to take me to my father's house. That was Agatha.

"To shorten the story, she managed to get on board, and refused to leave. She had all that remained of my mother's wealth, and that was the cost of her passage. You have seen the man Trevellyn's house? I would guess many of the stones of his walls were purchased by my mother's jewels. A sobering thought, eh?"

"What became of your mother?" asked Simon.

"She died, I hope," said the Bourc shortly, and Baldwin gave the bailiff a quick glare to stop him asking more. Time enough later, the knight thought, to explain about the horrors of capture by the besiegers of Acre, about the multiple rapes, the slow and painful murders—or, worse, the lifetime of slavery, owned by a fat merchant or prince. Far better, as the Bourc said, for the poor woman to have died quickly. Perhaps she was in the Temple when it collapsed, mercifully crushing all those who could not escape together with the remainder of their protectors, the last of the Templar Knights in the Holy Land. They were all buried together, in the one massive tomb.

"And you said that the ring you wore was the token of your position?" asked Baldwin.

"The ruby? Oh, yes. My father gave it to my mother, she gave it to Agatha, and she used it to prove who I was when she finally got me to my father."

"You are not wearing it . . ."

"No, I gave it to her when I saw her on Tuesday."

"You gave it to her?"

The surprise in the knight's voice made the Bourc glance up at him. "Yes. She was not wealthy, and I thought it could be useful to her. I gave it to her as a

token that my family would always remember her protection of me. Now . . . Well, now I wonder whether
that is why she died."

"What do you mean?"

"Perhaps Greencliff saw the ring and killed her
for it. She might have died because of the present I
gave her."

Baldwin untied his purse and withdrew the ring, setting it on the table before the Bourc, whose eyes grew
large and round as he stared at it.

"But . . . How did you find it?"

"It was not stolen. Greencliff did not see it—or did
not care about it. We found it in her house after her
death."

The Gascon gingerly picked it up and studied it for
a moment. "That is a relief, I suppose," he said at last
and passed it back to Baldwin. "At least I know I was
not responsible for her murder."

"I'm sure you were not," said Baldwin. "But the ring
is yours. Take it!"

"No. Let it be buried with her. She has little else. At
least that way her act toward me will always be with
her." Baldwin nodded and replaced it in his purse.

"Why were you here to see her?" asked Simon
frowning thoughtfully. "Was it just to give her the
ring?"

"I have no reason to hide it. For many years I have
sworn to find the woman who saved me, to thank her
and to find out more about my mother. But where do
you begin to search? She had left my father's court
when I was weaned, many years ago. Where she had
gone seemed a mystery to all, but then a letter arrived."

"A letter?"

"Yes. It said that Agatha Kyteler was here. As soon

as I heard, I set off to find her. It did not take so very long." He settled back in his seat as if that explained everything.

Now Baldwin leaned forward. "This letter," he said. "Who was it from?"

"We weren't supposed to know," the Bourc said smiling, then shrugged. "It was not signed, but it came from England, that much we found from the messenger."

"And the messenger came from . . . ?"

"He came from a town just outside Bordeaux, from a wealthy family. I asked them. They said it had come to them in a letter from their daughter, with a note asking them to send it on to me."

The knight mused, wrapping his right arm around his chest and resting his chin in the palm of his left so that it covered his mouth. Shooting a quick glance at the Bourc, who sat imperturbably sipping at his pot, he said, "There's more, isn't there? Why did you disappear? And why did you go down to the moors?"

The Bourc explained that he had thought it would be faster, and then paused. With a short laugh of pleasure, he set his pot down. Looking up, he stared at the knight, resting both hands on the bench at either side of him. "There is no reason not to tell you now, sir. Not now that the boy confessed to the murders. I admit it! When I stayed with you that night I was thinking about killing Trevellyn!"

"What?" said Simon, sitting suddenly upright and spilling his drink in surprise. "In God's name, *why*?"

"Simon, have you not heard a thing the man has been saying?" said Baldwin curtly. Then, to the Bourc, "So, you would have killed the man who had caused your mother's death. What stopped you?"

"Agatha was not at all how I had imagined. She was bitter and cruel, all she wanted was what she called revenge. But when I came to think about it, there seemed little point. Would the man be able to remember my mother? She was probably nothing more to him than just another refugee. And he did not touch her. She decided not to pay the price he demanded, but he did not actually do *anything* to her!" Under the stern gaze of the knight, he gave a quick shamefaced grin. "I don't know, sir, whether you have been in a position where you have had control of refugees. I have. I know that it is easy to take advantage when you have power like that, power to give or take away life."

Baldwin nodded. "So the choice did not seem so easy once you realized what Agatha wanted you to do for her?"

"No, it was not at all easy. But one thing was odd."

"What?"

"She never wanted the message to be sent to me. It came from a friend of hers, and was not Agatha's idea."

"You are sure of that?"

"Oh, yes. I asked Agatha. She was surprised to see me on the Monday when I explained who I was. She had not expected to see me again."

"And she told you all this on that Monday?"

"Yes, sir. Some of it she told me later, on Tuesday, when I went to say farewell. I thought I should return home and leave the merchant. I had done what I wished. I had given her the ring and found out more of my mother. But when she asked me to kill this man Trevellyn, on the Monday, I had to have time to think about it. She said it would be revenge for what he had done to my mother. I thought, and made my decision: I could not."

"And you left her well on the Tuesday? You saw no one else there?"

"No, there was nobody there that I saw."

"What about when you left? Which way did you go? Along her lane?"

"No, I left in among the trees. Agatha told me that she was often having people go to see her, and I might scare them away! She asked me to stay hidden, and I did as she asked."

"On your way back from seeing her? Did you see anyone?"

"Ah, yes. Coming back I saw a woman." He smiled. "It was Mrs. Trevellyn, Agatha told me that! She thought it was quite funny. The woman went to see her often, she said, and she found it amusing. Alan Trevellyn wanted children, but his wife did not."

Simon heard his friend draw in his breath. "But I thought . . . Was it Mrs. Trevellyn who sent you the letter saying where Agatha was living?"

"Yes. I suppose she had heard of me from the old lady and thought I could ease her last years."

"So, you say Agatha wanted you to revenge your mother?" said Baldwin.

"Yes. But I couldn't. Oh, I had seen the man, and I disliked him, but that's no reason to kill, and as for my mother . . . I am a soldier. I have seen what happens when a city is captured, and I have taken part. How can I condemn or kill a man because he took advantage of his position, when I have done so myself? No, I decided that I should leave him."

"And then you left?"

"Yes. She asked me to go."

"It's interesting that the man she wanted you to kill

died only days later," said Baldwin pensively, and the Bourc nodded and shrugged.

"I have nothing to hide. It is more strange than you realize." He explained about his meeting with Trevellyn at the inn, the ambush, and his subsequent visit to the merchant's house. "He tried to whip me, and I wasn't expecting that, but I think he was used to whipping men who would do his bidding: his servants, maybe even sailors. He worked in the east, perhaps he ran a galley for a time . . . I do not know. Anyway, the blow caught me on my back as I ducked, and that made me very angry."

His eyes misted as he remembered the lash sweeping back ready for another strike, and as he told them, he saw it all in his mind's eye: the way that the pain had lanced across his back like a slash from a razor, the way that he had sprung forward before the merchant could attack again. He had not even drawn his sword, the rage and pain were too intense. As the handle of the whip came forward again, the Bourc had swiped a gauntleted fist and caught him on the cheek and temple, felling him like a sapling under the axe.

By the time the merchant came to again, the Bourc had calmed, but Trevellyn did not know that. All he could see was the heavy blade of his sword at his throat. That was when the Gascon told him who he was and saw the terror spring into the small, black eyes.

"He honestly seemed to think I was a ghost," he said. "He was horrorstruck at seeing me." He gave a short laugh. "I don't know what he thought was worse: that I had reappeared from his distant past, or the fact that I had bested his men!"

"Did you do anything else to him?" asked Baldwin. The Bourc glanced at him and grinned. "What? Cut his throat, you mean? No, my friend, I'm afraid I did not! I left him there when I heard some of his men coming back, then made my way back to Wefford. Next morning I started south. I was happy that Trevellyn would not try anything new." He went on to describe his journey south and the attacks from the wolf pack.

When he had finished, Simon leaned back in his chair and gazed at his friend. "Well? It fits with what we know, doesn't it?"

"Yes," said Baldwin pensively. "And now Greencliff has confessed, that is an end to the affair, isn't it?"

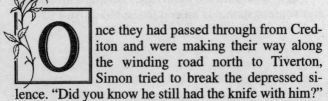

nce they had passed through from Crediton and were making their way along the winding road north to Tiverton, Simon tried to break the depressed silence. "Did you know he still had the knife with him?"

"Eh?" Baldwin's face registered bafflement.

"I said: the knife—he still had it with him. It even had the blood on it."

"Oh, you mean Greencliff. No, I didn't know that." he returned to his gloomy perusal of the trees ahead.

"Baldwin?" Simon attempted. *"Baldwin!"*

"What is it?" the knight turned to him irritably.

"What the hell's the matter?"

At the exasperation in his voice, the knight smiled apologetically. He looked as though he was about to deny any concern, but then, after a quick glance around, seeing that Edgar and Hugh were some distance behind and that Mark Rush was a little way in front of them, he dropped his voice conspiratorially and leaned over toward the bailiff.

"This is very difficult, old friend. I think I might have . . . No, that's not right . . . I feel that there could be a . . . Well *now,* since . . ." He suddenly broke off, and Simon almost laughed aloud at the sight. Here was a brave and resolute modern knight, completely lost for words. His eyes met Simon's and the bailiff saw near panic in them.

"And what does *she* say?"

"I haven't . . . How did you know?"

This time Simon did laugh. "Baldwin, did you really think you had kept it secret? God in heaven! The very first time you saw her it was like watching a cock with a hen. It was obvious what you were thinking . . ."

"Please, Simon, save my blushes," the knight murmured.

"So you have not yet said anything to her?"

"How can I, after the death of her husband?"

"Baldwin, at the very least you must get to know her better. Otherwise she may not even think of you. If you don't let her know you are interested, how can she tell you are?"

"*You* did!"

"That's different. I *know* you."

He digested this in silence for a moment. "But what should I do? I can't just go to her house and say, 'Hello, Mrs. Trevellyn, would you like to be my wife now your husband's been murdered?' can I?"

The bailiff sighed. "Look," he said, "you need to find ways of getting to know her. Ways to get her alone so that you can both talk. Maybe take her hawking, or just out for rides sometimes."

"Is that how you won Margaret?" the knight said, his eyes clouded with anxiety and doubt.

"No, I simply asked her father."

"Well, shouldn't I . . ."

"No, Baldwin. I was winning a young girl. You're trying to get a woman, one who knows her own mind, possesses her own household, has her own land and wealth. You have to win *her,* not her relatives."

"Oh. I see."

"Then why do you look so worried?"

"I'd rather be riding into a battle than trying to take on this role, old friend. That's why!"

Simon laughed, but then his face grew serious for a moment as he gazed ahead with a pensive expression, chewing his lip. "We're not far. Come on, we'll drop in on her now."

"No, Simon, I think . . ."

"Come on, Baldwin. To battle!" the bailiff laughed, and to the knight's abject misery, he turned to the servants and called, "Hugh! Edgar! We're going to the Trevellyn house first, before going back to Furnshill."

The bailiff was still grinning as they clattered up the hill to the Trevellyn manor, and his good humor did not fade as he banged on the door with his fist. It was only later, after they had entered, that the doubts began to assail him, but the thought had its inception with the opening of the front door, the rest was merely the gestation period.

When the door swung open, Simon found himself confronted by a pretty maidservant, a slim young woman of maybe twenty, with pert breasts and a cheeky smile. Her face was prettily framed by curling brown hair, and her lips parted in a smile as she saw him. Acknowledging her, Simon led his friend through to the hall, where both waited for the lady of the house to enter. Their servants waited with the horses in the stables, feeding them.

Upon the arrival of Angelina Trevellyn, Simon glanced at Baldwin expecting to see him step forward, but seeing his friend transfixed, he instead took a half-pace back. The knight appeared to be tongue-tied, standing as if in a dream as she approached, and Simon was pleased to see the way the woman's face changed on seeing Baldwin. It was as if her features were lighted by a subtle glow, and her step quickened as though she was keen to be close to the knight.

Looking at her, Simon felt a warm delight. It was not only her obvious pleasure at seeing Baldwin, it was also partly the sight of a woman in the perfection of her youth. There was no hardness to her. Her face, her body, all were composed of soft curves. Under the rich-looking blue tunic, her body moved with the grace and elegance of a well-bred Arab horse, all controlled energy carefully harnessed. Her hair was pulled back and today she was bare-headed, emphasizing her wide brow, unmarked by lines, above narrow eyebrows. It was the eyes that immediately caught the interest, though.

To Simon they looked like twin chips of emerald, glinting in the firelight, not with cold arrogance, but with a warm and calm joy. Self-confident, self-possessed, she radiated a distinct and deliberate sexuality, and even Simon found it difficult to take his eyes from her.

While she chatted inconsequentially, she kept her eyes on the knight, hardly seeming to acknowledge the bailiff, and led them to chairs before the fire. Then she ordered wine, and it was then, when the maidservant returned with a jug and three pots, that Simon's eyes quickly hardened. It was then that the idea took root.

Suddenly the whole room felt full of danger and risk, the warmth of their welcome hollow and empty. The bailiff's eyes glazed for an instant as he reviewed every moment since he and the knight had entered the place, and then focused back on his friend. He was talking to her and stammering as he invited her to join him in a day's hawking. The bailiff watched the maid as she walked to the door, having filled their pots. Picking up his own, he rose.

"Excuse me, madam, but I find it a little warm. I'll just go out for some air," he said, though the others hardly noticed him. Leaving the room by the screens, he saw the girl walking into the buttery, and quickly strode after her.

In the little room, filled with pots, jars and barrels, he found the maid drawing a pot of beer for herself. As he entered, she turned quickly, then, seeing who it was, she gave him a quick smile, shooting a glance to the door behind him.

"I wanted to speak to you. What is your name?"

Her eyes dropped demurely. "Mary, sir."

"You seem a very happy girl, Mary."

"Thank you, sir. This is a happy household."

"It is now, isn't it?"

"Now, sir?"

"When I first came here, you were very different, you know."

Her fingers began to play with a cord dangling from the neckline of her tunic. "I don't understand, sir."

"Oh, I think you do, Mary. I think you do." He sat on a barrel. "Did he beat you often? I suppose that was not all he did, either, was it?"

"Beat me?" Her eyes seemed to grow large in her face as she stared at him, but not with confusion. There was complete understanding there.

"When I first saw you, you were a nervous, shy thing, scared and fretful. Not now, not since he died.

Not since he stopped hitting you, is that it? And what about his wife? Did he beat her too? She wasn't sad to see him dead either, was she?"

"No, I wasn't."

He spun around. There in the doorway was Angelina Trevellyn.

"You can go, Mary." When the girl had scampered past, relieved to be free, the lady turned back on to the bailiff. "Well? Do you wish to interrogate me here, or shall we go back to the hall?" She picked up a jug, filled it with wine, and motioned with her hand toward the door.

Entering the room, the bailiff found Baldwin standing before the fire, his back to it, and staring at the door hopefully. Seeing Simon, his face fell a little, but then he grinned. At the sight of Mrs. Trevellyn behind, his face cleared and he smiled again.

"Please sit down, Baldwin," she said, and pointed Simon to another chair before filling their pots with wine. "I have some things to tell you; things you may not like."

The knight's eyes moved over her, then flashed to Simon, black with suspicion. She carried on softly, sitting and resting her hands in her lap with an almost deliberate attempt at composure.

"Your friend is most astute, Baldwin. He has noticed the change in my house since your first visit. It is not surprising, really, but I should have admitted it to you before. It was not fair to let you think . . ." She paused for a moment, as if in sadness. Taking a deep breath, she carried on.

"Anyway, he is right to think that we are all much happier now. My husband, Baldwin, was a monster! He was a brute. He took me when I was young, and forced me to marry him. He trained the servants well, and beat them often when they displeased him, but he treated me the same! He thrashed me as if I was one of his hostlers! When he wished to, he ignored me and took the maids to his bed—and they dared not refuse him, just as I dared not complain."

Baldwin stared at her in silence, but Simon was sure that there was pain in his eyes.

"So, my friend," she continued, "when you found his body, I think none of us here were sad. Oh, no! How could we be?"

Leaning forward, the bailiff gazed at her intently, but she kept her eyes downcast, refusing to meet his. "Mrs. Trevellyn, why did you stay with him? You could have left him and gone home again."

She looked up at that, with an unmistakable look of sadness. "Could I? How? My home is in Gascony, a little to the south of Bordeaux, so yes, I am English, the same as any other Gascon. And my father was always loyal to the English king, so I should be able to get home. But when your husband owns ships and knows all the people in the ports, how can you gain a passage? And even if there was someone to take me, how could I pay? My *husband,*" it sounded as if she wanted to spit at the word, "kept control of all our money. He even refused me permission to keep my jewels. Oh, no. There was no way I could leave!"

"Why did you agree to marry him in the first place?"

"I did not." Her voice dropped and her head fell to her breast, as if slumping with exhaustion. "How could I marry a man like him? No! He captured my parents and me when we were travelling from Normandy to our home. He took all our cargo, *everything,* and then bargained with my father. He would have me, and let my father keep half of his goods. I was bartered like a slave! But that is how hostages are treated: whether the daughter of a merchant or the king of a province, all are treated the same."

Nodding, Simon contemplated her. It was common enough for a man to be held until his ransom had been paid, and if her father saw a way of retrieving half of his cargo, paying the rest as a dowry, he might well consider it a good arrangement. "I understand, madam. Could you tell me what happened on the night your husband disappeared as well, please?"

"Simon, you don't think she had anything to do with the killing of her own husband!"

Looking at his friend, the bailiff was saddened to see the anguish in his eyes. He gave Baldwin a grave shake of his head, and then faced the woman once more. "Madam?"

Her eyes rose to meet his again, and she spoke simply, expecting to be believed. "I was outside and walking. It appears that my husband came running inside. He had decided he wanted to speak with me, and he asked all the servants where I had gone. When they said they didn't know, he beat two of them, including little Mary, my maid. Then he stormed out. I came back inside an hour or so later, and spent the evening in trying to calm the servants. When he didn't appear, I thought little of it. He often went out to visit the inns of the area. Usually drinking made him violent toward me, but when he went to an inn he was often too drunk, when he finally got home, to be able to hurt me."

"And the next morning?"

"I awoke as usual. He was not with me, but that was not unusual. I was surprised, though, when I found he was not asleep in the hall. When he was incapable of making his way to the solar, I usually found him there, spread out on a table or a bench. Still, it was no real surprise, not when I saw how much snow had fallen over the night. I would have sent out a man to ask at the village, but the drifts were too deep. I was surprised when you managed to get here."

"Tell me, madam. When Agatha Kyteler died, why were you there that day? You are not with child, and you have not had any children, is that right?"

"Yes. We . . . We were not lucky with children."

"So why were you seeing the midwife?"

Her face rose in a faintly haughty manner. "I cannot tell you that. I did not kill her. Or my husband!"

Simon held her gaze for a moment, his face serious. "Very well," he said at last. "I will not force you. But I would like to know this. Did you see anyone that night? The night that your husband disappeared. Was there anyone here?"

She seemed to become even more pale as she stared at him, her eyes wide and seeming to hold a secret fear as her lips mouthed the word "No."

It was then that Baldwin stood decisively and bowed to her. "Madam, I think we should leave you in peace now. I am sorry that we have caused you distress. Simon, come on. We must leave."

The bailiff rose and walked to the door behind the impassive knight. At the screens he turned, partly to take his leave of the woman, perhaps also to apologize, but when he caught sight of her face, he turned and left.

Her features were contorted with loathing, and it was concentrated and focused on him.

They had ridden almost to the door of Greencliff's house before Baldwin turned to face the bailiff.

"Simon you can't believe that she was involved. How could you think . . . ? After all, Greencliff's confessed . . . And she's far too beautiful to be a murderess. God! Why did you have to be so hard on the poor woman?"

"Baldwin, be still! Calm down." Simon stared at his friend and the knight could see his misery. Baldwin was torn between his strong attraction to the woman and his friendship to the bailiff, but although his loyalty to Simon was intense, he was so moved by Angelina Trevellyn that he felt a sense of near disgust for Simon after the interrogation he had just witnessed. Even so, the signs of misery on his friend's face compelled him to be silent and wait for the explanation.

"Look, we *know* she was there. She was with the witch on the day the poor woman was murdered, after the Bourc had left. She won't say why. We *know* she hated her husband—she hardly hides the fact, does she? Even her servants were not with her when her husband disappeared, from the sound of things."

"Simon, for the love of God! You can't believe this! How could a woman like her kill? It's not possible— it's mad!"

"Listen to me, old friend. You know as well as I do that there have been warlike women before, women who could kill, or wage war. You know this. Why should Mrs. Trevellyn be different?"

"But Simon . . ."

"You recall how her husband's body was? Lying as if outstretched? You remember I said it was as if he was pleading? Couldn't she have got Greencliff to cut his throat while he was begging *her* not to kill him?"

"But Simon! You cannot believe that, surely! A woman like her . . ." Through his horror, Baldwin, realized that his friend was pleading with him, his face set, his eyes intense.

"Baldwin, I don't know, I don't know! That's the point! I have to make sure she's innocent of the murders."

"But *you* said that Greencliff admitted to them."

"Yes, and he had a knife with blood on it, but even so, he might have had help . . . Or he might have helped another. I don't know. All I do know is that she *is* involved somehow. I don't know how or why, but I'm sure she knows what happened. Baldwin, I must know what she has done. So must you!"

Margaret was worried by the sight of the two men. She had expected Simon's return to be a joyful occasion, not miserable like this. The two men were hardly talking.

They entered the hall together, but almost immediately Baldwin muttered about wanting to change out of his clothes, damp as they were from his journey, and left them alone. Simon stood and watched him go, then sighed and dropped on to a bench.

"Simon, what has happened?"

Briefly he explained, telling her about their visit to Mrs. Trevellyn, and his conclusions. Margaret listened with misery. She could not comprehend the feelings of the knight, who at last appeared to have found his ideal woman, only to have his best friend suggest that she could have been involved in a murder—maybe two.

When the door opened, both looked up. Seeing it was Hugh, she turned back to her husband. "But you only have some suspicions against her, nothing concrete, nothing that should make Baldwin doubt her. Why not leave him to make his own choice. If she is as beautiful as you say, then . . ."

"But that's the point!" he exclaimed despairingly. "If I'm right, she might have been involved not just in one murder, but two! And one of the dead was her own husband. If she killed her own husband, would she not be a danger to Baldwin?"

To Hugh it looked as if his master was ravaged by doubts. It seemed as if he was pulled in different directions, by his friendship to the knight and the wish to see him happy, and by his confusion over the woman's role in the death of her husband. Clearing his throat, he interrupted. "Sir?"

"What?"

"I don't know if it's important, sir," the servant said, and quickly explained what Jennie Miller had said about Harold Greencliff and Mrs. Trevellyn.

It was one of the few times he had ever been able to shock his master, and Hugh rather enjoyed it.

"You mean Jennie Miller thinks that Mrs. Trevellyn herself killed old Agatha?"

Their evening was quiet. With Baldwin's reserved and withdrawn manner, there was little conversation. Simon and Margaret sat opposite Hugh and Edgar at the great table. Baldwin was at his place at the head, but he was unwilling to talk, and soon after he had finished his meal, he announced that he was ready to go to bed.

Before he could rise from his seat, Margaret went to him and poured him more wine, then stood beside him. "No, you need to talk with Simon," she said, and motioned to Hugh to clear the table. Sighing he got up and began to collect the plates. After a glare from Margaret, Edgar stood too, and began to help. Soon they were taking out the dishes, and when they had both disappeared, Margaret turned to her husband.

"Right, Simon. Tell Baldwin what we heard today from Hugh."

He gazed at her in surprise, and then looked apologetically at Baldwin, who stared back impassively as he was told of the rumors in Wefford about Mrs. Trevellyn and Harold Greencliff. Then, with a sigh, he picked up his pot and sipped at his wine.

"All right, but there's no proof that she has been unfaithful to her husband, no proof of an affair, and certainly nothing to suggest that she killed Agatha or her husband. It's pure gossip, as you say."

Margaret sat down again, looking from one to the other. "Baldwin," she said, "did you think her evidence was strange?"

"Strange?" he glanced at her in surprise. "How do you mean?"

"From what Simon told me, Mrs. Trevellyn will not say what she was doing at the old woman's house. And there really isn't anyone else who seems to have had a reason to want to kill her husband. Doesn't it seem strange?"

"Well . . ." He shrugged, dubious.

"And yet this boy has admitted to it. I don't see why he would do that unless he was involved, but I think you should question him and see what he has to say."

"There's no point trying to do that," Simon interrupted. "I tried to get him to speak about it yesterday and all the way back today, but I got nothing from him. He just didn't seem to want to talk about it at all."

"What?" Baldwin frowned at this. "Not at all?"

"No. He refused to talk about it. He wouldn't talk about Agatha Kyteler's death or Alan Trevellyn's. As soon as I mentioned either he went as silent as a corpse and said nothing until we spoke of something else."

"But he *did* confess to killing them?"

"Oh, yes. In fact, when we asked him, he kept reminding us that his knife had their blood on it. And it did—well, it had *some* blood on it, anyway."

"That *does* seem odd."

"What does?" asked Margaret.

The knight glanced at her. "The fact that he confessed without giving any reason why. Usually people boast of the reason why they murdered someone if they admit to it. 'He robbed me,' or 'he threatened me,' they say, and use that as justification for the killing. If they don't confess, and it's more common that they don't, they deny all knowledge of the crime. At least, that's *my* experience."

"So you think that because he said he *did* do it, it looks odd?" she said slowly.

"Yes. Nobody wants to surrender themselves to a punishment of death for no reason. It would be mad, stupid—or . . ." He suddenly broke off, and his eyes turned to the fire with a frown that spoke of a level of intentness Simon had not seen before. It was as if he was consumed with a total concentration which absorbed him completely. A low gasp escaped from his lips, almost a moan of pain.

"What is it? Are you all right?" asked Simon, and was surprised to be silenced by a curt wave of the knight's hand.

There *was* a reason, Baldwin thought to himself distractedly. If a man was committed, or if he was devoted in his life, tied to a cause, he could subject himself even to death. Who could know that better than he, he who had seen his comrades sent to torture and to death by the flames. They were all dedicated because they all believed in their cause: in the honor and purity of the military Order, in the Poor Fellow-Soldiers of Christ and the Temple of Solomon: the Knights Templar. They had refused to agree to the confessions put to them by the Inquisition, they had suffered and died, not for a lie, but because they believed: in themselves and their masters and their God. And now Harold Greencliff was behaving in the same way, as if he too had a cause. A *love,* greater even than his own love for life.

Simon's eyes flitted from his wife to the knight in his bewilderment. What Baldwin was thinking was totally hidden from him. What had he been saying? Something about not surrendering to something not done? That was it, he had been saying that anyone would be mad to admit to something that they had not done. The bailiff's eyes narrowed: was that what he was thinking? That Angelina Trevellyn had killed her husband and would be mad to admit it? That she would never confess, that someone who *did* confess to a crime must be a fool or mad? And she was neither?

He felt his eyes drawn to the fire. But why kill old Agatha Kyteler, he wondered. Then a quick frown pulled his brows down and he gave an angry sigh as he felt the frustration rise: why, for God's sake, *why* was he thinking about *her* still? She was irrelevant; unimportant—just a sad little old woman. Why did her murder keep impinging on his brain? As he glared at the flames, he found that with no effort he could again conjure up a picture of her from his dreams, dressed in her hooded cloak, her eyes glittering with bright red fire, her expressions intense—and yet not threatening.

It was not a terrifying face. Instead it was sad, as if she was trying to help him, nudging and prompting him toward her murderer.

This was foolish. Thrusting the thought aside, he

considered. The only thing that mattered was finding the killer of Agatha Kyteler and Alan Trevellyn. And right now he was not sure that they had the right man in the gaol. Glancing up he saw Baldwin's face set into a pensive scowl.

Right, the bailiff thought, so who wanted the witch dead? Even Harold Greencliff did not appear to have a motive. And who could have wanted to kill Alan Trevellyn? To find that out the bailiff would need to know more about him. Could one of his servants have wanted to see him dead? It sounded very much as if they all suffered under him. Who knew the man well?

He gave a start, making the brown and black dog stare at him in sudden reproach for waking him before dropping his head down again. He said, "I know what we have to do. Tomorrow we need to see Jennie and Sarah again and check a couple of points—I think I'm getting close to the truth at last!"

22

After leaving their horses with the hostlers at the back of the inn, they entered and took a table near the front of the room. Baldwin haughtily summoned the innkeeper with a curt wave of his hand, while the bailiff stared round the room. After hearing what Hugh had to say about his conversation with Jennie Miller, he was interested in seeing her again, and putting some other questions to her.

But today the inn was quiet. Although it was lunchtime, there were few people there, and Simon reflected that the people from the village would still have many tasks to perform. Even with the fields under snow, there would still be animals to look after, tools damaged over the year to be repaired, and some jobs, no doubt, to be done in their houses.

There was no sign of Jennie Miller. Over by the fire there was a little group of four men, one of whom Simon recognized as Samuel Cottey, but that was all. Perhaps it would become more busy as men finished their lunches and went to the inn for a quick drink before getting on with their afternoon duties.

Wiping his hands on a thick rag, the innkeeper strolled to them. "Sirs. What can I offer you?" he said.

Simon raised an eyebrow toward Baldwin, who shrugged. "Two pints of ale, and food."

"We have cold meats, sir. Is that all right?"

Nodding, Simon turned to his friend as the publican left to fetch their order. "Well, Baldwin? Come on, what do we do next?"

The knight glanced up at him, and gave him a wan smile before returning his gaze to the matted rushes on the floor. "I don't know, old friend," he admitted. "Everything we have heard would seem to support your doubts about Mrs. Trevellyn. But Greencliff had the knife, and the prints led to his door after Alan Trevellyn's death. Then there's Agatha Kyteler's death. He was there, we know that."

"So was *she,* though!"

"I know, I know. She confessed to that. But I wonder . . ."

"What?"

"I was just thinking: why did she want to see the old woman? Agatha Kyteler was supposed to be a midwife, but Angelina Trevellyn says she has never had a child."

Just then their food arrived, and they set to with gusto. Breakfast felt like it was a long time ago. Speaking between mouthfuls, Baldwin's eyes narrowed as he peered at Simon. "If Harold Greencliff was having an affair with Angelina Trevellyn, isn't it likely that he was trying to kill her husband so that he could take her for himself? It would make more sense than thinking that she was involved."

"I'm not so sure, Baldwin. I don't know her that

well, but if she really hated her husband that much, especially after the way that he apparently abused and mistreated her, I think she could easily become angry enough to kill. And don't forget, she *is* a Gascon. She's French."

"French?" the knight stared at him open-mouthed. "What on earth's that got to do with anything?"

"You know," Simon's eyes were suddenly hooded and he glanced around, quickly. "They do tend to get overexcited, the French."

"God in heaven! Simon, you and I must talk soon. You believe in witches, you trust to all the old superstitions, and now you think all the French are mad as well!" The humor had returned to the knight's eyes, Simon saw with a degree of bitterness.

"No, not all French. It's just that . . ." Simon shrugged. He knew he would not win this argument, so he changed the subject. "You know, I think I'm beginning to understand dimly what actually happened."

"There's still a lot we need to find out."

"We need to talk to the people of Wefford again and find out what they haven't told us."

"How? We've already spoken to most of them. How can we find out more?"

"Well, first I think we ought to go back and see Sarah Cottey—especially," he nodded toward the group in front of them, "especially while her father's in here. Then we must see Jennie Miller. She knows more than she's told us, she seems to know all the gossip in the village, if Hugh's right. And I want to speak to Harold Greencliff again. I don't know how to get him to talk to us, but he *must* know more."

"That's a lot of work. It'll take time to get into Crediton to go to the town gaol."

"Have him brought up to the manor, then. The innkeeper can get a man to fetch him and Tanner. It'll save us a journey, and probably do them both some good to be able to stay in a warm place, compared to that cell."

Having decided on their course of action, they finished their drinks and made their way to the Cottey holding, but when they arrived, there was no sign of life. Simon hammered on the door, and rode round to the back, but there was no sign of anyone, apart from the thin streamers of smoke drifting idly on the wind from the roof. After looking all over the plot, they decided to go on to Jennie Miller's instead.

Here they were more lucky. As soon as they came through the trees into the clearing, the sound of voices, shrill and laughing, met them. Coming to the small bridge, they could see the Miller children running and playing tag over at the line of the trees, their mother sitting on a stool and watching as she plucked the feathers from a chicken, laughing every now and again and calling to them to urge them to greater efforts.

At the sound of the horses, she spun round, and Simon was vaguely sad to see the happiness die from her features as she recognized her visitors. The cries from the children faded too, as if the slight breeze was taking away their pleasure and enjoyment with its gusts. The bailiff urged his horse on with a rueful grin. Such was power, he thought. To bring joy, but also to destroy it. Sighing, he brought his horse to the door, to where Jennie Miller had now risen, the fowl forgotten beside her, wiping her hands on her apron to rid herself of the tiny feathers clinging to the blood on her skin.

It was the knight who greeted her, sitting and watching her gravely from his horse. "Jennie, we have come to speak to you again about the death of Agatha Kyteler. Can we come in?"

At her shrug of apparent indifference, they dropped from their horses and followed her inside. Sitting at the same place, she watched them take their seats and sat back, waiting for them to begin with a slightly nervous mien, as if she was anxious of what they wished to know from her.

"Jennie, we wanted to find out from you anything that could help with these two murders," Baldwin began, and her eyes swiftly sought his face.

"What do you mean? You already have the killer, don't you?"

Simon gently interrupted. "You mean Harold Greencliff?"

"Yes," she nodded. "You have him held in gaol, don't you?"

"Yes, but do *you* think he could have killed them?"

"No!" The answer was categoric.

Baldwin stared at her. "But why? Who else had a chance?"

At this her gaze dropped and she stared at the floor in silence. Simon tried again.

"Jennie, you must tell us anything you know. After all, you wouldn't want Harold to be sent to trial and executed if he had nothing to do with it, would you?"

She shook her head, but no words came.

"Jennie, it's obvious you have some idea about this. Why? Who do you think it was?"

She started to speak in a low and halting voice. All the time her eyes remained downcast, and her features anxious. "I knew after I'd spoken to your man at the inn . . . I would have been better to hold my tongue . . . It was the drink got to me . . . But it's true, I'm sure of that."

"What . . ." Baldwin started, but Simon cut him off with a short movement of his hand.

"Carry on, Jennie."

She gave a sigh, a massive effort that looked as though it rose from the very soles of her boots, then looked at Simon and held his eyes. "When I came out of the woods, I was sure who it was I'd seen. I was certain it was Angelina Trevellyn. At the lane, I saw Harold Greencliff. And I know Sarah Cottey saw them too. She's a good girl, is Sarah. But she has not been able to admit to herself what sort of a boy Harold is."

"What sort of a boy do *you* think he is?" asked Baldwin. She ignored him, her eyes staying fixed on the intent bailiff before her.

"You see, Harold and Sarah, they've grown up together, been with each other for years, and they've always been very fond of each other. But now Sarah wants to marry and settle, she thinks Harold does too, and he doesn't. He never has, really. He's always been a boy for enjoying himself, and no girl ever could say no to him, he was always such a good-looking lad . . ." As if in answer to an unspoken question in Simon's eyes, she suddenly reddened and half-turned away in apparent embarrassment, but then faced him once more with an air of defiance, as if she knew her words might shock, but was now careless of effect.

To Simon it looked as though she was almost proud, and he realized with a quick insight how she must feel, working every day to bring up her family, toiling as she tried to help her husband keep the mill profitable so that there would be bread on the table for them. Would it be a surprise if a few kind words from a "good-looking lad" like Greencliff could remind her of a time when she was free of worry and had the opportunity to enjoy the comfort of another man? "And?" he asked softly.

"There are many he has known in the area. Sarah was one. But over the last few months, he has been seeing another woman, one who was not from Wefford. She was married, so he said . . ."

"What? Harold Greencliff *told* you this?" Baldwin cried, leaning forward suddenly.

"Harold?" There was a faint sneer on her face at this. "Oh, no. Harold didn't tell me. No, but there's been a few he did tell. Like Stephen de la Forte. *He* told me."

"What exactly did he say?" asked Simon gently.

She frowned in concentration. "When was it? Oh, yes." Her brow cleared a little and she glanced up at Simon quickly, looking as if she wanted to confirm that he was concentrating. "It was at the inn. Maybe . . . Maybe a month or so ago. He was laughing and joking about his friend, that is, Harold. Harold wasn't there at the time, and Stephen said that he was out with his new lover. He said that her husband was a fool to be cuckolded like that by Harold, but he said there's no fool like an old one. Stephen said he wished his friend good luck, and drank a toast to him. Well, as you can imagine, we all wanted to know. We asked him who it was, and at first he refused to answer, but later, when there was only a few of us left, he swore us all to silence, and then told us."

"He actually said who it was?" asked Simon.

"Well, he hinted. But it was impossible to miss who he was talking about. He said it was a woman he knew, someone married to a man close to him, someone wealthy, living close to the village. It could only be Mrs. Trevellyn."

"Do you think it was *her,* then?"

She looked up with a fire of bitterness glinting angrily in her eyes. "Who else? She hated her husband, everyone here knew that. And it's not surprising either, the way he treated her and his servants. I'm sure she loathed him enough to kill him or to have someone else do it for her. I'm sure it wasn't Harold."

"You said," Baldwin said pensively, "that you saw them at the woods. Did Sarah?"

"Oh yes. She must have done. And she knew what the rumors were about Mrs. Trevellyn and Harold, too. So when we saw her in the trees on the way to the witch's house, and then him at the roadway, she went quiet. She put the two together. Why else would they be there like that?"

Now it was Simon's turn to frown. "I don't understand, do you mean that she was ill and . . ."

Jennie Miller gave a sudden harsh laugh. "Ill? It's no illness to be with child, Bailiff!"

He stared at her open-mouthed. "You . . . You mean the woman was pregnant? That she . . . She was to have Harold Greencliff's child? They went to the midwife to get her help with the delivery?" he stammered, but it was Baldwin who answered, with a tired kind of sigh to his voice.

"No, Simon, not like that, anyway. I should have realized. It's obvious, now I think about it. A midwife can be useful to a woman to help in bringing a child into the world, but she can also sometimes be of help in stopping a child. That was why there was yew in Kyteler's cottage. Yew can be used to make a mixture that will make a pregnant woman lose her child. It forces a miscarriage."

When he looked at Jennie, she nodded. "Yes. I think

that's why Angelina Trevellyn was at the witch's house: to lose the child she and Harold had produced."

They were both quiet as they rode away from the mill toward the road, and they had travelled some way before Simon dared to interrupt the knight's thoughts. When he looked over at Baldwin, he could see that the knight was deeply troubled. The evidence of Jennie Miller had thrown the whole matter into a different light.

"Well, Baldwin?" he asked as they turned into the Cotteys' lane. "What do *you* think?"

Looking up, the knight's face registered a bleak sadness. He felt that the evidence was so overwhelming now that there was certainly good cause to doubt that the boy had confessed honestly. But what teased at his mind was why the boy should have admitted to a crime he had no responsibility for. And whether Angelina Trevellyn could have killed her own husband. It still seemed impossible somehow that such a beautiful woman could be capable of such a deed.

But then his mind went back to the chronicles he had seen and read when he had been in Cyprus and other countries while he was still a member of the Order of the Temple. There were many examples there of women prepared to take up weapons, from women who killed and threatened to take control of lands they wanted, to others who were more subtle and devious in their approach. Alice of Antioch was one, Constance another. Both had tried to take over lands and rule them alone. It was possible that Angelina was struck from the same mold.

"I have no idea, Simon," he said heavily. "All I know is that it seems that there is some reason to doubt whether the boy Greencliff was truly responsible for the murders. And we need to hear from the lady herself why it was that she went to Agatha Kyteler's house. I don't know."

They had almost arrived at the cottage now, and Simon nodded thoughtfully as they made their way to the door, through the flocks of chickens that scrabbled at the dirt for any food missed by their sisters. Dismounting, he lashed his reins to a tree and banged once more on the front door. This time there was only a short pause before it was opened to show Sarah Cottey, whose eyebrows rose at the sight of her guests.

"Sarah," Simon said, "we have come to ask you about the day you went to the witch's house again, and about Harold Greencliff." To his horror, she immediately burst into tears.

Baldwin was still on his horse, but swung down and walked over to join them with a grimace of sympathy twisting his mouth. Throwing a disdainful sneer at Simon, who stood staring at him with frank amazement at the response to his words, the knight barged past, took the girl by the shoulder and gently led her indoors.

"Come on, Sarah. Don't worry, we know most of it already." He helped her to a bench at the table and sat before her, holding her eyes with his, and she began to calm, sniffling. Eventually, rubbing at her nose and drawing in gulps of air, she glanced up at Simon, then began to weep again.

"Come now, child," Baldwin said. "We must know what really happened. Otherwise, you know what will happen, don't you? Harold must die. He has admitted both killings. He has confessed to them both. *You* can't believe he killed them. Tell us the truth."

Looking up, she found herself gazing into the knight's dark eyes. Under that solid stare she found herself relaxing, as if she was becoming entranced by their deep brown depths. "He can't have meant it. None of it."

"Meant what, Sarah?" the knight asked softly.

"What he promised me," she said, her eyes filling again with tears, one huge drop forming in her right eye and slowly descending like a feather dropping in a clear air. "He promised me he would marry me as soon as he could."

"When did he promise, Sarah?"

"Months ago. He said he loved me, that he wanted to live with me forever. But he was lying. I heard about him and that French cow, and how they were carrying on . . ."

"Where did you hear that?"

"At the inn. They were all talking about it up there. But when I asked him about it, he said it was untrue! He said it was all lies, that he'd never seen her, there was nothing in it. He said he still wanted *me*!"

Baldwin looked at her steadily as the tears fell in a constant drizzle, but he could almost feel her pain and it was only with an effort that he stopped himself from touching her to try to offer some comfort. "What happened to make you doubt him? Why did you think he was untrue to you?"

"Because he was *there*! He was at the road to that woman's house. I didn't realize at the time, I couldn't really see . . ."

"Did you see the woman in the trees? Did you see Mrs. Trevellyn?" Baldwin interrupted quickly, and saw with relief that he had brought her back to her story again.

"*Her?* Oh, yes, I saw *her*! She was there in the trees, hiding a little back from the lane, dressed so clean and expensive, like a lady, she was. But she was still there for the same reason . . ." She broke off suddenly, and her eyes glanced away.

"I think we know why she was there, Sarah," said Baldwin. "You had gone there for the same reason before, hadn't you?"

Her head came up once more and she looked him full in the face with a kind of pride as she said, "Yes."

"Why did you think she was there at the time? Is that what you thought immediately, or did you think she was there for some other reason at first?"

"I . . ." Her eyes lost their focus with the effort of recollection. "I didn't think *anything* at the time. I think it was just like seeing anyone. No, it was later, when I came to the lane and saw her horse there that I knew."

"What do you mean? Why?"

"I never saw Harold, he had dropped back into the trees, but he must have been there holding the horse."

"Why do you say that? Surely it could have been anyone there holding her horse—she might have brought an hostler to do that. Why do you think it was Harold?"

There was withering scorn in her eyes as she sneered at him. "Why? Because *I* may not have seen Harry at the time, but when I spoke to Jennie later, she admitted she saw him there, before he ducked back into the trees. He hid when he saw me. I'm not surprised he wanted to stay hidden from me."

Leaning back, Baldwin gazed at her with doubt. "So Harry Greencliff was definitely there—but as far as you could see, he was alone? You saw no one with him?"

"That's right. She must have been in the trees on the

way to see Agatha by then. There was only one reason for him to be there—he was there to give her comfort after she had been to see Agatha. And then she killed the poor old woman."

"*What!*" It was almost explosive the way in which the word forced itself from his lips.

"Well, of course she did. Just like she killed her husband. And with both killings, she tried to blame other people!"

"But why?"

"Why?" Again he could see the disdain in her eyes. "Because when the witch knew she was pregnant, Mrs. Trevellyn had to kill her so that her secret was kept. Then she killed her husband too."

"Wait!" Baldwin held up a hand and sighed. This was becoming impossible, the suggestions and allegations were flying around too quickly for him to be able to think them through. "Why would Mrs. Trevellyn have killed the old woman? Surely she could rely on her to keep the thing quiet?"

"Oh, I don't think so. How could she trust the poor old dear to keep her mouth shut? It's one thing for me, an unimportant woman, unmarried, I knew *I* could trust her. But her? Angelina Trevellyn? She had lots to lose." Her head tilted and she looked as if she was giving the matter judicious consideration. "I imagine she never thought of killing her husband, but then she realized how easy it was after killing old Agatha, and then I suppose the next time her husband tried to threaten her, it seemed like the best thing to do."

Baldwin threw a glance of desperation at his friend, and Simon leaned forward. "Sarah, when you knew Harold, did he always carry a dagger?"

"Yes, of course!"

"What was it like?"

"Just an ordinary ballock dagger. A thin blade with one sharp side. The handle was wooden, I think, and the sheath made of thick leather."

"And he always kept it with him?"

"Yes. Of course he did."

"So it comes to this, then," said Simon at last as they rode back to Furnshill Manor in the creeping darkness of the twilight. "We know that Mrs. Trevellyn was there. We think she was obtaining the same kind of medicine as Sarah, and she had some sort of reason to keep the witch quiet."

"But why did the boy run off? And why would he admit to the crime?"

"Baldwin! If you were young and in love, wouldn't *you* protect the woman of your dreams, even if you *did* think she could be a murderer?"

Drawing up his horse, the knight stared at him. "What do you mean? That *he* thought *she* had done it?"

"Yes!" Simon stopped his mount and turned to face Baldwin. "If you were him, and you had gone with her to see the witch, waiting for her with her horse, only to hear later that the witch had died around then, you'd wonder, wouldn't you?"

"Yes, I'd wonder, but I wouldn't run away immediately, though. Why did he do that?"

"I don't know, but I think the second time, after Alan Trevellyn had been killed, I think that was because he found out that the man had died. Maybe he came across the body in the snow? Or perhaps she told him she had done it and that revolted him so much that he decided to leave. The fact that he admitted to doing it seems to show that he was trying to protect her. After all, if he had not run away, if he had not confessed, it would not have been long before you and I began to wonder about her, would it? We would have to begin to think that she must have been involved, surely, after hearing about the way her husband used to beat her, and the way that she and the servants suffered.

"But the knife? It was covered in blood!"

"Ah! There's a simple reason for that, I'm sure."

"And why confess to doing it himself? That was madness!" said Baldwin incredulously.

"Why confess? That's the easy part. Because he loves her! It may be misplaced, but he wanted to protect her because he still loves her!"

23

Entering the hall, they found an unkempt-looking Greencliff tied to the beam of the middle of the floor, watched by an attentive Tanner who was reflectively drinking from a large pot of warmed ale and sitting by the fire. As the two men walked in, the constable stood quickly, conscious of his position compared with the two officers. Setting his drink aside, he greeted them.

"Hello, Tanner," said Baldwin, acknowledging the constable's nod before turning to the huddled form of Harold Greencliff. Striding across the floor, he carefully seated himself in his favorite chair and fixed a narrow-eyed glower on the unfortunate man. Seeing the frown of concentration on his face, Simon grinned to himself as he crossed over to a bench nearby. He had seen that expression on the knight's face before. It looked as if Baldwin was wearing a magisterial attitude of distaste, but the bailiff was sure that it was no more than a front to hide his bafflement.

But as he sat, he caught a glimpse of something deeper. There was pain in his friend's eyes, a pain that struck at the knight's very soul, and Simon realized what was so affecting him. The knight was a man of honor, who would want only to see that the law should be upheld. He would not want to convict the wrong person and he would not want to let the guilty go free. But that may well mean that he must find this farmer innocent, and if so, there was only one conclusion: Angelina Trevellyn must be guilty. The Bourc had confirmed she was there.

"Harold Greencliff, do you know why we had you brought here?" the knight began, and the shape by the beam stirred.

To Simon it looked as if the youth was beyond fear. His pale face stared back at the knight, but without any apparent care. He seemed disinterested, unfeeling, as if whatever happened to him was irrelevant now. Nothing could shake him more than the events of the last few days. It was as if he had already decided that his life was forfeit, and that there was no point in even hoping for any reprieve. Seeing the look in the knight's eyes, he appeared to recover a little, though, and struggled to get up, rising from a sprawl to kneel beside the post as if he was drunk and embracing a support. He nodded.

"You have admitted to killing Agatha Kyteler and Alan Trevellyn. Do you still affirm your guilt?"

"Yes." It was said with a note of contempt, as if the knight should not have harbored any doubts.

"When did you kill Agatha Kyteler? Was it after Angelina Trevellyn went to . . ."

"Leave Angelina out of this . . ." The pain of his expression and the suffering in his voice were all too obvious, and Simon nodded to himself. That barb touched a nerve, he thought.

"Leave her out of it?" Baldwin's voice was deceptively soft at first, but then it hardened as he leaned forward and continued more harshly. "How can we leave her out of it when she must bear part of the responsibility? If you killed them both, you killed them *for* her. You murdered the old woman so that your secret should be safe and you murdered Trevellyn so that his wife could be free of him, didn't you?"

The boy stared at him, mouth gaping in shock as he slowly shook his head from side to side.

"We know why Mrs. Trevellyn went to see Agatha Kyteler. We know that she went to get rid of the child she did not want."

"No." It came as a low moan, but Baldwin continued doggedly.

"She went there to keep her pregnancy secret, to hide it from her husband."

"No!"

"And then your knife was used to kill Alan Trevellyn as well, I suppose because he found out about the secret. We know you were there with her at the time. We followed your trail back. Your knife was still covered in blood when Simon here arrested you."

The knight paused. The look on the boy's face had become contemplative, and now a faint smile tugged at his lips. He nodded slowly. "Yes," he said. "That's what happened. I had to kill the witch after she realized that Mrs. Trevellyn was pregnant, and I had to kill Trevellyn when he heard about our visit to the witch."

"How?"

Greencliff stopped and stared at the knight at the simple question. "How? What do you mean?"

"How did Alan Trevellyn hear about the visit to the old woman? Who told him? I doubt whether *you* did, after all!"

"I . . ."

"And why did you need to kill Agatha Kyteler?"

"To keep her quiet!"

"But she always kept quiet before, didn't she?"

"Oh, I don't know, I . . ."

"But you *did* know, didn't you? You knew that Sarah Cottey had been to see her, didn't you? And you knew that no stories had spread afterward."

"No, that's not true . . ."

"No? Do you mean you didn't know that Sarah had been to see old Agatha?"

"I . . . No, I didn't know, I . . ."

"You knew." The flat statement cut him off, and he sat with a red face as the knight continued. "You knew full well that the old woman never spoke of the women who visited her, just as she never spoke of the men who went to see her. She always held her tongue, unlike others. No, you would not have killed her for that. And Alan Trevellyn? Why would you have killed him? So that you could have his wife?" The youth opened his mouth as if to agree, but the knight made a terse gesture with his hand to cut him off. "That's nonsense. Why kill the man and then leave? Why kill him to win his wife and then leave her behind? You broke yourself off from your life and your woman at the same time. Are you really that stupid?"

Now the boy was staring blankly at the knight. Looking at him, Simon was reminded of a hare gazing at a harrier. He was left with the impression that he and Tanner need not be present.

"So why, then? Why did I do it? Tell me that."

It was almost as if that simple demand for factual reasoning was enough. Harold Greencliff seemed to relax, nearly slumping back against the post, with an almost contented, a smug, expression on his face.

But his face changed as soon as the knight rested his

chin on his hand and gazed at him, saying, "Very well. I shall tell you what happened. I shall tell you *why,* but not as you mean. I don't think you killed anyone.

"When Agatha Kyteler died, you were standing by Angelina's horse. She left you and went to the old woman's house. You waited there and when she returned, you both went home. You didn't go to the house and kill. You couldn't have! When you went to the Trevellyn house, you didn't see Alan Trevellyn. You went to see your lover, and she took you to the places where her husband could not be. She was not stupid enough to take you somewhere he could see you together."

"Then how did my dagger get his blood on it?"

Baldwin waved a contemptuous hand. "There are many ways for a shepherd to get blood on his blade! What did you do that morning? Kill a ewe? A lamb? I'll bet it was something other than Trevellyn's blood on the knife!"

Simon pursed his lips. It did not seem likely. No, it was more probable that it *was* Trevellyn's blood. If a shepherd killed a sheep—if any man used his knife— he would clean it before putting it away again.

"No! It was me! I did it! I killed them both, I . . ."

But if that was the case, Simon frowned, if that was so, then why was the blade still dirty? Everyone always cleaned their blades, didn't they?

Could it be because someone wanted it to stay bloody? Harold must surely have cleaned it if he had used it, but if another had used it to murder, would they have left it filthy to prove Harold's guilt? Was it to put the blame on him?

Now the knight leaned back as if exhausted, his features seeming somehow older, his face sagging as if through old age, his features seeming to become gray and ancient. "No," he said softly. "You aren't a killer. A man, certainly, but not a murderer. You couldn't have killed the old woman and Trevellyn later, not even for the love of a woman like Angelina. But you could lie for her. You could lie and say that you *did* kill for her. You could do that and make us believe you. So that *she* was safe. So that she went free."

"No!"

"Because all along, all the time, you knew who had really done it, didn't you? All along you knew that only one person *could* have done it. Only that dear woman, only dear, sweet Angelina could have had the chance to kill both the old woman and her own husband. Nobody else had the chance. Did they?"

And it was then, as the knight asked the question, that Simon suddenly realized. "Oh, my good God in heaven!" broke from his lips in a soft cry that was almost a prayer as the truth dawned and he saw what had truly happened.

As if he was looking at a sequence of pictures that built up a large tapestry, he saw in their turn the house of the old woman Kyteler, her body, the form of Alan Trevellyn under the snow, the tracks in the snow leading from the Trevellyn house back to the Greencliff house, and the footprints that he had followed down south toward the moors. Snatches of the comments he had heard with Baldwin struck him and now they seemed to build a tight framework around the killer, with threads as strong as hempen rope around a neck.

He leaned forward and gazed at the boy with an intensity that Harold Greencliff could almost feel. He turned to face the bailiff slowly and nervously.

"Harold, I think I can prove that the killer was not

who you thought it was. If I can show it most certainly was not Mrs. Trevellyn who killed either of these two people, would you tell us the truth?"

There was a cynical question in the lifting of the boy's eyebrow as he stared at the bailiff, but then, as Simon suddenly gave a wolfish smile, he thought he could discern a slight puckering of Greencliff's brow as if in confusion.

"What are you talking about?" asked Baldwin. They had both gone outside and were standing at his front door where the youth in the hall could not hear them.

"We can clear up two suspects in one session. Send a boy to ask Mrs. Trevellyn to get over here for an early lunch tomorrow. Make sure there is no mention of us having Greencliff here. I think we should keep that quiet for now. Then we'll need to go out for a ride, I think."

"Simon, you can be exceedingly unpleasant on occasion, especially when you are smug. Tell me what is going on!"

But the bailiff refused. He ignored entreaties and threats alike, and merely smiled to himself as Baldwin tried to prise the truth from him. "You have heard and seen the same as me, Baldwin. I think I may have seen something you haven't, that's all. I won't tell you what until I've had a chance to see whether I'm right or not," he said and changed the subject.

By the time Margaret came out to see what they were doing, they had stopped talking, and Simon was gazing out over the scenery toward the moors with apparent calm contemplation, while behind him the knight was meditatively kicking at the ground with a face like thunder.

"Are you two all right?" she asked anxiously. She had never seen them like this before. When they glanced at her, she could see that they were both deep in thought, though her husband's thoughts appeared more pleasing to him than Baldwin's. Simon gave her a quick grin, while the knight appeared preoccupied and apparently hardly noticed her.

"What is it?" she asked, not sure whether to laugh or show sympathy, they both looked so absorbed.

In the end it was Simon who answered. Speaking slowly, as if still considering his words carefully, he said, "I think I may have discovered who could *not* have killed either of the two victims. I *think* we are almost in a position to arrest the real murderer!"

"And . . . ?"

"And I'll tell you both tomorrow when I'm sure!"

The next morning was clear and calm. The sky was filled with enormous clouds that floated past slowly and majestically like massive ships under a low but steady breeze, and the sun occasionally burst out from between them to give a wintry glow to the land.

It only served to heighten Simon's expectancy as he walked slowly at the front of the house, trailing aimlessly along the track that led back to the road, then turning off to wander on the snow that still lay over the grass at the side. Every now and again his eyes floated to the lane itself, as if they were being pulled there against his will, as he searched for any sign of approaching horses, and Angelina Trevellyn. Baldwin had been like a boar with a spear in his side all night. Tetchy and fractious, he had snarled even at his servant when Edgar apparently failed, in the knight's opinion, to meet his usually high standards of service. It had little effect on Edgar, who simply smiled, and even threw a knowing glance at Simon, to his faint surprise. It looked as if the man was acknowledging the bailiff's presence, and giving Simon his approval. When the bailiff gave him a slight nod, the servant's mouth twitched, as if he was trying to show a degree of sympathy for the guests in the strained atmosphere.

Smiling again at the memory of Baldwin's petulant expression when he had refused again to answer the knight's questions, he slowly ambled over to a tree trunk that lay not far from the woods. Wiping away the excess snow, he sat down.

He was still there when Margaret came out, followed by Agatha Kyteler's dog, who jumped up at the bailiff with every indication of delight, then, after managing twice to slobber on his face and making him turn away in disgust, began to walk around with his body bent like a strung bow, wagging his tail and panting.

Margaret watched the dog's antics with a small smile. The previous evening had been miserable. She hated dissension, and her husband and their friend had both been so edgy: though for very different reasons, that much was obvious.

It was curious that Simon wanted to keep the matter to himself. That was not like him, especially if he knew, as he must, that the affair was causing Baldwin real discomfort. And the fact that it was distressing the knight was plain to see. Usually Simon would leap at a chance to calm a friend, but with these murders he seemed almost to be taking a perverse pleasure in keeping his friend in suspense, and the ploy, if it was a ploy, was working. Strolling thoughtfully, she went to her husband's side and sat on the trunk with him, and he glanced up at her as he patted the now quickly calming dog.

"Hello, my love," he said, smiling at her. She did not return his welcome, but sat quietly with her hands in her lap. "What is it? Are you all right?"

"Yes, Simon. I'm fine, but I'm worried about you."

"Me? Why?"

She looked up into his smiling gray eyes, searching them for a sign as she spoke. "What you're doing is so cruel. Can't you see what it's doing to Baldwin? The poor man's in a torment. He has no idea what you're thinking of doing today or why! You're making him mad—*why*?"

"I'm sorry, Margaret, I didn't mean to worry you. It's nothing that you need fear," he said, but then his eyes drifted to the view again. "It's just that I'm not sure myself how it's going to go today. I'm fairly certain that Harold Greencliff is innocent, and I think we'll show that today, but the trouble is, what will the result be for Angelina Trevellyn? I think maybe she *did* have something to do with it, and if so, it's quite likely that today I'll have to hurt Baldwin's feelings. And I don't want to."

"What makes you think young Greencliff didn't do it?" she asked matter-of-factly after a moment.

Glancing at her, he smiled. It was typical of his wife to get straight to the main issue without being sidetracked. He considered, but before he could speak there came the tinny jingling of harnesses from the lane before the house. "Come inside, and you'll hear all about it any moment now," he said and, rising, gave her his hand. Looking briefly down to the road, he confirmed it was Angelina Trevellyn before he turned and led the way to the house.

Baldwin appeared at the door as they approached, peering past them to the people on horseback. Watching him, Simon saw the concentration, the intensity of his stare. He felt his belly churn at the thought that the woman might be involved. Oh, God, he prayed, please let it be someone else. I couldn't face Baldwin if I made it clear it was her!

24

When Angelina Trevellyn and her manservant arrived at the door, they were met by the stern-featured Edgar, who took her horse and pointed her to the front door. She curtly passed him the reins and entered. In the screens, she found herself glancing up and around, assessing the property. It was clearly not as good as her own place, neither as new nor as spacious, but it was warm and appeared to be comfortable. She could see rooms off to her left, but before she could investigate, a taciturn, dark-faced glowering man came out from the furthest and indicated the door near her that led into the hall itself.

She haughtily looked him up and down briefly, and when her gaze returned to his eyes she was angered to see that he stared back. If he had been one of her own servants, he would have been whipped, then thrown out of her house for his presumption. At least Alan had always treated the men correctly, she reflected, even if he was wrong to beat her and her maid. After staring at him for a moment, she condescended to enter, but she had only gone a few paces when she felt her legs begin to falter.

To Margaret it looked as if the poor woman was close to fainting. At first she entered as if she owned the place—and if she was as aware of Baldwin's infatuation with her as everyone else was, Margaret thought, she had good reason for arrogance. But her steps began to stumble at the sight that met her gaze. The brown and black dog seemed to understand this too, and walked to her with his tail wagging as if trying to sooth her, but she recoiled from him, and he withdrew, offended, to sit beside the figure of Harold Greencliff.

Looking at her husband, Margaret suddenly realized how well he had arranged the benches and tables. Simon had insisted on pulling the table to the far end of the hall so that Mrs. Trevellyn must walk across the length of the floor to get to a chair. Ranged opposite at the table were Baldwin, then Simon and Tanner. Margaret was at one end, and at the other sat Harold Greencliff. Thus, as she entered, the woman saw the knight at first, directly in front of her, then as her gaze ranged over the other people, it met the unflinching stares of the bailiff and constable. Only after meeting their eyes could she glance over at the last actor in the sad little drama: Greencliff.

Whereas the representatives of the law were sitting grimly pensive, the youth had at first looked enthusiastic. He appeared to want to leap up and greet her, but realized that it would not be right. Seeing how her gaze flitted over him, and seeing the contempt in her eyes, his face fell. When she looked back at Baldwin, the boy almost fell back as if suddenly nerveless.

They had exercised no torture, no cruelty against him, but the seriousness of his position was clearly apparent in the dejected way that his body slumped, an elbow resting on the table top, his head hanging as he stared at the floor. Now he understood he had lost her too. He looked up and all she could now see in his eyes was a pathetic, total and abject misery before his eyes fell, full of shame.

The look had not gone unnoticed by the others. Simon cleared his throat authoritatively and motioned to a chair set before the table. "Please be seated, madam."

She strolled to the chair, then stood beside it while she tugged off her gloves with a contemplative air. Sitting, she raised an eyebrow and stared at Baldwin. "So, sir? I thought I was asked to come here as a friend, to join you in a meal. Why am I subjected to an inquiry? I assume that this *is* an inquiry?"

The knight opened his mouth to speak, and she thrilled to see his expression of hunted apology. He clearly had not had much desire to see her here like this, then. Glancing at the others, her gaze fixed on the bailiff, and she knew she was right. It must have been him that organized this.

"You will be welcome to join us at our lunch as soon as we have sorted out a few problems, madam," said Simon smoothly. "We have been talking to Harold Greencliff here, and we would like you to help us with a couple of points."

To Baldwin it looked as though the blood immediately drained from her face.

"Well?" she asked composedly.

"In the first case. On the day that the old woman died, Agatha Kyteler, you went to see her. It was to arrange for a miscarriage, wasn't it?"

At his words, Greencliff covered his face with his hands, but the woman merely stared back silently, her face as rigid as a mask. After a moment she stiffly inclined her head in agreement, her lips pursed into a thin, bloodless line of rage.

"And while you were there, you left Harold minding your horse, didn't you?" Again there was a slow nod. "While you were there, what happened?"

Shooting a look at Harold Greencliff, she seemed to steel herself. "When I got there, the old woman was fine. I had seen her the previous Saturday to ask for the . . . medicine. She had said that it took time to collect the leaves and herbs, so she could not make it for some days, but it would be ready on the Tuesday. I went there, paid her, and took the draft. I did not wait, I drank it there, with her watching."

"What then?"

"Then? I returned to my horse. Harold was there, and he gave me back my horse and I made my way home."

Greencliff stirred, and his hands fell from his face. Staring at her bleakly, he said, "No. That's not how it was. She told me she was going there to get a potion to make a child—*our* child—strong and healthy. She said she believed the rumors about old Agatha."

"Harold!" she cried, suddenly scared.

"She thought Agatha was a witch, she said. She said the old woman could help her to have a strong baby. I didn't think she was right, but I wanted her to be happy, so I agreed. I held her horse for her while she went to the witch's house, and I waited until she came back. But when she was there, she looked sort of smug, and I knew something was wrong!

"Then she told me. She said she'd bought a draft and our baby would die. She'd always promised me we'd live together, that we'd run away to her family in Gascony, where her husband wouldn't dare to come for us, and when she said she had gone there to drink a mixture that would kill our baby, I was horrified."

"What did you do, Harold?" asked Simon, angrily cutting off the sudden attempt at interruption by the woman, who now sat with her magnificent eyes wide in her horror as she stared at Greencliff, shaking her head slowly from side to side.

"I tried to talk her out of the idea, tried to tell her we'd be all right, that we could get away and we'd be safe in Gascony, but she just laughed, and that was when she told me she'd already taken the potion. It was too late! She said that I was mad if I thought she was going to leave a wealthy husband to live the life of a pauper in another land. She rode off, and I was sort of struck dumb. Well, I had to do something, so I went to the inn and had a drink. I was mad, furious about the witch taking away my child. She'd killed him, sure as anything, because if she'd not given Angelina the mixture, she could have had our child."

"Harold!" she murmured softly with a catch in her voice. He ignored her.

"Well, I hadn't been there for long when a friend arrived, frozen from the weather. He had not expected it to be so cold and had left his surcoat behind. When he saw what sort of a state I was in, he asked what was the matter, and I admitted to him what had happened, and he said that I should see the witch and make sure she kept her silence, otherwise she could make great trouble for me and for Angelina. I still hoped that she might change her mind, you see, and thought that if we could make sure that there was no gossip about us, she might decide to come back to me.

"We left straight away. It didn't take long to get to

the old hag's place, and when we got there we went in . . ."

"Who went in first?" said Simon, frowning intently.

After a moment's consideration, he said, "Me. I went inside while he saw to his horse, and the . . . She was on the floor covered in blood. The dog, *this* dog, was on the floor by her head, whining. I think he had been hurt too. That was when I realized . . . Well, I thought . . ."

"You thought Mrs. Trevellyn had killed old Kyteler to keep her mouth silenced permanently, didn't you?" The boy nodded dumbly. "And you immediately thought that she must be suspected as the murderess?"

"Yes, I thought that if the body was found there, there would be bound to be an inquiry, and someone may have seen her going there and then what chance would she have? They would be bound to guess it was her, and I didn't want that. So I sent my friend away, and took the body to hide it. My friend, he was . . ." His voice trailed off uncertainly.

"You might as well tell us it all. Your friend will not be hurt for trying to protect you," said Baldwin.

"I think he was sure that I must have killed the old woman. He thought I had done it while he was seeing to the horse. When he came in, he saw the body and stared at me, saying, 'Why, Harold? There was no need to kill her!' He was very shocked. Anyway, he left me, shocked, and I took her body back to my house. It was too dark to do anything with her that night; the earth was solid, I would never have been able to bury her, so I was going to hide her the next morning. Then I went back to the inn as if nothing had happened. He was in Wefford, and I met him on the way, so we entered together. Next morning, when I was going to hide her somewhere in the woods old Cottey arrived and found her before I could, and that was when you were called."

"I see," said Simon, frowning as he concentrated. "And what of the night when Alan Trevellyn died?"

"I had been trying to see Angelina ever since the day that old Kyteler had died, but she always refused. Then my friend managed to get a note to her, and he told me we could meet. He came with me through the snow and when we saw her, he left me to speak with her alone. I swear I didn't see Alan Trevellyn. Or kill him. I spoke with Angelina and tried to persuade her to come away with me, but she laughed at me. She told me she would never leave her husband while he was alive and told me to leave her alone."

"Then what?"

"I went back home and tried to sleep. But no matter how much I tried, I couldn't. I just kept thinking of her and how my life would be. I couldn't face it. Knowing I would be always seeing her in the village, or out in the fields and the woods, it made me sick to think of it. So I decided I must leave. I decided to go to Gascony without her. At least there I could forget her and start a new life. I packed some things and went. I went . . . Well, you know the rest."

Simon was nodding. Certainly it matched the facts that they had so far managed to piece together. Shooting a look at the woman, he said, "Well?"

She started. For the last few minutes she had seemed to lose herself in her thoughts, staring into the fire roaring close by. "Yes? Oh, I suppose it's true. It is how I remember it. But I didn't know it at the time. After I had been to see that old hag, when I heard she had been found dead, I was sure that it must have been Harold who killed her. Especially when I heard that she was found in his field. It was obvious. I was scared to see him after that. I thought he might try to kill me. That was why I insisted that he came without a weapon when he came to see me."

"You insisted he came without a weapon?" Simon said.

Greencliff said, "Yes. She took my dagger and gave it to my friend before we met. She refused to see me alone while I had my dagger with me."

Simon leaned back in his seat, both hands on the table top, and stared wide-eyed at the youth. For a moment he was silent, but then he spoke with a voice slow and deliberate. "When did you get it back? When did your friend give you your dagger back?"

"My ballock knife? When we left the Trevellyn house, I suppose. Oh, no. No, he must have set it down at my house. That's right, I found it on the floor in the house when I was packing. He must have put it there for me."

"Tell me one last thing. This friend, it was Stephen de la Forte, wasn't it?"

The misery in his eyes was plain to see as the boy answered simply, "Yes."

After they had checked the story to make sure that they understood it, Baldwin told Tanner to hold both Greencliff and Mrs. Trevellyn at Furnshill, and then led the way out. Simon and he quickly donned thick jackets and cloaks. The bailiff also grabbed a woollen scarf which he wrapped round his neck before tugging on his gloves. Then he went back to the hall to see his wife before leaving. Having given her a hug, he turned, and caught a glimpse of Baldwin.

He was standing by the doorway, and Mrs. Trevellyn had crossed to his side, as if expecting to receive a similar farewell to that which Simon and his wife had exchanged. It felt as if his heart would stop when Simon saw the knight look at the woman without recognition, only to turn dismissively on his heel and make his way to the front door. Not from sympathy for the woman, but because he could see how much his friend was hurt at the story he had just heard. As if recognizing the knight's despair, the thin figure of the black and brown dog followed at his heels.

Outside, Edgar was already mounted on his horse, and Hugh stood nearby, holding Baldwin's and Simon's. They swung up, took their reins, and made their way down the driveway toward the lane. The dog followed behind as, once on the road, they turned their faces to the south and set off to Wefford.

Whenever Simon glanced at his friend, Baldwin's face was set as solidly as the brass plate on a tomb. Although he maintained an expressionless demeanor, Simon could see the pain in his eyes. It was too clear, and it made him try to think of something to lighten his friend's mood. But what can soothe a wounded heart? In the end he gave up the struggle and stared ahead glumly, sadly aware of his inability to offer any comfort.

25

They clattered up to the entrance of the house in the early afternoon, halting and dismounting before the front door. Soon hostlers appeared and took their horses while Baldwin tied the dog to a hook by the door. Then they entered. In the hall they found the lady of the house, sitting alone in front of her fire and looking up at them with fear in her eyes.

"Yes?" she said, her voice quavering.

Baldwin stepped forward, but Simon interrupted him quickly and, pushing in front, bowed quickly to the lady. "Madam, we need to speak to your son. Is he here?"

She shot a glance at Baldwin and Edgar, her eyes wide and fearful, before they rested on the bailiff once more. "You want to speak to Stephen again? But why? He told you all he knew the last time you were here, what more do you want of him?"

"I'm sorry, madam, but we need to ask him some questions. Is he here?"

"No . . . No, he's in Crediton. He left some time ago. He should be back tomorrow, though, so if you want to come back then . . ."

"No, I think we'll wait."

"But why?"

Simon looked at her sympathetically. He was beginning to feel that all he could do today was try to offer support to those he was bound to upset. Trying to smile, he said as soothingly as he could, "We have to ask him about the death of Agatha Kyteler and Alan Trevellyn. We think that . . ."

He paused at the sight of her pale, terrified face in which the eyes appeared to have grown to the size of plums, huge and startling against the pallor of her skin. "Are you all right? Can we get you anything?"

Waving a hand in irritable dismissal of the offer, she held his gaze, and to his sudden distress, he saw a large tear roll down her dried and wrinkled cheek. It was as if he had upset his own mother, and he felt her pain like a band constricting his chest. Yet there was nothing he could do to make it easier for her. If her son was, as he believed, responsible for the two murders, she would live to see her only son die, and in a cruel and degrading manner.

He averted his gaze and settled to wait, but he had only just made himself comfortable in a small chair, while Baldwin and Edgar stood lounging against the screens, when Walter de la Forte came in, closely followed by the thin and perpetually anxious manservant.

It was apparent that he had not seen the knight and his man to his left as he entered, because he immediately strode to the bailiff and stood before him bristling with rage.

"What is this? I understand you're here to question my son again? What gives you the right to invade my house? You may be an officer, but you're not an officer *here*!"

"I am an official. I can . . ."

"Not in my house, you can't. I've a good mind to teach you not to molest a man in his own home. I could kill you now, and all my servants would swear that you attacked me and . . ."

At the sound of Baldwin clearing his throat from behind, he underwent a sudden transformation. His anger disappeared to be replaced by a kind of cunning sharpness before he risked a quick glance over his shoulder and found Baldwin and Edgar to be close behind him. He slowly turned back to Simon, who did not move or respond, but merely sat and stared up at him with an expression of faint disbelief. When it became apparent that the man was still wondering what he could say, Simon softly spoke. "You just threatened an officer in the presence of two other men of high honor. You will sit and be silent. We shall deal with you later."

At first it looked like he was going to attempt an attack on Simon. His eyes bulged with his emotion, and his hands clenched, but then the fire died. His shoulders dropping, he looked as though he recognized defeat. Turning away, he stumbled to a bench and sat, his face in his hands.

Looking up at Baldwin, Simon saw that his eyes were on the fire. However, Edgar was aware that the man could be a problem, and when the bailiff gave a quick nod, the servant walked round to take up a position behind the merchant.

On Simon's cloak there was a twig caught among the threads. Reaching down, he lifted the heavy cloth and studied it. Pulling at the stick, he murmured softly, "It must have been hard, having to be suspicious of your own son. I don't suppose you really wanted your partner killed so that your son could take over his position. It sets a rather unpleasant precedent to have partnerships dissolved by death. I must admit, though, I don't understand why he wanted to kill old Agatha Kyteler." He plucked the twig free and gazed at it ruminatively for a moment before tossing it into the fire.

The older man stared at him for what seemed a long time, then he turned to gaze at the fire, as if debating with himself whether to tell his story or not. After a minute or two, looking up, he said to his wife, "You had better leave us." She stared at him, and appeared to be about to say something, but then thought the better of it, rose, and swept out.

It was some more minutes before Walter de la Forte began to talk. "It was so long ago, we never thought it could hurt us. You don't worry like that when you're young, do you? You think you're immune to any problems caused by your actions. You don't realize that they can return to haunt you in your later life. In our case, we thought the past was far behind us, but it was lying dormant, waiting until we should be so arrogant as to think ourselves safe. Then it pounced."

The room was silent apart from the crackling of the logs on the fire, but even they looked subdued, as if the flames too were listening.

"When Alan and I were much younger, when we were beginning our business, we set up as traders from the money we made during the evacuation from Acre. There were no English knights to take over our ship, Alan and I did it ourselves. Our captain had died in the city. He was hit by shrapnel from a catapult's stone. We took charge of the ship. It was so easy!

"There were people thronging the docks, trying to escape, looking like ants swarming over all the land, streaming on to any old cog or carrack that would carry them. We were careful, we took on board only those who had money or gold. With the wealth in the city we could afford to be choosy. We had no need of furs, so if that was all the people had, they stayed. We took men and women and children. The children were best. They took little space and the mothers were often glad to see them sent away safely.

"There was one couple, a mother with her boy, who tried to persuade us to take them. She was a little older than us, a strong girl, but what a beauty! The boy was only a baby. Well, I was happy enough to take her for the jewels she carried, but Alan took a fancy to her. He was adamant. He wanted *her,* and that was to be her price for freedom. He always was a randy fool. I think it was because he had never managed to father a child. If it had been me, I would have taken her on board and then raped her, but he always was a fool about that sort of thing. He told her what the price of her passage would be and she refused. And with obvious loathing. So! He refused to take her or her child, no matter what she said. That was that!" He glanced up bleakly.

Sighing, he continued, now holding the bailiff's eyes as he spoke. "Later, another woman came, one who was not the same in looks or in position. She had a young child, and she had money. We let her aboard. How were we to know that she had the son of the first? And we could not tell that the first was the woman of a powerful man in Gascony, the Captal de Beaumont, who had been in Acre to help defend the city.

"The boy was his son—his bastard, apparently. The woman was his nurse: Agatha Kyteler, curse her! When we let her off the ship at Cyprus, she managed to make her own way back to Gascony and delivered the boy to his father. The mother must have died. To our shame!" His head dropped into his hands, and although he did not weep, his emotion was all too clear.

Sighing, Baldwin tried to keep the contempt and disgust from his face as he watched the man. That any Christian man could have condemned a woman to the mercy of the Egyptians was horrific enough, but for so paltry a reason? It would have been kinder to have simply killed her. He sighed as the man began talking again.

"And there the affair ended, as far as we were concerned. Alan and I began our new lives. We had made plenty of money in the escape from Acre, and we used it wisely. We bought new ships—heavy cogs for bringing wine over the channel—and spent years trading peacefully between Gascony and England. But then, of course, the troubles began to get worse in France, and our ships started to get attacked. We lost one ship sunk by pirates and another captured, with all the men aboard murdered. That only left us the one, and we needed finance to keep it going, which is why we had to go to the Genoese. Doing that we managed to survive until about ten years ago."

His face was almost wondering now, as if in amazement at how far he and his partner had fallen after the high point of their lives. "It was that bitch Kyteler, the old hag!" he declared, his head shaking slowly from side to side.

"I had only just built my house when she came to town. I don't know how she got here or how she found out where we were, but she did. She came here, to my house and introduced herself. Then she recalled the trip from Acre and told me whose son the boy was. I was horrified! I thought that at any time we should expect to have the Captal's men storming the house, but that was nonsense. When I told Alan, he said we should kill her, but I was against the idea. I thought we had enough dead on our hands already, so I said I would have no part in her murder.

"He went and tried to threaten her. He wanted her to leave the area, but I think she had decided to stay as a constant reminder of our action at Acre. A living token of our guilt. She threatened to tell the Captal if anything happened to her. That was why Alan built his house up and had the castellations added. He was scared of being attacked by the Captal's men."

"So all she did was stay nearby? She only lived here, and that made Trevellyn go in fear of his life?"

"Yes! The Captal de Beaumont is a powerful man. If he wanted to attack us, we could hardly protect ourselves. Alan said we ought to have had her killed off years ago, it would have been easier, at least we'd have known where we stood. But it was too late after a while.

"Stephen got to hear about it somehow. He felt that she was a danger to us all. He wanted her gone, but what could we do? And then, when she was out of the way, he decided that our partnership was useless as well. He told me that Alan must be bought off. He said that Alan was a harmful partner, that he was destroying the business, that there would be nothing for Stephen to inherit if Alan remained. When I asked him what he meant, he told me to have Alan killed. At first all I could do was stare at him, and then I lashed out. That was where he got his bruise. It was after that I heard Alan had been killed."

Just then they heard a horse approaching outside. The merchant looked up as if searching for sympathy, staring at Simon with a kind of desperate yearning, as if he was pleading for understanding.

He was surprised to hear the old woman's dog begin to snarl and then growl and bark savagely out by the front door. There was a sudden flutter in the screens, and then they heard the front door thrown open. Almost before Simon could comprehend what was happening, Baldwin had uttered a most uncharacteristic curse and hurled himself at the door, and Edgar had followed, leaving the bailiff and the merchant sitting in astonishment.

"Don't kill him, Bailiff. He's a good son," said the man softly, and then Simon's senses recovered. Realizing what was happening, he lurched to his feet and ran at full pelt.

26

Outside, the mother was standing and staring at the disappearing figure of her son, riding fast for the road. Baldwin stood fuming, waiting for Edgar to return with his horse. When he did, there was only his own and Baldwin's. Snatching the reins from him, Simon snarled, "Get inside! Keep the father there until we get back!" And, somewhat to his surprise, Edgar obeyed.

Whipping their mounts, they launched themselves down the road at a gallop. They had their target some hundreds of yards away and all they need do was catch him. They could see him riding over the snow-covered grass to the right of the lane, then turning north as he hit the road. Whipping their horses, they kept their speed, although every now and again the knight glanced down at the snow rushing past their horses' hooves, wondering what would happen if they were to fall at this sort of pace. And it was likely that they would. While the snow was soft enough, he knew that a layer of ice could lie beneath its white covering, as slippery as oil on a metal breast-plate, and if they were to hit such a patch, they would be hurt.

And it was not long before he was proved correct.

He felt his horse's hindquarters slip, and felt the great creature falter as if nervous, knowing that he was losing grip. It was only with care that he managed to stay in the saddle. When he heard the high whinny and gasp from his side, above the whistle of the wind in his ears, he knew that Simon had fallen, and turning and throwing an anxious glance behind, he saw the bailiff sitting in a drift and rubbing his head with a grimace of angry pain.

It was then that Baldwin felt the anger rising. Now this young fool had caused his friend to be hurt as well. With his jaw set and his eyes staring, he set spurs to his mount's flanks and raced on.

They had entered the cold shade of the woods now, and Baldwin felt that the dark trunks rising on either side and flashing past looked almost like disapproving spectators. He set his teeth at the thought. Why should they approve? This was a race to the death, after all. The boy would die, whether during his flight or later, and the knight must catch him or die in the attempt, now that there was only him left.

Then the trees seemed to pull back from the track as if in dismay, and Baldwin drew in his breath. They were coming into the village. The open space by the inn came toward them, then they had flashed past, leaving two surprised men trying to calm their horses at the entrance, startled by the speed of the two riders.

Leaving the village, Baldwin became aware that his mount was beginning to tire. He could feel the breathing becoming more labored, the steps starting to lose their rhythmic pattern, and the head was straining as it stared forward. Biting his lip, the knight frowned ahead. Could the boy escape? No, he mustn't. He must be caught and made to pay for the murders.

The horse ahead was a blur against the white of the road, the youth a darker smudge on its back. All Baldwin could see was the snow whipped up by the hooves and the wind, flying upward into a cloud like a trail of feathers in their wake. It was already becoming colder and the breath felt like it was freezing his lungs as he inhaled. It smoked as he breathed out, the cold damp mist being snatched away from his mouth by the wind as he rode. Every now and then he would catch a whiff of the dank breath of his horse as the gray exhalation was drawn past his nostrils, but he kept his eyes fixed now on the figure ahead: his prey.

He was aware of the light fading. The sun was gradually sinking behind the protective covering of clouds, and there was a pink and orange glow in the west, flecked with purple and blue, which he could glimpse on his left. But then they were suddenly out of the trees and into a clearing. Here the youth sensed he had an advantage, and Baldwin saw his arm rise and fall in a steady rhythm as he beat his horse's flank. "Fool!" the knight thought. "All you'll do is lose his concentration if you keep hitting him. Leave him be."

But it worked, and the boy reentered the woods at the far end of the clearing with a greater advantage. It was obvious that the knight would not be able to catch him. The youth was smaller in body, his horse faster, while the knight's mount was larger and slower. The contest was too unequal. He was about to rein in, when he saw a larger splash of snow, and then, when it settled, the horse and rider seemed to have disappeared. Uttering a quick prayer, Baldwin slowed to a canter, then a trot, and went forward hopefully to investigate.

"Get up! Get *up!*" he heard as he approached, and then he saw the boy. Stephen was kneeling and struggling in desperation to make the horse rise, but the horse was lying dazedly, both forelimbs outstretched, and whinnying softly, clearly in great pain. When he was close, Baldwin saw that one leg was bent at an impossible angle from the forelock. It was broken.

"Shut up, Stephen," he said as he dropped from his saddle, and the youth rose, to stand anxiously, eyes wandering from the knight to the woods. "Don't even think it," Baldwin continued evenly. "If you try to run, I'll catch you. And if you were wondering about taking my horse, don't bother. He doesn't like other riders. He'd throw you within yards. Sit down over there, while I see to your horse."

While the boy stumbled to the patch of ground Baldwin had indicated, the knight studied the horse. There was nothing he could do. The leg was broken, and it was easy to see why. Riding in among the trees, the horse had been unlucky enough to put his leg into a rabbit hole hidden by the snow. There was nothing else for it. Baldwin drew his dagger and cut the horse's throat with a single, quick slash that opened the artery. Leaping back, he could not avoid the fine spray and then thick gouts of blood that gushed. The knight was liberally spattered. It was soon over, and when the creature's shivering death throes were done, he cleaned his knife on the horse's flank before he stowed it away. Stephen de la Forte was still seated where he had been told, resting with his hands on the ground behind him, although now his panting had reduced. Baldwin kept an eye on him while he mounted, then cocked an eye back the way they had come. "I think it's time we started back, don't you?" he said affably.

The youth slowly rose to his feet and glanced at the dead horse. Without moving, he said musingly, "I suppose you know how wealthy my father is? He would pay well for my freedom. All you have to do is let me go now."

"You have a long walk ahead of you, Stephen. Save your breath for that."

It would have been foolish for the boy to try to escape. Similarly, he seemed to realize that it would be impossible to try to deny his guilt. He strode along amenably enough, hands clutching his cloak tightly around his body as they made their way back. Their mad race had taken less than a half-hour, but it took them nearly that long to get to the village with Stephen on foot, and Baldwin's better judgment might have persuaded him to stay and enjoy a drink, but he decided to continue. He wanted to see how Simon was after his fall.

It was almost another hour before they came to the track on the left that wound its way up to the house, and here for the first time the youth faltered.

"Do we have to go there? Can't you take me straight to the gaol? I don't want to see my parents like this." There was a plaintive tone to his voice, the spoiled child who cannot have his own way.

Baldwin's sympathy was limited. "Get a move on. At least you can get a warm drink inside you at the house."

The last thing on the boy's mind was an attempt to break away and make his escape, but he was reluctant to arrive at his home, and the knight cursed the youth's slowness under his breath. Now he was nearly there, he wished to complete their journey as quickly as he could.

At the door they waited, and when it was pulled wide, it was Edgar who stood there to welcome them.

Taking Stephen by the arm, he waited while his master dropped from his horse. When an hostler arrived and took the reins from him, they all passed inside.

"Simon! How are you?" Baldwin cried at the door, and crossed the floor to his friend, who sat swathed in cloak and blankets like a new-born child. The bailiff smiled, but his pleasure at seeing the knight could not hide the yellowish pallor of his features.

"I'm fine," he admitted. "But I landed on my head, and it jarred me." He stopped and stared. "My God, Baldwin! Are you all right? You're covered in blood, did he stab you?"

"I'm fine. I had to kill his horse: broken leg."

"Thank God! I . . ." He stopped, his mouth open in apparent revelation, and Baldwin heard him mutter, "Of course! That was why he was cold! Why didn't I realize before?"

Barging past the knight, Stephen stepped up to the fire and ignored the gaze of the others. His father was sitting with his mother on a bench by the hearth, his arm around her, and to Baldwin it looked as if they had both aged in his absence. She was sniffling and trying to hold back her weeping, while her husband sat stoically and expressionlessly, swallowing hard every few minutes as if trying to keep the tears at bay.

When the youth turned from the fire, Baldwin saw him glance at his parents for a moment. In that quick look, he saw only contempt and loathing, and he felt a cold chill at the sight of it. How long would it have been, he wondered, before this boy decided that his father was too weak or ineffectual to be his partner as well?

It was Walter de la Forte who broke the silence. "Are you going to tell us why?"

"Why, father? Why I killed them? *You* know the reasons why. And I did it then because I had the opportunity, I thought, of getting away with their deaths. After all, they both deserved their ends."

He walked over to a small chair and sat, staring at his father with apparent surprise, as if he expected that he at least should understand. "She had been a threat for ages, and that was hardly right, especially now the business has been suffering. No, it was only right that she should die. She was a danger, and had been for many years."

"But why Alan? He was our friend, your friend! Why kill *him*?"

"He was weak and a fool. He wanted us to keep on with the trading when it was clear we needed to change, to move into banking, beat the Genoese at their own game. That's where the money is going to be in the future. But he wouldn't see it. He couldn't. He was going to ruin our business, Father. I couldn't let him do that to my inheritance. I had to kill him."

Simon interrupted. "You knew what you did was going to put the whole blame on to Greencliff, didn't you? Did you want him to die for what you had done?"

"Harold?" The youth's face showed momentary confusion, near anger as he frowned, but then he seemed to realize that the bailiff was genuinely unaware of the truth and gave him an comprehending smile. "Oh, no. You don't understand. I told Harold to go and escape, I knew he *could* be in danger otherwise. That was why I went to his house after the witch died, to make sure he had gone. I had to make sure he would be all right after I killed her. Then, when I had seen to Alan Trevellyn, I made sure he left for good. He was my friend; I was looking after him."

27

I t was late when they finally made it home, and both were ready to drop straight to sleep, but there was no opportunity for them to do so. Margaret, Tanner, Greencliff and Angelina Trevellyn were still in front of the fire, and their eyes rose to the door as the three men entered.

Margaret went to Simon as soon as she saw him, with a sigh of relief, hugging him with her eyes closed. "I thought something must have gone wrong," she whispered, and then, as she squeezed tighter in her joy, she felt him wince and heard his quick moan, and stood back. Now she could see his pain, and the paleness of his face. Even as she saw him try to smile, she turned an accusatory glare to Baldwin. "What's happened to him?" she asked, and then gasped in horror as she saw the gore over his tunic. "Baldwin! What has happened to *you*?"

The knight grinned. "Very little, the same as your husband. But I fear we shall all three of us soon die of the cold if we do not get inside and sit before the fire."

While Margaret bustled, calling for Hugh and helping Simon to a chair, Baldwin walked to his own chair by the fire and sat, pensively watching them. Hugh did not appear—he had fallen asleep in the kitchen by the fire—so Edgar went to fetch food and drink for them. It was only when he had left the room that Baldwin found his eyes being drawn to Angelina Trevellyn. Seeing her condescending smile as she watched the husband and wife, the knight nodded to himself as he turned his face to the fire once more. It confirmed his decision, reached with such difficulty on the ride homeward.

"Come on, then! What happened? And Simon, how did you guess it was him?"

The bailiff smiled at his wife. "There were a number of things that made me start to think of Stephen de la Fort," he began. "I think the first thing was how so many people started saying how much of a friend he was to Harold, and how they were always together. It seemed as though they had no secrets from each other—Jennie Miller even said that Stephen knew who Harold's wealthy lover was." At this, both Greencliff and Angelina Trevellyn stirred, but Simon ignored them.

"Then there was the fact that at both murders, although Harold was there or nearby, he was apparently alone. It did not occur to me at once for, in affairs of the heart, most men will leave their friends behind when they go to see their lover. But there was something odd about the prints back from the Trevellyn house on the afternoon we went to Harold's house after discovering Alan Trevellyn's body. It only came to me late. There were the prints of a man *and a horse*!"

He glanced at the farmer. "You never owned a horse, did you? That's what Jennie Miller said too. What use would a shepherd and farmer have for a horse? And if you did have one, why walk the horse home? To avoid ice, maybe, but it would be rare for a man to walk unless his horse was lame, and this horse did not limp. No, I became certain that there was another man with you. You confirmed that yesterday.

"So what about the day of the death of Agatha Kyteler? Once again, you were seen while you stood with Angelina's horse, once again, you were alone there. Was it likely? Later, at the inn, you were seen with Stephen de la Forte again, but *he came in after you*. You did not enter together. If he was with you when you went to see your lover, when Alan Trevellyn died, surely it was possible that he was with you when Agatha died as well? In which case, where had he gone?"

Nodding, Baldwin leaned forward. "Yes, I think that this is what happened. You two, Harold and Angelina, agreed to meet, but Stephen went with you. Harold, you waited with the horse while Angelina went to see the old woman. When she left, Stephen made some excuse . . ."

"He said that after seeing the old woman, Angelina would want my company, but he would probably be unwelcome," said Harold dully. "He rode off as if he was on his way home."

"I see. So he went a short way, then tied his horse in the woods, and made his way to the old woman's cottage. When he saw Angelina leaving, he went inside and found her still at her table. He pulled out his knife and killed her."

"I knew none of this!" the boy cried, and his face dropped into his hands.

"No, that much is obvious," continued the knight. "What happened was that Angelina told you what she had done, and you were shocked, horrified, by what she had done, when you had been looking forward to raising the child."

"She said she wanted nothing more to do with me when I asked her to leave the village and come away with me."

"Yes," said the knight and threw her a glance. She appeared to be gazing at the youth with a small contemptuous sneer. "I imagine she did. Anyway, feeling as you did, you went to the inn to get drunk. Half an hour later or so, Stephen arrived . . ."

Eagerly, the bailiff interrupted. "And he was cold, you said! You said he had no surcoat!"

"Yes," the boy nodded with surprise.

"Look at Baldwin's tunic, after killing Stephen's horse!" said Simon triumphantly. "Stephen may have been able to clean his face at a stream in the woods, but he couldn't clean his clothes. That was another thing that stuck in my mind!"

"Thank you, Simon," said Baldwin with an imperceptible frown of irritation at the break in his tale. He paused, trying to regain the threads, but Simon was too quick.

"So," he said, "Stephen appeared, heard what Angelina had said to you, and then started to speak about how the old woman would be sure to talk about such a wealthy woman going to see her, or something, yes?"

The boy nodded miserably. "He said that Agatha never could keep her mouth shut. He said she had told everyone in the village about me and Sarah Cottey. I *had* to do something to keep her quiet."

"Yes, that was when you were overheard talking about silencing the old witch!"

"Yes. And Stephen offered to come with me."

"That's the interesting bit. I suppose he wanted someone to confirm that it was a shock to him to find her body there."

"I don't know. He came up to the cottage, but when I opened the door, and found her there, her dog came out and started to attack him. He said we'd better go, and I held the dog back, for it would have taken him by the throat otherwise. When he had gone, though, I began to think, and . . ."

"You thought Angelina had done it," said Baldwin flatly. "So you chose to drag the old woman's body to your field, so you could bury it and hide the proof of the murder."

Nodding again, the boy looked up with frank sadness. "I went to the inn first, with Stephen. I left the body there at the house. I didn't even tell him what I was going to do, I thought it would be wrong to involve him. Then, when we left the inn I took her back with me, through the woods, and left her in the field. I was intending to bury her the next morning. But Cottey found her first."

"Why did you run away?"

"I still loved—I still love—Angelina. But she made it clear that she did not love me. I was going away. I was going to leave the area and find my fortune elsewhere."

"I see."

Simon musingly poured himself some wine. "Who suggested that you should go and see Angelina later? When Alan Trevellyn died?"

"Angelina did," he said.

"I did not!" she declared hotly. "*You* asked to see me!"

"I assume, then," interjected the knight suavely, "that Stephen told you, Harold, that Angelina wanted to discuss things with you, and told you, Angelina, that Harold must talk to you?"

They both nodded, and she seemed to consider as she said, "He threatened me. He said that Harold would tell all in the village about us if I did not agree to meet him one last time."

"But you refused unless he came without a weapon?" asked Baldwin, leaning forward.

"That was Stephen's idea. He said that Harold was so depressed he could do anything. He said I should be very careful, and he offered to take Harold's knife if I agreed to see him. Stephen said he would stay nearby so that I should be safe."

"So in that way he managed to get your knife, Harold. He used it to kill Alan Trevellyn. I don't know how."

"He came to the house and asked for wine. Maybe he told my husband that he had seen me with a man up in the woods? The servants were all terrified by my husband's temper before he left to search for me. He was in a terrible rage."

"It's quite likely. Yes, he knew your husband well, as the partner of his father, so if Stephen saw Alan, Alan would probably have believed his story. And he could have promised to lead him to you, as well. It would not have taken much to drop back behind, and cut his throat as he stood in the trees. Then he covered the body with snow to hide it a little, and went back to see you two."

"Why wasn't he covered in blood this time?" asked Simon frowning.

"This murder was better planned. He knew that blood would cover the whole area after killing the old woman, so maybe he carried a fresh tunic with him,

one that he only put on after leaving these two together. I don't know, but he's bright enough to manage
that."

"And then," Simon finished, "he joined you, Harold,
after your meeting with Angelina, and went home with
you. It was his tracks and yours that we saw. Your feet,
his horse."

"Yes, he came back. He stayed with me a while, I
think, but I hardly said anything to him. Angelina had
confirmed that she would not leave her husband to live
with me, not even if I could get us away, to over the
sea. I felt that I had nothing to live for in Wefford any
more. After he had gone, I packed and left. The rest, I
think, you know."

In the silence that followed, Margaret found it difficult to keep her eyes from the miserable figure of
the farmer. He sat huddled, deep in thought, but
none of the thoughts seemed to give him any joy.
The woman was different, she could see. Angelina
Trevellyn sat with a measuring gaze in her green
eyes, and they were fixed intently upon Baldwin,
who appeared to be unaware of her presence. The
story of love and misery had struck him with its
despair.

"Oh, don't take her, Baldwin," she found herself
thinking with a shudder. To her surprise she found that
the wish was so intense it struck her almost as a prayer.
"She's vicious, uncaring and grasping. Beware!"

As if he had somehow caught the drift of her
thoughts, Harold Greencliff suddenly rose. Without a
word, he swept from the room, his face downcast and
his eyes avoiding meeting the gaze of any of the other
people there. When she looked at her husband and the
knight, Margaret saw the sympathy there, but the boy

appeared not to have noticed as he slammed the door and stalked out into the open air.

After a moment, Baldwin stood and followed the boy.

Outside, the night was a gray curtain that hid the land around, and Greencliff was invisible in his dark tunic. But it was easy to find him from the sound of tortured sobbing that came from the side of the house. Baldwin stood undecided for a moment, not sure whether to go and interrupt the boy in his misery or not. He made up his mind. Steeling himself he strode on.

The boy was leaning against the log pile, eyes thrown upward at the star-filled sky, heaving great breaths and sobbing them out again in his despair and misery. He did not turn as the knight came up beside him, but continued his solitary skyward stare.

"What will you do, Harold?" asked Baldwin softly after a few minutes.

"Do? What *can* I do? What is there for me here? I've lost my only friends: my best friend is a murderer who tried to put all of the blame on to me; my woman, the one woman I thought wanted me as her husband, has made up her mind I'm not good enough for her! Not good enough to sweep her stables! What is there for me? What can I do, where can I go to find peace?"

Remembering Sarah Cottey and her spirited defense of him, Baldwin considered. He said slowly, "There are others who may be better friends or lovers, Harold."

"There's no one. I have no one. No friends, no family, nothing." The tone was definite, the finality as certain as the slam of a tomb closing. In the face of it, Baldwin felt unequal to any further battle for the boy's confidence. Turning, he stared away as he thought for a minute.

"Harold, if you need help, tell me. If you want to leave the area and go to Gascony like you said before, I'll release you from your villeinage. But remember, you can only run from things you leave behind, not from things inside you. If you go but take the woman and your friend with you in your heart, you'll never find peace. There must be another woman here that would be better for you, someone who can ease your life and . . ."

It was this that finally made the boy spin to face him. "Why? So *you* can take my woman? She's told me that already, that you want her. It's obvious why—a wealthy merchant's widow and the wealthy knight— but don't try to tell me it's better for *me* when all you're trying to do is look after yourself. Don't try to tell me you're trying to help me when what you're doing is stealing my woman!"

Simon was sitting alone in the hall when the knight came back.

"How is he?"

Dropping into his chair, Baldwin gave him a grimace and puffed out his cheeks in a sigh. "There's nothing *I* can say. He doesn't trust me. I think if he stays for a week he'll be here forever, but if he goes far away I wouldn't be too surprised. You never know, it might be best for him. It certainly did me good when I went abroad."

There was a slight noise, and the door from the screens opened to show Angelina Trevellyn. She walked in as slowly and gravely as a nun and sat opposite the knight, her face showing a sad and compassionate concern. "How is he?" she asked softly, her voice low.

"I think," Baldwin said, staring at her skeptically, "that you should find out for yourself, madam."

"What do you mean?"

"He was your lover."

Simon wriggled in his seat. He had no desire to be here for this. He glanced at the door in mute appeal, but no one entered, and he dared not interrupt them himself. Cringing back, he tried to make himself as small as possible.

"That was before," she said calmly.

Baldwin spoke dryly. "What, before you realized you were about to become a widow and could have your choice of the men—or should I say knights?—of the area, madam? Before you thought you could do better for yourself? Before you thought it would be pleasant to own a man with a title in preference to a mere merchant whom you had always feared and disliked?"

"That is hardly fair," she said, giving a slightly nervous smile. Baldwin did not smile back.

"Isn't it? I think it probably is. When did you decide on me? Was that some time ago too? Or was it a snap decision, like choosing to take a local farmer as your lover? It must have been funny until you got pregnant. That was the one thing that surprised me. Why were you so upset about being pregnant? Why should a married woman be so fearful that she is prepared to go to a woman reputed to be a witch to force the child to miscarry before her husband can find out?"

"I thought it would be wrong to bring up a child as his own when it might not be," she said with a hint of defiance.

"I doubt that, I doubt it a great deal. I think it was because you knew that he could not have children. Oh, yes," he carried on as her face colored, "Walter de la Forte knew about that too. He told us. Tell me, though: when did you choose me? Was it when you saw my house here and realized how large my estates were? Or was it before, when you first saw me and thought I might be more enjoyable than a mere farmer?"

"I don't have to listen to this!" she said, standing and glaring at him angrily, the light reflecting from her eyes in green glints of cold fury.

To Simon, it seemed that the knight stared at her for a moment as if trying to remember something, perhaps how he had felt when he had first seen her and been so enamoured of the beautiful green-eyed Gascon lady. "No," he said softly, "you can go whenever you want, can't you? Do whatever you want. You are wealthy now, and have money and lands. Well, go then. I wish you well."

As his friend turned back to his fire, Simon thought he saw doubt in the woman's eyes, but then her rage took her over and she flounced from the room. Soon her voice could be heard outside, shrilly calling for her horse and servant, then shrieking when she felt that she was being thwarted.

"I think that you have probably just had a very lucky escape!" said Simon meditatively, but when he glanced over at him, the bailiff caught a fleeting glimpse of the deep sadness that passed over the knight's face.

The door opened and Margaret walked in, a tray with wine and minted water in her hands. "Have you seen Angelina Trevellyn?" she asked in bewilderment. "She's demanding her horse, and when I suggested she might be better to wait here the night and leave in the morning, I thought she was going to launch herself at me in her rage! What have you said to upset her? Baldwin, why what is it?"

But even as she set the tray down and leaned toward him with a compassionate frown on her face, even as he tried to smile, he found he could not. And only by blinking could he stop the tears that suddenly threatened.

28

When they had been back in their drafty castle for almost two months after the murders, Simon and Margaret received a letter from Baldwin. Of course, Margaret could not read or write, but Simon had been fortunate enough to have been schooled by the priests at Crediton when he was young, and he and the educated knight often exchanged letters when they had the opportunity.

"What does he have to say?" she asked, not bothering to rise as she once had done. Before, the novelty had made her look at the indecipherable characters over his shoulder, but now that he had been bailiff for a little over a year, she was well used to seeing missives arrive, and the event was not such as would make her leave her plate of food. Funny, she thought vaguely, that being pregnant can make one so hungry all the time.

"It confirms that young Stephen de la Forte is dead. Apparently he went to the gallows well enough, but he took his time dying and the executioner had to help. Anyway, it seems that Greencliff has announced in church that he is to wed Sarah Cottey. Baldwin thinks it's a good idea, even old Sam is happy with it. He'll be grateful for an extra hand, and Greencliff is a good strong lad."

"Anything else?"

"His manor is ahead of itself already, and he's looking forward to a good harvest at last." His face frowned suddenly, and he leaned forward.

"What is it?"

Glancing up, she saw a smile spread over his face. "Angelina Trevellyn," he said. "She's decided to return to Gascony, apparently. And Baldwin has made some comments about her that I don't think I should relay to you! It's enough to say that he seems relieved to see her go. What he does say is that she was somehow embarrassed. It seems that some men took to heckling her in the street. Apparently, news of her affair with Greencliff got around the village, and spread further afield. Baldwin thinks it might have been Jennie Miller."

"That's not very funny. It's not very chivalrous to treat a woman like that."

"No, but it seems that the result was her choosing to leave, so it had a good outcome. It seems to have made quite a stir in the area. Anyway, he goes on to say that there's a widow over at Crediton that Peter Clifford is trying to get Baldwin interested in, who appears to be very suitable."

"How suitable? Do stop grinning like that!"

"She is known to be generous with her alms and supports Peter's little hospital, so she seems quite sensible and kindly."

"And?"

"And she's older than Baldwin, uglier than his mastiff, and he's begging us to invite him here for a holiday to escape her clutches as soon as possible!"

"Tell him I look forward to seeing him soon," Margaret sighed. "It'll be good to see him again. But tell him to come here in the summer. It's too cold in the winter! Oh, and ask him if he wants to bring this lady with him. After all, he might find things very boring here otherwise!"

Dark mayhem and foul murder in the Middle Ages—

THE KNIGHTS TEMPLAR MYSTERIES BY

MICHAEL JECKS

> *They were warrior monks dedicated to the protection*
> *of pilgrims in the Holy Land—until stories spread by*
> *an avaricious king destroyed the order.*
> *There was one knight, however, who escaped the stake,*
> *vowing justice as he watched his innocent brothers die.*

THE LAST TEMPLAR
0-06-076344-2 • $7.50 US

In the year 1316, Simon Puttock, bailiff of Lydford Castle is called to a nearby village to examine a burned-out cottage and the dead body within. But it is the newly arrived knight, Sir Baldwin Furnshill who discerns the deceased was, in fact, murdered prior to the blaze.

THE MERCHANT'S PARTNER
0-06-076346-9 • $7.50 US

When the mutilated body of a midwife and healer is discovered, a frightened local youth is suspected. But Sir Baldwin Furnshill, once a Knight Templar, has doubts about the boy's guilt and enlists his friend Simon Puttock in the hunt for a murderer.

A MOORLAND HANGING
0-06-076347-7 • $7.50 US

Cold-blooded murder has transformed Simon Puttock's official obligation into something horrid—and he will need the able assistance of his friend Sir Baldwin Furnshill to draw a criminal out, even if their search exposes extortion, foul corruption and killers eager to shed still more blood.

Available wherever books are sold
or please call 1-800-331-3761 to order.

AuthorTracker
www.AuthorTracker.com

MJ 0105

Coming soon!

Eye of the Needle: For the first time in trade paperback, comes one of legendary suspense author Ken Follett's most compelling classics.
0-06-074815-X • On Sale January 2005

More Than They Could Chew: Rob Roberge tells the story of Nick Ray, a man whose addictions (alcohol, kinky sex, questionable friends) might only be cured by weaning him from oxygen.
0-06-074280-1 • On Sale February 2005

Men from Boys: A short story collection featuring some of the true masters of crime fiction, including Dennis Lehane, Lawrence Block, and Michael Connelly. These stories examine what it means to be a man amid cardsharks, revolvers, and shallow graves.
0-06-076285-3 • On Sale April 2005

Now Available:

Kinki Lullaby: The latest suspenseful, rapid-fire installment of Isaac Adamson's Billy Chaka series finds Billy in Osaka, investigating a murder and the career of a young puppetry prodigy.   0-06-051624-0

First Cut: Award-winning author Peter Robinson probes the darkest regions of the human mind and soul in this clever, twisting tale of crime and revenge.   0-06-073535-X

Night Visions: A young lawyer's shocking dreams become terribly real in this chilling, beautifully written debut thriller by Thomas Fahy.   0-06-059462-4

Get Shorty: Elmore Leonard takes a mobster to Hollywood—where the women are gorgeous, the men are corrupt, and making it big isn't all that different from making your bones.   0-06-077709-5

Be Cool: Elmore Leonard takes Chili Palmer into the world of rock stars, pop divas, and hip-hop gangsters—all the stuff that makes big box office.
0-06-077706-0

Available wherever books are sold, or call 1-800-331-3761.

Don't miss the next book by your favorite author.
Sign up now for AuthorTracker by visiting
www.AuthorTracker.com

PERENNIAL

An Imprint of HarperCollinsPublishers
www.harpercollins.com

DKA 1104

"A fabulous new voice."
New York Times bestselling author Cindy Gerard

"Her novels are twenty-first-century *noir* with guts and heart and a wicked sense of humor."
Jonathan Maberry, multiple Bram Stoker Award-winning author of *Patient Zero*

"Dane's smooth style, believable characters, and intense pacing will remind readers of Lisa Jackson, Lisa Gardner, and Tami Hoag. . . . Her tight plotting and male characters are exceptional, bad guys and good."
Publishers Weekly

"Jordan Dane will make you think twice before you ever walk alone in the dark again."
Robin Burcell, award-winning author of *The Bone Chamber*

"Thrills and chills that blend beautifully with human pathos and emotions. A wonderful author who sets you up on a roller coaster, rising, falling, twisting."
New York Times bestselling author Heather Graham

"Jordan Dane will wring your emotions dry as she takes you on a wild ride . . ."
USA Today bestselling author Merline Lovelace

"Non-stop action, hold-your-breath suspense, terrific characters . . . what more could you ask? I cannot wait to have the next Jordan Dane in my hot little hands."
Mariah Stewart

By Jordan Dane

RECKONING FOR THE DEAD
THE ECHO OF VIOLENCE
THE WRONG SIDE OF DEAD
EVIL WITHOUT A FACE
NO ONE LIVES FOREVER
NO ONE LEFT TO TELL
NO ONE HEARD HER SCREAM

ATTENTION: ORGANIZATIONS AND CORPORATIONS
Most Harper paperbacks are available at special quantity discounts for bulk purchases for sales promotions, premiums, or fund raising. For information, please call or write:

Special Markets Department, HarperCollins Publishers, 10 East 53rd Street, New York, New York 10022-5299. Telephone: (212) 207-7528.   Fax: (212) 207-7222.

JORDAN DANE

Reckoning for the Dead

A SWEET JUSTICE NOVEL

HARPER

An Imprint of HarperCollinsPublishers

This is a work of fiction. Names, characters, places, and incidents are products of the author's imagination or are used fictitiously and are not to be construed as real. Any resemblance to actual events, locales, organizations, or persons, living or dead, is entirely coincidental.

HARPER

An Imprint of HarperCollinsPublishers
10 East 53rd Street
New York, New York 10022-5299

Copyright © 2011 by Cosas Finas, LLC
ISBN 978-0-06-196969-0

All rights reserved. No part of this book may be used or reproduced in any manner whatsoever without written permission, except in the case of brief quotations embodied in critical articles and reviews. For information address Harper paperbacks, an Imprint of HarperCollins Publishers.

First Harper mass market printing: October 2011

HarperCollins ® and Harper ® are registered trademarks of Harper-Collins Publishers.

Printed in the United States of America

Visit Harper paperbacks on the World Wide Web at
www.harpercollins.com

10 9 8 7 6 5 4 3 2 1

If you purchased this book without a cover, you should be aware that this book is stolen property. It was reported as "unsold and destroyed" to the publisher, and neither the author nor the publisher has received any payment for this "stripped book."

To my uncles and aunts—
Loren, Beth, Larry, Joyce, and Lorena.
Laughter is like taking a vacation
without returning home ten pounds heavier.

ACKNOWLEDGMENTS

In this fourth book of the Sweet Justice series, I was influenced by the escalating violence along the United States/Mexican border. And after researching how the drug cartels work through the gangs on the U.S. side, I had to write a story to shed light on that. Covert operative Alexa Marlowe goes off the grid when her former lover and boss, Garrett Wheeler, goes missing under mysterious circumstances and is suddenly replaced by someone she doesn't trust. And when surprising DNA evidence surfaces on an old cold-case murder in Wisconsin, Jessie Beckett learns more about her already frightening past as her relationship with Seth Harper deepens. Will Jessie let Seth into her life enough to help her through the ordeal? I love writing about strong women and the men who love them. As a writer, it's my job to throw roadblocks in their way even though I feel bad when I do so. The characters in this series have become very dear friends. And I feel blessed to have them be a part of me.

And speaking of blessed, I'm fortunate to have friends and family who bring joy to my life. My dear husband constantly surprises me with the many ways he supports my work. And my parents have always nurtured each of their children in unique ways. I'm truly blessed to have them. And my weapons wizard, Joe Collins, is a real-life hero that I'm lucky to have as a friend.

Special thanks to my amazing editor, Lucia Macro. Your collaboration is remarkable. As always, you bring everything together and make it fun. And thanks to all the staff at Avon Books who played a part in this project, with special recognition to my agent, Meredith Bernstein. I'm so happy to have you in my life.

And finally I want to express my profound gratitude to my readers. I love hearing from you through my Web site at *www.JordanDane.com*. Except for the many voices I hear in my head, writing is a solitary activity, but finishing a book is only part of the equation. The most important part is for you to read the book and take a journey with me. You complete my creative circle, and I'm especially grateful for all of you who have been following this series and enjoying my books. The passion I feel for writing is made richer by your continued and cherished support.

Reckoning
for the Dead

CHAPTER 1

El Paso, Texas
Nearly midnight

After he'd sent a text message on his cell phone, twelve-year-old Ruben de los Santos did as he'd been ordered to do. He followed the man from a safe distance as he left the cantina, heading for his car. The parking lot was down two blocks and around a corner if the man stuck to the well-lit streets. If he knew of the shortcut, he would use the alley.

That was what Ruben prayed he would do.

When the stranger looked over his shoulder, Ruben ducked into the shadows of a doorway and waited until it was safe to move. With his heart racing, he counted to five before he emerged from the shadows. By the time he did, the man was gone.

"Ay, Dios mio," the boy muttered, with his eyes alert.

Ruben looked down the lit street and saw no sign of the man, but when he turned toward the alley, he caught a glimpse of movement. It had to be him.

He ducked into the alley and stepped up his pace to catch the man. When he got to the end of the alleyway, he stopped and held his breath. Slowly he inched closer to the corner and peered into the darkness.

That was when a hand grabbed his shirt collar and pulled him off his feet.

"Please . . . don't hurt me," he begged.

Ruben covered his face with his hands and raised his voice higher, sounding more like the boy he was.

"Why are you following me, kid?"

The tall, muscular man kept ahold of him. His body was cast in nothing more than a bluish haze. Ruben couldn't see his face. And although the boy felt the heat of the man's breath on his cheek, he tried not to be afraid.

Ruben de los Santos wasn't alone.

"You will see soon enough, *señor*." The boy forced a smile with courage he didn't feel.

The big man released his grip on Ruben and pulled away. He reached for his weapon, but it was too late. Members of Ruben's gang emerged from the shadows like ghosts rising from the grave. The stranger was surrounded.

"Who are you? And what do you want?" the man demanded. He aimed his weapon into the crowd, shifting his barrel from face to face. He was outnumbered and outgunned.

"Lower your weapon, *pendejo*. You will not be asked a second time." Arturo, one of the older boys, stepped forward and held his gun sideways, aiming between the man's eyes. Ruben held his breath, unable to take his eyes off the two men. If one of them fired, many would die. And Ruben had no doubt he would get caught in the cross fire.

The standoff continued, neither man backing down, until the one Ruben had trailed into the alley finally lowered his weapon. The boy let out a ragged breath and made a quick sign of the cross, but it wasn't over.

After they'd taken the man's weapon, every gang member of *Los Chupacabras* beat and kicked the stranger until he dropped to the asphalt.

After he was down, lying unconscious and bleeding on the ground, Ruben searched his pockets for his wallet. He pulled out the few hundred dollars he had in cash and gave it to Arturo, the boy in charge. And Ruben got a look at the man's driver's license and saw his name and where he lived.

"I'll need that." Arturo held out his hand. "Cash is ours, but his ID goes with me."

One of the other boys pulled a van into the alley. They loaded the wounded man into the back and carried out the rest of their orders. The man was to be taken across the Mexican border and delivered to someone linked to the Pérez cartel in Juárez. Ruben's gang in El Paso had powerful connections on the other side of the border, men who supplied them with drugs to sell. And in return, *Los Chupacabras* carried out execution-style killings, acted as drug mules, and bartered for weapons with their brother organization. That was why Ruben had taken the risk to follow an armed man into the alley.

He had passed his initiation. And the unconscious man in the back of the van had been his ticket in, but what the American from New York City had done to piss off the cartel and earn him a one-way trip across the border, Ruben didn't know.

And didn't care.

Outside Ciudad Juárez, Mexico
Three hours later

Ramon Guerrero's footsteps echoed as he walked the shadowy corridors of the rancho, guided by the meager light from flickering torches. The old hacienda belonged to his family, handed down through the generations. Although it had no electricity, and its only source of water was an old well on the property, it served its purpose by sheltering him and his men. It had been a good location to hide the many hostages who were held for ransom as a funding source for his drug operation. And being remote, the ranch enabled him to carry out the unsavory side of cartel business without anyone's knowing what went on behind its adobe walls.

An armed guard stood at the end of the long passage. The man had been slouched in a chair but now stood at attention as Guerrero approached.

In his native tongue, he asked the guard, "Has he admitted anything of value?"

The man only shook his head.

"Then it is my turn. Unlock the door," he ordered. The guard did as he was told.

A dark silhouette of a man was backlit by moonlight from the only barred window, with eerie shadows, cast from a single torch, undulating against the wall. The hostage had been stripped of his clothes. Completely naked, hanging from a metal bar, his body sagged from its own weight. Ropes cut into his wrists, and blood had run down his arms. Deep contusions were visible on his taut belly and rib cage, an aftermath of the beatings he had endured before and after he'd been delivered to the hacienda.

In the corner of the cell was a wooden bucket. Guerrero picked it up and threw dirty water at his prisoner.

"Ah." The man groaned and tried lifting his head, without much success.

"My name is Ramon," the drug lord said in English. "Your fate is in my hands."

"Go to . . . h-hell."

Guerrero grimaced at the prisoner's lack of respect.

"You will make it there well before me. I can assure you."

When Guerrero got close, he held his breath. The stench of blood and other distasteful smells made it hard to breathe. He grabbed the man's dark hair and yanked his head back. The prisoner's face was battered and bleeding. And one eye was swollen shut. Guerrero had allowed his men first crack at the hostage.

The man had brought unwanted interest. He'd been asking too many questions across the U.S. border in El Paso, calling attention to Guerrero's Juárez operation. After receiving reliable intel from a number of sources, Guerrero figured he had an edge to exploit that could expand his reach. He gave the order to take the man alive and deliver him, and any identification he had on him, to the rancho's gate. Perhaps the hostage would be Guerrero's way of gaining more power within the cartel.

Like many, Guerrero had ambitions. The hostage had crossed his path for a reason. His appearance could not merely be chalked up to good fortune. He preferred to think of the opportunity as his fate, his much-deserved due.

"I am surprised you took such a risk. Did you not think we would find out what you were doing in Texas? Did you think being across the border would protect you?" Guerrero walked around the naked man, taking in every old scar that marred his body. One scar in particular had caught his eye. No doubt, the man had seen his share of fights, but the prominent burn scar on his back had betrayed him. And, given what Guerrero already knew, he had enough to get what he wanted without the man's cooperation. It was one thing to have the man's ID but quite another to truly know who he was and what he did for a living.

"Surely someone of"—he paused for effect—"your stature would have others to take such risk."

The hostage flinched only for a second, but Guerrero was certain he'd seen a reaction.

"I don't know . . . w-what you're t-talking about."

"That doesn't matter. Not anymore." He leaned closer, and whispered, "You see, I know who you are . . . who you really are. And that will be enough to get me what I want."

"You don't know shit, Raymond."

"The name is Ramon." He gritted his teeth at the man's insolence. "And if you wanted your real identity to remain a secret, you should have removed that scar from your back."

The hostage glared at him but didn't say a word. Even beaten as he was, he mustered enough contempt to provoke Guerrero.

"Why are you pissing on my turf?" he pressed. "What did you hope to gain?"

The man did not hesitate. "I'm looking for a man . . . to kill him."

Guerrero stared at the hostage in disbelief at his gall before he burst into laughter. The sound echoed off the walls of the cell—a foreign noise in a place where screams were more common.

"And how is that going for you?" Without waiting for an answer, he shook his head, and said, "You Americans have such arrogance, but we shall see how long that lasts."

Under his belt at the small of his back, Guerrero pulled out a black hood and covered his prisoner's head. The hostage jerked and fought it, but he didn't say anything. The American didn't have the good sense to cower. He held his head up, and the black cloth moved with every breath of his defiance. When Guerrero pictured the smug look on his face under the hood, he balled his fists to make his point about who was in charge.

In the stifling heat, he punched the hostage in the gut. *Once. Twice.* The prisoner clenched his stomach muscles and took the blows without uttering a sound, withstanding the abuse in silence.

"We shall s-see"—Ramon panted—"h-how strong . . . you are."

It took all his willpower to lower his hands. He stopped the beating only because he had a call to make. "Th-there are far worse . . . things to endure."

When he had first communicated his part in the capture of such an influential American, his cartel boss had sent word promptly. He had ordered him to make a journey to a rendezvous point, bringing the prisoner with him. Guerrero would make a gift of the American and, hopefully, reap rewards for his efforts.

Gasping and winded, he walked across the cell and spoke to the guard on the other side of the door. In minutes, his man returned and, between the bars, handed him a loaded syringe. With a smirk on his face, Guerrero shoved the hostage's head to one side and injected the needle into his neck. The man struggled, making a futile attempt to fight back. As his prisoner fought the drug, Guerrero hit speed dial on his cell phone and contacted the man he hoped would be very grateful . . . and generous.

As he listened to the phone ring in his ear—waiting to report he'd confirmed ID and give the details of how he would transport the prisoner—Guerrero wasn't done tormenting his hostage. Before the man drifted into a merciful oblivion, he leaned closer and whispered in his ear.

"Your name is Garrett Wheeler." He spat on the man's bare chest. "And I know who you work for, *cabrón*."

"I'm picking up a cell-phone signal from inside the walls of the residence outside Juárez. No ID on the caller, but I can track the GPS signal. If the guy with the cell moves, I'll know it." The handler for the mission had made contact with the man who had ultimate control over the op. From an encrypted international phone, he spoke to him now, nothing more than a voice on the other end of the line.

"Did we get a visual? Do they have the hostage inside?"

"Yes. We got a visual confirmation from team two."

After the hostage had been taken by a group of young thugs known as *Los Chupacabras* in El Paso, surveillance tracked the movement of the van the gang had used to cross the border into Mexico. Once they left U.S. soil, the handler rotated surveillance teams, so they wouldn't lose their target.

"Your order, sir?" the handler asked.

"Make contact with team one in Juárez. Tell them you have a signal you're following. It's their backup plan, in case something goes wrong on their end. If that GPS signal moves, I want eyes on it. Keep me informed."

"Copy that."

Short and sweet, the man taking the lead on the operation gave his orders and ended the call. The handler's part in the mission had ramped up. He made his call to team one and followed orders.

New York City
Before dawn

Dressed in gray slacks and black cashmere sweater, Alexa Marlowe stared out her apartment window, located on the third floor of a brownstone on the Upper East Side. For the last week, she'd been restless, and sleep hadn't come easy. In her line of work, that was a hazard of the trade, but she had another reason to worry. And after getting a call from Tanya Spencer yesterday, arranging for an early-morning meet at Alexa's place, she wondered if the Sentinels' analyst had been losing sleep for the same reason.

When she heard the soft knock on her door, she rushed to answer it.

"Good morning, Tanya." She forced a smile. "Please . . . come in."

"Thanks for accommodating my crazy schedule."

Even before dawn, the woman was impeccably dressed, in a navy Burberry blazer and a pencil skirt. Her black skin looked radiant, with only a hint of the flawless makeup she wore. And her Southern drawl could melt butter. That voice had calmed Alexa on many covert-ops missions when she had needed analytical support . . . and a friend.

"Sorry to get you up this early, but I thought we should talk somewhere away from headquarters. And your place was on my way to work."

"No trouble. Can I get you coffee?" Alexa asked.

"Yes, please."

Alexa already had a pot made and served Tanya a cup before they sat in the living room.

Being a covert agent, Alexa viewed the world differently from most people. She looked for ulterior motives and conspiracies under every rock. It was how her brain worked, out of necessity. Her survival sometimes depended on it. And since Tanya Spencer had a similar background—

having worked many years with the privately funded Sentinels and served as Garrett Wheeler's right hand for the last decade—Alexa figured the woman's cryptic words meant she was only playing it safe.

"So tell me what's on your mind, Tanya?"

"I'm not sure if I should be saying this, but . . ." the woman began. " . . . I haven't heard from Garrett in almost ten days. And that's not like him." When Alexa didn't act surprised, Tanya said, "What's going on? Do you know anything about this?"

"No, I don't." Alexa shook her head and heaved a sigh. "But I've noticed the same thing. I thought it was me. After I broke it off with him, our relationship changed. It had to, but I haven't heard from him either. And that's got me losing sleep."

Tanya was one of the few people within the Sentinels who knew about Alexa's personal relationship with her boss, Garrett. She considered the woman a trusted friend.

"Isn't anyone else concerned about this?" Alexa narrowed her eyes. "He's head of our organization. What's he been working on?"

Tanya had been Garrett's senior analyst and advisor for the last ten years. She usually kept close tabs on him. And he trusted her with every aspect of what he did. They were a team.

"That's just it. I don't know." The woman shook her head and put down her coffee. "And it's got me worried sick. He's never done this, Alexa. He's always involved me with anything he touched. That's why I wanted to talk here, at your place. Something's been going on, and I've been cut out of the loop. The people Garrett answers to, they have to know something, but they're not clueing me in."

"So who's in charge with Garrett gone? I've never seen him work with anyone in particular who could step into his shoes."

"Yeah, I haven't either, not with the secrecy above his level. But this can't go on forever. If Garrett is AWOL, someone's got to assume his duties."

"You have any idea who?"

Tanya only shook her head. She was normally unflappable, but seeing the grimace on her face told Alexa all she needed to know about how concerned the woman was.

"We'd have to be careful looking into this. We could blow his op and put him in danger if we barge in without knowing what's going on."

"Does that mean you and Jessie will be looking into this?" Tanya asked. "I've tried tracking Garrett, but I've got nothing. Maybe if we trace other movements within the organization, we'll have better luck."

Tanya was right. If Garrett was involved in a covert op that excluded his top analyst and his most trusted agent, it had to be really big. But that also meant the Sentinels' resources would be dedicated to the operation. And if Alexa could hand-pick someone to dig through the veiled secrecy of the Sentinels—an organization of international vigilantes who operated off the global grid to dole out their brand of justice—she would have Tanya Spencer at the top of her list. The woman had connections in and out of the organization. And with her internal-systems knowledge, she could slip through virtual back doors without anyone's noticing.

"I'm meeting Jessie later for breakfast. She's pretty new to how things work within the Sentinels, but we'll see." Alexa sat back on her sofa and crossed her arms. "If we do this, we'd need your help."

Tanya nodded, and said, "Count on it."

Alexa knew that what she was planning on doing—using the organization's resources to trace a covert operation involving her boss and former lover—would not be a sensible thing to do. It could turn into a career ender, at best. Or a death sentence, at worst. And to involve her new partner, Jessie, would not be wise either—especially for Beckett's sake.

Relying on her gut instinct, she'd have to make that call when she talked to Jessie. If she read anything in her that raised a red flag, she'd let it slide and go it alone with Tanya. But one way or another, she'd take the risk for Garrett—because he would do the same for her.

New York's Lower East Side

The ringing of a phone early in the morning was never a good thing.

Jessie Beckett pulled the bedcovers off her face and fumbled for the light switch. And after she flicked on her lamp, she squinted at the alarm clock on her nightstand.

"Six twenty? Who the hell—" She winced and grabbed the cell phone off her nightstand and flipped it open without looking at the caller's number. "You better have a damned good reason for breaking into my beauty sleep."

The sun had barely made an appearance. And that meant she didn't give a rip about winning Miss Congeniality.

"Jessie? It's Sam."

She recognized the voice of her best friend. Samantha Cooper was a vice cop in Chicago. And she had better sense than to call her at this hour if it wasn't important.

"Sam? What's up? Is Seth all right?"

Her worry barometer worked double time when it came to Seth Harper, a guy who had nestled into her heart and made a home. The whacked-out computer genius had a habit of getting into trouble, and not only because he knew her. The boy had a serious way of attracting it on his own. And with his recent recruitment into the Sentinels for his mad skills with a keyboard—the same organization Jessie worked for—Seth had more than doubled his gift for luring trouble.

"No, Seth is fine, I guess. I haven't seen him lately, but I was calling you about . . . something else."

"Oh?"

Her friend cleared her throat and stalled. And that wasn't like her.

"Spit it out, Sammie."

"Chicago PD received a bulletin from a police chief in La Pointe, Wisconsin."

"Where the hell is that?"

"It's at the northern tip of Wisconsin. On Madeline Island in Lake Superior, to be exact. I looked it up on a map."

"Thanks for the geography lesson." Jessie ran a hand through her dark hair. "Explain why I should care about this?"

Sam cleared her throat again. Definitely stalling.

"You should care because the police there are working an old cold case. A pretty gruesome murder that happened over twenty years ago."

"Twenty years. We were both kids back then. Why are you calling me about this, Sam?"

Jessie didn't like where this was headed. Twenty years ago, she was a kid in the hands of notorious pedophile, Danny Ray Millstone. At least, that was what she believed. She had been too young to really know the truth about how she ended up with him—or maybe she'd blocked it out. And insult to injury, after she was rescued by Detective Max Jenkins of the Chicago PD, no one from her family stepped up to claim her. Not even the national media coverage afterward shed light on what had happened to her. That aspect of her past had remained a black hole. And she'd given up trying to find where she'd come from.

Looking into the details of her childhood nightmare had always been too painful.

"Yeah, well, back then DNA wasn't used to solve crimes like it is now," Sam said. "But an old case caught the eye of this local police chief. And he sent in evidence he had stored in archives to the state crime lab. When the lab ran its findings against the CODIS and NCIC databases, the chief told me he got a hit on DNA evidence—and his first new lead in over twenty years."

Jessie's mind worked double time, thinking how a DNA test would link to her. The FBI maintained both the Combined DNA Index System and the National Crime Information Center. The first held DNA profiles in a database, while the other was a repository for specific criminal records on known fugitives, missing persons, stolen property, and other details. Such database information was available to state and federal law-enforcement types and was meant to be shared across jurisdictions. Since she'd been a missing person as a child, her gut twisted with the implications of where Sam might be going with this.

"He got a hit . . . on what?"

"Since you were a missing kid, your DNA is on record, Jess. The Wisconsin crime lab got a hit on your DNA. It puts you at that crime scene over twenty years ago."

"What?" Jessie grimaced. "I don't understand."

"I didn't either. That's why I put in a request for that DNA report. I could have our crime-lab boys take a look at it, decipher what it means. When I get it, I'll let you know."

"That's great . . . I think."

"I also called that local LEO in La Pointe. His name is Tobias Cook. I only asked questions and didn't tell him anything. I wanted to talk to you first," Sam told her. "According to him, that DNA hit on you was a dead-on match. Unless there's a serious mistake, it looks like you're connected to that murder somehow, but that's not all."

"Oh, great. The hits keep coming."

"Chief Cook was asking about your mother. He's looked into your story, Jess. He knows about Millstone and what happened to you as a kid. He asked why no one ever came forward and claimed you after the rescue."

"What did you say?"

"I told him I didn't know anything about that. And he'd have to talk to you about it."

"You did good, Sammie. Thanks." Jessie swallowed hard. "Did he say why he was asking about my mother?"

Hearing the word "mother" always flashed her back to a haunting memory that had been with her since she was a little girl. She remembered a sunny day with fall colors and a woman's smiling face. She held those images close to her heart, of a woman playing with her in a park. She must have been someone very special because the memories always made Jessie happy. Although she still couldn't be sure the woman in her dreams was really her mother, Jessie needed to believe she'd once had someone who loved her like that.

She'd always fantasized that if she saw the woman again, she'd know it. Something in her eyes would give it away. At least, she'd always hoped that would be true.

"The chief only told me that he was running down leads, something about kids being seen at the house where the murder took place."

"Was the murdered woman . . . my mother? I mean, did my DNA match . . . hers?"

She ached with the thought that her mother might have been dead all these years. And the very thing she'd longed for was never going to happen.

"Sorry. He didn't tell me anything more about his case. Believe me, I asked, but he got a call and had to jump. That's why I wanted to see that DNA analysis myself. I swear, Jess. The minute I get that report, I'll call you. Promise."

"Yeah, thanks."

"We don't know if your mother was there at all. Without a peek at the DNA report, there's no sense buying into more trouble. Even if she was there, she could have been a witness."

"Or a suspect."

Jessie had a hard time thinking about her mother after all these years, but she had an even tougher time considering what dark scenarios had put her at that crime scene.

"Don't go there, Jessie."

"Either way, I don't see a family reunion in my future. My luck doesn't work that way."

"You're still breathing, aren't you? I'd say your luck is better than most." Sam heaved a sigh. "Besides, if your mother had been connected in some way to a murder, that would explain why she never came forward after you were rescued."

What Sam said made sense. It had always pained her that no one had claimed her after her ordeal with Millstone, especially with all the national media coverage. Given the scant memories she had of a woman she believed to be her mother—a child's wishful thinking—Jessie didn't want to even think about the woman's being involved in a killing. The life she led before Millstone had been a black hole so far, but maybe this local cop could fill in the gaps. Jessie would have no way of knowing anything for sure unless she contacted him.

"So now what?" Sam asked. "People here at CPD know we have a connection. They're letting me handle this bulletin request for information, but I can't stall them."

"No, and I don't expect you to." Jessie chewed the inside corner of her lip. "Give me the 4-1-1 on this chief dude."

Sam gave her the man's name and phone number.

"Chief Cook asked you to call him. He thinks he can clear things up over the phone."

"Not good enough. Not for me."

"What are you saying?"

"I'm flying to Chicago as soon as I can arrange a flight, Sam. I'll call you when I get there."

"You want me to pick you up at O'Hare?"

"No . . . I'll get Harper to do that. But I'll call when I get a chance, okay?"

"So what are you going to do?"

"I'm driving to La Pointe. You can tell Chief Cook that I'll see him face-to-face late tomorrow. I gotta know what evidence he's got on that case. And if there's a connection to my mother, or a reason why I ended up with Millstone, I have to know."

"Look, Jess. I know this is hard for you, but if you need to talk, call me."

"Thanks, I will."

Her past never went away. For the first time in her life, Jessie had a future and prospects, working for the Sentinels. She wasn't just a bounty hunter drifting from case to case, living in a crappy apartment on the fringe of society in Chicago. And since Seth Harper had nudged his way into her life, she also felt good about herself. He had known about her past and accepted her. The scars she carried on her body and on her soul weren't an issue with a guy like Harper.

So why now? Why did this damned cold case in Wisconsin have to bite her in the ass now?

It scared her to think that her only memory of someone who could be her mother might have been wrong. Was she ready to kill the only good thing she remembered of her past?

"I can never catch a damned break," she muttered as she got out of bed.

Dressed in a tank top and boxers, Jessie trudged into her living room and logged onto her laptop to look for a flight to Chicago. She had breakfast plans with Alexa Marlowe that she could still make on her way to LaGuardia. Her new partner would need to know that she was leaving town, but Alexa didn't need to know everything.

Very few people knew the details about the nightmare of her childhood ordeal, and she preferred to keep it that way.

Two hours later

Norma's Restaurant in Midtown West was packed. Bright and bustling, the place had high ceilings, wood paneling, and faux-silver-edged tables that gave a modern yet comfortable feel. It was a popular café for breakfast and lunch, located in the Le Parker Meridien Hotel lobby. Norma's was too expensive and trendy for Jessie's taste, but Alexa knew her partner had suggested it for her sake. Being a former bounty hunter, Jessie had dealt with the dregs of humanity and would have been satisfied with any hole-in-the-wall greasy spoon.

When Alexa arrived, she noticed that Jessie had gotten there early and scored a table, a small carafe of coffee, and two shot glasses of the restaurant's complimentary smoothie du jour. After her partner waved her over, it didn't take Alexa long to notice the carry-on luggage under the table.

"Planning on staying the week? The blueberry pancakes are good, but come on," she joked to cover up her surprise . . . and disappointment.

"I'm on my way to the airport, heading for Chicago. Something personal has come up." Dressed in a T-shirt and jeans, Jessie leaned across the table. "I know this is short notice, but I don't have a choice."

Alexa narrowed her eyes and dropped her smile. "Anything I can do?"

"No, nothing." Jessie shook her head. "I've got it covered."

Jessie had hesitated, enough to tell Alexa her trip to Chicago wouldn't be for pleasure.

"And I'm guessing you probably don't want to talk about it."

"Bingo." Jessie grabbed her coffee cup and hid behind it.

Her partner was a woman with secrets, and Alexa respected her privacy. The scar over Jessie's eyebrow had a story behind it, one Alexa had never been privileged to hear. Even though not too long ago, Alexa had gotten a glimpse into something Jessie had barely survived as a child, her partner had never confided in her, and she hadn't pushed.

And Alexa also guessed that Jessie had feelings for the computer genius, Seth Harper. Maybe her trip had something to do with him. The guy was a new recruit for the Sentinels, but he'd opted to stay in Chicago rather than move to New York, so he could stick close to his mentally deteriorating father, who lived in a nursing home. Those had been her first thoughts about Jessie's trip; but with her partner, she might never know for sure.

"How long will you be gone?" she asked. "I mean, in case something comes up."

"Maybe a few days. Not long."

"Okay." She nodded. "Will you call me if you need anything?"

"Yeah . . . I'll do that. So what's good here?" When Jessie flipped open her menu, her eyes grew wide. "Oh, my God! They have a lobster-and-caviar omelet for a thousand smackers. Who the hell are they kidding? That's just . . . insane."

As fast as Jessie stuck her nose in the menu and changed the subject, Alexa knew her partner would never take her up on her offer. Jessie had a tough, independent streak. It was one of the things she liked most about her, but sometimes that made it hard for anyone to get inside. As a partner and a friend, Jessie was an acquired taste.

But with Jessie going out of town—completely distracted by her personal agenda—Alexa knew she'd be working with Tanya alone. Once her partner got back and could focus, Alexa might ask for her help, but for now, Jessie was out of it. And there was no sense telling her anything about Garrett. Jessie had enough going on in her life without adding the guilt trip of leaving her in the lurch—because that was exactly how Jessie's mind worked. She'd feel guilty over something she'd have no control over.

As if she'd read Alexa's mind, Jessie looked up from her menu, and said, "You look tired. You getting enough z's?"

Alexa ran a hand through her blond hair and heaved a sigh as she propped her elbows on the table.

"I'd be doing better if you'd dose me up." She forced a smile as she shoved over her empty cup. "Pour me some coffee, will ya?"

While her partner filled her cup, Alexa turned her thoughts to Garrett. Something was terribly wrong. As an experienced operative, she sensed it in her bones, especially after talking to Tanya and hearing that Garrett's top analyst hadn't heard from him either. That clinched it. She had to do something.

When they were together, Garrett had been an attentive and aggressive lover and quickly become her obsession after she'd come off the high of her near miss with fellow operative Jackson Kinkaid. Her one-sided feelings for Jackson had been tough to let go. They had chemistry, no doubt, but she needed more than he had to give. And, after working with him on a hostage-rescue mission in Cuba not too long ago, the emotional roller-coaster ride with him had not changed for her. She still had it bad, especially after Jackson told her why he'd kept her at a distance.

There had been another woman. A dead one.

Jackson was still deeply connected to his murdered wife and the child he had lost. He had nothing to give her, or anyone. He'd changed. He wasn't the same man she had known years before. It broke her heart to walk away from him after the Cuban op, but she had to. Forcing Jackson to deal with his grief before he was ready to let go wouldn't have been good. He would always resent her for it. And that was no way to live, for either of them.

After she'd first met Kinkaid years before, Garrett had been a rebound fling for her, but he'd been a distraction she needed at the time. He had unleashed her insatiable need and been a much-needed diversion after the pent-up feelings she had for Jackson. And even though the urgent passion she had with her boss, Garrett Wheeler, had run its course, she still cared for him deeply. She owed him more than her unflinching loyalty.

Where are you, Garrett?

Somewhere in Mexico

"Is it . . ."

"Is it . . ."

" . . . him?"

A woman's voice echoed in his head and filtered through the fog in his brain. Her words overlapped like undulating ripples across still water, mixed with the faint distant echo of a child's laughter. The sounds nudged his faltering consciousness or tapped into a sliver of memory. He didn't know which, nor did he care. He had to concentrate to hear anything at all. He didn't know where he was or how he got there. In this place, he had no past, no future, and barely remembered his own name. Yet in his shadowy existence, he felt certain that he was completely deserving of whatever fate had in store.

When he felt a cool velvet touch on his fevered

cheek, he heard a moan, unsure if the sound came
from him. He forced his eyes open a crack and
caught a glimpse of light. Shadows eclipsed a dim
glow, but he was too weak to move. With the drug
still so strong in his system, he wavered on the razor's edge of darkness and took the only comfort
he could. He imagined the woman's voice he had
heard morphing into a more familiar sultry one
and pictured running his fingers through a soft
tumble of blond strands as he gazed into pale blue
eyes.

His lover's throaty voice stirred him, and her
haunting eyes lingered, along with a trace of her
perfume. He felt her kiss and her whisper in his
ear as she trailed a finger down the bare skin of
his chest and onto his stomach. Her touch made
him flinch, and his body reacted.

He wanted her. He needed her. And when he
willed the beautiful woman to stay—*she did*.

CHAPTER 2

New York City

After breakfast, Alexa arrived at the Sentinels' headquarters and went through the high-tech security measures to access the elevator that would take her to the belowground stronghold. Running on autopilot, she had her mind on Garrett as she headed for Tanya's office and walked through the massive computer area, where analysts manned global surveillance systems.

Black walls encircled the room, and the overhead lights were purposefully dim, so computer jockeys could better see the array of colors on their monitors. And with the tight acoustics in the room, the cavernous space had the feel of a planetarium.

With Jessie out of town, Alexa would be working alone with Tanya to dig into Garrett's whereabouts. Following the physical and electronic trail to find him would be tricky. Any search would cover sensitive information and involve tapping into restricted resources within the organization, something she'd be willing to chance if it meant finding him.

Plenty depended on her trust in Tanya's instincts and her own when it came to Garrett. And her experiences with the man and his covert organization told her their search should be low-key until they dug up something more substantial to go on.

When she got to Tanya's office, the door was open. She strode into the room but stopped when she saw that her friend wasn't alone.

"I'm sorry." Alexa stopped in the doorway and turned on her heels, heading out. "I'll come back later."

"No, please. Come in, Marlowe." A deep masculine voice called after her. "I was just leaving."

Alexa turned in surprise when she heard her name coming from the stranger. She narrowed her eyes and looked at the man. And from what she could see, Tanya appeared stressed. The analyst made eye contact and tried to communicate something Alexa couldn't read . . . yet. But knowing Tanya, that wouldn't take long.

"Have we met?" She stepped back into the office and closed the gap between her and a tall man dressed in an impeccable charcoal gray suit. "How do you know my name?"

"Your dossier." He flashed a slick smile and extended his hand. "Quite impressive. My name is Donovan Cross. I'm an old friend of Garrett's."

Alexa took his hand and fixed her eyes on him. Few people in the world knew her real credentials. Once she'd become a member of the Sentinels, her background had been sanitized or erased. If this man had seen her dossier, he had to be part of the organization—and a high-ranking agent at that. Yet this was the first time she'd heard his name or crossed his path. And she hated being at a disadvantage.

"Funny. He's never mentioned you. Why are you here, Mr. Cross?" She shifted her gaze toward Tanya, who only raised an eyebrow. When the analyst allowed it, her face could be an open book. And just then, she made for an easy read. Something about this man annoyed her.

"Please . . . call me Donovan. And as for why I'm here, Tanya can fill you in. I'm sure you'll have plenty to talk about once I leave. Good day, Marlowe."

Cross had an arrogant swagger, and he moved with the confidence of a man who had been in the business for a long time although he didn't look to be older than his mid-to-late thirties. In some ways, Donovan Cross reminded her of Garrett.

He had short dark hair and the same keen intense

eyes that took in everything, except that Cross's eyes were hazel, not the steel gray of Garrett's. He was tall and athletic-looking. And although he had the same taste for expensive clothing, he had a rougher edge than Garrett. His face told her that. He'd seen a fight or two and broken his nose more than once. He wasn't classically handsome, but any woman would notice him in a crowd.

"What was that all about?" she asked Tanya, after Cross left.

"I'm sorry I didn't have time to tell you. I only got the official word an hour ago, direct from Mount Olympus. And that's when he walked in, complete with access codes and security clearance."

Without Garrett at the helm, they had no one above his level to trust. Tanya was the only one who had communicated with the upper echelon, but she'd never met anyone face-to-face. Alexa didn't like what was happening. And maybe a small part of her knew what Tanya would say next.

"He's Garrett's replacement, Alexa. And I'm not sure it's temporary."

Chicago
Afternoon

Once Jessie exited the secured area at Chicago's O'Hare airport, she looked through the sea of expectant faces of those waiting for friends and family coming off flights. She searched the crowd for tall, lanky Seth Harper, a guy who wore his hair a little long in soft dark waves and had honey brown eyes that made her weak in the knees. His boyish good looks had always captivated her.

Jessie peered at dozens of faces, looking for him. When she didn't see him anywhere, she felt a twinge of disappointment. She couldn't believe how eager she was to see him. And, completely unlike her, she had primped on the plane and made sure her breath smelled minty fresh, behaving like such a . . . girl.

In her haste to leave New York, she'd only given Seth her flight number and arrival time, resorting to text messages after they'd played phone tag. And she'd told him if they missed each other—which would have been easy at the massive airport—that she'd see him on the curb outside baggage claim.

With airport security these days, it was easier to make arrangements to meet on the arrival ramp although a part of her had hoped he'd surprise her by showing up inside the terminal.

She hoisted her overnight bag over her shoulder and followed her fellow passengers toward baggage claim, but as she rounded a corner beyond security, she saw Harper leaning against a column outside a gift shop. He had a big grin on his sweet face and was holding flowers.

The boy looked damned good.

Without a word, she walked toward him. When she got close, she dropped her bag at his feet and collapsed into his arms. He smelled good—like soap on warm skin—and he felt even better. And all she thought about was how good it felt to be home.

Harper was home.

"Oh . . . you feel so good," she whispered into his shoulder. "You have no idea."

Her ear tickled with the sound of the soft laughter muffled in his chest.

"Yeah, I've missed you, too."

He pulled back long enough to raise her chin with a finger and kiss her. Sweet tenderness heated to a slow burn. People walked by, and the noise of the airport faded. None of it stopped her from showing how much she loved him.

"I've got a new place. And I can't wait for you to see it," he said, as his kiss turned into a big hug. "I got a deal on it."

"Yeah, I hear you're connected." She grinned.

When she reached down for her bag, he had already grabbed it and put his arm around her as they walked through the busy airport, with her holding the flowers he had given her. On the surface, they looked like a damned Hallmark card; but given their pasts, they were the polar opposite of ordinary.

"Tony carved out a piece of real estate for me downtown, one of his renovation projects, but the beauty of it is—I actually own it, Jess. Guess that makes me an official adult."

Harper said that like it was a good thing.

"You've done it now. You've crossed the line, Harper. I'm not sure I can hang with someone like you. Too rich for my blood."

Tony Salvatore was a local business developer in town, head of the Pinnacle Real Estate Corporation, a major player in the real-estate market. And he'd been a good friend to Seth and his family.

"Don't worry. It hasn't gone to my head. I have a roommate. He needed a place to stay for a while." Harper stopped and reached into his jeans pocket. "I better give him a call now, let him know we're on our way."

Jessie stood with her mouth open as Seth hit speed dial and walked away. *Harper has a roommate?* He was the original lone wolf. When she had first met him, the guy lived off the grid. With his computer expertise, he'd wiped his background clean and avoided any way to trace him. And he lived out of luggage as he moved from place to place with Salvatore's vacant high-dollar real-estate ventures.

Keeping a low profile had been Harper's way of dealing with the strained relationship between him and his father, a former cop who suffered from a form of dementia, the aftermath of a job that had consumed him. Seth's actually putting down roots shocked her, but the whole roommate thing was really over the top. Way too normal for Harper.

Living in downtown Chicago was expensive. Giving him the benefit of the doubt, Jessie knew it made sense that Harper had someone to share the cost, even if it was only "for a while," whatever that meant.

But it was hard to deny she had been disappointed when he told her about his roommate. She had high hopes of spending real alone time with him. And Harper was excited about her coming to Chicago, too. She'd seen it in his eyes. Before she arrived, he'd loaded up her phone with text messages, telling her about his special plans for their time together.

She chalked it up to bad Karma. A dark, surreal cloud had followed her from New York, after Sam's phone call. And after seeing Harper, she didn't have the heart to blurt out the real reason she'd come. Eventually, she'd have to; but before she ruined everything by leaving town again, all she wanted was to enjoy his company.

When Seth rejoined her after calling his roomie, she took a deep breath and shook her head, trying to hide her disappointment in sharing her quirky computer genius with anyone else. He had connections in Chicago, and not all of them were wealthy land barons.

Harper was a magnet for anyone strange. His innocent charm had a lot to do with it. Like her, he knew more than his fair share of fringe dwellers. And curiosity had her wondering whom he trusted enough to share his place.

Harper led a weird life. He was a guy she still thought had a borderline aptitude for crime. His sense of right and wrong was squishy and . . . adaptable.

In a word, he was "perfect" for his new employer, the Sentinels. Garrett Wheeler, the head of the clandestine organization, had recruited him personally. And as for her, Harper was like a pistachio. She couldn't get enough of him.

Jessie narrowed her eyes. "Does your new roomie know what you do for a living?"

"Yeah, he's got a vague notion, but he doesn't hold it against me. Someone's got to work." He shrugged. "Besides, I trust him."

Typical Harper. And she wouldn't have him any other way.

Jessie rolled her eyes. "If you say so, Harper."

New York City
Sentinels' Headquarters

When Alexa Marlowe crossed the threshold of Donovan Cross's new accommodations—Garrett's office—he was expecting her to make an appearance. The tall, athletic blonde made a point not to make an appointment or call ahead. He knew he'd have to earn her respect, and that would be a difficult task. And if the woman had something on her mind, she would say it. Marlowe had a reputation for being anything but subtle.

Cross didn't bother to stand. He slouched in his chair behind the desk, staring at the woman who he knew would not be intimidated.

"Good, you saved me the trouble of sending for you." He forced a smile. "Your work is exceptional. I've been looking forward to meeting you, Marlowe."

"I wish I could say the same. All I've got is your word that you have a pedigree. You've seen my dossier. The least you could do is return the favor and show me yours." The striking woman stood in front of his desk with arms crossed, not bothering to sit.

"And if I say no, what then?"

"Then you would seem like a man with something to hide."

"Well, here's a novel concept. You could give me a chance. I assure you, I'll grow on you."

"Look, I just want to know what happened to Garrett. Is it true you're replacing him?"

"Yes. I follow orders, same as you."

"Where is he?"

Cross raised his eyebrow and didn't answer at first. He made her wait, until he finally said, "I can't say."

"Can't or won't?" She leaned across his desk and fixed her icy blue eyes on him. "Big difference."

Cross smirked and rocked in his chair.

"We work for a covert agency. Everything is on a need-to-know basis. Surely you understand how that works."

"I do, but surely you understand a man like Garrett doesn't just disappear, not without people asking questions."

From what he'd read of her file, a woman like Alexa Marlowe wouldn't let her questions go unanswered. She was stubborn. Her inquisitive nature and undaunted spirit made her a good agent. Cross knew he'd have to go beyond protocol to satisfy her. And what he had to do wouldn't be easy—for him or her.

"Sit down, Alexa." He softened his voice and gestured toward a chair. The woman begrudgingly complied and sat on the edge of her seat. Her eyes were fixed on him with a stern expression on her face. Cross took a deep breath before he said, "I hate to be the one to tell you this, but . . ."

"But what?" She clenched her jaw.

"Garrett is dead. He was killed on a covert mission." He swallowed and found it hard to look into her eyes. "I'm sorry. I know he was your friend."

She fought to stay in control.

"No, this can't . . ." She shook her head, and her eyes watered. "How?"

"I don't have the details. And there are things we may never know."

"What are you . . . s-saying?"

"I'm saying . . . that his mission was highly classified. And we may not even recover his body. Witnesses say he was killed in an explosion, Alexa. A bad one, but we've confirmed his DNA at the scene. I'm sorry."

Cross had delivered his message and waited for her reaction. With a trained operative, he'd only get a glimmer if he got any response at all. Alexa Marlowe stared at him for a long moment with only small flinches to her facial muscles. He knew she was deciding what to believe, but when she gritted her teeth and stood without another question, her move surprised him.

Without a word, she left his office.

It took all Alexa's strength for her to walk away from Donovan Cross when she wanted to scream. Screaming might wake her up from the living nightmare her life had suddenly become.

This couldn't be happening.

Numb, she shook her head as she closed the door behind her and headed down a hallway toward the elevators in a fog, not knowing where she was going. She wanted a stiff drink to dull her senses and slow the rush of emotions that crowded in on her, but her training and her loyalty to Garrett wouldn't allow it.

In all the operations she'd worked with Garrett, she found it hard to picture him dead . . . until now. He was such a resourcefully strong man who had lived through some amazing missions, many of those with her by his side.

Donovan Cross was another story. She didn't know him or trust him. Her first impressions of him weren't good. He was cagey and had a hard time answering a direct question, the opposite of Garrett.

But the biggest ache she felt was about Garrett

and the connection they shared. If he was dead, surely she would know.

Wouldn't she?

When he was alone, Donovan Cross picked up the phone and made a call. On the second ring, his call was answered by a familiar voice. Forgoing any customary greeting, he simply said, "I gave her the news, and she just left."

"Do you think she believed you?"

Cross leaned back in his chair and stared at the ceiling before he answered.

"Actually . . . I have no idea."

"Assign someone to tail her. If she finds out what's going on, she'll interfere, and we can't afford that. Not now."

"Agreed. And already done."

He ended the call and stared at the door Alexa had closed after leaving the room. The woman intrigued him. He suspected that she and Garrett had shared a special bond.

And he had no doubt Alexa Marlowe would be trouble.

Downtown Chicago

After Harper had parked his vehicle in underground resident parking, he showed Jessie to an elevator, and they rode up to his floor. His developer friend hadn't missed a trick. He'd built another urban retreat in the trendy heart of downtown Chicago, with a view of Lake Michigan and close to shops, restaurants, and bars.

"I hope you don't mind, but I made us dinner. Nothing fancy."

"You've never really cooked for me." She smiled. "You know I'm a sure thing, right?"

When Harper grinned, his face turned red. Blotches colored his cheeks as he ran a hand through his dark hair.

"I hope you like my place," he said. "I mean, it's not finished, you know. It's a work in progress."

"I think you've forgotten where I used to live. I'm sure your closet is bigger than my old dump. The trick is, always have low expectations, Harper. You'll never be disappointed."

Jessie found his shyness completely disarming. Innocent charisma came naturally for Harper. His physical beauty never ceased to amaze her, but he never seemed aware of his looks. And he never had to work at it. Harper was an original, always.

Driving from the airport, he had rambled about lots of stuff. He told her the latest on his dad. And he had funny stories about Tony Salvatore helping him find his new place. She'd never seen him so chatty, except when he talked about RAMs and gigabytes. In Harperworld, she usually needed subtitles, but not tonight.

His nonstop stream of consciousness meant only one thing. Harper was nervous.

When they got to his floor, Seth unlocked his front door. Still looking a little on edge, he let her walk in first. And her jaw dropped when she saw what he'd done.

"Oh, Seth. This is . . . beautiful," she gasped.

Harper had his place lit with white candles, flickering romance wherever she looked. And she smelled fresh flowers. He'd placed bundles of colorful lilies and roses throughout his loft. Wine had been poured. Music was playing softly in the background. And a silver tray of appetizers was on a bar near the kitchen.

Seth had staged everything.

"That call you made at the airport. Your roommate lit all these candles, didn't he? Either that, or you didn't pay your light bill."

"Someone else did it. My roommate isn't much of a romantic." He grinned. "So, you like it?"

"Like it? Harper, I love it." Jessie walked into the loft with her mouth open. "You did all this . . . for me?"

Everywhere she looked, he'd done something special. He'd enlarged photos of them in New York and placed them on shelves. And he'd framed striking black-and-white images of her favorite spots in Chicago and hung them on the walls, places she'd told him about. Even the music he had playing was more to her taste than his.

"Why not?" He shrugged with a smile. "You came all this way to be with me. I wanted your visit to be special."

The old Jessie would have beaten herself up with guilt. She hadn't come back to Chicago for Seth alone, not exactly. Even though she had missed Harper terribly since his trip to New York, she had another personal reason for coming, and she dreaded having to tell him. But the new Jessie fought the sting of tears and the lump in her throat, accepting Seth's beautiful gift.

No one had ever done something so thoughtful for her. And before she met Harper, she never thought she deserved to be happy. Her abused past had been a lifetime prison sentence, without the possibility of parole. But seeing herself through Seth's eyes had allowed her to hope things could change. Maybe it was okay to let someone good like him into her life.

Maybe she had a chance at being normal if she let it happen. Harper was a heaping helping of normal compared to *her* crazy standards.

"I want you to be happy." He wrapped his arms

around her and kissed her neck, as if he'd read her mind. "Actually . . . I was hoping that if you liked it, you might want to . . . move back to Chicago and live here with me. I've missed you, Jess."

She turned and looked him in the eye. Now his nervousness made sense. Seth had more on his mind than spending a few days with her.

"I've missed you, too, Harper." She heard the catch in her voice. "But I need to tell you—"

She wanted to explain the main reason why she'd come, but Harper stopped her. He touched a finger to her lips and pulled her close.

"You don't need to tell me anything. Not tonight. I just want us to be together. Keep things simple, you know?" He kissed her forehead. "I'm not pressuring you. Just promise me you'll think about it."

"I will. I promise." She nestled into his arms and breathed him in.

The truth was that she had thought a lot about moving back. She'd never gotten used to living in New York City. She was a Midwest girl, and Chicago felt more like home.

Until Harper came along, she'd never thought about putting down any real roots. Her old South Chicago apartment had been more of a self-inflicted wound. She never thought she deserved better, but Harper made her want . . . *more*.

"But if I move in, what will your roommate say?"

"Absolutely nothing. Beggars can't be choosers."

"So where is he?" she asked.

"I banished him for tonight. I wanted you all to myself." When he grinned, his cheeks colored pink. "You can meet him tomorrow."

Jess didn't have the heart to tell him she wanted to be on the road early. The trip to La Pointe, Wisconsin, would take most of the day. The police chief would be expecting her, but after seeing everything Seth had done, she kept that information to herself for a while longer. He'd asked to keep things simple, and she knew what he meant.

For one sweet night, no drama.

When morning came, she'd find a way to tell him. Harper would want to go with her, but this was one trip she had to take alone.

Mexico

Last night, Ramon Guerrero had awakened fifteen-year-old Estella Calderone in the middle of the night, the way he usually did lately. He took what he wanted like an animal, without saying a word.

When he was done, he forced her to get dressed and come with him, ignoring her questions. When they got outside his hacienda near Juárez, two cars were waiting in front with headlights blazing. And his men were nothing more than dark silhouettes, without faces.

"You ride with them." He waved a hand, barely looking at her. "Watch over the American in the back. He's your responsibility."

Guerrero gave his order and told her to ride in the van. That was the first time she had seen the wounded man.

"What's happening? Who is he?" she asked, but no one answered, not even Guerrero.

Estella was shoved inside the van and did as she was told. She would not be traveling with Guerrero. His car would follow at a safe distance behind the van. And she would be alone with two men she didn't know.

Now that it was hours later and nearly dusk, Estella had had plenty of time to think. She realized she was as much a prisoner as the American who lay unconscious at her feet in the back of the moving van. She stared down at the man with his hands tied behind his back, experiencing a strange envy.

One way or another, his incarceration would one day end. She could not say the same.

Her thoughts turned to Ramon Guerrero, the man who had owned her for the last two years.

He'd traded drugs for her. And her mother had been too strung out to say no.

At first, she had been glad to have a roof over her head and food in her belly. Guerrero had her clean his house, do his laundry, and cook for him and his men at his hacienda near Juárez.

But all that changed two weeks ago.

One night, Guerrero had staggered into her room without putting on the lights. He'd been drinking. She'd smelled it on his breath. He forced her to take off her clothes, and he hurt her, covering her mouth as she cried. After that, he didn't ask her to clean or cook for him.

She'd become his whore.

What she had done with him had been a sin. And now she was no more than a common criminal, too. If she got caught with the American, she'd spend the rest of her life in prison, blamed for what Guerrero had done. It would not matter to the authorities that she'd been ordered to take care of the wounded man and keep him quiet if he got delirious.

She'd been given a canteen of water and an old rag. Not knowing what else to do, she kept his lips moist and dabbed the wet rag on his forehead and neck to keep him cool in the sweltering heat. If the man died while in her care, she'd be accused of far worse than kidnapping.

Hot air swept into the open windows of the van and sucked in suffocating billows of dust, forcing her to squint and hold her breath. Every now and then, she gazed through the windshield and caught a glimpse of road signs, the only way she knew they were heading south, deeper into Mexico.

Estella made the sign of the cross and shut her eyes tight as her lips moved in prayer. She had her doubts that God listened to a whore, but it gave her comfort even if it was only for a moment.

"We'll stop for gas." One of the men turned and spoke to her in Spanish. "You stay put. If you have to pee, squat in the corner. And don't let anyone see you. Understand?"

The man's eyes trailed down to her breasts. She hated how he looked at her.

"What is your name?" he asked.

She gritted her teeth and took a deep breath before she answered him.

"Estella."

By the way the man stared, she wondered if there was another reason she'd been told to go with them—and taking care of the American had only been an excuse to distract her. She had a bad feeling that Guerrero had grown tired of her, and that meant only one thing. She was no longer just *his* whore. Maybe he'd promised her to these men.

"This one, she has a pretty mouth," the man said to the driver. When they both laughed, Estella crossed her arms and looked away.

That was when she saw that the American was awake.

One of his eyes was swollen shut, but with the other, he stared straight through to her soul.

Estella gasped.

Although she wanted to talk to him, she didn't dare. She waited until Guerrero's men stopped the car and got out at the gas station.

When she was alone with the injured man, she whispered in English, "Who are you?"

The man blinked and opened his mouth to speak, but nothing came out. She reached for the damp rag and held it out to him.

"This may hurt."

With a trembling hand, she dabbed his forehead with the rag and water trickled down the man's swollen cheek. The American winced as he stared at her, accusing her with the unrelenting glare from his good eye.

"I did not do this. I swear. I am a prisoner, like you."

Estella didn't know if he believed her. He let her touch him and cool his brow before he slowly closed his eyes again. Before he drifted to sleep, she leaned closer and brushed his damp hair off his face.

"If I can, I will stay with you, *señor*," she whispered, only loud enough for him to hear.

Estella didn't know why she had felt such a strong urge to comfort the man with a lie. If Guerrero was involved, the American was as good as dead, especially if he was being taken to Guerrero's powerful boss.

The American didn't stand a chance. And she knew exactly how that felt.

CHAPTER 3

Downtown Chicago
The next morning

Before she opened her eyes, Jessie couldn't help but nudge the corner of her lips into a faint smile as she remembered making sweet love to Seth Harper into the wee hours of the morning. Images of Harper in the shower, running his soapy hands over her body, melded into flashes of memory when they'd made love by candlelight in his bed under white sheets.

Harper had always been beautiful to her, but by candlelight, he was unforgettable. And her skin flushed hot with the thought of him inside her, the urgency of his body filling her need for him. He made her feel wanted and loved and . . . beautiful. In the dim glow of candles and seeing herself in his eyes, she could forget the scars on her body and the deeper wounds she carried in her heart.

Even now, with eyes shut, she sensed the gray of morning and moaned with pleasure as she rolled toward Harper, wrapped in his comforter. But when something wet and cold nudged her chin, she flinched and opened her eyes with a start.

"What the hell . . . ?" she blurted out, running a hand over her face to clear the cob webs.

"You know, in some states, you could get arrested for that." Harper's voice came from across the room.

If he was over there, then who was in the bed with her?

With eyes wide, Jess sat up and pulled the sheets over her naked body. And she found herself staring into the face of the ugliest dog she'd ever seen—a brown-and-black-striped, brindle-colored pit bull with a large square head marred with scars. Its muzzle and paws were white, and the tip of one bent ear was gone. The dog sprawled on her lap and cocked its head, whimpering. Its tiny dark eyes were dwarfed by the size of its huge, panting grin.

"Meet my roommate, Floyd." Harper grinned. "I know you're gonna find this hard to believe, but he's not just another pretty face."

Dressed only in worn jeans, Seth joined her on

the bed. His hair was damp from the shower, and he flopped down on the mattress. Not even his enticing aroma of citrus soap cut the smell of warm dog breath.

"Floyd?" she asked.

"Yep, that's it. No last name. Just Floyd." Harper ran a hand over the dog's head. "He adopted me."

"Lucky you."

Jess scratched behind the dog's ear. The pit bull moaned and leaned into her hand until it flopped onto the bed, chest up and legs flailing.

"He's easy," she said.

"Yeah, he takes after me." Harper brushed back a strand of hair from her eyes. "Have I mentioned how much I love having you here? I love it even more than my towel warmer."

"Thanks, I think." She did a double take. "Wait a minute. You have a towel warmer?"

He grinned. "Come on. I've got breakfast started. Hope you're hungry. I couldn't decide what to make, so I kinda got carried away."

"Ah, Seth. You didn't have to . . ."

"I know, but I wanted to."

She opened her mouth to tell him what was on her mind, about the trip she had planned to Wisconsin, but Seth's face was an open book, and he looked like he had something more to say.

"Listen, Jess. Tanya Spencer assigned me a new

project. Sounds pretty important to her, something below the radar. I'm expecting her call. I wanted to spend the day with you, just the two of us, but I may have to work, so I'm officially apologizing now."

"Well, get in line, Harper, 'cause when it comes to official apologies, I owe you a big one."

Seth ran a hand through his wavy damp hair and shrugged.

"Not before coffee. House rules." He got off the bed and headed toward the door, with Floyd close on his heels. "Come on. Get dressed, Jess. Sounds like we've got talking to do."

Before he left the room, she called out, "Hey, Harper. Have I told you how much I love you?"

When he turned, he flashed a crooked grin, and his cheeks blushed pink. "Not today, but feel free to make that up to me."

Jessie knew Seth would be disappointed that she couldn't stay, especially after he surprised her with his new place—a home he wanted to make with her. She wished things could have been different, too, but she couldn't stop thinking about the mother she never knew and a dark past that still haunted her.

Harper would want to help, but she knew that he'd respect her wishes. This trip was something she needed to do alone.

New York City

Alexa had stayed up all night, working her own contacts. She'd made countless phone calls and even worked local sources by hitting the streets and visiting old haunts of Garrett's. No one knew what he'd been working on before he vanished.

"Damn it, Garrett," she muttered as she checked her cell for messages.

She resisted the urge to stay angry at him. The bastard had always been secretive. It was his nature, but that made it hard for her to feel the intimacy she had always craved with him—a closeness he probably had never shared with anyone—not even with lovers.

Sipping Starbucks coffee that she'd grabbed on the go, she navigated the Upper East Side on foot, heading back to her home. It would be the first time since yesterday afternoon that she would cross her own threshold, but not before she talked to Tanya to see if the analyst had had any better luck in tracking Garrett.

After she hit speed dial, Tanya picked up on the second ring.

"Hey, Tanya, it's me. I suppose you heard?"

"Yeah, I heard what that man is sayin'."

Alexa heard the contempt in Tanya's voice, contempt meant for Donovan Cross. The Sentinels had replaced Garrett without causing a ripple on still water. It was business as usual, but not for her or Tanya, maybe others. Replacing Garrett would be hard, but she didn't trust Cross. Something about him left her wary. Call it gut instinct. And she had to admit, trusting anyone after the tight connection she had with Garrett would be next to impossible.

"Do you believe his story . . . about Garrett being dead?" she asked Tanya, resenting the doubt she heard in her own voice.

"Do you?" the woman shot back.

Before Alexa answered, her friend softened her tone.

"Look, I don't know what to believe, except that I want all this to go away. All I know is that if he's dead, I need proof. That's all I'm sayin'. Guess I don't trust that wannabe, Cross. Garrett Wheeler he ain't, honey."

Tanya's Southern drawl always intensified whenever her attitude flared.

"Yeah, guess I'm not willing to give up hope either. Thanks for the pep talk."

"Anytime, sugar. Now what have you been up to? Talk to me."

Alexa tossed her empty Starbucks cup into a trash bin on the street, happy to get back to business.

"I've covered all my contacts, locals and otherwise. I've come up dry so far. If anyone knows anything, they're not talking. Something's up. I can feel it." As the traffic light changed ahead, she found a quieter spot away from the crowd. "How about you? You got anything?"

"Yeah, maybe. I've got a lead, but you're not gonna like it."

"Why?" Her voice edged with worry. "What did you find out?"

"A guy in Logistics told me Garrett had taken a small team on a mission, but he can't find any record of it. Whatever he had seen is gone now. And there's no trace of the cover-up either. He's working from memory."

"And how good is that? Can we trust this guy?"

"I trust him, but I'm also looking for confirmation. Give me a little time. If there's something out there, I'll find it," Tanya said. "My contact thinks Garrett was working off book, something I haven't seen him do before. And according to my guy, no one knows anything about it, not even those who should. It's really strange, Alexa. It's like he's dropped off the planet, and no one is talking."

"So did your contact have the names, the guys he took on his team?"

"Not yet, but he's working up a list of operatives who are AWOL without a specific assignment. A process of elimination. He'll call me later with that intel. It's the best we can do without more to go on. What are you thinking?"

"Garrett is too cagey to leave a trail, but maybe someone on his team wasn't so careful." Before Tanya could respond, Alexa heaved a sigh. "The thing is, why would he do anything without you knowing about it, Tanya? What could be so damned important to break protocol?"

"Good question, honey. I wish I knew." Tanya commiserated with her in silence before she said, "There's something else I have to tell you. I got a call five minutes ago. And you're not gonna like this either."

Tanya had mastered the art of the understatement. If she was concerned, that meant things were usually far worse.

"What's up, Tanya? Spill it."

Alexa shut her eyes, feeling a headache coming on. Her brownstone apartment was a few blocks away. She'd be home soon and could use the second wind that a long hot shower could deliver.

"Donovan Cross is looking for you. He wouldn't tell me what it was about, but I don't like it."

"Why didn't he call my cell?"

"He strikes me as someone who'd rather come at you sideways rather than head-on, like one of those sidewinder snakes." Tanya was spot-on with her analogy. "What do you want me to tell him?"

"If I was a suspicious person, I'd say he's working you to get to me. I don't trust him."

"You got that right. As far as I'm concerned, the jury is still out on Cross. I don't trust him either," Tanya said. "So what do you want me to do?"

"Stall him for now. Tell him you can't reach me. That'll give me time to get really lost, but I'll need you to be my eyes and ears. And when you find a lead on Garrett's last-known location, I'll need a way to get there. I'll call you when it's safe."

"You got it."

When Tanya ended the call, Alexa made up her mind to avoid her apartment and rely on her instincts to work off the grid. No one could know what she was doing. No one, not even Tanya. She didn't make such a decision lightly. There was risk in what she planned to do, but she'd already set up for such a contingency. Most covert operatives had a similar backup plan, out of necessity.

Heading west, she walked across the street, tossed her cell into a trash bin, and took the first step to sever ties to her life. An operative always had a fallback plan if all hell broke loose. Cash was stashed away with prepaid cell phones, fake IDs, and passports stowed in safe-deposit boxes. It was time to utilize what she'd set up long ago.

And it was time to find out what had happened to Garrett, even if the news wasn't what she wanted to hear.

Outside Guadalajara, Mexico

Estella crept down the murky corridor but ducked behind a stone wall when she noticed the guard outside one of the jail cells. If she got caught, Guerrero would punish her, whipping her for disobeying his order to stay in her room. She had no doubt that she wouldn't have been alone for long. Guerrero's men would finally come for what their boss might have promised, and Estella would rather die than sit and wait for that to happen.

But why she had come to find the American, she had no idea. The man had one foot in the grave. He wasn't strong enough to help her escape her fate, yet she followed her instincts to find him. She'd come to see where they had him. And even from where she stood, cowering in the shadows, she heard what they were doing to him. And it made her sick.

One voice stood out from the rest. And the sound of his cruelty raised the hair on her neck.

"Do it. Now!"

With the help of another man, Ramon Guerrero followed orders and grabbed the head of the naked prisoner. He shoved the man's face into a tub of filthy water. With his hands in shackles, Garrett Wheeler bucked to break free, sloshing water to the stone floor. When he stopped struggling, and the last bubbles erupted to break the surface of the water, Guerrero looked over his shoulder at the man who had given the order.

Miguel Rosas, number two man to the head of the Pérez cartel, had a reputation for brutality, with the body count to prove it. The Pérez cartel was a splinter group making a name and expanding its reach. And Rosas had played a big part in the Pérez family's growing reign of terror in the country. Guerrero had no appreciation for the politics within the organization. He was only a soldier within its ranks, only wanting to carve out his piece of the pie. A manageable piece.

Guerrero had transported the drugged American to a heavily guarded villa outside Guadalajara, Mexico. Being allowed to remain with Wheeler had been a good sign that powerful men had taken notice and trusted him to get the job done. Participating in the interrogation was another good sign. He didn't care if Wheeler died, but it made no sense to kill him before they got him to talk.

Finally, Rosas nodded, and the prisoner was yanked from the water. A loud, guttural gasp reverberated off the walls, but when Wheeler said nothing, his reprieve was short-lived.

"Again," Rosas demanded.

"No," the bound man gagged as his head was shoved back under the murky water. This time, when he was brought up, Rosas stepped closer and looked down at the gasping man.

"You make this harder than it needs to be. Who have you come to kill? And why are you here, in my country?" When Rosas spoke, his voice echoed. "Tell us what we need to know, and your misery will be over. Are you not hungry? Would it not feel good to sleep?"

Wheeler had not been allowed to rest after the drug had worn off. He'd been forced to stand naked in his cell and had been drenched with water every time he could no longer open his eyes. And he'd not been given food or drink. A local doctor had been on call to keep the American alive as the torture escalated.

And still, Wheeler had not told them anything.

Guerrero grabbed the American's hair and yanked his head back. The man's jaw fell slack as he panted for air, his chest heaving.

Mustering his contempt, he glared at Rosas. "Go to . . . hell."

"Very well. You leave me no choice."

In Spanish, Rosas gave an order, and the American was hung by his arms, suspended in chains from a massive wooden beam, and his body was doused with water. When an electrical generator was powered up, Guerrero knew what would come next.

Garrett Wheeler would be taken to the edge of death by electrocution. The American flinched when he saw one of Rosas's men touch two metal paddles together. A loud pop erupted, and a spark of electricity cast an eerie light into the murky cell.

The American narrowed his eyes and glared at his tormentor, Rosas. When Wheeler tensed his jaw, he didn't say a word, mustering what little defiance he had left. All that changed after the order was given. When the paddles sparked, volts of electricity shot through the American's body, making him jerk like a macabre puppet. Smoke drifted in the stale air, and the smell of burning skin and hair hit Guerrero's nostrils.

With a dismissive wave of his hand, Rosas eventually ordered his men to stop. Wheeler's body collapsed, still rippling with spasms. After he grunted in pain and fell unconscious, Rosas walked toward Guerrero and stood at his shoulder, speaking in a low voice.

"You do not approve of my methods. I can see it in your eyes."

Guerrero kept his dislike for Rosas in check. Looking into the man's eyes reminded him of the time he had confronted a rabid dog, an animal he would never turn his back on. With a man like Rosas, he had to tread carefully. One wrong word could ruin everything he had hoped to gain, or worse, put him in the crosshairs of a man he would rather not cross paths with again.

"It is not my place to approve or disapprove." Guerrero avoided looking at the man standing next to him.

"It is good that you know your place," Rosas said.

If the man had not looked so smug, Guerrero might have kept his mouth shut. But when Rosas ordered one of his men to awaken the American with a bucketful of water, Guerrero said what was on his mind. He could not help himself.

"It's just that this American, Garrett Wheeler, has many secrets worthy of your efforts. My sources tell me he is the leader of a very influential U.S. agency sent to spy on us. And who knows what someone would pay for a man like this."

"Yes, I know what you reported, but Pérez believes this American might be a diversion for a bigger assault on the cartels. The United States would do anything to stop the violence in our country."

"What are you saying?"

"What if the CIA or this agency Wheeler works for is planning to assassinate the leaders of the cartels, pick them off one by one, making it look like a drug war? Pérez doesn't care about what happens to the other cartels, but having advance information is very important."

"And I suppose if the competition is eliminated, that would not be a bad thing."

"Yes, of course." Rosas smiled. "So as you can see, our job here is very important."

Before Guerrero replied, the man looked over his shoulder at the waking prisoner hanging in chains. He ordered his men to hit him with the paddles again. Wheeler's body jerked with another jolt of electricity. He cried out, unable to hold back.

In reflex, Guerrero grimaced and noticed that Miguel Rosas was watching him. With the American dangling and jerking like a caught fish, Rosas only smiled at Guerrero, displaying a strange cruelty that caused the hair on the back of Guerrero's neck to stand.

At that moment, he knew that Miguel Rosas was a man who truly enjoyed his work.

Outside Guadalajara, Mexico

"We lost his signal, sir," his man reported as he knelt by him in the dark.

Following a burst transmitter signal, Hank Lewis and his team had crossed the border into Mexico and were positioned on a nearby ridge overlooking a large hacienda near Guadalajara. The estate was located on the northern shore of Laguna de Chapala, where his team was conducting a covert surveillance operation for the Sentinels, tracking an operative under deep cover who was being held prisoner inside.

As to who their operative was—or the purpose of their mission—Hank had no clue.

His team had been monitoring thermal imagery, tracking the movements of the men inside the compound, when he got the bad news about the transmitter. The device sent a burst of data at regular intervals via satellite, transmitting coordinates for his team to follow once an hour, but it also served a secondary purpose. It recorded the operative's vitals to make sure the unlucky bastard was still alive. From what Hank had been told, the transmitter had been implanted under the skin of their target.

The tracking device was damned small, an upgraded, high-tech version of the ones used to track the migratory patterns of wildlife. And unless someone knew what to look for, the transmission frequency was very hard to trace since it wasn't a constant signal. This version passed a bug sweep without a problem for the same reason. It only powered up once an hour, long enough to gather vitals, compress the data, and transmit it. That also meant the battery power would be minimal, which translated into a tracking device that could be injected under the skin with a hypodermic needle. A perfect piece of technology for this mission, until it failed.

"What do you think happened?" he asked his man.

"Don't know, sir. I'm trying to figure that out. Got cut off midtransmission."

"Keep trying, son."

"Yes, sir."

Hank didn't like being in the dark on a sensitive mission like this one. His team was on the front line of the op. If they couldn't find out what had happened, the mission could be scrapped. And Hank didn't want that to happen on his watch.

"What about our target's vitals, Doc?" Hank directed his question to the medic on his team. "Did we get a reading before we lost the signal?"

"I saw enough to know the target is an extremely agitated state. His breathing is irregular, and his heart rate is erratic. Up one minute and down the next. From my experience, the lower heart rate comes when the body is fighting off torture. It's a natural instinct."

"Is he in danger from a medical standpoint?" Hank asked. "Do we need to pull the plug?"

"I can't tell you. I didn't get enough of a data feed to form an opinion other than his body is under a great deal of stress, and one other thing." The medic fixed his gaze on Hank. "If we had to attempt a rescue, we'd probably have to carry him out."

Hank narrowed his eyes, considering what the man had told him.

"Thanks, Doc." And to his communications man, Hank said, "Let me know if Guerrero leaves the compound. We're still tracking his cell-phone GPS, right?"

"Yes, sir. If he moves, I'll know it."

Ramon Guerrero was their backup plan. Intel tracked a cell-phone signal from the moment the target had been taken hostage. One of the gang members had initiated a call to report what had happened. And Hank's team was already set to take advantage of that mistake. His team monitored any cell-phone signal detected in the general vicinity. Once they eliminated any legitimate cell-phone user through a background check, they narrowed their search to phones that could not be linked to a name. It was a surveillance tactic that had paid off in the fight against al-Qaeda.

Coupled with ground surveillance of the abduction, they eventually tracked the signal into Mexico, near Juárez, the stronghold of Ramon Guerrero, a known drug-cartel leader. After another sweep of cell-phone usage inside the compound, they used the process of elimination to isolate Guerrero's cell phone and had followed him and his men to Guadalajara, to the estate of another drug kingpin in the organization. Odds were that if the target was still alive, Guerrero would be close by. It was the best they could do without knowing more.

Hank's team had been fed coordinates through a handler, a man who monitored the transmission via satellite. Until now, they had stuck close to the target, moving as ordered. But with the target being in danger, and the burst transmitter potentially compromised, Hank knew the handler would have to kick the problem to the next level, the decision maker who was running the op.

Hank reached for the encrypted phone he'd use to communicate with his handler, a middleman in the operation. Although Hank was in command of the ground team, he didn't know who they were tracking inside the drug cartel or why the mission had required the secrecy. That bit of intel was on a need-to-know basis. Only one man knew all the details and would make the final call on every aspect of the mission. Communicating through the handler, he would direct Hank's team to carry out his orders.

But if the burst transmitter's signal was gone, they were flying blind. And the poor bastard on the inside would be on his own.

"Damn it," Hank cursed.

CHAPTER 4

New York City
Evening

Instinct had Alexa fixing her eyes on the reflection in a store window as she walked down Broadway. Display lights and neon signs cast enough light for her to see something she didn't like. She'd stopped suddenly, pretending to have an interest in a pair of Jimmy Choo stilettos.

That was when she caught the exchange.

A man had stopped short and looked across the street. Two men were following her, one in a dark business suit and the other in jeans, a Yankees ball cap, and a white T-shirt with a logo across his chest, too small for her to read. Their reaction had been subtle, but it was enough to trigger her survival instincts. From experience and training, she knew to trust her gut and take action. Indecision was not an option. And in the field, to hesitate might get her killed.

Without turning around, Alexa assessed her situation. If the men were connected to a surveillance team, they'd have a backup plan if she hailed a cab. And they could track the cab through the taxi company. Without thinking, she quickly ducked into the store and made her way to the back. When she saw a salesclerk heading for her, she smiled and waved her off.

"You got a way out back? I'm trying to avoid an old boyfriend. You know how it goes."

"Sure do, honey." The sharply dressed saleswoman pointed toward the dressing rooms. "We got a loading dock through those doors, and good luck ditching the jerk."

Within a minute, Alexa was on foot down an alley. She cut through another store and changed course again until she had lost the two men tailing her, but that didn't mean she was in the clear.

When she found a main thoroughfare, she took a risk and hailed a cab. She was already late. If she didn't rush, the bank would be closed when she got there.

And without the contents of her safe-deposit box, she'd be dead in the water.

Sentinels' Headquarters

"She tried to ditch us, but we picked her up again."

"Where is she?" Donovan Cross asked the agent who headed the second surveillance team tracking Marlowe.

"Bank of America. We've got eyes inside the bank. She's in the vault, accessing a safe-deposit box. What do you want us to do?"

Cross didn't like the sounds of this. If Marlowe was like any other good agent, she had a plan to ditch her identity and become someone else. And the contents of her safe-deposit box would help her do that. He knew from personal experience that she'd have fake passports and IDs, cash from several countries, and myriad ways for her to stay off the grid. A seasoned field agent like Alexa Marlowe would have stashed plenty of ways for her to get very lost.

"Don't let her out of your sight, do you understand?" Cross found it hard to keep the urgency from his voice.

"Copy that. When she leaves the vault, we'll be on her sweet ass."

"Just call me when she leaves." Cross ended the call and tossed his cell onto Garrett's desk.

Arrogant son of a bitch! Cross had more respect for Alexa than the pompous jerk following her, and he hoped he wouldn't regret giving the assignment to a young agent with something to prove.

"What are you up to, Marlowe?" He sprawled in his chair and stared across Garrett Wheeler's office. "And what have you got stashed at that bank?"

Cross had a bad feeling he wasn't going to like the answer to that question.

Sentinels' Headquarters
Twenty minutes later

"We lost her." Donovan Cross hated failure, especially when he had to be the one to admit he'd underestimated Alexa Marlowe. "I had a team on her when she left headquarters, but she gave them the slip."

"Do you think she knew she was being followed?"

The man on the other end of the line was his contact deep within the Sentinels' organization, one of the anonymous members of the elite council who secretly ran the covert group from a discreet distance.

"In a word . . . yes. Bank video footage showed

she entered the vault to access a safe-deposit box, but the surveillance team lost her coming out."

"How is that possible?" The man on the phone asked the same question he had only moments ago.

"Apparently, she had a change of clothes and a wig in that box. She ditched the stuff she had on in a vault trash bin. And the disguise she used was good enough to give our team the slip when she left the bank. She was dressed like an old woman."

Cross knew that field operatives could be real cagey and downright paranoid. If the hair on their necks got goosed, it wouldn't matter if they actually saw anyone tailing them. They'd follow their instincts and get lost in a crowd. And they had the training to carry out that slick maneuver easily enough.

"What about her apartment?"

"The surveillance team had someone there, too, but she never showed. We still have it staked out, but I don't think she'll go there now."

"This isn't good, Cross. What are you doing to rectify the situation?"

"We may have a line on her. When I get something definitive, I'll call you."

Cross told the man how his surveillance team had scoured digital camera feeds from all over the city after they'd hacked into the municipal traffic system. They'd picked up Alexa again—once they knew what disguise to look for—and although they hadn't pinpointed her exact location, they were getting close.

Very close.

"I don't have to tell you how sensitive our operation is at the moment. Find her, Cross. Do it, now."

After his call ended, Cross gritted his teeth. He hated losing. And Marlowe had bested him from day one, but with the success of the mission on his shoulders, that had to stop.

Outside New York City
10:40 P.M.

After Alexa felt safe enough, she grabbed a quick bite from a fast-food drive-through and hit a twenty-four-hour pharmacy before she found a place to spend the night. Without prying eyes, she changed her hair color to brown and took a quick shower. After a couple of hours' sack time, she'd hit the road again. But before that happened, she checked in with Tanya Spencer, her only lifeline.

"Hey, it's me." Alexa didn't say her name. "You got anything new?"

She'd used a prepaid cell, a number that Tanya

wouldn't know, but she figured the analyst would recognize her voice and take everything in stride like the pro she was.

"Yeah, I think I found something." Tanya dispensed with the usual formalities of asking questions and kept her focus. "But it doesn't make much sense."

"What do you mean?" With a towel wrapped around her wet hair, Alexa sat on the corner of her motel bed, a room she'd paid for in cash.

"Someone with access to our internal resources is using satellite time to track a cell-phone GPS signal in Mexico. And as far as I can tell, no one at the Sentinels has an operation in that country. Normally, I wouldn't make a big deal about this, but since we're looking for anything out of the ordinary, it piqued my interest."

"Do you have a name of the owner of the cell, or maybe the coordinates of that GPS signal?" she asked.

"No name, but I do have coordinates." Tanya gave her a location outside Guadalajara, Mexico. "And I've got Seth Harper working this on the QT. With him being located in Chicago, he's got no one looking over his shoulder to see what he's up to."

"Good call. Not many people connected to the Sentinels know Harper, and the guy can keep a secret." Alexa tightened the towel that she had wrapped around her body. "So what's near there? Can you tell if the signal is coming from a residence?"

"Did some digging on that. It's not just a residence, it's an estate, honey. And the property had a few layers of corporations heaped on top of the name of the real owner. I had to call in a few markers to dig that deep."

"And? Who's playing the shell game?"

"Manolo Quintanilla Pérez is the owner of record. He's the head of a drug cartel, an upstart group that's trying to make a name. What they lack in longevity, they more than make up for in brutality. A fun bunch."

"So if you can't find any record of this op, what makes you think Garrett is involved?" Alexa asked.

"My Logistics contact came up with those AWOL operatives who don't have a specific assignment. And one name got my interest. Hank Lewis. Besides you, Hank is one of Garrett's 'go to' guys. It's just a gut feeling, but I think this is the thread of information we've been looking for. We may not get anything better, Alexa."

For the first time since she had learned of Garrett's disappearance, Alexa felt the pang of regret. Whatever Garrett was involved with, he hadn't included her. He'd chosen Hank Lewis to confide in and lead the team that would back his play.

Why hadn't Garrett asked her?

"I know what you're thinking," Tanya said after her silence left an awkward wake in the conversation. "And when we find him, you can ask why he was so bullheaded about not making you a part of his team, but right now we've got work to do."

"Yeah, you're right." Alexa took a deep breath and rubbed her temple. The tension headache that had started earlier in the day had gotten worse. "I'm going to Mexico, Tanya. I don't think we've got another choice."

"Honey, I knew you'd say that."

Tanya had already worked out the logistics for her trip to Guadalajara. She'd leave at first light. If Garrett was in Mexico, she would find him.

She had to.

Northern Wisconsin

Jessie gulped down the last dregs of cold coffee from a lidded styrofoam cup and ate what was left of the Cheetos as she drove through Wisconsin. With orange fingertips, she gripped the wheel of her rented Taurus sedan and watched the center stripes roll by under its high beams.

The sun had gone down hours ago, taking with it the last of the scenery worth seeing. Rolling green hills dotted with picturesque dairy farms and placid lakes that mirrored the waning sunset had been replaced by darkness and miles of self-doubt. She had plenty of time to think. In her state of mind, that wasn't necessarily a good thing.

She had paid the price for getting a late start on her drive to La Pointe. Thinking of Seth had made the trip easier, but it was hard to ignore the nagging thoughts about her past. She had talked with Seth over breakfast and explained why she'd come to Chicago. And like she had expected, Harper had plenty of questions as they sat at his dining-room table.

"Do you really think this old case might give you a lead on your mother? That's huge, Jess." Harper leaned closer, elbows on the table, as he grabbed her hand. "I mean, how does that make you feel?"

Jess shook her head, and said, "I don't know, exactly. After all this time, a part of me wants to know what happened, but maybe this will make things worse."

If she had to let go of the only good memory she had—the only shining moment of the woman she believed was her mother—Jessie wasn't sure she could handle that. Her whole life had been about abuse—what one sick man had done to her and what she had done to herself when she didn't feel she deserved to be happy. Jessie wanted to believe she had gotten past it, but she knew that wasn't true.

She never would.

"I can come with you," Seth had offered. "I can have someone look after Floyd while we're gone."

"But what about that assignment you have with Tanya?"

Harper launched into geek speak, telling her about his new laptop, courtesy of the Sentinels. He had plenty of juice to keep in touch with Tanya Spencer on the road.

"My new laptop is ubersexy. I can stay connected with New York. No worries." He squeezed her hand and fixed his gaze on her. "I just don't think you should make this trip alone."

Looking into Harper's eyes made anything possible. Jess thought about his offer as they sat in silence. She'd have to keep her explanation simple and something Seth would understand. She would avoid telling him the real reason she needed to make the trek to Wisconsin alone, mostly because she didn't want to hear the words come out of her mouth.

If her mother had anything to do with how she ended up with a serial pedophile, Jessie wasn't sure how she would handle that. She'd rather face that reality alone and deal with it on her own terms. And if there had been a reason why she was never claimed by a family after her ordeal as a child, maybe Chief Tobias Cook might know what it was.

"I appreciate the offer, Seth, but I think this is something I'm gonna do on my own. I hope you understand."

Of all people, Harper would understand her need to uncover the truth about her mother by herself. For years, he'd been dealing with the fragile relationship he'd had with his father while growing up. In her eyes, Harper's father would always be a hero, but that hadn't been the way Seth saw it.

His old man was a retired cop who had been an AWOL dad when Harper needed him. It didn't matter that his father had sacrificed his personal life for the sake of his job. To a small boy, that didn't matter. And in a strange show of irony that life often dished out, now Harper was responsible for his father's care after dementia had sidelined him at a nursing home with no one else to take care of him. Seth had dealt with his burden on his own, too, even after he and Jessie had met and grown close. Sometimes, family problems hit too close to home to share with anyone.

"Yeah, guess I do. Family stuff can really mess with your head," he said. "But I want you to call me, anytime. You hear?"

"Yeah, I will."

"Don't say that unless you mean it, Jessie. Swear to me."

"Pinkie swear." She raised her hand and offered her pinkie. When Seth took it with his, she added, "I'll call you."

Under the table, Floyd sprawled at her feet and groaned. When he moved, the dog passed gas. Jessie tried hard not to take it personally.

"Oh man, Floyd. Give it a rest, big guy." Harper grimaced as he waved his hand. "Sorry about that. He must like you."

"I'll be sure and send him a thank-you note."

Although Seth had covered up his disappointment well with a soft chuckle, his eyes mirrored everything he felt. She knew he was worried about her and had been disappointed she hadn't asked him to come. In the end, he had to settle for feeding her, arranging for a reliable rental car, and stocking her sedan with Harper-worthy munchies. Field-tested eats, he'd called them. Jess didn't get on the road until early afternoon and had nearly nine long hours ahead of her.

She'd arrive well after dark at a remote location she'd never been to. And the only ferry making the trek to Madeline Island stopped at midnight. If anything went wrong, it would be close, but lingering with Seth in Chicago had been worth it.

She ached, having to leave Harper behind. Even Floyd had grown on her. She tried to imagine living with someone else, especially someone like Harper. She kept odd hours, took risks, and had never answered to anyone. The abuse she had suffered in the past was a strong driver for the woman she had become. Could she change the way she looked at the world for him? Despite the fact that she loved Seth, how would she feel about sharing her life?

Self-doubt had always been her number one enemy. It was easier to picture Harper getting tired of her than the other way around. When anything good happened, her first response was to beat herself up over it. And things hadn't changed much over the years. By the time she made it to Bayfield and the ferry, she had a wad of tension in her stomach the size of Floyd's head.

"Why do you keep doing this to yourself?" she muttered.

Jessie bought passage on the Madeline Island Ferry Line and pulled her vehicle onto the loading zone behind a guy in a red pickup. In no time, she was waved onto the ferry and told where to park. She could have stayed in her rental car for the half-hour ride to the island, but the moonlight dappled on the water was far too enticing. Jessie headed for the bow of the ferry and let the cool breeze tousle her hair.

In the distance, she saw the lights from La Pointe, a small town shining its beacon along the shoreline of Lake Superior. No big-city lights spoiled the incredible canopy of stars over her head. She took a deep breath and leaned against the railing, feeling incredibly small and inconsequential.

Whatever she learned the next day from Chief Cook would change everything she knew about her mother. She felt certain of that. She wanted to brace herself for what would come next, but she had no idea what that might be.

She had just begun to think her life had turned a corner, with Seth and Alexa and her best friend, Sam Cooper, in her life. And working for the Sentinels had been a step in the right direction, too. It meant she had a steady income and could leave behind her ratty Chicago apartment and the scumbags she had tracked for money as a bounty hunter, working one bail jumper at a time.

If she learned that her past was darker than she could have imagined, what new ways would she find to punish herself for coming from a crappy gene pool? Jessie shut her eyes when she felt the sting of tears. Wallowing in self-pity had its appeal, but the ferry had docked, and she'd arrived at La Pointe.

After she'd disembarked from the ferry, she got a better look at the small harbor town. The place wasn't much more than a few dimly lit streets that intersected. A visitor would have to work damned hard to get lost.

Except for a few bars, La Pointe was closed for the night. Most of the other businesses were geared for the tourist trade. Gift shops, quaint cafés, realty offices, and motels with self-serve Laundromats lined the narrow streets. When she located the police station, it was on the main drag across from a diner and a local watering hole, with a motel only a short walk away.

"Looks like I've struck the mother lode."

Jessie pulled into a parking spot near a motel that had a flashing red neon sign claiming it had a vacancy. Once she got out of her car, the sound of waves ebbing against the shoreline haunted her memory like a tune she was desperately trying to remember. La Pointe had triggered something in her that she couldn't quite put a finger on.

Only occasional laughter and jukebox music coming from a nearby bar interrupted her trip down memory lane. The remote location and the small size of the town made her wonder about her connection to it all. The place probably had a thriving tourist trade, and, during the day, it no doubt had its merits; but at night, it left her feeling lonely and on edge. Every shadow held demons from a past she needed to know more about.

How did you end up here, Beck?

Standing outside her car, Jessie looked around. There wasn't much to see this time of night, but she got a real hinky vibe when she thought about living in a town like this. There'd be no place to hide from who you were, and everyone would know your business, or think they knew it. Living in a place like La Pointe would be a disaster for someone like her. That was why living with hordes of strangers, like she had in Chicago and New York, had been a major relief. Except for Sam and Harper, no one knew her story. And she could reinvent herself whenever she felt the need.

Jessie looked into the window of the motel office and saw the light of a TV cutting the shadows in a room behind the counter. Someone was up. Her hiking boots crunched gravel until she hit the wooden boardwalk in front of the motel. When she stepped inside the front door, a doorbell tinkled overhead. The cramped space was filled to the rafters with knickknacks for sale, small-sized containers of toiletries, gum, and breath mints, and plenty of snacks even Harper would endorse.

"You come off the last ferry?" The motel clerk stepped out from the room where she'd seen the TV.

Jessie spied the clerk's name posted on a wall plaque behind the counter. Byron McGivens.

"Yeah, as a matter of fact, I did. You got a room, Byron?"

"Sure do." He worked the keyboard of his computer and kept talking. "If you came off that ferry, did you drive from somewhere or just walk on?"

"I drove up from Chicago." She was tired enough to let Byron's prying get to her. "What's with the twenty questions?"

"I didn't mean anything by it." He shrugged and had a hard time looking her in the eye. "Living in a small town, you get curious, that's all."

Jessie hadn't noticed before, but the guy got a little antsy when she pushed back on his questions. She'd probably overreacted.

"Sorry. Guess I'm a little tired."

After an awkward moment, the guy broke the ice.

"Okay, I've got another question, but this one's business. How long you stayin'?"

"Not sure." Jessie narrowed her eyes. "Can I tell you later?"

"Yeah, no problem."

The guy had on a royal blue T-shirt with the name Madeline Island printed in white across his chest. He looked to be in his thirties, with dark thinning hair and a day's worth of scruffy growth. After she handed him her credit card, the clerk had another request.

"I'm gonna need to see some ID."

"Sure." She fished for her driver's license and handed it to him.

"You can never be too careful these days," he said after he'd taken a good look at her ID and handed it back. "I've got you in number 12. Less road noise there. You can park around back."

"Thanks."

Jessie took her room key and headed to her car. She drove around back and carried in her one bag. The motel room was basic. Near the front door was a window with an air conditioner below it. One table was tightly squeezed next to the queen bed, with the bathroom toward the back and plenty of shag carpet in between. The room smelled moldy, like every other low-rent place she'd ever stayed in.

"Just like home."

Before she unpacked, Jessie reached for her cell phone and hit her speed dial, making a call to the one guy who could make her feel better.

Harper.

"Hey," she said quietly, finding solace in the sound of his sleepy voice. "It's me."

Shoreview Motel
After midnight

"You told me to call. A woman checked in just now."

Byron McGivens spoke low. Even though no one was within earshot at this hour, it seemed like the thing to do. He didn't expect the rapid-fire questions that came at him before he had a chance to think. This time of night, his brain wasn't working on all cylinders.

"Yeah, I checked. Her name's Jessica Beckett. And I verified that by her driver's license. She drove up from Chicago."

The motel clerk stepped out from behind the counter and walked toward the window, looking down Main Street.

"You need me to do anything else?"

Before he even got his question out, he was left listening to nothing but dial tone, with not so much as a good-bye. He would have been irritated with the rude way he'd been treated, but with the cash he'd been given, he overlooked it. Spying on a guest was easy money. And he hoped he hadn't seen the last of his newfound good fortune.

If his services were needed again, he'd be ready.

The Pérez Compound
Outside Guadalajara, Mexico

Estella had stayed as long as she dared, but after seeing bright light erupting from the make-shift jail cell and hearing the screams of a man in pain, she knew they were torturing the American, and she ran.

She tore down the stone corridor, back the way she'd come. There was nothing she could do for the man, not now. Tears clouded her eyes, and she had never felt so alone. When she hit the night air, she sucked it into her lungs, fighting back the sadness that threatened to choke her.

After Estella closed the door behind her, she leaned against it before she collapsed. Trembling, she made the sign of the cross and slid to the ground, clutching her arms around her. How did she end up here? And what would become of her? A small part of her had hoped the prisoner would be strong enough to escape and save her, but now she knew that would never be.

If her mother had known this, would she still have sold her to Guerrero?

Estella knew the answer to that question, and it made her sick. Her own mother had betrayed her. And she would've done it again if it meant more money for her next fix. When she had the strength to walk, Estella stood and headed for her room in a building next to the main house. She crept through an adjacent patio garden and stuck to the shadows, which would hide her from the guards patrolling the grounds. When she'd made it to the hallway—and knew her room was at the end of the hall—she breathed a sigh of relief. No one was waiting for her outside.

Her room was next to the maid's quarters, not much more than a closet, with only a bed and one lamp on a small wooden table. There was no lock on her door. Even if she wanted to hide, she couldn't do it.

She slowly turned the knob of her door and peeked inside. When she saw that the room was dark, she slipped in with hands outstretched as she fumbled for the lamp.

When she touched the chest of a man, standing in front of her, she screamed. An arm tightened around her neck, cutting off her air.

"No, please . . . d-don't hurt m-me," she begged in Spanish, not recognizing her own voice.

"You should have thought about that before."

When the man whispered in her ear, she recognized his voice. And his smell had haunted her nightmares. Ramon Guerrero had her by the throat. She couldn't breathe. In the dark, she never saw his face, but Estella knew Ramon took pleasure in her fear.

CHAPTER 5

The Pérez Compound
Before dawn

Ramon Guerrero had found a new way to get the attention of Manolo Quintanilla Pérez, head of his cartel. And the psychopathic tendencies of his number two man, Miguel Rosas, would aid him in doing so.

He had wanted to surprise Estella Calderone in her room, but when she wasn't there, Guerrero had waited. Every minute that ticked by made him angrier. With her disobedience, she'd forced him to punish her. He had no choice if he wanted to retain his reputation.

"Open the cell of the American," he ordered as he hauled the girl down the corridor, by her hair.

A guard did as he was told and stood back as Guerrero shoved the girl to the stone floor inside.

When she hit the ground, she cried out in pain. And as he expected, Miguel Rosas was waiting in the corridor.

"String her up," Guerrero demanded, but when the jailer hesitated, he yelled, "Now!"

After the man reached for the chains, Guerrero waved his hand.

"Use that rope, over there." He pointed. "Her wrists are too small for the chains."

He didn't have to see Rosas's face to know that the man was enjoying this.

"You surprise me, Guerrero, but in a good way." Rosas smiled. "Since this is your idea, you take the lead, and I shall watch. Please, carry on."

Although Rosas stepped into the shadows, Guerrero felt his eyes on him. He would have preferred Rosas take charge and do what came naturally to a man like him.

Estella had disobeyed him. He owed her nothing, but when Guerrero saw that Rosas wasn't going to take over, he took a deep breath and thought about what would come next. How far would he be willing to go to impress a man he didn't respect?

"Please . . . don't do this," the girl begged, with tears glistening in her eyes. "I swear. I only left my room for a little while. It was too hot inside. I needed fresh air. Please."

"You're a lousy liar." He glared at her and pretended to be angrier than he truly was.

When the guard hoisted her off the ground, she cried out in agony. That was when Guerrero turned toward the American, who could barely lift his head. No matter what would come next, the blame would not be his.

"You see? You have done this," Guerrero yelled, and grabbed the man's hair, forcing him to look in his eyes. "Are you willing to let this innocent girl die in your place?"

Guerrero found himself pleading for Estella in earnest. He hoped the American would take pity on her, something he could not afford to do, not with Miguel Rosas watching. If the prisoner cooperated, he could release her without looking like he'd compromised. Sure, the girl needed to be taught a lesson; but if Rosas had his way, she would pay with her miserable life.

When the American opened his mouth to speak, Guerrero hoped he would let him off the hook, but that wasn't the case.

"Using that girl? You're a ... c-coward, man." The prisoner could barely speak, but he'd said plenty.

Guerrero had no choice now. He had to save face in front of Rosas and his own men.

"Very well. This is on you."

He slid his knife from its sheath and slowly walked back toward Estella. Tears streamed down her face as she sobbed.

"Oh, no . . . Please. Don't do this, Ramon." Her plea echoed off the walls in the small cell. Guerrero gripped the hilt of his blade and clenched his teeth.

Whatever came next wouldn't be *his* fault. Estella had brought this on herself. And everything would depend on what the American would do next.

LaGuardia Airport—New York City
Dawn

The morning sun was making a valiant effort at its first appearance, but the night sky was conspiring with a menacing storm to keep dawn at bay. The dark clouds left Alexa feeling tense, as if nature foreshadowed the approach of something ominous.

Closing her eyes, she pushed the thought aside and sank into her seat on the US Airways jet as it pulled from the gate. She took solace in the fact that she was finally on her way to Mexico and breathed a sigh of relief. By late afternoon, after a change in carriers to Mexicana Airlines, she'd be in Guadalajara after layovers in Charlotte, North Carolina, and Mexico City.

Seeing herself in the reflection of the small window over the wing, she hardly recognized her face. She'd changed her hair color and used contact lenses to alter her distinctive blue eyes to hazel.

She had used fake ID to get past TSA security. And if someone came looking for her image on security cameras, she'd be impossible to recognize. On her neck and arms, she had fake tattoos applied with ballpoint pen, and she walked with a pronounced limp. And her secondhand clothes made her look like a homeless bag lady. Alexa had picked a disguise with layers of clothes in case she had to change on the run, literally.

In her line of work, being a chameleon came with the territory. And it was a skill that would come in handy where she was going. After a fitful sleep last night, she'd had plenty of time to think about her encounter with the two men on the streets of Manhattan. She knew they'd been sent to track her. And she also knew exactly who had sent them.

Donovan Cross.

She didn't have to know the man, only the type. He had pretended to be sincere when he'd told her how Garrett had died. That had been the mark of a real player with a streak of mean. She'd seen the act before. Hell, she'd played the part herself a time or three.

All she had to do was stay one step ahead of that bastard. And with the coordinates and location in Mexico that Tanya had given her, maybe she'd have an edge before Cross knew she was out of the country.

But one other thing was perfectly clear, and it was strangely comforting. If Garrett were dead, Cross wouldn't have sent a team to track her. More than ever, she felt certain her instincts were dead-on.

Garrett was in trouble. And Donovan Cross had no intention of letting her throw him a lifeline.

The Pérez Compound

With Miguel Rosas watching, Ramon Guerrero had to make it look good, even though he hated cutting into the tender flesh of Estella Calderone. She'd been a virgin when he first came to her bed. Her skin had been untouched and perfect.

But now, as he tightened his grip on the knife, he knew she would bear his marks forever. When the tip of the blade cut into her skin, the girl cried out.

"Please . . . don't do this. I beg of you, Ramon."

Under the flickering flame of a torch, he watched a stream of her dark red blood trail down her arm and leach into her blouse. And when she pleaded for him to stop, Guerrero saw the American flinch.

"Using that g-girl, you're a c-coward, Raymond."

"My name is Ramon. And you are the coward, not me. You are the one who is allowing this to happen to her."

"Turn your blade on me. I'm the one you want."

"And still, you do not talk. Why is that?" Guerrero turned toward his hostage and pointed the knife at his eye. "This girl does not have to suffer because of you. All you need to do is answer our questions. Is that so difficult? This could all be over if you would only cooperate."

"You mean we could all be friends? Well, why didn't you just say so?"

Guerrero clenched his jaw and glared at the man. He was tired of his insults.

"Always with the smart mouth. You think this is a game?" He shook his head, but when Guerrero turned his back on the American and stepped closer to Estella, the man spoke up again.

"You work for Pérez." He said it with certainty, as if he knew that for a fact.

"Who?"

"Now who's playing games?"

Guerrero took a risk and glanced at Miguel Rosas, Pérez's watchdog. The man's dark eyes glared back, yet he remained in the shadows, content to let him hang himself.

"Go on," Guerrero said. "What were you going to say?" He turned back toward the American and kept his face a blank slate.

"Before you go past the point of no return, you should contact your boss. Tell him about me."

"What makes you think you are worth his time . . . or mine?"

"You do, or you wouldn't have brought me here."

Without warning, Guerrero slashed his knife across the chest of the American. Caught off guard, the man cried out and gritted his teeth. Although his sudden show of violence seemed to redeem him in the cruel eyes of Miguel Rosas, Guerrero wasn't pleased with the fact that his hostage knew where he was. It made him all the more determined to push the man to talk. Everything he hoped for would depend on it.

"Pérez knows me. If you get him here, he'll tell you that." The American winced in pain as his chest bloomed with fresh blood. "I'll talk to Pérez, no one else."

Guerrero gripped the knife tighter in his hand, ready to cut the man again, but Rosas stopped him. He didn't say a word. He only tilted his head, ordering Guerrero to come with him. He resented being called like a dog, but he followed anyway.

When they got outside the cell, out of earshot of the prisoner, Guerrero spoke first.

"Do you believe him? You think he knows Pérez?"

"No. He's only stalling for time," Rosas said.

"But shouldn't we let Pérez decide?"

Rosas was an arrogant man who presumed too much. And Guerrero resented him for it.

"We don't need to waste his time." Rosas put his hand on Guerrero's shoulder and softened his tone. "You showed good instincts to bring the girl into this. The American reacted to her pain, I saw it."

"So what are you saying?"

"We let him think he has won, for now." Rosas smiled. "But I will return later, to pick up where you didn't have the stomach to continue."

Guerrero started to speak, but Rosas held up his hand.

"This is what I do, Ramon. Let me do my job, and we shall both get results."

Rosas didn't wait for his reply. He turned his back and headed down the corridor, back to the main residence. Rosas had dismissed him, like a servant who was beneath him.

Guerrero had no doubt that Rosas would kill Estella, just to make the point that he was in charge. And Guerrero would be no closer to getting recognized for his efforts than he was before. Letting Rosas take over wasn't an option.

Guerrero knew he had to do something, but did he have the balls to contact Pérez himself and go around the cartel boss's number two man?

"Hell, yes."

La Pointe, Wisconsin
Two hours later

Dressed in a Chicago Bulls T-shirt, jeans, and a hooded navy sweatshirt, Jessie hunched over her first cup of coffee, barely looking up at the waitress who poured it. She hadn't paid attention to the name of the hole-in-the-wall diner either, but she'd seen that kind of place many times on stakeouts. The clank of plates and the incessant chatter of the patrons were background noise to the thoughts roiling around in her head, thoughts that hadn't stopped all night long.

After spending the night staring at the ceiling of her motel room and catching the blur of red digital numbers on the nightstand alarm clock count down her boredom, Jessie was glad when dawn came. It gave her an excuse to be upright. And her motel was next door to the diner. All she wanted was coffee, but the waitress was hoping for a better tip.

"You know what you want, honey?" A woman with overpermed gray hair leaned across a Formica counter, popping gum. From the look in the woman's eyes, she'd seen it all and had lent a hand to invent the best parts.

"Not yet, but I'm sure it'll come to me."

"It'll come to you if I bring it. You see, that's how it works here. You tell me what you want. Joe back there cooks it like he knows how. Then you eat it, pay, and give me a big tip so I can retire to the Bahamas."

"What have you been smokin'?" Jessie mumbled as she took her first gulp of caffeine.

"What was that, darlin'?"

"Nothing." Jessie set down her mug and grabbed a menu, giving it a quick eyeball. "Gimme two eggs over easy with bacon and toast."

"You might as well take the hash browns that come with that. I hear they're sublime."

Jessie narrowed her eyes at the woman, who had polished her attitude to a fine sheen. And flinging it so early in the morning was a skill Jessie had come to respect.

"Fine." She held out her coffee mug. "Top me off, will ya? And keep it coming."

"You got it."

After the waitress called out her order, Jessie saw her own face in the mirror behind the counter. Under the fluorescent lights, she looked tired. Dark circles under her eyes made the scar across her eyebrow more pronounced and ugly.

The words "sullen" and "unfriendly" came to mind, which was fine by her. Not everyone was a frickin' ray of sunshine in the morning. When she gulped down more coffee, she noticed another pair of eyes staring back.

A uniformed cop with a newspaper under his arm was throwing bills on a booth table. She guessed that local law-enforcement officers kept an eye out for strangers sporting an attitude.

LEOs in small towns were like that. That was why she preferred the anonymity of getting lost in the masses of Chicago or New York City. She didn't appreciate getting rousted by the local law, especially before she had finished her coffee.

"You Jessica Beckett?" the cop asked as he walked toward her.

Before she said anything, Jessie looked down at the name badge on the man's uniform. Chief Cook, the man she'd come to see. She crooked her lips into a lazy grin, knowing from experience that the gesture would come off looking more like a sneer than hospitable. Even though she and the law seldom saw eye to eye, she reined back her usual cynicism to greet the man proper.

"Yes, that'd be me. How's it goin', Chief?"

The man ignored her attempt at small talk. With a stern face, he eyeballed her like the cops in Chicago usually did. And he got down to his agenda, the real reason he'd struck up a conversation in the first place.

"You have a permit to carry that concealed weapon under your sweatshirt?"

"Yeah, I do, but I guess you won't take my word for it." Jessie reached into the back pocket of her jeans and pulled out a wallet. "I'm a licensed fugitive recovery agent out of Chicago. Carrying a gun is part of the job."

"So you're a . . . bounty hunter."

"That's not what I said," she corrected.

For the police chief, her carrying a concealed weapon in his town had been like waving a red flag in front of a bull. And cops usually saw her former occupation the same way. The chief was no different. His disdain showed on his face and in the way he said, "bounty hunter." No, Chief Cook didn't bother to hide how he felt as he looked over her permit, but him seeing her as a bounty hunter was easier than concocting a lie to explain her current employer.

"Have a nice breakfast, Ms. Beckett. When you're ready, you know where to find me."

"Yes, sir. I do."

"And when we're done"—he leaned closer and lowered his voice—"I think it's best that you leave town. Am I making myself clear?"

"Abundantly. Guess you've got your welcome wagon in the shop, out of commission." Jessie raised her mug of coffee in mock salute.

Chief Cook gave her the stink eye and turned on his heels without saying another word. He left the diner, with Jessie watching him go. Even though her first encounter with the local police chief had been brief, she could tell already. Chief Cook had made a snap judgment about her. She saw it in his eyes because she'd seen it plenty before from other cops. He'd have no tolerance for any woman who would encroach on his territory and take up bounty hunting for a living. And a woman carrying a gun, legal or otherwise, got his testosterone all riled up.

"Great . . . just great."

"You know the chief, honey?" the waitress asked as she set down Jessie's breakfast and freshened up her coffee.

"Not yet, but that's about to change, unfortunately."

Before she'd finished her first cup of java, Jessie

had been kicked out of town. That had to be a new record.

Forty-five minutes later

Chief Cook made Jessie wait while he pretended to take an important phone call. Like most cops she'd known, the man liked being in charge and made sure she got that point. Jessie was on her second cup of the swill he called coffee when the chief finally gestured her into his office, shutting the door behind her.

"So how do you know Detective Samantha Cooper in Chicago?" he asked.

The chief sat behind his desk and invited her to sit in one of his visitor chairs while he made small talk and pried.

"In my line of work, I meet a lot of cops."

"It's just that she seemed to know you . . . beyond the job."

She could have offered him more, but the fact that she and Sam Cooper had been friends since childhood was none of his business, and her gal pal had nothing to do with why she'd come. Jessie had her secrets and had gotten really good at being evasive.

"Don't know what to tell ya." She shrugged. "Chicago PD told me you scored a hit on my DNA from an old murder case. I just came to check it out, see if I could help."

"What makes you think I need your help? From what I can see, your attitude could use an overhaul."

Something in his smug expression flipped a switch in her. And even though it would have been better for Jessie to keep her mouth shut and stifle her cynicism, she just wasn't good at that. Diplomacy was a skill set she didn't have.

"I'm a recovering smart-ass. Guess I've fallen off the wagon." After she realized how she sounded, Jessie heaved a sigh and tried to reel it back a notch. "Look, I think we've gotten off on the wrong foot. I'd appreciate seeing what you've got."

"That's not how it works around here." The chief leaned back in his chair and crossed his arms. Real defensive. "This is my case. I ask the questions."

Jessie held up both hands, and said, "I didn't mean to step on your toes, Chief. It's just that I'm an investigator. And I thought that having another set of eyeballs on the murder book might help."

Jessie had never called herself an investigator—until now—but if her argument swayed the stubborn man behind the desk, then she'd beef up her résumé to include anything that would get her a foot in the door of his case.

"No offense, but that murder book is off-limits to civilians. Now I know you were only a kid at the time, so I won't be needin' your help. All I need is your cooperation. Big difference." He narrowed his eyes. "Now what can you tell me about your blood evidence being found here in La Pointe?"

Jessie didn't know squat about how her blood had wound up in Wisconsin. She knew less about her past than most people since she'd blocked out the trauma of her childhood. And forget about old family albums. She didn't have relatives or the usual trappings that could help trigger a memory.

"When we got that hit on your DNA, I looked at your missing-persons file." The chief pursed his lips, letting what he'd said sink in. "Terrible thing happened to you."

Jessie saw the look of pity in his eyes, and she hated it. That look was the reason she never talked about what had happened to her.

"That Danny Ray Millstone case hit national news. I didn't need to read your file to remember that sorry excuse for a human being. He got what was coming to him."

Guess the chief thought that commiserating over the serial pedophile who had tortured her and so many other kids was a way of breaking the ice. Well, she didn't need that. *Ever.*

What she *did* need was a look at the chief's investigation. Seeing what the local law had accumulated would give her a glimpse into a past she knew nothing about. And maybe, for the first time, she'd get a lead on the woman who might be her mother.

The way she figured it, she had a fifty-fifty chance of discovering that her mother had been involved with Danny Ray Millstone and given her up or had loved her the way a mother should and hadn't been given the choice to keep her child.

But to get a look at the cold-case file—or gain the trust of the man behind the desk—would require her to do the one thing that didn't come naturally. She had to open up to a stranger, or her business in La Pointe would be done—over, out, *finito*.

"All that took place after your murder, Chief, but I don't know how your case would be connected to what happened to me."

"To find that out, you may have to talk about things you don't care to. You okay with that?" He furrowed his brow.

When the chief leaned forward in his chair, she knew she had his attention, making what she was about to ask him more difficult.

"Since you did DNA tests, was the woman who was killed . . . was she related to me?" Jessie cleared her throat, unable to look him in the eye. "Was she . . . my mother?"

"You don't remember anything about your mother?" His voice softened.

"Bottom line is that I don't know how my blood got here in La Pointe because I've blocked out a big chunk of my past. Either I was too young to remember stuff, or I didn't want to know what had happened. I don't know which, but I came here to see what you had, hoping I might learn something about my family . . . my mother, actually. That's why I want to see what you've got on this case. Do you think you can help me, Chief?"

At first, the man stared at her as if she had two heads. Like the boy who cried wolf, she was about to find out if the guy believed her when she finally told him the truth. When his expression softened, he leaned back in his chair and heaved a sigh. He kept up his silent stare as if the truth would appear on her forehead.

Eventually, he broke the stalemate. "You have time to take a ride with me?"

The Pérez Compound
Outside Guadalajara, Mexico

Ramon and his men had left them alone, for hours now. Estella Calderone listened to every sound coming from the corridor outside, waiting for the footsteps that would signal that her nightmare wasn't over.

And in the stillness of the cell, she also heard the labored breathing of the man next to her. They'd given him loose-fitting clothes to wear, pants that tied at his waist and a shirt that had not been buttoned. Since they'd taken his shoes, his feet were bare. Suspended by chains, he looked more like a ghost in the darkness of their cell. That was why Estella was shocked to hear the American speak to her for the first time.

"I'm s-sorry."

His voice had been so soft, she almost missed what he said.

"For what, *señor*?" Estella found it hard to breathe. Hanging by ropes made it hard for her to fill her lungs. And when she tried to relieve the pain by moving, her body ached with every exertion.

"What they've done to you, it wasn't s-supposed to go d-down like this."

Estella didn't know what he was talking about, but she heard the sincerity in his words. The man looked at her with his face half-swollen and saw the knife wounds Ramon had cut into her arms. The sight looked as if it truly pained him.

His reaction made her more aware of what Ramon had done to her. She would never be pretty to another man. Ramon had ruined her in more ways than one.

The smell of her own blood filled her nostrils in the small cell. And whenever she moved, she opened the wounds and more warm blood oozed down her skin. Estella felt the sting of new tears and fought them off by talking to the man she shared the cell with.

"I was born under an eclipsed moon. No good can come from that, my mother used to say." If her hands hadn't been tied, she would have made the sign of the cross. "Besides, Ramon owns me. He can do whatever he wants. My mother sold me to him."

It had embarrassed her to admit what she was to this stranger, but since they were both about to die, she did not see the point in hiding the truth.

"That bastard might've given m-money to your mother," he mumbled, trying hard to catch his breath. " . . . but he can't own you."

The American was weak. She strained to listen to him, barely hearing his words when the sound of his voice echoed off the stone walls.

"He's got n-no right to do w-what he did to you." He grimaced with the pain of speaking. "What's your name?"

"Estella Calderone. And you are Garrett Wheeler, is that right?" She'd heard his name when he was being tortured, before Guerrero had come looking for her.

The American barely nodded.

"If we are to die today, then it is good we know who we are." She felt a single tear roll down her cheek. "But in God's eyes, no names are necessary."

He knew the girl was scared even though she was trying to sound brave. It was one thing for him to withstand torture, but seeing what they had done to Estella had ripped him up. Any plans he had for revenge had been challenged the minute Ramon Guerrero touched that girl with his knife. It left him with a burning question that he had not yet found an answer for.

How badly did he want to kill the man who had taken everything from him?

La Pointe, Wisconsin

"So this is where it happened?"

Sitting outside in the passenger seat of Chief Cook's patrol car, Jessie stared through the windshield at a dilapidated old clapboard house that was set back into the woods, off an unpaved road. The yard was overgrown, with vines and weeds making an effort to reclaim the property.

Massive old trees dwarfed the abandoned house, casting the place in shadows. And old crime-scene tape fluttered in the wind, a sad reminder of what had happened. A strong feeling of déjà vu hit Jessie, even though a day ago, she would've sworn she'd never been to La Pointe.

"Yeah," the chief said. "It's been on the market a few times, but they haven't had much luck in selling it. In a small town, rumors get more exaggerated as time passes. And it's damned hard to whitewash a murder."

"Well, that's true enough." Jessie got out of the squad car, keeping her eyes on the old house. "What was her name? The woman who was murdered here."

"Angela DeSalvo. She was twenty-eight years old." When the chief got out of his car, he had a file with him. After Jessie got caught staring at the manila folder he had under his arm, Chief Cook added, "I was a rookie at the time. Didn't know her, but she was a pretty little thing by all accounts."

After an awkward silence, he said, "Let's go inside, and I'll show you where it happened. And you can ask your questions."

She nodded and walked in silence to the front steps. When she got closer, she stared up at the second-floor windows. One in particular caught her eye. Something about it was familiar, but it also stirred a tight knot in her belly.

"You look like you've seen a ghost," the chief said. "You okay?"

Without taking her eyes off the window, she replied, "Yeah, guess so."

When they got inside, the chief didn't say a word at first. He let her walk through the musty old rooms by herself, with her boots echoing in the emptiness. And every time a flash of memory hit her, she shut her eyes and clung to it as if she'd lose it forever if she let go.

Too much was familiar. As she walked through the rooms, too many recollections bombarded her for the unsettling feeling to be purely coincidental.

"I think I've been here . . . before," she whispered, hardly realizing that she had spoken at all. "Where did it happen?"

"Up here," the chief called to her from another room. When she joined him, he pointed up a set of stairs.

As Jessie followed him, her stomach tightened, especially when she got to the second floor and made the turn she knew would come. If Chief Cook hadn't been leading the way, she still would have known where to go. That window she had seen outside had been important to her for a reason.

She'd been there before.

"She was found in her bedroom. Right there."
He didn't need to point to where Angela DeSalvo
had died. Bloodstains marred the old floorboards.
The pooling wasn't red anymore. It had turned
dark brown with age.

When Jessie knelt by the stain and put her
hand to the floor, she felt an overwhelming sense
of loss. And flashes of violent images came from
nowhere, bombarding her with a past she didn't
realize she had buried. The darkness of it gripped
her hard. And she fought a lump in her throat. She
didn't want to break down in front of the chief,
but a part of her didn't care.

"You ready to see a photo?"

Jessie looked up in shock, unsure what to say.
After she took a deep breath, she stood and waited
for him to fish out a photo from his file. When he
handed it to her, she looked into the face of Angela
DeSalvo.

"Oh, my God." Jessie couldn't help it. She gasped
with a hand to her lips, her fingers trembling.

"You recognize her?"

"I don't know. I'm not . . . sure."

The woman in the crime-scene photo stared
back at her, forever immortalized in black and
white, a look of shock frozen on her face. The
photo was a close-up, and a dark pool of blood

was congealed under her head. Despite the image being graphic, Jessie had lied to the chief.

She'd recognized the woman from the many times she'd come to Jessie while she slept.

A flash of her smile and the sound of laughter jarred Jessie from her stupor, memories of the only happy moments she had when she was a child. The woman in her dreams had played with her in a park, on a swing.

When Jessie heard a steady squeaking sound coming from outside the bedroom window, she turned her head, trying to listen for the noise, and her breath caught in her throat.

"What's that?"

It took the chief a minute to realize what she was asking.

"That squeaking sound is from an old swing out back. You want to go see . . ."

Jessie didn't wait for him to finish. She ran down the stairs and headed for the backyard until she stood next to an old rusted swing, blowing in the breeze. The play set stood under a large tree, squeaking every time the wind blew. An eerie trigger for her memory.

Jessie knew right then that she had been there before. This had been where Angela DeSalvo had pushed her on the swing. That memory hadn't been from a park. It had come from right there, within steps of where Angela would later be murdered.

"Was she my mother? Can you tell me that?"

Avoiding the chief's eyes, Jessie looked down at the swing as she wiped away a tear with the back of her hand. He'd never answered her before when she questioned him on the DNA found at the scene, but now she had to know.

"Not sure how to answer that." The chief's voice was low. Feeling numb, she really had to listen to hear him when he said, "Biology doesn't always determine a real parent, but if you're asking if your DNA is a match to Angela's . . ."

Jessie found that she was holding her breath, waiting to hear what he'd say.

" . . . I'm sorry to say . . . No, her DNA didn't match yours."

Jessie was crushed. She couldn't help it. If Angela's DNA had matched, it would have meant her mother was dead, which would have felt just as bad. Yet without having a biological connection to Angela, everything she thought she knew about the sliver of memory she'd always associated with her mother was gone.

She had a strong feeling that Angela had loved her, but if she wasn't her mother, then who was she?

And why had she crossed paths with a killer?

CHAPTER 6

Guadalajara, Mexico

Situated twelve miles southeast of the city, Guadalajara International Airport had only one terminal, with domestic and international flights coming into the same facility. That meant more traffic for Alexa to blend into. A tall blonde would have stood out in a sea of brown skin and dark hair, but after the dye job from last night, she was a brunette. Having changed disguises at the last two layovers and scrubbed off her fake tattoos, she now looked like a conservative schoolteacher on vacation.

She didn't need to fight the crowd at baggage claim since she carried only one bag. Keeping things simple also got her through Customs without a hitch. Now she stood on the curb, waiting in line for a cab.

But she couldn't shake the feeling that someone was watching.

As a trained operative, she had learned to pay attention to her instincts. Using every tactic she had in her arsenal of tricks, she discreetly searched the crowd outside the airport. Tourist buses and yellow-and-green-striped taxicabs lined the arrivals ramp outside baggage claim, with the vehicles clouding the muggy air with diesel fumes. And men in uniform blew whistles and waved traffic through, yelling out orders in Spanish. Nothing looked out of the ordinary.

Yet she had the unmistakable sensation that someone was keeping tabs on her. If they had followed her to Mexico, after the many ways she'd covered her tracks, they were plenty good. Whoever got the hair on the back of her neck to stand at alert, they had her complete respect. She'd have to find a way to lose them, *pronto.*

"You need a taxi, lady?" A short, brown-skinned man in uniform smiled at her.

"Yes . . . please." Alexa adjusted her dark glasses and didn't look him in the eye.

She could have told the man she was also looking to rent a vehicle, but the fewer people who could trace her movements, the better.

"And can you recommend a good hotel in the city?" she asked.

"Oh, yes. The Hotel de Mendoza is very popular."

The man grinned and rattled off a location in the heart of Guadalajara—a place Alexa had no intention of staying. If anyone had eavesdropped or traced her movements, they'd be running down bogus leads. She needed a good smoke screen to ditch whoever was watching her now.

"Thank you," she told the man as she tipped him and got into the cab that he'd waved to the curb.

"*Gracias, señorita.*"

After the taxi pulled into traffic, Alexa told the driver to take her to the Hotel de Mendoza. From there she would find another place to stay. On pure reflex, she moved to where she saw the traffic behind her, using the driver's mirror. Although nothing looked out of the ordinary, Alexa had been in the field long enough to know looks could be very deceiving. And instincts carried much more weight than merely trusting her eyesight.

"How long to the hotel?" she asked the driver, to distract him from noticing her obsession with his mirror. As the man talked, she thought about her next steps.

She planned to get lost in the city of Guadalajara, traveling off the grid, using her fake passports and paying cash for everything. Once she got situated in town, she'd lease a rental car and make contact with the local Tanya had given her. For a price, he'd have what she'd need to conduct surveillance in a foreign country. She needed the right gear and enough firepower to make a good first impression.

Soon she'd be on the hunt for Garrett Wheeler, staked out near the compound of Manolo Quintanilla Pérez, the leader of a ruthless drug cartel. But if she couldn't shake whoever was following her, she had to come up with a better plan. No one was getting in her way, not when she was so close. If Garrett's life was at stake, she'd never forgive herself if she did nothing.

La Pointe, Wisconsin

"Were there any witnesses?" Jessie asked Chief Cook as she stood by the swing set in the backyard behind the abandoned old house where Angela DeSalvo had been murdered.

"Only a yardman who found the body three days later. The smell, you know. His name was Luke Brenner."

"Was?"

"Yeah, he died three years ago. Hunting accident."

"What about neighbors? Did anyone see anything?"

The deserted house was on a spur off the main road. And given the rural setting, the nearest neighbor would have been too far to hear much, but asking the question was worth a shot.

"When we get back to the station, I can let you look at the case file, but I don't need an outsider second-guessing the work of my men. I've had my guys go over every detail, and I questioned most of the key people who were living here at the time. I came up empty. DNA evidence is my last shot at reviving this case, but without anything to compare it to, this investigation has run out of gas."

Jessie believed Chief Cook when he told her that he'd been over the case, reexamining every scrap of evidence. A murder like this would have been a black eye on his years of service. And it probably still haunted him, like it would have bothered her. But even if she wouldn't get a long look at the murder book back at the station house, she had another way to look into the case. If the local library carried old newspapers in its archives, she might find something intriguing to look into.

"When I talked to Detective Cooper about your case, Chief Cook, she mentioned something about children being reported at the DeSalvo house. What can you tell me about that?"

"Not much. We interviewed folks who lived close to the crime scene and one or two mentioned something about seeing kids at the residence the week prior to the murder, but none of that could be substantiated." He pursed his lips and avoided her eyes. "Now that I think about it, if your DNA was found at the scene, what those folks saw was probably you."

"But kids doesn't mean one child," she argued. "And with my DNA being at the scene, there's proof that at least one child was there. Doesn't that give a new perspective on all those people who claimed to see children there?"

Chief Cook heaved a sigh and shook his head.

"Like I said, none of that could be substantiated. We saw no evidence of a child or children at the DeSalvo house. For all we know, if there were kids there, they could have been visiting one day. That's it. We just don't know. And, quite frankly, I don't see how it factors in."

"It factors in because I ended up in the hands of a serial pedophile, Chief. If I was in La Pointe, how did I end up in Chicago? Someone had to take me there."

Cook narrowed his eyes as he leaned a shoulder against a tree.

"I don't mean to sound insensitive, and I certainly wish I had answers to your question, for your sake, but backtracking who brought you to Chicago won't solve my murder." He softened his expression. "That would bring closure to you. And I pray you find it, but I'm not sure what more I can do for you."

"Can I see a copy of the DNA analysis?"

Sam had already sent for the analysis, but Chief Cook didn't know that. Jessie wanted to see how forthcoming he'd be.

"I'll see what I can do. After I got a look at it, I sent it to be filed. It should be in the evidence box, but maybe that hasn't gotten done yet. Why do you need to see that?"

"DNA brought you the first lead you've had in the case in nearly twenty years. Bet that made you feel pretty good." After he nodded, she made her point.

"Well, think how I felt when I finally got a lead on a past I'd given up on knowing about. After I got rescued in Chicago, no one ever came forward to say they knew me. The Chicago PD posted my face in the news all over, and no one contacted them except the lunatic fringe. This is the closest I've come to knowing where I came from. I just can't walk away from this. I can't."

"I'm sorry, Ms. Beckett. I truly am, but I'm not sure what you expect me to do for you."

"You said you'd let me look at the murder book, that's a start. I don't want to interfere in your investigation, but maybe I could talk to those people who reported kids at the DeSalvo house."

"You can read the interviews. I don't want you talking to the people of this town unless I'm with you. But after nearly twenty years, the memory of some of these folks may not be so good. The best you'll get is probably in those interviews, when their minds were fresh."

"You're probably right. And thanks, Chief."

Jessie followed him back to his squad car in silence. For the first time in a long while, she was stumped for anything to say. The harsh reality was that the death of Angela DeSalvo might only be another piece to the puzzle of her life. The case had gone cold for a reason. Getting her hopes up now would only make it harder later if the answers she'd hoped for couldn't be found.

She knew she had been at that crime scene before. That had been real, but none of this explained why she'd ended up with Danny Ray Millstone.

At least, not yet.

Guadalajara, Mexico
Two hours later

After Alexa had been dropped downtown, it didn't take her long to find suitable accommodations. She'd checked into the Villa Ganz, a quaint boutique hotel on the west side of the city near

Avenida Chapultepec and the beautiful Zona Rosa district.

With the hotel catering to a discreet clientele, the average tourist couldn't afford the luxury accommodations, but she'd picked the hotel for other reasons. Her room had a good view of the street, and there were plenty of ways to bail in a hurry if she had to. And anyone who came looking for her, without an invitation, would get noticed if they weren't a guest.

While she waited for the sun to go down, Alexa had gotten familiar with the hotel layout, looking for viable egress plans in case she needed them. She had also made a few calls and arranged for a rental car to be brought to her. A dark SUV with tinted windows was waiting downstairs, but before she left the hotel, Alexa called Tanya to check in.

"I'm here. Anything new?"

"I had Seth do a little digging into the use of that satellite. Whoever is behind this off-book mission isn't only using it to trace one cell GPS signal at the Pérez compound. Harper backtracked their trace."

"Oh? What else are they working?"

"Something happened in El Paso that triggered all this. And from the satellite imagery, they were following a moving signal that ended up at the Pérez estate."

"Do we know what they were interested in?"

"Yeah, and Harper sent me the images. From what I can tell, a man was abducted on the U.S. side in El Paso and taken over the border to Pérez. We're trying to figure out who he is, but that's a long shot."

"You think it's Garrett?"

"Don't know. He's been missing longer than this man was abducted, but no telling what this off-book job is. I've forwarded the images to you on your cell. There's not enough detail to see faces, so no luck there."

Alexa couldn't help but let her disappointment get to her. They had plenty to be concerned about but nothing real to go on.

"Harper told me one other thing," Tanya added. "It seems phone chatter inside the compound was picked up once the hostage was delivered. Whoever this man is, it's a big deal to the men who took him."

"Do you think our team is there to rescue this guy?"

"From what we can tell, they haven't made their move," Tanya said. "It's like they're waiting for something."

"Or someone," she speculated.

"Maybe, but none of this makes sense from where I'm sittin'. I'm worried."

"Yeah, me too. Thanks. I'll call you when I can."

"Be careful."

After Alexa ended the call, she sat on the edge of her bed, thinking about what Tanya had told her as she stared at the satellite image she'd been sent. Tanya was right. There wasn't enough detail to see faces. All they had was proof of a kidnapping. Only her gut made her believe that Garrett was the abducted man.

But if this was a Sentinels' operation, why would anyone sit on the sidelines watching a kidnapping and do nothing about it? She had a feeling Donovan Cross knew about this mission. And since he'd tried to stop her, that had given her another reason to fear that Garrett was the guy in the hands of that drug cartel.

But something else bothered her.

If Hank Lewis was on the ground in Mexico, why would he sit still and let anything bad happen to Garrett? Like Tanya said, none of this made sense.

No matter how things played out, she was in the right place to do something about it.

Alexa grabbed her stuff and headed for the lobby and her rental car. Dressed in dark jeans, hiking boots, and windbreaker, she tipped the valet and dropped the nearly empty duffel bag she carried on the passenger seat next to her.

Before she headed for the coordinates Tanya had given her for the Pérez compound, she'd make contact with a local that the analyst had given her, an arms dealer who would have what she needed to fill the bag she'd brought.

She wanted to acquire a com unit to keep in touch with Tanya, a full surveillance package, body armor, grenades, two MP-5s, and a couple of handguns with ammo. If someone was tracking a cell-GPS signal inside the compound of a drug cartel, they'd soon have a shadow.

Alexa only hoped her efforts would lead her to Garrett—and that when she found him, he'd still be alive.

Police Station
La Pointe, Wisconsin

"You plannin' on stayin' the night?"

Jessie looked up to see Chief Cook standing in the doorway of the small conference room they'd allowed her to use. She'd been poring through the murder book and had photos, interview notes, and other evidence spread over the table.

She'd officially taken over part of his station house.

"Oh, wow."

When she looked past him toward a window, she saw that the sun had gone down, and it was dark outside.

"Sorry. I didn't realize what time it was."

"You've been so quiet in here, I didn't want to interrupt," he said. "You have any questions before I head out for dinner?"

The chief told her he would be working a little OT, catching up on paperwork, but eventually when he left for the day, she'd have to leave the case files behind.

"I noticed a folded map with notes on it. What did you use that for?" she asked, pointing to the aged paper map that she had pinned to a corkboard near the door. The town map had been laminated with red circles and notes in black marker on it.

"That map was used by me mostly. I kept track of who we'd interviewed, the neighbors who lived closest to the crime scene. With the properties so sprawled out, I wanted to make sure we got everyone."

"Looks like you did make contact with everyone who lived around the DeSalvo place."

"Yep, all those red circles. Once my men told me they'd made contact, I circled the location. What are you getting at?"

The chief narrowed his eyes, and she felt a distinct chill in the room after she questioned his investigation. The map had been loaded down with small, abbreviated notes from the chief. A lot of detail, but something was missing.

Before she answered the chief, one of his deputies poked his head into the conference room. Deputy Tyrell Hinman had introduced himself before when he got her a coffee refill.

"You need me, Chief. I'm fixing to head out."

"Ah, no. You go on, Tyrell. I'll see you tomorrow."

"Sure thing. Good night, Ms. Beckett. It was nice meetin' you."

"Yeah, you too." Jessie barely looked at the deputy. She had kept her eyes on the chief. While the deputy interrupted, she saw the wheels of Cook's brain working. The man was leaping ahead, trying to figure out where she was going with this.

"What's wrong with my map?" he asked.

"Nothing's wrong with the map exactly. It's just that when I went through the evidence box, I sorted everything by type. All interview notes are here." She put her hand on a stack of papers. "But when I matched up the interviews to the neighbor's residence and this map, that was when I noticed one interview was missing. Can you help me locate it?"

"What? No, that can't be." He stepped toward the table and looked down at the map where she pointed. "Which one is missing?"

"There's a note here. See it? The Tanner place. Sophia Tanner." Jessie stepped toward the table and pointed to the interview-report pile. "But I can't find an interview with her, just references that one of your guys missed her, a couple of times. Do you know if anyone actually conducted that interview? Maybe it was misfiled."

One missing interview wasn't exactly a home run, out of the park, but Jessie had scored a solid base hit. A murder investigation had a lot of moving parts, especially one as shocking as the DeSalvo killing would have been in a small town. The chief would have had a lot on his mind. And with the evidence spread out in the conference room, the magnitude of his job was very clear.

Jessie wanted to give him the benefit of the doubt that he might have missed something minor, but the neighbor living closest to the DeSalvo house was a key interview to miss. She hoped he'd tell her the paperwork had been misplaced and that he'd remembered it; but after seeing his reaction as he looked through the files on the table, Jessie had a bad feeling that a critical interview had never happened.

"Are you sure it's not here?" The police chief

helped her look through the paperwork, but they came up empty.

"I've searched through all this, too. Were there any other evidence boxes?"

After the chief shook his head, he slumped into a conference-room chair and stared at the papers stacked on the table in front of him.

"Well, I remember seeing it. It must have gotten misfiled . . . or something."

"If you saw it, what did she say?"

"Nothing. She didn't hear anything. And she hadn't seen any kids." Chief Cook shook his head. "I forgot about that map."

"What?"

"That was good detective work . . . you comparing that map to the interviews, I mean. I should have . . ."

He never finished. He only stared across the room, avoiding her eyes.

"Is Sophia Tanner still living in town?" she asked.

"Yeah, she is." Chief Cook looked dazed. "She used to work part-time at the police station a few years ago, after she retired from teaching. I can speak to her tomorrow . . . for all the good it'll do now."

Jessie knew what he was thinking. The chief claimed to have seen that interview, but he might have been covering up the truth. If that interview had never been completed, that was a pretty big hole in the investigation. And if Sophia Tanner was still in La Pointe, how much would she remember from so long ago?

Someone had screwed up, big-time.

Most people would have the urge to comfort him, but not Jessie. If he was anything like her, nothing would make him feel better. Chief Cook had owned responsibility for this case. Even if one of his men had dropped the ball, he knew it was all on him.

And she respected him for taking the responsibility.

"Who knows? Maybe something will come up," she said in commiseration. "You mind if I tag along when you talk to her?"

"No, I mean, yeah I mind. This is an official police investigation. I can't have civilians looking over my shoulder."

Jessie was dumbfounded by the chief's sudden about-face. She was getting the worst of his cold shoulder, and that was getting her hackles up.

"But I was the one who uncovered this missing interview. Some people might say you owe me one."

"Well, some people might be wrong. This is my case. And I'll handle it."

When Chief Cook stood, he grabbed the stacks

she had so carefully put in order and stuffed them back into the evidence box, piling them up helter-skelter. If she'd been lucky, he would've been done talking, but that didn't happen. Cook opened the door to the conference room and waited for her to leave, but not before he said what was on his mind. And the attitude he'd shown her when they first met was back in full force.

"I'm sure you'll be heading out of town now since there's nothing more you can offer. Leave a number where I can reach you. And I'll call."

"Be still my heart."

Jessie glared back, but the man wasn't intimidated. She walked out the door with her mind in overdrive. What the hell had just happened? She'd been kicked out of town twice in one day. A lesser person would have taken it real personal.

But unfortunately for Chief Tobias Cook, that wasn't Jessie.

CHAPTER 7

Alexa had parked down the street from a seedy-looking bar on the outskirts of Guadalajara, called La Cucaracha. A row of motorcycles was parked in front, with more parking in the rear of the stucco building that had been marred with black and red graffiti.

"Nice ambience." Alexa sighed. "Guess I can forget the umbrella drinks."

Tanya had told her about the bar. An arms dealer operated out of La Cucaracha, a man known by the street name, *El Puma*. In English, his name translated to Cougar. Clearly the man wasn't concerned with the negative image of his branding efforts, especially if he hung out at a bar named for the cockroach.

While she sat in her SUV, watching who came and went from the local watering hole, she pulled back her hair and tucked it into a ball cap that she'd brought in the canvas bag. Pulling the hat down over her eyes, she wanted to minimize the fact that she was a woman. In a dump like La Cucaracha, her precautions might not make a difference. Once she got inside, Tanya had given her specific instructions. If she did as she was told, *El Puma* would make contact with her.

"This better work."

After Alexa entered the murky bar, every head in the place turned toward her. At least, that was how it felt. She avoided eye contact and found an empty table to the left of the smoke-filled bar. The place smelled of cigarettes, sweat, and booze. Eventually, a waitress came over and dropped a napkin on the table and asked to take her order in Spanish.

"Sorry, I don't speak the language." Alexa kept her voice low, only loud enough for the young woman to hear. "Just give me a beer. Dos Equis with a lime, thanks."

After the waitress left, Alexa took out a pen and wrote on the napkin. When the girl came back with her order, Alexa handed her the note she'd written. The young woman looked at it, then locked eyes with her before she went back to the bar. Her exchange with the bartender left Alexa with little doubt that she'd gotten her message across. She wanted to meet with *El Puma* to talk a little business.

Alexa took a sip of her beer and kept her eyes alert for any sign of trouble. The place gave her the creeps. The only women in the bar waited on tables or looked like hookers working the room. La Cucaracha didn't exactly cater to the tourist trade. And with the abundance of ink in the bar, she was feeling left out, not having enough tattoos to fit in.

It took nearly twenty minutes before the bartender caught her eye and nudged his head toward the back. His gesture had been so subtle, she almost missed it in the dimly lit bar. Alexa noticed a doorway to the right.

"Showtime," she muttered.

When she got to the door, a man dressed in jeans and a black T-shirt stood in the hallway. He was armed and carried a Beretta in a shoulder harness. As big as he was, she couldn't see past him, making her edgy.

"Lead the way," she said with a wave of her hand.

"After you, *señorita*."

Although Alexa didn't like turning her back on *El Puma*'s man, she did as she was told and walked by him toward a door at the end of the hall. When she opened it, Alexa was surprised to see who was in the room.

A familiar face smiled back at her. And she couldn't hide her shock.

"Hello, Alexa. I usually prefer blondes, but seeing you as a brunette could change my mind."

Sentinels' operative Hank Lewis was leaning against the far wall of the office with his arms crossed. And a man she didn't know sat behind a desk like he belonged.

"What are you doing here, Hank?" She narrowed her eyes. "And who's your friend? *El Puma*, I presume." Alexa extended her hand to the guy behind the desk.

He had a wide barrel chest with broad shoulders and slicked-back dark hair. When the man stood to take her hand, Alexa noticed he was dressed in a navy sport coat, open-collar white shirt, and khaki pants. Except for his penchant for gold chains worn around his neck, *El Puma* looked like any businessman on the street.

"*Sí, Señorita* Marlowe. I have a street name for business purposes, but you can call me Victor, since we are all *compadres* here." The man remained standing. "Can I get you another *cervesa*?"

"Unless Hank gives me a good reason to stay, I'll pass on the beer, but thanks, Victor."

When she turned her attention on Hank, the short, muscular man with the burr haircut grinned, and said, "You mind giving us some time alone, Vic? We need to talk."

"No problem. My office is yours, *mi amigo.*" Taking his bodyguard with him, Victor left them alone.

"Thought you were on assignment, Hank."

"Yeah, I was. Mission interruptus."

"Were you the one who's been following me since the airport?"

Hank furrowed his brow and shrugged.

"Sorry. Don't know what you're talking about."

Alexa watched every detail of Hank's reaction. His body language, and what she knew of her many missions with the man, made her believe he was telling the truth. And he had no reason to lie. Not now.

Had she gotten so paranoid that she'd imagined being followed?

"I've been . . . working, until now." Hank cocked his head. "I got pulled off an op to talk to you."

"Talk to me. About what?"

"I'm here to ask you to back off, Alexa. We're in the middle of a sensitive operation. We don't need the distraction."

"Just tell me about Garrett. Where is he, Hank? Is he involved in your assignment?" Alexa crossed her arms and stood her ground. "I just need to talk to him, make sure he's okay."

Hank thought about what she'd said before he answered, "As far as I know, Garrett isn't part of this."

"But you don't know for sure," she guessed. From his hesitation, she knew how things went when a mission was run on a need-to-know basis. Hank might not know who was calling the shots.

"Why are you here, Alexa? Straight up." He stepped closer and fixed his gaze on her.

Alexa had to give him enough so he'd believe her, but not so much that it would implicate Tanya's involvement. If anyone got pegged for interference, it would be her alone. She wouldn't let anyone else go down with her.

"Garrett's gone AWOL. He hasn't come up for air with me, and I checked with Tanya. She hadn't heard from him in a couple of weeks now. I'm worried, Hank. And I have reason to suspect there's an op going on down here off book. Is Garrett involved in any way?"

"I couldn't tell you that, Alexa, even if I knew myself."

"Did you know someone is using unauthorized satellite time to track a cell-phone GPS signal inside the estate of Manolo Quintanilla Pérez, a drug-cartel boss?" She pressured him to let her in on the mission by spouting what she knew. "Your op is south of the city at the Pérez compound, right?"

"I can't talk about the mission, Alexa. You know that."

"I just gotta know he's okay. That's all." Alexa took a risk and pretended to know more than she did. "Is he inside that estate? Is that who you're tracking? I've seen the satellite images of the kidnapping. What's going on, Hank?"

From the look on his face, she knew she'd hit on the truth.

"Damn it. How did you . . ." Hank shook his head but stopped before he said too much. "Look, the best I can do is run this up the food chain, see if they want to bring you into this."

"Who's running the show?" she asked.

"Don't know, but if they want you gone, you gotta follow orders." Hank headed for the door like everything had been settled. "In the meantime, give me a number where I can reach you. And stay put until you hear from me."

"Not good enough, Hank. I've got business with our mutual friend, Victor. Unless I hear from you, I've got my own agenda."

Hank turned and faced her, unable to hide his frustration. She'd seen that look before.

"Guess I knew that's what you'd say." He pulled a gun and aimed it at her, a move she didn't expect.

"Since I can't trust you to behave, you're coming with me."

"And just where are we going?" Alexa gritted her teeth, feeling more than a little pissed that she hadn't seen this coming.

"You'll see soon enough. Now move."

An hour later

Hank always did know how to entertain a woman. He had her stashed in a cheap motel room a few blocks from the sleazy bar he'd just abducted her from—at gunpoint. The place rented by the hour, which explained the low-rent décor . . . and the smell.

Slouching in a chair by the bed, Alexa had eavesdropped on a few of his cell-phone calls, but they were so cryptic, she hadn't learned much. The only thing she really knew was that after the last call to the handler for the mission, Hank was more nervous than she'd ever seen him.

When she saw a huge roach crawl across the floor, she watched it until Hank noticed it, too.

"Friend of yours?" she asked. When he didn't find her amusing, she said, "Hey? What's eating you?"

When Hank glanced at her sideways, Alexa cocked her head and batted her eyelashes, playing it real coy just to piss him off. Midpace, he stopped and did a double take.

"You're kidding, right?" he asked. "You come down here and mess with my op, forcing me to leave my men and make a call I never wanted to make to my handler. Now the head honcho in charge of this mission is coming here, breaking all protocol, to fix this screwed-up mess because you can't leave well enough alone. And you wanna know what's wrong with me?" He ran a hand across his short hair and shook his head. "That's just rich."

"Hey, you made the choice to bring me here. I had my own party goin' on." After Hank rolled his eyes, Alexa pressed him for more. "So why are you sitting this one out? You know they have a hostage. You've seen proof off the satellite. What are you waiting for? The guy could be dead, and you'd never know it. What kind of mission are you on?"

She hated grilling Hank, but she was bored and more than a little antsy.

"I'm following orders, Alexa. And if that hostage was in real trouble, we'd know it."

"What are you talking about?"

Before Hank could answer, a knock on the door stopped him cold.

"So who's at the door?" She leaned forward with her eyes darting between him and the closed door. "Come on, Hank. In a second, that won't be a secret anymore."

"That's just it, Alexa. I don't know." He rubbed his palms across his shirt to dry them off.

"Don't you know who's heading up the op?"

"No. I follow orders, Alexa, something you should consider doing from time to time." Hank reached for the door and pulled his weapon. After he nodded at her, making sure she was ready to back his play, Hank opened the door.

"What the hell . . ." He lowered his gun. "So *you're* in charge of this mission? Well, I'll be damned."

And Alexa stood with her mouth open. She couldn't help it. She was stunned.

"I thought you were . . ." She shook her head, staring at the man standing in the open doorway.

"You two better have a real good reason for risking this mission, especially you, Alexa."

Larger than life, Garrett Wheeler filled the threshold and lowered a weapon of his own.

CHAPTER 8

Alexa was completely shaken. After seeing Garrett Wheeler standing in front of her, she didn't know if she should be happy he was alive or be mad as hell. And he had the nerve to point the finger at her, accusing her of messing up his op.

"And you better have a damned good reason for breathing." She pulled him into the room by the arm and after she gave a quick look down the hall to make sure he was alone, she closed the door and turned on him.

"What's going on, Garrett? And why all the secrecy?"

"You ever look up the word 'secret,' Alexa? You should try it sometime."

"I was worried that something bad had happened to you. Sorry for caring." She glared at him. "If you're here, then who is Pérez holding as hostage?"

"What do you know about that?"

Typical Garrett. He had shifted gears by going on the offensive.

"Don't change the subject. Answer me."

She knew she was pushing it with the man who was her boss, but she was in no mood to be diplomatic.

"Give me one legitimate reason why I should? You're not part of this mission, Alexa. And from the way you've barged in here, I think that was a good call."

"Whoa, now. I don't wanna get hit in the cross fire." Hank raised both eyebrows and backed off. He found a corner in the room and crossed his arms, playing it as neutral as Switzerland. When Alexa saw Hank's reaction, she mumbled under her breath, "Coward," before she directed her anger back at Garrett.

"I was worried about you. If I had gone missing like that, what would you have done?"

"Touché, but jeopardizing a mission in progress? That's . . ." Garrett searched for the right word. " . . . irresponsible."

"So is disappearing without a word. And I refuse to apologize for caring about you." When Garrett softened the stern expression on his face, she knew he was finally listening. "Tell me about this mission. I'm down here. You might as well use me."

"I can't." He shook his head and turned his back on her. "The reason I didn't ask you to join us hasn't changed."

"What's that supposed to mean?"

"Damn it, Alexa. I need you to walk away from this. You came here looking for me. Well, you've found me. And I'm telling you to go home."

When Garrett looked her in the eye, he flinched for an instant. His reaction was enough for her to realize he was holding back. And it was personal.

"You're hiding something. What is it?"

When Garrett looked to Hank for support, the guy shrugged, and said, "Hey, don't look at me. This op is on a need-to-know basis. And, apparently, you didn't want me to know anything either."

"Not you, too." Garrett raked a hand through his dark hair as he thought about what to do next. His jaw tightened, and he avoided looking at either of them.

"I got a call a few weeks ago," Garrett began. " . . . a guy telling me that he had an operation already in play. He told me he would be infiltrating the Pérez cartel, the hard way. He had personal reasons for wanting to kill the son of a bitch."

"Who? Pérez?" Hank asked.• When Garrett nodded, Hank narrowed his eyes. "Didn't know you needed a reason to kill that sorry bastard."

"Yeah, well, this guy had two good reasons. Pérez had ordered a hit on him several years ago, but his family got killed instead."

Alexa saw the pained look on Garrett's face and knew there was more to this story than what he'd told them.

"That's horrible, but why did he call you?" she pressed, moving close enough to look him directly in the eye.

"Because I owe him. I was the one who'd ordered the protection detail on his wife and little girl. His family was killed on my watch."

Alexa's next breath caught in her throat. She'd seen the same look of guilt on Garrett's face before. And a face from her past emerged from the shadows of her mind. Green eyes she'd seen not long ago, eyes filled with a never-ending sadness that had haunted her since she'd last seen him.

"I know this story," she whispered, not completely sure she had spoken aloud.

"Yeah, you do. And that's why you weren't asked to come along, Alexa. You're too close to this."

"Would someone please clue me in?" Hank asked.

"Jackson Kinkaid is the guy inside." Alexa felt numb. Saying Kinkaid's name made it all real. "He's on a suicide mission to kill the man who murdered his wife and child. And damn it, Garrett, you should've told me."

"Why? So you could watch him die? You're as crazy as he is, Alexa."

"I could've talked to him, made him listen to reason. Getting hijacked by Pérez, that's a one-way trip."

"You know how Kinkaid operates. He didn't give me any choice. By the time I got our team deployed, he was in the thick of it, with no way to back out. The guy doesn't know how to back down. I've known him longer than you have. He's been living for this. In his mind, it's all he has left."

Kinkaid wasn't with the Sentinels now, but he used to be. And after what had happened to his family while he had worked for their organization, she figured Garrett had authorized the mission based on the obligation he felt toward a man who had suffered as much as Kinkaid had.

"I can understand going after Pérez if the guy killed his wife and kid, but how do we know what's going on in there?"

"We have a burst transmitter on him, embedded under his skin," Hank told her.

"Don't tell me. Let me guess," she interrupted. "That was his idea, right?" When she looked at Garrett, all he did was nod and shrug.

"Unbelievable."

"That transmitter has been sending us his vitals, as well as his location, so we can track him via satellite," Hank continued. "I'm in charge of the ground team, and we're located right outside the compound, ready to go in once we get the green light. And as for his vitals? The medical doctor on our team thinks Kinkaid is being tortured."

"Tortured? What for? If they knew who he was, Pérez would just have him killed. I'm not arguing for that, mind you, but killing him would tie up a very big loose end. What am I missing?" she asked.

"That's just it. He got abducted when they thought he was someone else. And that's who they think they're interrogating, a bigger fish in their eyes."

"Oh, yeah. Who?"

"Me," Garrett said. "The Pérez drug cartel, they think they have me."

Shoreview Motel
La Pointe, Wisconsin

After the surreal trip she'd taken down a shadowy memory lane with Chief Cook at the crime scene earlier, Jessie was desperate for anything that closely resembled normal. And the chief's sudden change of heart, about wanting her help, had left her feeling more than a little lost.

She took a hot shower, got ready for bed, and made a call to Seth. He'd become her life preserver in the turbulent sea of her past. He steadied her and made her feel safe. With Harper, she had a shot at "normal," at least a taste of it.

When he answered her call on the second ring, she simply said, "Hey, it's me."

Jessie heard a soft rustle and knew he was in bed, too.

"Hey, you," he said. "What are you wearing?"

Jessie couldn't help it. She had to grin.

"Nothing but a smile. And you?"

"I'm wearing . . . Floyd, actually. He's such a bed hog."

"What did he do today? I could use a good Floyd story. And I know you've got one."

Harper told her that Floyd had learned how to open doors by standing up and flipping levers with his paws.

"I've got a reason for telling you this," he said.

"Oh?"

"Yeah, the next time you're alone in our bathroom and you feel a cold nose on your butt, you'll know who it is."

"A cold nose, huh? Why would I assume Floyd is the culprit?"

"Very funny."

She listened to the sound of his soft chuckle as she pulled the comforter over her shoulders.

"Should I be worried?" he asked.

"About what?"

"You seem to have this thing for Floyd. Do I detect a little canine envy?"

"That's it, Harper. You've nailed it." She sighed and ran a hand through her wet hair. "Have I told you how nice it is to hear your voice?"

"Yeah, but feel free to remind me whenever you feel like it."

After a comfortable silence, Seth had more to say.

"You've done a fine job avoiding what's on your mind. So what is it?"

"Can't fool you." She tried to smile, but couldn't. "This place, I know that I've been here before, but those memories are just beyond my reach, you know?"

"You met with that cop today. What did he have to say?"

"He kicked me out of town . . . twice. Is that what you mean?"

"Wow, that must be a record."

"Yeah, that's what I thought."

She told him about the police chief taking her to the crime scene and how he'd later allowed her to see the murder book until he erected a wall and suggested she leave town . . . again.

"I've seen you in action. Guess I'm not too surprised."

"Thanks a lot, pal. Whose side are you on?"

"Yours. You've got the gun. But what do you think happened? Sounds like you were BFFs until you mentioned that missing file."

"Yeah, that's what I thought, too."

Harper had the same take on the situation as she had. *Great minds . . .*

"You're gonna see that Tanner woman, aren't you?"

"You know me, Harper. Never leave a good turn unstoned."

"Wait, I gotta write that down," he said.

She heard him fumbling for a paper and pen, like he was seriously taking notes.

"Are you sure that Angela DeSalvo was the woman you remembered from your dreams?" he finally asked, taking a detour down Serious Lane. "Maybe seeing the dead woman's face forced you to make that leap."

What Harper had insinuated made sense, but

Jessie felt sure that she had remembered Angela's face on her own, without the help from an old crime-scene photo.

"No, I'm sure it was her." She sighed. "I've never felt so . . . down. Seeing her face and thinking she was my mother was the only bright spot to my childhood, and now all that is gone."

"I knew I should have gone with you. You shouldn't have to go through this alone."

"But I don't feel alone, not when I can look forward to your abuse. I mean, your support."

Even though she'd poked fun at him, hearing Seth's voice on the phone made her feel like he was right in the room with her. Of course, nothing would replace the feel of his arms around her—or the many other things he did to make her feel warm and happy—but having him to talk to at the end of her day was the next best thing.

"So, with the chief taking back his key to the city, what're you doing tomorrow?" he asked. "Is there something you need me to do?"

"I'm planning on making a royal pain of myself."

"Stickin' with your strengths. Always a good strategy."

"And thanks for the offer to help. I may take you up on that."

"For you? Anytime."

"I'll call you tomorrow," she said. "And give a big sloppy kiss to Floyd."

"That's an image I didn't need."

Even as lousy as she had felt that day, Harper could always make her laugh. And now he had an accomplice.

Guadalajara, Mexico

In the cramped motel room, Alexa listened to Garrett as he told what he knew about Jackson Kinkaid. And from the looks of Hank, he hadn't had a clue about any of it. She guessed that since she and Hank both knew Kinkaid, Garrett had kept the truth from them and added a higher level of secrecy to the mission.

"Kinkaid lied to them and set up a pretty big ruse, pretending to be me," Garrett told her. "He even made fake ID to back up his story."

"What made him think they'd believe that?" Alexa asked. "And how would they know who you are? You keep a pretty low profile."

"Actually, that was a thing of beauty." Garrett almost smiled. Almost. "He ran the whole thing like a con artist running a scam. He set up a fake online trail and made sure rumors got out on the street before he even got to El Paso. By the time he hit the ground, they were waiting for him, but that was what he wanted. All he needed was a way in, and a street gang on the American side of the border gave him that. He made himself a damned Trojan horse. Once he got inside, he had a plan to bring down the bastard who ordered the hit that got his family killed. Guess he wanted to look the guy in the eye before it all goes down . . . even if it put him at risk, too."

By the way Garrett shook his head, Alexa knew he hadn't had a say in how Kinkaid had orchestrated his own abduction.

"And in order for his plan to work, that meant you had to disappear," she said. "If anyone saw you living large in New York, word might get back to the border, and Kinkaid would be a sitting duck."

"Yeah. That's why I couldn't say anything. It had to look as if I'd gone undercover, on a mission of my own. If anyone knew what was really happening, Kinkaid's life would be more at risk than it already was. I backed his play because he left me no options."

"This is crazy. You gotta get him out of there," she insisted. "I mean, what are you waiting for?" Her frustration got the better of her, and she knew it. "There's gotta be another way to get at Pérez. We'll find it and bring him down."

"No, we're too close, Alexa," Garrett argued. "For now, we're doing it Kinkaid's way. All he has to do is hold out a little longer."

"Hold out, for what? He's not you. He can't tell them anything." She heard the anger in her voice and didn't care. Anything involving Kinkaid was personal. No wonder Garrett had left her in the dark.

"Yeah, but they don't know that. Kinkaid is holding out until Pérez gets there. From our intel, that son of a bitch is in Mexico City, conducting business as usual, but he's heading to his estate tomorrow. That's what Kinkaid has been waiting for."

"So what happens after Pérez is in the picture?"

"I know what I'd like to see happen, but I don't think Kinkaid has any intention of taking Pérez alive. He's got another plan that I don't know about."

"Then why did he ask you to back him up?"

"We're his insurance. If he can't finish what he started, he wants to make sure I do."

"That's insanity. We could have done this clean, with minimal collateral damage." Alexa shook her head. "But he doesn't care about that, does he? If he's got a shot at killing the bastard, he's gonna take it, no matter what happens to him. Damn it, Jackson."

She knew Kinkaid didn't care what happened as long as he got what he wanted. Garrett was right about his having nothing left but revenge. And how much of Kinkaid's mercenary days had been a part of his scheme to find the man who'd ordered the hit? Had he gotten involved with the drug cartels, hoping to find out who had been responsible for the murder of his wife and child?

His obsession had consumed him. That was what she sensed the last time she'd seen him on their mission into Cuba during a hostage-rescue operation, but after hearing what Garrett had to say, Alexa felt an overwhelming sadness for Kinkaid. *What a waste!*

"I want in." She turned her attention to Garrett. "I understand your concerns about my objectivity when it comes to Kinkaid, but I've got to be a part of this."

Garrett sighed and stole a glance toward Hank. The ground-team leader only shrugged his version of an endorsement.

"You're in on one condition. What I say goes. You're following orders, understood?" Garrett pointed a finger at her. After she nodded, he said, "And when this turns ugly, don't say I didn't warn you."

Alexa knew that if Kinkaid was on a suicide mission, odds were that she'd see him die. And that thought fueled an ache deep in her belly, but that was a far cry from letting him go it alone. The least she could do was back him up.

And that meant taking down Pérez on his turf—in the stronghold of his estate.

CHAPTER 9

La Pointe, Wisconsin
Next morning

Jessie had taken a chance and gotten up early to catch Chief Cook at the police station. She didn't intend to talk to him, knowing how far that would get her. This time, she parked down the street, playing a hunch. And when she saw his patrol car leave the station parking lot, she smiled.

"Gotcha."

The man could have been making a donut run, but Jessie had a gut feeling he was up to something else. When he headed toward the DeSalvo house and turned onto a back road, she knew her hunch had paid off. True to his word, he had gone to see Sophia Tanner, the trip he had wanted to make alone.

"Sorry, Tobias. You can't be the Lone Ranger, not today."

But before he turned into the Tanner driveway, the chief spotted her in his rearview mirror and stopped in the middle of the drive, blocking her way in. When he got out of his vehicle, she did, too.

"I'm not breaking any laws, Chief. This is a public road. And I'm a tourist."

"You're loitering."

"I'm bird-watching." She glared at him, going on the offensive before he did. "What changed, Chief? One minute you're talking to me, the next, you're ready to slather me in hot tar and roll me in feathers. What gives?"

"Look, I don't have to explain myself to you. What part of 'this is my case' don't you understand? Is English not your first language?"

"Oh, I'm getting your message loud and clear, Tobias. And for the record, if I were bilingual, I could ignore you in two languages." She stood toe-to-toe with him, her arms crossed. "Who's Sophia Tanner? And why are you protecting her?"

"What? That's ridiculous." Chief Cook glared at her and worked his jaw like it pained him. "Anyone ever tell you, you're a pain in the ass?"

"Yeah, but if it'll make you feel better, you're the first one today."

Before Cook could mount a second wave of

ornery, Jessie looked beyond him and waved her hand and smiled.

"She looks real friendly."

Chief Cook turned to see Sophia Tanner standing on the porch. She was returning Jessie's wave with one of her own.

"I might have to come back, to say hello."

"Now I told you . . ."

"I know what you said, Chief, but the way I see it, you have two choices. You could invite me to stay, and both of us talk to her, or I can come back later—alone. Your choice?"

"There is another way to go. I could arrest you."

"For what? Bird-watching?"

Cook dropped his chin to his chest and let his shoulders slump. None of this was going like he'd planned, but before he thought about things too hard, Jessie's mouth was making promises it couldn't keep.

"If I promise that I won't say a word, will you let me sit in?"

Chief Cook clenched his jaw, and finally said, "Fine."

The Tanner residence was the closest acreage to the house where Angela DeSalvo had been murdered. It was a mirror image of the DeSalvo place except that it was in better shape. The green clapboard house had a well-maintained yard with wooden steps that led to the front porch. Potted flowers hung from a cedar pergola near the front door. And Sophia Tanner was a collector of yard art, anything that spun in the wind.

By the time Jessie and Chief Cook parked their vehicles and got out, Sophia Tanner came out to meet them. She was wiping her hands with a washrag, wearing khaki slacks with a blue floral top.

"Hello, Sophia. Thanks for making time for me."

"I didn't expect you to bring a visitor, Tobias. Not with you wanting to talk about . . . that DeSalvo murder."

Mrs. Tanner did not look happy with the chief, but when she turned her attention on Jessie, the woman smiled.

"I'm Sophia Tanner." She extended her hand and waited for Jessie to reciprocate. The woman's hand was icy cold.

"My name's Jessie. Jessie Beckett."

"You're not from around here, are you?"

"No, ma'am. I'm not. I drove up from Chicago. I'm an investigator, helping Chief Cook with an old case."

The woman squeezed her hand and held it a little too long. And the way she looked at her, it made Jessie feel uncomfortable. Chief Cook must have felt it, too. He cleared his throat and put his hand on Mrs. Tanner's shoulder.

"Let's go inside. Would that be okay?"

Mrs. Tanner blinked, almost as if she hadn't heard him.

"Yes, of course. Please . . . come in." The woman led them into her living room. "How's that arthritis of yours, Tobias? You walking like I told you?"

"Sophia used to push me to walk at lunch when we worked together," the chief told Jessie. "And she wasn't a woman you could say no to, at least not often."

Mrs. Tanner listened to Cook and smiled, but when she thought Jessie wasn't looking, the woman stole glances at her. Jessie felt like a damned lab rat. The staring made her uncomfortable until she got distracted with the woman's house.

The Tanner house was real homey inside, especially with the smell of coffee and cinnamon lingering in the air. And she collected antique furniture, good-quality stuff, and had lace and pastel frills everywhere. But when Jessie saw all the family photos in the living room, the smiling happy faces reminded her of what she'd never had—a family.

She'd been a ward of the state of Illinois and had never been around a real family, except for those in the foster-care system that she'd stayed with when she wasn't in an institution or halfway house. All of her belongings had been kept in a trash bag, ready to move when the state ordered it. That was no kind of life for a kid.

"Can I get you some coffee?" the woman asked.

"None for me," he said.

Taking a cue from Chief Cook, Jessie shook her head and said, "No thanks."

"Please, sit." Mrs. Tanner took a seat and folded the washrag on her lap, something to do with her hands. "How can I help you?"

The chief sat in a wingback chair, and Jessie took a spot on the sofa.

"Like I said on the phone, I'm lookin' into the Angela DeSalvo murder case," he began.

"I don't know. That's been so long ago. I thought I read somewhere that you'd closed that case, Tobias."

"That case never went to court. And murder cases stay open until they do. You remember how that works, right?"

"Terrible thing." The woman shook her head. "I had nightmares over that for such a long time."

"I can understand that."

"So why are you here . . . talking to me, Tobias?"

"I hate to admit this, but we're missing some paperwork on the case. Everyone whose property was adjacent to the DeSalvo house got interviewed, except for you. And I've come to rectify that."

"But I did talk to someone. One of your men, I think." She wrung the cloth in her hand. "Maybe that old paperwork will show up. Maybe it was misfiled, is all."

"I understand what you're saying, Sophia, but while we're here, I'd like to ask you a few question. Will that be all right?" Without waiting for her reply, he continued as he opened a notepad, "What can you tell me about the night Angela DeSalvo was murdered? Did you see any strangers or hear anything out of the ordinary?"

Sophia Tanner told Chief Cook all she remembered. The more she talked about Angela De Salvo, the more her fingers worked the washrag she still held in her hands. And she avoided eye contact as she spoke. She was uptight about something more than recalling the murder of a neighbor.

While the police chief made a note, Jessie had a question of her own.

"How well did you know Angela?" she asked.

Chief Cook gave her a sideways glance, and, under his breath, he said, "So much for not saying a word."

When Jessie saw him raise an eyebrow, she ignored him and turned her full attention on Mrs. Tanner.

"I knew her as well as anyone would know a neighbor, I suppose. We didn't socialize, if that's what you mean. We talked on occasion, as neighbors. That's all."

"Do you remember seeing any children at the DeSalvo home?" From the corner of her eye, Jessie saw Chief Cook shift in his seat, and she heard his sigh, but that didn't stop her. "Maybe she had kids at her place that week prior to the murder."

"Tobias, what is she talking about? Kids? You never said anything about wanting to talk about children."

Sophia Tanner's eyes watered, and she looked confused. If Chief Cook had been doing his job, he might have attempted to calm her down, so he could continue his questioning, but that's not what he did.

"I think I've got everything I need." He stood and reached for Jessie's arm, heading her for the door. "Thanks for your cooperation, Sophia. If you think of anything else, give me a call."

"I will. I promise." The woman forced a smile. "Have a good day, both of you."

When they got outside, out of Mrs. Tanner's earshot, Jessie had plenty to say.

"You call that an interview? You clearly don't watch *Castle*, to see how it's done."

"And you clearly make promises you have no

intention of keeping. I think we're done here. Have a good day, Ms. Beckett. And if I hear that you've come back here to harass this poor woman, I'll arrest you. Is that clear?"

The man was done talking. He got in his squad car and waited for her to get in her rental. Any hope she had for his cooperation had dried up, and she had no idea why. She'd hit a wall that she had never seen coming.

Now she'd have to scramble, and she had a good idea where to start.

La Pointe, Wisconsin
Twenty minutes later

If Chief Cook wouldn't give her any more information on the murder of Angela DeSalvo, Jessie knew how to dig up stuff on her own. And a good source for a story nearly decades old was the town library and the newspaper archives.

She took a corner of the archives and worked over the digital images of old newspapers until she was bleary-eyed. With only the occasional bathroom break and a raid on the snack machine, where she finished off the Cheetos and KitKat bars, she searched the digital records, looking for anything pertaining to the murder of Angela DeSalvo. And seeing the newspaper evolve over time gave her insight into the community and people of La Pointe.

TV detectives always had miraculous databases to help them solve cases in a make-believe world where DNA results could be done in minutes, and the killer always confessed in the last five minutes of the show. In real life, it didn't work that way. Most cases involved "beating feet" on pavement and tedious grunt work that could be butt numbing.

When she'd located a string of articles that encompassed months after the murder, Jessie made copies of the best ones with the most details. Since this was a small town, the newspaper took liberties with its reporting. It deviated from the typical sparse style of journalistic writing and sometimes focused on the more emotional aspects of the story.

She scanned the pages and didn't see anything that she hadn't expected, but she'd go over the articles later when she had more time to read.

When the last article had printed, Jessie sorted through her pile and placed the most important pages on top. Once she got back to her motel room, she wanted to read them first. And considering the stack of paper, it would be a long night.

She headed out of the library with her gold mine of old articles on the DeSalvo killing rolled up in her hand. When she got outside, it was the first time she realized that she'd spent almost the whole day ratholed in the archives. But after she filled her lungs with cool dusk air and caught glimpses of the sunset glittering on the churning waters of Lake Superior, she got a second wind. And her stomach reminded her that she hadn't eaten much all day.

She followed the main drag, walking toward the water. From what she remembered of her ferry trip, the harbor area had some inviting restaurants near the shore. That made her belly rumble, but as she turned down a side street, she caught a glimpse of movement in the waning sunlight. A shadow had moved behind her.

La Pointe was small, a tourist town. Why she flinched at the sight of someone behind her, she didn't know. Maybe her wariness had been a by-product of digging into the DeSalvo murder all afternoon. And being in the very town where it had all happened had caused her jumpiness.

The way Jessie figured it, it didn't hurt to be careful. When she picked up her pace, she paid closer attention to the sounds coming from behind her and kept a watchful eye on any suspicious movement. Under her windbreaker, she carried her Colt Python. And with the adrenaline coursing through her veins, she felt the weight of her weapon as she ducked around another corner. If someone was following her, she'd have precious seconds to expand the gap between them and look for a place to confront the bastard.

Jessie had no intention of losing him, not when she wanted to look the son of a bitch square in the eye.

CHAPTER 10

La Pointe, Wisconsin

Jessie spotted a darkened alleyway ahead. The sun was low enough on the horizon to leave shadows in its wake. The alley separated two storefronts. One place was still open, a small gift shop. And the other had lights out and was closed for business. Before the guy who was tailing her rounded the corner, she darted into the alley and shoved her back against a brick wall.

Come on, you sorry son of a . . .

She didn't have to wait long.

When the guy thought he'd lost her, he'd picked up his pace. The sound of his footsteps grew louder. Jessie waited for him to run by the alley where she was hiding. All she saw when he jogged by was a blue plaid shirt, jeans, running shoes, and a navy baseball cap pulled low over his face.

After she'd turned the tables on him, she fell in pace behind him, tailing him instead. But the guy must have seen her make the move, because with barely a look over his shoulder, he made a run for it.

"Damn it!" she cursed under her breath as she chased him. "If you make me break a sweat, I swear . . ."

There was only one good thing about the guy hauling his ass down the street. With him running, it confirmed that he'd been following her. She hadn't been overly paranoid after all.

But with the guy having a lead on her, Jessie had to make up ground. Her lungs were burning, and the muscles in her legs were on fire. With her arms pumping, she carried the rolled-up newspaper articles clutched in her hand. And when the bastard ducked around a corner without hesitating, she saw that he was taking her through a deserted part of La Pointe, a place she didn't know at all.

The guy knew where he was going. It was his town. He had an advantage. And with him out of sight, she had to be careful. Jessie slowed up, bracing her body in case he reached out and grabbed her. With her chest heaving, she tucked her newspaper articles in the waistband of her jeans before she pulled out her Colt. She gripped the weapon in her sweaty hand as she neared the street corner.

Jessie slowed her breathing and stepped lightly so he wouldn't know exactly where she was, but once she made her move, that was the end of her game of finesse. When she swung around the corner, with both hands on her Colt, she saw that the street was empty. An abandoned old gas station was positioned on her right and an auto repair place stood on her left, secured by a cyclone fence that was locked.

Jessie walked slowly down the street, keeping her gun aimed into every shadow. And after she'd checked both sides of the street, she lowered her weapon.

"Damn," she cursed under her breath.

The bastard had found a place to hide, like the cockroach he was.

Pérez Compound
Outside Guadalajara, Mexico
10:20 P.M.

On day two of surveillance, Alexa had changed her clothes to more practical attire—camo BDUs. Garrett always came prepared and had brought extra gear. She was hunkered down in the foothills outside the Pérez estate, with her elbows propped on a boulder, using high-tech night-vision binoculars to monitor the security patrols inside the compound. On instinct, she timed and tracked the intervals at which the armed guards patrolled the grounds and how many men made the rounds.

She felt dirt on her skin, but she kept perfectly still and didn't fidget. And when something crawled up her ankle, she didn't panic. She brushed the scorpion away by moving with slow deliberation to avoid any sudden moves, a practice honed from years of training and discipline. Hasty moves and unexpected noise in the stillness could make her a target.

She'd picked an isolated spot away from Hank's ground team and kept to herself. She melded into the terrain as the moon cast a bluish haze that looked like a dusting of fine blue powder over the rugged landscape outside the estate, covering trees, boulders, agave plants, and yuccas. And she listened to the sounds of the night, the forlorn hoot of an owl in the trees and the baleful cries of a pack of coyotes.

Most people might have been tense, hiding in the dark, but Alexa got off on the isolation, a complete departure from New York City. Yet despite the serene setting, she couldn't forget why they were there. Jackson Kinkaid had crossed her path once again. And she hoped, given the situation, that it wouldn't be for the last time.

Rapt in her thoughts of Kinkaid, she hardly noticed that Garrett had joined her. He hadn't said a word, and neither of them felt uncomfortable with the silence between them. He'd only slipped next to her and didn't feel the need to say anything at all. The reason for his secrecy had vanished, so he joined Hank and his men, and Alexa had become part of the team. Having Garrett with her felt comfortable, and it reminded her how close she'd come to losing him. But swapping her fears from Garrett Wheeler to Jackson Kinkaid wasn't exactly making progress.

It wasn't until she heard a steady thump in the distance that she'd realized the intruding noise was man-made and mechanical, and stood out from the sounds of nature.

"What's that?" she whispered, only loud enough for Garrett to hear.

"Helicopter."

As if on cue, lights in the distance cut through the darkness. She lowered her night-vision binoculars—not wanting to be blinded by the onset of the bright lights on the horizon—and watched as a helicopter rose over the mountains. The aircraft circled the estate below and hovered behind the hacienda, kicking up dust as it landed.

"Pérez," she said under her breath and edged closer to Garrett, feeling the warmth of his arm against hers.

Without responding to her, Garrett spoke into his com unit to Hank and his men.

"Anyone with confirmation, speak up. If the big man is there, I want to know it."

"Copy that."

Alexa watched as Hank's team shifted positions to utilize long-range surveillance gear. Even with her night-vision binoculars, she couldn't see well enough to ID a face. Not even the full moon helped. All she could do was sit back and let Hank's men do their jobs.

"What now?" she asked Garrett. "How do we know when to move in?"

"If we can't make an ID, then Jackson has to confirm that Pérez is on-site. He said he'd give us a signal."

"What kind of signal?" she asked.

"He said we'd know it when we saw it, but until then, we're to stay put on the ridge outside the estate." Garrett gave her a sideways glance and didn't say anything more.

Even in the murky shadows, she saw Garrett tighten his jaw as he watched the estate below. He didn't like this either.

An hour later

No one on Hank's team had confirmed that Manolo Quintanilla Pérez had been one of the people who'd flown via helicopter to the estate outside Guadalajara. Too many men had rushed to the helicopter to usher the new arrivals inside. And so far they hadn't seen any sign from Jackson Kinkaid, if he was even still alive, that is.

"I can't believe you went along with Kinkaid's self-destructive idea of a plan." The words were out of her mouth before she could rein them back in. The instant she'd said them, she knew she'd done the wrong thing. It wasn't Garrett's fault that Kinkaid had a vendetta against a drug kingpin in Mexico and that he was being held by Pérez and his vicious pack of dogs. Jackson had done that on his own.

"It's not like he gave me a choice, Alexa," Garrett said, unable to hide his annoyance. "If we don't see anything soon, I'll make the call to go in. Understood?"

"Yeah, understood." Alexa took a deep breath. She only had to understand, she didn't have to like it. "So what now? We wait?"

"Yeah," he whispered back. "We wait."

She knew that waiting was a big part of surveillance, but she didn't have to like that either. While the team watched the activity below—with some of Hank's men closer to the action, so they could confirm any sighting of Pérez—Alexa took advantage of having Garrett next to her.

And she wanted to get her mind off Kinkaid's suicide mission.

"Was it you who followed me from the Guadalajara airport? At first, I thought it was Hank, but later he told me it hadn't been him."

She hated admitting she didn't know who had tailed her, but if it had been Garrett, that would explain why she only felt him and never saw him. Garrett was an experienced agent who could make himself a ghost if he wanted to.

"No, wasn't me." He shook his head and furrowed his brow. "Someone followed you? Did you see 'em?"

"No, only felt them. If it wasn't you, I have a pretty good idea who ordered it."

"Who? What are you talking about?" he asked.

"Donovan Cross." She fixed her gaze on him, waiting to see if the name meant anything. "So what's up with that guy? What's his part in all this?"

"Donovan Cross? I know who he is, but what's he got to do with it?"

She stared at him for a long minute, trying to read if he was lying again. Since he'd clued her in and made her part of his team, now he had no motive for keeping her in the dark when it came to the mission with Kinkaid, but she had no idea if that extended to his past with Donovan Cross.

"He took over your job and told me you were dead, killed in a classified mission. He made up a story about how you got caught in an explosion, and your body would never be recovered. Ring any bells?" When he didn't say anything, she stared at him in disbelief. "You mean he wasn't part of your disappearing act?"

"No, he wasn't." Garrett narrowed his eyes and got strangely quiet.

When he finally glanced at her, he must have seen the worried look on her face, because he said, "I'll put out some feelers, figure out what's going on. It's probably nothing."

He tried for nonchalance, but she wasn't buying it.

"Yeah, right. It's probably just a coincidence. And you know how I feel about those." She sighed. "You better watch your back with Cross. He's got to have support within the Sentinels if he stepped into your job so quickly. Who would do that?"

"I'll take care of it."

The way Garrett said it—as if he had made a promise to himself—it left her cold inside. In a covert agency like the Sentinels, it paid to have solid support within the organization, from the top down. But if Donovan Cross had slipped easily into Garrett's job, she had to wonder. Who had undermined Garrett's authority? Doing something like that wasn't a one-man show. Who was backing Cross as the new head of the Sentinels?

And how far would they go to keep him there?

"Cross doesn't strike me as someone's puppet." She couldn't let it go. "And he's got to be working with people who have the balls to seize an opportunity when they see it, with you missing. I'm just . . . worried, Garrett."

"I know you are," he began as he stared into her eyes, "but I've got to handle this my way. I don't want you getting stuck in any cross fire. That would . . . kill me."

For the first time in a long while, Garrett looked into her eyes like he used to. She'd ended their relationship and moved on after she'd caught him with someone else, but the intimacy between them had never truly been severed. And that had never been more apparent. Alexa blinked and cleared her throat, breaking his connection with her.

"Just remember that you've got friends, too. Don't go it alone, tough guy."

Garrett smiled, a quick fleeting curve of his lips.

"Good to know. Thanks."

* * *

"What was that? That sound, did you hear it?" Estella's voice cracked.

She turned her head toward the only window in the cell and squinted into a piercing light that vanished as quickly as it had come. A powerful engine roared across the night sky as the sudden brightness stabbed the dark and left its phantom image in her mind.

Something was happening outside.

And after the engine noise faded, she heard the distant voices of Ramon's men and hoisted herself high enough to see out. But her sudden moves started the aching pain again. Her shoulders were on fire, caused by the weight of her body. And her wrists were raw from the ropes.

When her question about the noise went unanswered, she looked over to the dark part of the cell, where only a thin stream of moonlight doused the stone walls. Estella saw the silhouette of the American. He had not moved in over two hours. And she barely heard his breathing.

"Please . . . don't be dead," she whispered.

Saying the words aloud didn't make her feel so alone, even if the wounded man couldn't hear her.

"No such luck," he mumbled.

"Oh, I'm . . . sorry. I did not mean . . ."

"Helicopter."

"Excuse me?"

"You heard a h-helicopter. That was . . . the n-noise."

It took all her concentration to hear him. Yet even though the man sounded weak, there was something in his voice that calmed her. And since he had answered her first question, she ventured another.

"What are they doing? Ramon's men. I hear them outside."

Her whisper hissed across the cell and echoed off stone, sounding garbled. When he didn't answer right away, she almost repeated her question, thinking he had not understood her.

"This is almost over. I'm sorry for how it turned out." Even though he choked out words plainly enough, she didn't understand what he meant.

"This isn't your fault, *señor.*"

"I wish you were right about that." When he spoke, she saw the glint in his eyes, a reflection of the moonlight . . . and something else.

Estella didn't understand the strange man, but for first time, she was afraid of what she saw in his eyes.

La Pointe, Wisconsin

After Jessie lost her footrace with the guy who had taken an interest in her, she had given up on her appetite. She'd stopped in at the motel office and scored enough snacks to satisfy her if she changed her mind. Byron McGivens wasn't behind the desk when she stopped in, even though his nameplate was still hanging on the wall as if he were on duty.

"Does Byron have the night off?" she asked. The minute she'd instigated the conversation, Jessie knew it had been a mistake. It only gave the guy behind the counter a reason to chat her up.

"Yeah, he had something to do. I fill in sometimes." The older man grinned back at her. "So . . . you new in town?"

Jessie fought the urge to roll her eyes. The clerk rang up the sale, between his attempts at making one-way small talk, and forced Jessie to smile as she headed out the door. When she got to her room, she set the brown bag with her snacks on the sidewalk near her door—and as a precaution—she reached for her Colt Python. After she unlocked her door, she flipped on the lights and aimed her gun from corner to corner.

Her room was empty. And her things were as she'd left them, except where the maid had touched. Jessie smelled the scent of pine cleaner, saw that the bed had been made, and noticed the maid had left her fresh towels. After she saw the room was clear, she went back for her bag of goodies and locked the door behind her, tossing her new stash of Fritos, Twinkies, and Red Bull onto the extra double bed.

She pulled out the newspaper articles from the waistband of her jeans and tried to straighten them, without much luck. Since the pages had gotten squashed and manhandled in her chase with the local yokel, she slipped them under her mattress to flatten them out while she got cleaned up.

Jessie took a quick shower and changed into the gym shorts and tank top she normally slept in if she wasn't spending the night with Seth. After she got in bed, she propped herself up on her pillows and spread out the articles she wanted to read as she ate a Twinkie.

Most of the articles about the killing were textbook journalism, but some were more dramatic, like an intriguing mystery. And some reporter even speculated on rumors. Anything was news in a small town.

Folks had wondered why Angela DeSalvo had kept to herself, not socializing much with the rest of the town. Someone had her pegged as a woman on the run from an abusive husband. And another local woman swore she saw her with kids and speculated that she was running an illegal adoption scam.

"Well, I'll be damned," she whispered.

Reading that, Jessie felt the hairs on the back of her neck rise. If Angela DeSalvo had been on the wrong side of the law, that could explain how she had ended up in the hands of a serial pedophile. The thought of Angela contributing to what had happened to her made Jessie sick.

"What were you up to? And did it get you killed?"

Jessie made up her mind to spend the next day talking to some of the locals mentioned in the articles, to see who was still living in La Pointe. And something about Sophia Tanner still bothered her. The woman had appeared edgy, and she had wrung the washrag so tight in her hands, it had made Jessie nervous just watching her. And when she'd mentioned kids, the woman freaked. She had immediately looked to Chief Cook for protection, and the local LEO obliged her, right on cue.

Jessie had no doubt that Cook would arrest her if he found out she had talked to Sophia Tanner one-on-one after he had specifically told her to leave the woman alone. When Jessie thought of how adamant he'd been, she smiled to herself.

Guess what he didn't know wouldn't hurt her.

Jessie turned out the lights and lay in the dark, her mind still working over all that she'd seen today, but when her cell phone rang, she had to get up to answer it. She had it recharging in the motel bathroom.

"Hey, Sam. What's up?" She'd recognized the incoming cell number and knew who it was. Her friend didn't call at this hour unless it was important.

"Hey, Jess. Sorry to wake you."

"Funny thing. I haven't been able to sleep lately. Imagine that."

"Well, don't kill the messenger." Detective Samantha Cooper forced a laugh, but since Jessie knew her well, she was familiar with Sam's strained attempt at humor. "Are you sitting down?"

Jessie looked behind her. The only place to sit in the tight bathroom was the toilet seat, and she had no intention of receiving bad news sitting on the commode. When she got to the bed, she took a corner and sat.

"Yeah, I'm sitting. Shoot."

"Remember that DNA report that I requested, the one Chief Cook claimed he got a hit with your DNA that tied you to his cold case?"

Jessie didn't like the sounds of this already.

"Yeah. What about it?"

"Chief Cook told me he got one hit on your DNA. Is that what he told you?"

"Yeah, he did. What's this about, Sammie? 'Cause you're shaking me up here."

Jessie's throat went suddenly dry. Her breathing had escalated, along with her heart rate. She had no idea where Sam was headed with her questions, but Jessie didn't like it.

"Sorry, Jess. I don't know why the chief wouldn't tell you everything. Guess you can ask him when you see him."

"Sam, spit it out. Please."

"I had my lab boys analyze that report, so I'd be sure of the findings. That's why I couldn't call you sooner, but Jessie, that report had two DNA samples on it. Your DNA wasn't the only one found at that crime scene."

"What?"

"The Wisconsin state crime lab found a second unidentified sample of DNA. And that sample showed a 95 percent probability match to yours."

"What does that mean?"

"It means that second sample doesn't have a match in the databases, so they can't ID who was there, but the DNA came from someone in your immediate family, Jessie. Your *real* family." Sam let that thought settle before she landed a second shocker. "And according to the crime lab and my CSI guys, that DNA has genetic markers that indicate it came from a male."

"You mean . . . my father?"

"I don't know, Jess. It could be your father or a

brother." Sam heaved a sigh. "I don't know if this is good or bad news, but maybe you can ask Chief Cook why he left out that second DNA sample. He didn't tell me about it. And apparently he never said anything to you either. I'd sure want to know why."

Terrible thoughts crossed Jessie's mind. And it left her reeling. She couldn't sit anymore. She had to stand, but when she caught a glimpse of her face in the mirror, she suddenly got nauseous.

With all the talk about kids being seen at Angela DeSalvo's place prior to her murder, Jessie had to wonder. She had to have been one of those kids since her DNA was found at the crime scene. And now it appeared her brother had been there, too. The joy of knowing she might have a brother mixed with a flood of dark thoughts.

Had her brother been taken the way she had been? Did Danny Ray Millstone torture her brother, too? Had he been in that house where she was held prisoner, and she hadn't even known it?

"No, that can't be." She swallowed, hard.

"What?"

"Oh, Sammie. Give me a minute here. I gotta process all this before I say anything." Her voice cracked as she paced the floor. "Just wait a minute."

Although Sam could check into the Millstone case, looking for names of the survivors or the

names of the kids the bastard had killed, that
would take time. Sam would have to pull the case
files and do legwork to find out what Seth Harper
would know in short order. Harper had his father's old murder book. And he'd been making
contact with the Millstone survivors. That was
how and why they'd met. Harper would know
what she needed.

"I've got to talk to Seth," she muttered.

"What? Slow down, Jess," Sam urged her. "Take
a deep breath."

"I know. And you're right, but I gotta think.
What did Cook tell me? I gotta remember." As she
ran through everything the chief had said, she
paced the floor and searched through her mind.

Chief Cook had told her that he'd looked into
the Danny Ray Millstone case and knew about
what happened to her as one of his victims.
Maybe he knew more than he'd let on. Or maybe
he only wanted to spare her feelings. Either way,
she hated that he'd kept the truth from her. And
what she was thinking was far worse than if he
had just told her what he knew.

Besides the possibility of having a brother who
might already be dead—or a survivor of abuse
like she had been—there was a darker scenario
that lurked in the back of her mind, one that made
her even more sick.

"Hold on, I gotta . . ." Jessie dropped her cell on the mattress and ran to the bathroom. She emptied her stomach until all she had left were dry heaves. Her face was hot, and beads of sweat clung to the skin of her arms. With trembling hands, she cleaned up. And when she could, she got back on the phone with Sam.

"Are you okay, Jessie? I'm so sorry."

It took her a moment to catch her breath and calm her racing heart.

"Can you do me . . . a favor?"

"Yeah, anything."

"Do you know if they have a sample of Millstone's DNA on file? I mean, maybe after he was caught red-handed and killed, no one bothered to collect it."

"That's hard to say. Back then, digital DNA records were hit-and-miss, and not every case got consistent treatment. Why are you asking about this, Jessie?"

"I need to know if Millstone was . . . my father."

It took everything she had to say those words.

She had no other explanation for how she ended up with the serial pedophile. Being related to that scumbag would be the worst she could imagine, and that was saying something. She knew it was a leap, one she didn't want to take, but if this trip had been about uncovering her past, she had to go the distance. She had to keep an open mind about the possibilities, or she'd never find the truth.

"Oh, my God, Jessie. I never thought . . . If Millstone's DNA wasn't on digital file that could explain why Cook didn't get a hit on that second sample. And if we can confirm that second sample is Millstone's, then odds are that Chief Cook can solve his old murder case." Sam rambled on for what felt like an eternity, trying to console her, but finally she said, "Yeah, I'll look to see what I can find. And I'll call you the minute I know something."

"Thanks, Sam."

Jessie ended the call, knowing she'd never get to sleep. She had too much to try to remember—and way too much she'd never forget.

She'd contact Seth in the morning, first thing, but confronting Chief Cook face-to-face weighed heavy on her mind. She had to know why he'd lied to her about the DNA analysis. Did he already know what Sam had promised to find out, about her possible connection to her childhood abuser?

According to Cook, his men had missed getting an interview with Sophia Tanner. The interview had been missing from the murder book, but what if that original document had been taken from the evidence on purpose, to cover up the truth?

And if Cook had been behind that cover-up, why would he have gone through the motions of interviewing the woman again? He could have blown Jessie off and made excuses. There was plenty for her to be suspicious about and not enough cold hard facts, but the chief of police in La Pointe would be the man to see.

Had he held back the truth to spare her feelings, or was he protecting someone? Either way, Jessie wanted to look Cook in the eye and dare him to lie to her again.

CHAPTER 11

Waiting had never been Alexa's thing. It gave her too much time to dwell on Kinkaid's predicament, but something else was eating at her. And she had to say something to Garrett. When she found him hunkered down next to Hank, she moved closer and spoke in a hushed tone.

"What happens when Pérez sees Kinkaid?" She didn't wait for Garrett to say anything. "If it's true that bastard killed Jackson's wife and kid, then he'd know Kinkaid on sight. Once he sets eyes on him, he'll know he's not you. The masquerade would be over. All Pérez has to do is pull the trigger, or order it done."

Garrett didn't act surprised to hear what she'd

said. He only heaved a sigh as he turned his back on Hank.

"I'm sure Kinkaid knew that going in," he told her. "I tried to warn you. He's not planning on walking away from this."

Until now, Alexa had thought of this as a rescue mission, but nothing could be farther from the truth. She turned away and didn't say anything more. She didn't want the moonlight to out her to Garrett as her eyes filled with tears. Whatever Kinkaid had planned, he was going out in a big way. And the odds were against him, even with Garrett's team being outside the stone walls of the Pérez estate.

Jackson Kinkaid was beyond saving.

1:10 A.M.

"What was so important that couldn't wait?" Manolo Quintanilla Pérez said in his native tongue.

Ramon Guerrero clenched his jaw as the drug-cartel boss stared at him and Miguel Rosas, his number two man. Pérez hadn't offered them a seat. He'd made them wait to see him while he relaxed. And now they stood in front of him as the big man sat behind a massive cherrywood desk in the study of his estate. He leaned back in his leather chair as he sipped a fine Cognac from a crystal snifter.

Rosas was about to open his mouth to speak first, but Guerrero couldn't let that happen. The American had been his to find, and he wasn't about to let Rosas take credit for his diligence or downplay his part, not after he'd made the call to Pérez that had brought him there.

"My men took a hostage in Juárez, a very influential American. His name is Garrett Wheeler and he claims that you know him."

"Oh? That name is not familiar to me." Pérez narrowed his eyes at Guerrero. "Tell me. How do I know him?"

When Pérez crooked his lip into a humorless sneer, Guerrero cleared his throat before he went on.

"He did not say, but I believe that if you see him for yourself, you can get him to admit what he's up to."

"So now, you want me to do your work for you?" The cartel boss cut a sideways glance at Rosas, who only shrugged with boredom.

"No, sir. That's not what I'm saying, but someone of your reputation has no doubt made an impression on this man. You have said that you fear this American is probably CIA, and my sources back this up, too. This man has probably been sent to assassinate the heads of the drug cartels for the U.S. government."

In an effort to make a big impression and beat out Rosas, Guerrero had blurted out a theory Rosas had told him about, something that had come from Pérez himself, but his boss's questions had rattled him. And now that his words hung in the air, without evidence to back him up, Guerrero had sounded like an idiot.

"Oh? How do you know all this?" Pérez asked, setting down his empty glass. "What proof do you have?"

Before Guerrero could answer, Rosas interrupted with a smirk.

"He doesn't have any. He is only trying to impress you. The American hasn't confirmed any of this."

"He carried a U.S. driver's license with him. I've seen it and so have you. It confirms his name and an address of his home in New York," Guerrero argued.

"Identification like that can be bought. It means nothing." Rosas looked at his boss with a dismissive shrug. "And do you think if he is some big spy, that he would have his real information so easily obtained? Like I said, his ID means nothing."

"Then you are also dismissing the messages I received from my contacts across the border? Wheeler was overheard, trying to buy information about the cartels . . . and you, in particular. He admitted who he was when he thought he was safe on the American side. And my sources in New York have confirmed that Wheeler is missing."

"That's the point. Only your sources say this, but I believe in other ways to arrive at the truth." Rosas narrowed his eyes. "When a man knows he is about to die, he will bargain any way he can to save his miserable life. That is the only source worth believing, forcing a man to tell you everything he knows when he faces death."

"Ramon, you told me that it was urgent I should be here. Is this all you have? That I should see this American for myself?" Pérez shifted his glare toward Guerrero once again.

"I assure you, sir. I believe the man has vital information that you can help us get from him. I swear on my sainted mother's head, it's only a matter of time before we get him to talk."

"So now you use the words 'us' and 'we.'" Rosas chuckled under his breath and leaned against a wall with his arms crossed. "A minute ago, you were running this show, single-handedly. Which is it?"

Guerrero suddenly saw himself between two very dangerous men. He'd gone around Rosas's back to have a face-to-face meeting with his boss, an encounter that had not gone as well as he had expected. If he didn't play his cards right, he would end up the big loser.

"You have been extremely resourceful in dealing with the American," Guerrero said to Rosas. "I'm sure he will tell us everything, in time. And my sources will be confirmed."

"Very diplomatic, Ramon." Pérez grinned and stood. "Cowardly, but diplomatic nonetheless."

Before Guerrero had a chance to redeem himself, Pérez focused all his attention on Miguel Rosas, his trusted death dealer.

"What has the American admitted so far?"

"Nothing of consequence, but he has told both of us that he has come to kill a man," Rosas admitted.

"Oh?" Pérez smiled. "Depending on who his target is, perhaps we should help him. Eliminating the competition, is that such a bad thing?"

"My thoughts exactly." Rosas glanced over his shoulder at Guerrero, rubbing in his advantage with the boss and taking credit where none was due.

"Take me to him then"—Pérez smiled—"this man I know."

Rosas escorted the cartel boss out of the study, toward the makeshift cells where the American was being held, with Guerrero following close behind. Without really trying, Rosas had made him look like a fool, but maybe he still had a way to redeem himself.

When Pérez came face-to-face with the American, perhaps the truth would come out, and his boss would see who he had personally delivered to his door.

1:35 A.M.

"I haven't told you the truth, but it doesn't matter now. It's too late."

He looked at Estella and saw the questioning look on her battered face. And before she opened her mouth to ask what he meant, he kept talking. He'd run out of time.

"My name is Jackson Kinkaid. I'm not Garrett Wheeler. That was a name I thought would get Pérez here."

"You mean . . . the man Ramon works for? He is coming here?"

Kinkaid didn't have to see the fear in the girl's eyes. He heard it in her voice.

"He's already here. He came in that helicopter. And he's probably on his way to this cell right now."

"He's a bad man, *señor*. A very bad man. If he's here, it will not be good."

"If I had known you'd be dragged into my fight,

I wouldn't have done this. I would've found another way, but now everything is in motion. I can't stop it."

"What's in motion? What are you saying?"

From across the cell, Kinkaid saw Estella's eyes glistening with fresh tears. If this girl died because of him, he was no better than Pérez.

Grief and his urgency for revenge had blinded him. He had tunnel vision when it came to settling the score. There had to be a reckoning, where the dead got their due. That was all that had weighed on his mind and heart and soul since his family had been killed. The murder of his wife and his precious little girl had haunted him beyond reason.

Revenge was the air that he breathed.

Garrett Wheeler and his team were waiting for a signal—only it wouldn't be what they were expecting. Kinkaid's own men had confirmed that Pérez had been inside the aircraft at takeoff. And now that the helicopter had touched down at the compound outside Guadalajara, it had tipped the first domino, which toppled the rest to the point of no return.

And Estella would pay a price for his indulgence. But there was nothing he could do about it.

"Open the door," a man's voice bellowed from the corridor.

After a key slid into the lock, the door creaked open. And a torch nearly blinded him. Kinkaid squinted and turned his head with a grimace. He braced himself for more abuse, his body taut and seething with adrenaline.

He had lived for this moment. Despite his regret for what this meant for Estella, he couldn't do anything about that, not now. And his need to see this through to the end outweighed his good conscience.

Hidden behind the bright flame of the torch, the shadows of several men entered his cell, but the big man stood out. His face emerged from the dark, as in the many nightmares Kinkaid had had over the years. Manolo Quintanilla Pérez stood in front of him with a despicable smirk on his face. After all these years, it was really him.

The man who had murdered his wife and child.

The man who had taken everything.

CHAPTER 12

Sweat trickled down Kinkaid's face and stung his eyes. And it took all his determination to lift his head and stare down the man who had killed his family.

It had taken him years to uncover the truth. And he had worked with other despicable men to find out who had given the order on the hit, an assault intended to kill him instead of his wife and baby girl. But after he'd learned the truth, that Pérez had put a price on his head, it was all he could think about and all he had lived for.

And it would be the reason he would die here.

"So you are Garrett Wheeler, a big man with the CIA." Pérez sneered and walked slowly, not taking his eyes off him. "I only want to know one thing."

The men standing behind Pérez shuffled and moved closer. They listened to every word the fat man said. They were waiting for the American spook to back down in front of their fearless leader.

"Why did you feel you had to lie to my men?" Pérez leaned in and whispered, "You are worth more to me than Garrett Wheeler."

"What?" The voices of his men echoed in the cell. "What do you mean? Who is this man?"

"His name is Jackson Kinkaid. He blames me for the death of his wife and child, but who is really at fault?" The man shrugged and shifted his focus back on Kinkaid. "You were the one who destroyed my first cartel. It took me years to rebuild. And what kind of man would I be if I didn't punish the one who nearly got me killed?"

Pérez grabbed Kinkaid by the throat and squeezed. "You are to blame for the death of your family. You brought that on yourself. I warned you what would happen."

After he let go, Kinkaid choked and gasped for air.

"Your beef was . . . with m-me, not them. You're a c-coward who murders innocent women and ch-children."

"So what did you hope to gain by getting

hauled here to me, like this? You are a stupid man, Kinkaid. A bullheaded one." Pérez grimaced. "And all this, for a mere woman? You are a young man. You could have had more children, no?"

"I missed killing you the first time. But now I'm here to finish the job."

"So the man you came to kill is Pérez?" Ramon Guerrero looked shocked, but it didn't take him long to make excuses to his boss. "I swear, I did not know."

"Unbelievable," Pérez said as he scowled at his man, but when it finally sank in what Kinkaid had intended to do, he laughed aloud. His men joined him, with each one looking at the other to make sure it was all right. In Pérez's eyes, he had the high ground—the advantage. Kinkaid was nothing, less than nothing.

"You turn me loose, and we'll see how un-fuckin'-believable it is." Kinkaid mustered all his strength. He lurched at the man, rattling his chains. "You don't have the guts to face me like a real man. You're soft, Pérez. You've grown too fat and too old."

Pérez stopped laughing. And from the shadows, Kinkaid saw the man glaring at him in the darkness. He didn't know if the cartel boss would take him up on his offer, but he had nothing to lose.

Outside the Pérez Compound
2:05 A.M.

"What are you waiting for?" Alexa crowded
Garrett's space, grabbing the sleeve of his BDUs to
plead her case. "What if there's no signal? What if
he can't . . . ?"

She didn't have to finish. From the look on Garrett's face, he knew what she was about to say. Jackson Kinkaid could already be dead. And if Pérez
got into that helicopter again, he'd fly off and get
away with murder . . . again. Kinkaid might not
care what happened to him, but Alexa did.

"I'm telling you, Alexa, I have a gut feeling
Kinkaid has got more up his sleeve than us. If we
go in hot, it might get him killed or put my team at
greater risk." Garrett's commonsense advice contradicted the concern on his face.

Alexa knew he was right. Garrett had more to
consider than one man. Being in charge of the mission, he carried a great weight on his shoulders.
And heaped on top of that, his guilt over what had
happened to Jackson's wife and little girl had been
eating at him for years. Now this.

His training and his instincts were at war with
the regret he had over the brutal annihilation of
Kinkaid's family. And from the pained expression on his face, she knew none of this would be

easy. Before this day was over—no matter how it turned out—Garrett would pay a steep price for any mistake he might have made years ago, when he thought he had protected Kinkaid's family and hadn't.

"We got a read off the burst transmitter," Hank emerged from the shadows and huddled next to Garrett. "Our boy's in trouble again. His heart rate is up. Something is happening in there, but at least we know he's still alive."

Alexa breathed a sigh of relief. Even though the whole situation reeked, knowing Kinkaid was alive had taken the pressure off Garrett; but she still had no idea what he would do. Waiting was not Garrett's strong suit either.

"Kinkaid had asked us to stay in the foothills and keep watch." Garrett took another look through his night-vision binoculars. "But if anything happens to him, and Pérez leaves his estate in a hurry, we won't be able to stop him in time, not from here."

"What do you want us to do, boss?" Hank stared at Garrett, with half his face cast in shadows and the other half in moonlight. "My men are ready."

"We move closer. I want us within striking distance."

Garrett gave his order and pointed where he wanted his men positioned. They'd split up, with

Hank and Alexa taking one team and Garrett taking command of the other.

Alexa waited for Hank to leave. When she was alone with Garrett, she took off her camo boonie hat and looked him in the eye.

"You watch your sweet backside. I don't want to lose you twice."

Before he came up with his usual smart-ass macho comeback, she kissed him on the cheek for old time's sake. Feeling the warmth of his skin on her lips opened a floodgate of emotion that she hadn't expected. She'd moved on, and she knew that, but a part of her would always love him.

"I wish you hadn't followed me to Mexico, but now that you're here . . ." His lips curled into a lazy grin. " . . . I'm glad you did. Guess that makes me a selfish bastard."

"One of your better qualities," she said.

Giving her one of his devilish smiles made more seductive under the moon, Garrett left her and vanished into the darkness. This mission could cost her both of the men she loved. And no amount of training and experience would ever make her ready for that.

"Damn," she whispered to no one.

2:20 A.M.

Pérez glared at Kinkaid as he clenched his jaw in silence, leaving Ramon Guerrero dumbfounded at the stupidity of the man he worked for.

"Surely you are not considering this." Miguel Rosas stepped between his boss and Kinkaid, putting a hand on the man's chest. "He's simply goading you into letting him out of those chains. You have the advantage here. Give the order, and I will kill him for you. And I will take my time. He will regret his insults to you."

Still, Pérez didn't speak or take his eyes off the prisoner. Guerrero had a bad feeling this would not end well. The American—Wheeler or Kinkaid or whoever he was—had been tortured and was weak. But Guerrero had learned long ago not to count a man out who had just cause on his side. He slipped behind Rosas and moved closer to Estella, but not so close that it would draw attention. The girl hung from ropes and looked more frightened than ever. He could do nothing for her, not anymore, but he felt less like a bastard if he pretended he cared what happened to her.

"You should listen to him, coward," the American taunted. "You wouldn't want to ruin a good manicure, lard ass."

Guerrero was close enough to see the spark of anger in his boss's eyes. He knew the prisoner had hit the mark. He'd pushed as much as he needed to. Pérez would either order his men to kill the hostage—a long, slow death—or he would remove his restraints and free him to fight one last time. Neither of those options looked as if it scared the prisoner. The man was beyond caring.

Dead was dead.

"Don't do this, boss." Guerrero made his case, not wanting to be one-upped by Rosas. "Leave him to us. We will take care of this dog."

"Us? You brought this man to my door, Ramon. Don't think I will forget that." The cartel boss scowled at him. "But I will handle him myself. Uncuff him."

Guerrero was shocked by the man's order. And so were the other men. No one moved. Each of them looked at the other until Pérez broke the stalemate.

"What's wrong with you? Are you deaf?" he yelled. "I said free this man. And someone give me a knife."

His boss shrugged out of his suit jacket, unbuttoned his collar, and rolled up his sleeves. Miguel Rosas was the only man who moved. He handed his boss a knife and stepped back, glaring at the American, who would remain unarmed. Even in the shadows, Guerrero saw the faint smile on the face of Miguel Rosas. The man didn't care what happened or who died.

Like the sick psychopath he was, Rosas only wanted blood.

2:30 A.M.

Garrett's team was positioned outside the front gates of the Pérez estate. When his men got into place, he found a spot behind a boulder and lay flat on his belly atop a slight rise near the main entrance. He communicated to the rest of his team, and each one checked in. When their voices came over his com unit, it sounded like he was beside them. Hank and Alexa were last to move into position.

"We have two lone wolves, taking high ground. They're mine." Hank's cryptic message meant he had spotted a two-man sniper team in a tower overlooking the main residence. They had clear sight of the perimeter and the grounds.

"Two watchdogs every fifteen, front and back. Clockwork." Alexa had been monitoring the guards walking the grounds. Two-man teams walked their territory front and back of the property every fifteen minutes, without deviation.

"On my mark. In three." Garrett took one final look through his night-vision binoculars before he gave his order to launch their assault on the drug cartel's stronghold. RPG rounds would take out the front gate and cause a diversion for Hank and Alexa to launch their simultaneous assault from the rear.

But something made Garrett stop. He lowered his night-vision gear and listened with eyes closed so he could focus. A distant sound droned in the background. Something familiar made him hesitate. And when he recognized the noise, he had no choice but to call off their assault.

"Stand down. I repeat, stand down."

"What's happening?" Alexa was the first to speak over the com, but Garrett didn't have time to answer. Within minutes, they all heard it, and Garrett was the first to break silence.

"Fall back. I repeat, fall back," he ordered. "And take cover. Now!"

If what he suspected was right, they'd have to find cover fast. From the sound of the turboprop engine and the brief glimpse he got of its sleek distinctive design, an MQ-9 Reaper UAV had targeted the drug cartel stronghold. The unmanned aerial drone had hunter-killer capabilities. With its sophisticated surveillance, it could hunt a specific target. And with its payload, it could definitely kill. It was loaded with up to fourteen Hellfire missiles and GPS-laser-guided bombs. In seconds, the UAV drone would be over the estate and dropping its payload.

"Damn, Kinkaid. That's what you call a signal?" Garrett fell back with the rest of his team, praying that Alexa and Hank had gotten away clean. "You sure know how to send up one helluva flare."

Kinkaid had always been a gutsy operative. Garrett should have trusted him when he said to wait for his signal. If anyone died because he gave the order to attack too soon, that would be on his head, not Kinkaid's.

2:47 A.M.

Estella struggled to see over the men who stood in front of her, despite the pain it took for her to move at all. Flickering torches were the only light in the stone cell. And men's voice echoed loudly as they yelled their encouragement to Pérez. They wanted him to kill the American. She screamed, "No!" and thought no one heard her, but she'd been wrong. In the noise and confusion, it took her a moment to realize that Ramon had come to her. He leaned close enough to speak in her ear.

"If you know what is good for you, you will keep your mouth shut and stay put."

He raised a knife, and she flinched. It had been

the knife he used to cut her, but this time he used it to cut her down. She collapsed in his arms, too weak to stand on her own. Her arms were numb, and every muscle in her body ached. She didn't want to touch him or feel his hands on her again, but she had no choice.

"Can you stand?" he asked. Ramon smelled of sweat and dirt and blood.

She only shook her head. She didn't think he would hear her. Ramon held her for only a moment before he shoved her aside to lean against a wall in the shadows. He raised a finger of warning for her to stay put before he joined the rest of the men.

Where would she go? She had no one to help her and no place safe to run.

Estella dropped to the floor and crawled away from the men, so she could see. She watched Ramon's boss come at the American, Jackson Kinkaid. The man was weak. He could barely stand or even lift his arms, but when Pérez came at him with his knife, the American lunged for the big man. She knew the agony he felt to fight. And her pain was only a fraction of what he had endured.

Both men fell to the floor of the cell, kicking up dirt as they wrestled for the knife. The circle of men moved tighter around Pérez and the American until they blocked her view. Estella couldn't see any more.

She was trapped, and there was nothing for her to do but watch the American die. Tears streamed down her face. She could not blame the brave man for wanting revenge. Pérez had killed his wife and child.

It took Estella a moment to realize that she was already doing the only thing she could. She prayed for both of them.

3:05 A.M.

Kinkaid grappled for the knife Pérez had in his sweaty hand. All Pérez had to do was give in. If he ordered his men to kill him, his fight would be over, but the big man never opened his mouth. He was too stubborn, something Kinkaid had counted on.

But he was no match for the fat man, not in his condition.

Every time Pérez rolled on top of him, he cut off his air. Kinkaid shoved the man aside and used his weight against him. And he kept both hands on the knife. The blade cut into his skin. And with the adrenaline racing through his system, he used his rage to keep fighting. His lungs burned, and every muscle in his body was betraying him. He had nothing left.

"To d-die . . . f-fighting. It is g-good." The drug kingpin felt Kinkaid's hands give way. And when he saw the blood draining down his arm, he knew Kinkaid was losing his fight. One last time, he rolled over him. And the sharp tip of the blade hung over his eye, with Pérez putting his full weight behind the knife.

"G-glad you . . . think so." Kinkaid felt the sting of the blade cut into his cheek. In seconds, his warm blood rolled down his skin and filled his ear.

He was staring up at the last thing he would ever see—the red-faced, sweaty, drug-dealing bastard who had murdered his wife and child. Pérez looked like a madman. His eyes were bulging from his skull, and his jowls were trembling with his exertion. Kinkaid shoved at the man, using his legs to topple him, but that wasn't working. He had no more strength left.

"It w-would be . . . easy." Pérez whispered as he struggled to make one last thrust. "Just let . . . g-go. You will . . . die quick."

The drug-cartel leader's face blurred above him. The tip of his blade hovered over his one good eye. If he let go, Pérez would drive the knife into his brain. The drug trafficker was right. He'd be dead in seconds.

"No, don't. Please!"

Kinkaid heard a faint voice, mixed with the shouts of Pérez's men. The angry shouts echoed in the cell and nearly drowned out the girl's voice, but eventually Kinkaid heard Estella.

"No, please don't kill him." She was the only one who was on his side. And she had the guts to cry out, even in the face of an angry drug-cartel boss and his men.

Her voice gave him the strength he needed to hold on. All he had to do was last a little longer, but when a deafening blast erupted and shook the ground and walls around him, he knew the cavalry had arrived. When the first missile hit, he saw the brilliant flames light up the night sky through the barred window in the cell. And he heard stone walls topple. Dust filled the room, and Pérez's men yelled and ran for cover.

"What's happening? What was that?"

One blast had them scrambling, but the second and third blasts had them running to save their miserable lives, scurrying like vermin into the dark.

Pérez eased up on his grip long enough for Kinkaid to breathe. Air rushed into his burning lungs as Ramon Guerrero and Miguel Rosas emerged from the shadows.

"We are being attacked. If we don't leave now, we will be trapped. We'll die here." Guerrero's voice cracked.

"Give the order, and I will kill this man," Rosas yelled as he pulled his gun.

Kinkaid couldn't let that happen, not now. He heaved against the drug boss one last time, shoving him into his men. In the confusion, he grabbed for the hilt of the blade and twisted it, bending the man's fingers back. The weapon slipped from Pérez's hands before he had a chance to fight for it.

"Kill him. Do it now!"

The drug dealer screamed his order as he crawled away like the coward he was, but he didn't get away fast enough. Kinkaid gripped the knife and thrust it hard into the fat man's leg. Blood spurted from the wound before the cartel boss clutched his leg to staunch the bleeding. When he cried out, Guerrero rushed to him and grappled with the man, lifting his weight off the ground.

"We have to go. Now!"

The night sky lit up with more explosions. And when the sound of automatic gunfire erupted, Rosas aimed his weapon. Kinkaid had nothing to defend himself with except the knife in his hand. On his knees, he grabbed the tip and threw it at Rosas. The blade spun end over end until it struck the armed gunmen's flesh with a meaty sound. It embedded in his chest, hilt deep.

Wide-eyed, Rosas staggered back, his jaw slack, staring down at the knife protruding from the center of his body. The hilt of the blade pulsed, moving in time with his still-beating heart. And as blood blossomed from the fatal wound, it saturated his shirt with a deep crimson. The man dropped to his knees, still aiming the weapon at the prisoner.

Kinkaid held his breath. If Rosas had the strength to pull the trigger, he'd be dead before the bastard took his last breath.

CHAPTER 13

Outside the Pérez Compound
3:20 A.M.

Garrett watched the air assault from a distance as his team fell back to the designated rendezvous point and checked in. One by one, he heard from each of his men but still hadn't seen or heard from Alexa.

Where the hell are you?

Garrett and his team were firing back when the armed men behind the compound walls got off a few rounds, but the attacks were sporadic. The air assault had split the drug cartel's forces, and some of Pérez's foot soldiers were running for cover and scattering into the hills, the ones who had had enough fighting an unmanned drone that could target their positions with precision. In this attack, they weren't after the small fish.

"Whisky Two, reporting in, sir." Hank's voice came over his com unit. "Not that I'm complaining, but who's operating the Reaper?"

"Don't know. One of Kinkaid's men, I'd guess." Garrett couldn't tell Hank who was operating the UAV, but he couldn't help smiling. He had a grin on his face as he watched more missiles hit the Pérez estate.

"If you take fire, return it, but stay put until the UAV is done. Wait for my order."

Even with the Reaper UAV's sophisticated technology, Garrett knew his teams would have a hard time joining the battle. They would have no way to communicate they were "friendlies." And a thermal-scanner surveillance didn't have the capability of distinguishing his team from Pérez's men.

But from the looks of things, apparently Kinkaid had thought about that. So far, the UAV was only blowing the shit out of Pérez's estate and punching holes in his stone walls. The Reaper was paving the way for Garrett's ground teams to clean up. Within minutes, the unmanned drone would let them get to work.

"Martini One, come in." Garrett kept his voice steady. "Do you need assistance, Martini One?"

When Alexa didn't answer, Garrett took a deep breath and focused on the rest of his team.

"Whisky Two, are you getting a transmission

from inside?" Garrett knew it was a long shot, but he had to know. "Is our boy still alive?"

He was breaking protocol by saying too much, but he had to know. If he got confirmation that Kinkaid was still alive, he'd push his men to move in as soon as the last rocket was launched. While he waited for Hank's response, Garrett got out his binoculars and searched the flaming rubble below for any sign of Alexa. Her men had checked in, but she was still missing. And the longer she stayed that way, the more he worried.

"Where are you?"

He had a bad feeling that she hadn't waited for the air assault to be over. If she thought there was a chance she could save Kinkaid from the fate he had planned for himself, she would go in with guns blazing. And she wouldn't risk her team to back her play. She'd go it alone.

"Damn it, Alexa," he cursed.

Garrett had the rest of his team to think about. He couldn't give a command that he knew would put his men at risk. He had no idea why Alexa wasn't answering him, but either option wasn't good. She was either dead or badly injured, or she'd gone in after Kinkaid on her own.

Alexa Marlowe and Jackson Kinkaid were two of a kind.

* * *

With her binoculars, Alexa had seen movement and a flash of light coming from a barred window right before the air assault. From the belowground prison cell, she had heard men shouting until the UAV launched its deadly payload—and she and her men had run for cover.

But in that split second, she had made a decision.

When the missile had blown a hole through a main wall, the initial blast had blinded her. She saw her team retreat, and she should have followed. They motioned to her, and she saw their mouths move, but her hearing was nearly gone. Instinct told her she should have gone with them, but her heart sent a different message. She couldn't leave, not without knowing what had happened to Jackson.

In the noise and confusion, she made a run for it, only she didn't do the smart thing like her men had done. She ran toward the breach in the stone wall that surrounded the Pérez estate. And when a second rocket hit the main house and sent stone and debris flying, she felt rocks pummel her body, and she had no way to protect herself. She went down, and everything went black.

It had taken her precious minutes to recover. She'd lost consciousness. How long she'd been out, Alexa didn't know. By the time she got to her feet, she stumbled deeper into the hacienda, with everything a blur. She'd gotten caught in the fall-out, and shards of rock had cut her face. Smoke from the intense flames billowed black into the night air, making it hard to see and breathe. And it took all her concentration to hold on to her H&K MP-5 assault rifle. Men escaping the burning estate ran into her, but they never looked back.

"What the hell . . . ?"

When she realized where she was and remembered what was happening, she had no choice. The air attack had escalated. She had to look for cover and go farther into the compound. That was when she remembered the prison cell where she had heard the angry men shouting before. Since Kinkaid had a way of riling people, that seemed like a likely place to begin her search.

"Damn it." Disoriented, she raised a hand to her ear and looked down the front of her shirt. "Where is it?"

It took her time to realize she'd lost her com unit back in the rubble where she'd fallen. Alexa knew her decision to search for Kinkaid alone hadn't been her finest hour. She wasn't thinking straight, but it was only her ass on the line now. Whatever consequences there would be, she would face them alone, and she could accept that. The last thing she wanted was to be responsible for anyone else getting dragged into the risk she was about to take.

"Kinkaid, I swear, you better be alive, so I can kill you myself."

3:32 A.M.

Kinkaid stared into the vacant eyes of Miguel Rosas. The crazed, bloodthirsty lunatic still had a gun pointed at his head.

Outside, the war raged on. Secondary explosions mixed with the staccato sounds of automatic gunfire. And dust and smoke clouded the stone cell. Wide-eyed, Estella stood frozen in place, staring at the man with the gun. Even Guerrero had stopped at the cell door. He had Pérez's arm over his shoulder as he helped the man escape, leaving a trail of the drug dealer's blood on the ground. He was bleeding like the stuck pig he was.

But all eyes were on Miguel Rosas.

And Kinkaid could do nothing except wait for the man to pull the trigger. He was too far away to lunge for the weapon. And he had nothing else to fight with.

"Kill him, Miguel. Do it!" Pérez demanded. "Pull the trigger!"

Rosas blinked. He gripped his weapon tighter

and steadied his aim. That left Kinkaid with nothing left to do but open his mouth.

"You're done, Pérez. This isn't the only place we hit tonight." Kinkaid forced a weak grin. If he was going down, he wanted the drug-cartel boss to know what he'd done. "We wiped you out."

MQ-9 Reaper UAVs had arrived in time to annihilate Pérez and his entire operation. Kinkaid's men had staged more than one attack, at multiple locations. By now, the second drug cartel that Pérez had worked years to rebuild was nothing more than massive holes in the ground.

Kinkaid and his men had been researching the drug dealer's strongholds and supply connections for years. Every key target that could be destroyed without jeopardizing innocent lives had been hit in simultaneous assaults across Mexico.

His taunt had been enough to force Pérez to make his move. The man grabbed for the gun Guerrero had stuffed into the waistband of his pants. He cursed and took aim. When Miguel Rosas saw his boss move, he turned and lowered his weapon as another missile tore through the stone wall near the makeshift cell.

That was the break Kinkaid needed.

As flames billowed through the barred window, and rocks rained down on them, Kinkaid lunged for Rosas and shoved him to the ground. He grabbed for the gun as he rolled behind the man. When Pérez fired his weapon, Kinkaid returned fire. And the only protection he had was Miguel Rosas. He heard the bullets as they riddled the man's body. And when he could, he shot back. He saw the drug boss stagger when he put a hole in his chest, but in the chaos, Kinkaid didn't know what happened.

He felt a punch in his shoulder, but kept shooting. Estella screamed and cringed in a corner, covering her head. When Kinkaid heard her, he got to his knees and shielded her from fire. And Guerrero had used the fat body of his boss to cower behind. Everything happened in slow motion.

Bullets ricocheted off stone, splintering wood and spraying shards of rock into the room. And when another blast shook the foundation, and the roof started to crack and break free, Guerrero had had enough.

"Let's go . . . let's go. Now!" The man urged his boss to move. And when the big man stumbled, Guerrero grabbed him by the collar and pulled him into the corridor, making a run for it. His motivation wasn't difficult to figure. Guerrero had no weapon. Pérez had taken it.

Guerrero had no choice but to get his boss moving, the man who was big enough to use as a human shield. And with the hacienda coming down, if they didn't get out now, the odds were they'd be buried alive where they stood.

"Move it! Now!" Guerrero yelled.

Kinkaid stood and looked for Estella in the haze of black smoke and suffocating dust. When he found her, he knelt beside her.

"Are you okay? Can you move?" When the girl nodded, he said, "We have to get out of here."

But it was too late. The minute Kinkaid had the girl on her feet, heading for the only way out, the roof caved in. He pulled her back and put his body between her and the falling rock. It was all he had time to do.

"Get down. Cover your head." He shielded the girl as best he could. Every stone that hammered his body sent a shock wave of pain through him. And after a brilliant burst of light blinded him, his body went limp. He fought to stay conscious, but lost his battle.

Darkness swallowed him whole.

CHAPTER 14

"The whole place is a house of cards, ready to come down. Heads up, people." Over his com unit, Garrett warned his men as they walked through the fallen stone wall at the entrance to the hacienda. They'd split into three-man teams and spread out, making tougher targets.

"Anyone who finds Martini One, sing out."

When the UAV had stopped firing, Garrett and his men breached the perimeter and went hunting for survivors. Most of Pérez's men had split, running for the foothills. And there had been only the occasional skirmish between his men and those still hiding within the walls of the estate.

The UAV flew wide circles around the vast property. Soon, the drone would have to leave.

Once Mexican authorities detected the battle, they'd have to evade capture. The longer they were there, the greater the chance of them getting caught, but Garrett hadn't found Kinkaid or Alexa yet. No matter how one-sided the attack might have been, any victory would be tainted if Jackson and Alexa had been killed in the assault.

And if he didn't have enough to worry about, what Alexa had told him about Donovan Cross had disturbed him. What was Cross up to? And who was backing him for the number one slot? One man couldn't do it alone. He had no doubt that Cross had help, but how far would Garrett have to go to protect his back? Returning to his old life, as head of the Sentinels, might be dangerous, especially when he had no idea who had supported Cross in his apparent attempt at a takeover. Someone within the Sentinels had made it easy.

"Found something. Over here." The voice of Hank Lewis came over his earbud, a much needed distraction from the conspiracies filling his head. When Garrett looked for Hank, he saw him waving in the glow of the burning hacienda. By the time he got to him, Hank was kneeling near a large pile of rubble, holding something in his hand.

"Found Martini One's com unit." Hank held the gear up toward the light and showed it to Garrett. "She didn't respond because she couldn't."

Finding her com link didn't mean she was alive. Her body could be under the pile of stones at their feet, but since they hadn't secured the compound, Garrett couldn't divert his men into a rescue mission for one agent. As he saw it, he had only one option.

"Put a team on this spot," he told Hank. "Have them trade off. Two men dig through this pile and one stands guard. Call out if they . . . find her."

"Will do, sir."

Garrett didn't want to think that Alexa was dead. She was a force of nature, a strong, intelligent woman who was a borderline adrenaline junkie. She thrived in his world, living on the razor's edge of danger. Imagining her dying before he had taken his last breath was something he couldn't handle. Even though he gave his order to Hank, it pained him to pretend he could conduct business as usual.

Loving her had been the reason he'd let her go. Neither of them had functioned in their jobs the way they should have. When the success of the mission should have been top priority, they each layered on the added complication of caring what happened to the other. They took unnecessary risks to protect one another, real over-the-top stuff like her risking her career and her life to come looking for him in Mexico.

So when Garrett had seen an opportunity to end it, he had let her find him with another woman, someone who didn't matter and could remain discreet. Although it had killed him to hurt Alexa that way, he had seen the writing on the wall and knew it was in her best interest to dump him so she could find a better man.

Quitting Alexa was the hardest thing he had ever done. And he'd failed at it. Now it would take all his concentration to focus on the rest of his mission, when all he wanted to do was find her.

But from the look on Hank's face, the man had more bad news.

"My communications guy just got a call from our handler," Hank interrupted his misery. "He's picking up chatter with the local police. They know we're here, and they're coming out to investigate. We've run out of time, sir."

Garrett stared across the compound. The Sentinels had survived for as long as they had because of their secrecy. He wouldn't break that code.

He knew what he had to do, but he didn't have to like it.

Before the last missile blew apart the main residence, Alexa had zeroed in on the prison cell she had seen from the outside. One corridor, partially belowground, had fit her memory of its location. But after the blast, the destruction had been devastating. Whole sections of the roof had collapsed, and flames lit the night sky. Clouds of dust made it hard to breathe, but she pressed on, aiming her MP-5 into every dark corner. With slow, deliberate steps, she made her way through the debris.

When she heard a moan ahead, and the sound of footsteps echoing down what remained of the stone hallway, she moved faster.

She peered through the dust and smoke and saw movement. The faint silhouette of a man caught her eye. She wanted to yell out, but she had no idea if the man was Kinkaid or the enemy.

The man she had seen hadn't been alone. Another wounded man was with him. With his back to her, the big man hobbled and needed help to walk. When Alexa got close enough to take aim, she shouted.

"Stop, or I'll shoot."

One man looked over his shoulder, the one helping the wounded guy, but neither of them slowed down. And when they disappeared around a corner, she'd lost sight of them.

"Damn it," she cursed under her breath.

But before she could chase them down, something caught her eye. When she crossed the threshold of the only chamber down that corridor—a room that had a massive door splintered by the blast and fallen rock at the entrance that blocked the way in—she saw a light.

A flickering flame burned through the debris. And eclipsing the fire was a barred window that had been cracked from its casing. The metal bars cut the light and were exactly what she had seen from outside. Gut instinct told her this cell was the one she had come to find.

"Kinkaid . . . you in there?" She took a risk and called out his name, but no one answered. While she kept her eye on the corridor where the men had vanished, she leaned closer to peer through the pile of rock.

Nothing moved inside.

"Jackson. Talk to me. Please." She yelled louder this time, but still, she heard nothing.

Alexa stood back from the cell and stared at the cave-in. Something made her stay. She couldn't explain it, but to move the boulders that blocked the door didn't make sense if there were no signs of life inside. She grimaced and shook her head as she held her assault rifle. She had the two men to follow. They were real. They should have been her target, but something kept her rooted where she was.

"Kinkaid. Give me a reason. Please!"

When her plea echoed in the room without a response and nothing else to show for it, Alexa reluctantly made up her mind to leave. She turned, but stopped when she heard it. The sound barely registered with her, and yet she knew she'd heard something.

A choking cough.

"Jackson, is that you? Come on. Answer me."

"Please . . . h-help him. I don't know what to do."

A girl's voice gripped Alexa by the throat. When she heard it, she didn't hesitate. She slung her weapon on her shoulder and dug into the rocks and debris blocking the splintered door.

"Hold on. I'm coming," Alexa cried out as she worked.

Sweat that had beaded on her skin now ran down her arms and back. It stung her eyes, but she kept working. And without gloves, the shards of rock cut her hands, and dust clotted the wounds.

"Is he alive? Please tell me," she begged the girl. And while she shoved at the door that hung off a hinge, she listened for any signs of life inside. When no answer came, Alexa worked harder. A minute later, she heard the weak voice again. The girl answered her, but Alexa didn't like what she heard.

"I don't know. I don't think h-he's breathing. Pl-please hurry. There's blood."

A slow rage burned under Alexa's skin. She hadn't come this close to Kinkaid to let him die. With her hands bleeding and raw, she strained to move the wall of stone that stood between them.

"Hang on, Jackson. Please . . . for once in your life, do as I tell you."

CHAPTER 15

Alexa heaved rocks one by one, trying to open a gap for her to squeeze through the toppled wall. Outside, she still heard the sounds of the skirmish, but things had died down. To avoid the Mexican authorities, Garrett's team on the ground and Kinkaid's UAV would have to clear out soon. She was running out of time, but she had no choice, not now.

The more she worked, the more her hands and shoulders ached.

She heard muffled sounds coming from outside. She tried calling for help, but no one heard her. Being in a collapsed part of the hacienda, Alexa knew it would take time for Garrett and his men to find her. And it would soon be dawn. In the harsh light of day, she didn't want to get stranded and have to explain to the Mexican government why she was there. Getting caught would land her in a Mexican prison, with the Sentinels throwing away the key. They wouldn't officially claim her, and that meant she'd be on her own, but all she could think about was . . .

"Jackson? Are you with me?" she called out.

"He's opening his eyes," the girl told her. "Can you hear me, *señor*?"

Alexa heard the excitement in the girl's voice when she began talking to Kinkaid. And with more of the rock shoved aside, Alexa heard the crunch of shoes on the stone floor. The girl was moving inside the cell. At least she was free and didn't have to be dug out. Alexa prayed that would be the same for Jackson.

"Is he okay?" she asked.

"I think so, but I see blood. I think he's been shot."

Alexa craned her neck to look into the cell. Torches had been tossed to the floor but were still lit. The flames gave off enough light for her to see a small girl kneeling by Kinkaid. Dust covered both of them.

"I'm coming. Hang on."

Alexa shoved at the last boulder that blocked her way. She squeezed through and worked her way back to where they were. The roof looked dangerously fragile. It wasn't safe, but she had to see how bad Kinkaid was before she moved them to a better location.

Jackson was sprawled flat on his back in a corner of the cell, covered in dirt and debris. Alexa had to lift rocks off his legs before she could get close enough. When she stared down at him, she saw his blood-covered shirt and went looking for the damage. He'd been shot in the shoulder, but that was the least of his worries. She'd seen men tortured before, but nothing like this.

She couldn't help but stare at him. He'd been beaten so badly that half his face was swollen, and one eye was nearly shut. His body was bruised with deep contusions, with knife wounds across his chest and stomach. He had to be in incredible pain even though he didn't let it show.

But Jackson was breathing. And that made him beautiful to her.

Alexa stared into his dazed eyes until she knew he recognized her. With trembling fingers, she touched his cheek, careful not to cause him more pain. She never thought she'd see him alive again.

She had walked away from him in Cuba when she saw in his eyes that he had nothing to give her . . . or anyone. He was too much in love with his dead wife and too empty inside from grieving over his only child. And from what she saw in him now, that hadn't changed, but she couldn't help how she felt about him. Loving Kinkaid had been her joy and her curse. And she wasn't sure she would change that, even if she could.

"You're a hard man to kill, Jackson." *Thank, God,* she wanted to add.

"You say that . . . like it's a b-bad thing." When he tried to smile, he winced from his cut lip.

"They tortured him. I heard it . . . and I saw what they did. It was terrible," the young girl said with fresh tears in her eyes. "When the rocks came down, he protected me."

"Don't make me out to be a hero, *chica*. No one who really knows me will believe you."

"He's got a point," Alexa said as she shrugged out of her shirt. "What's your name, little one?"

"Estella Calderone."

"Thanks for helping him, Estella. Now we need to get both of you out of here. Can you walk?"

"Yes." The girl nodded.

This time, she turned to Jackson. "And how about you? You look a little rough, big guy."

"Took one in the shoulder. Is the bullet still in there?"

She helped him rise enough to see his back. Without an exit wound, the bullet was still lodged in him. Someone would have to cut it out. But something else caught her eye.

"What's that old burn scar? When did you get that?" Before he answered, she remembered where she'd seen that burn before. "Actually, that looks like Garrett's scar. You didn't . . ."

By the look on Kinkaid's face, she knew what he'd done. He'd burned his own skin to make it look like a scar Garrett had, in case the drug cartel had heard about it.

"Seemed like a good idea . . . at the time." He shrugged.

"You're insane. Plain *loco*," she said, noticing that Estella was nodding behind his back. "And that bullet is still in there. Garrett brought a medic. He'll have you patched up in no time."

"No way. Pérez just left. He's wounded. I can catch him, but I gotta go now." When Kinkaid struggled to sit up, rocks and debris fell off him. Alexa helped him brush off as she thought about what to say.

"When I saw him, he wasn't alone. By now he could have plenty of help. And you're in no shape to chase after them, not anymore."

"Ramon Guerrero is with him," Estella told her. "He's a dangerous man."

"There, you see? Listen to her." When Jackson tried to stand, Alexa helped him to his feet, but the guy was real shaky. "Look at you. You have a bullet in you. Your face looks like raw hamburger meat. And you're barefoot. How far do you think you'll get like that?"

It took Kinkaid a moment to straighten up. And when he did, he looked her in the eye and ran a finger through her hair and tugged at a strand with a nod, his only acknowledgment of her changed hair color.

"I'll get as far as I need to." He softened his tone. "Now please . . . tell me where he went?"

When she didn't answer right away, he glared at her with his one good eye. No matter what shape Kinkaid was in, he still looked intimidating. His handsome face was battered and bruised, and his broad shoulders and tight abs were covered with bloody cuts and contusions. He'd been tortured for days, and it showed on every inch of his body.

He was barefoot and dressed in a thin pair of pants and an oversized shirt that made him look like a refugee from a prison camp, but the fire in his eyes was still there. Seeing him like that made Alexa a believer.

Jackson Kinkaid wanted revenge. He had come to take down Manolo Quintanilla Pérez and annihilate everything he stood for. Alexa understood that. The drug-cartel leader had brutally taken everything that Kinkaid held dear and loved—his wife and precious child.

From their last hostage-rescue mission in Cuba, Alexa had seen firsthand the pain of Kinkaid's self-imposed exile from the rest of humanity. He hadn't always been that way, but he'd changed after his family had been killed.

He'd alienated everyone who had mattered in his life. Her included. And he'd banished himself to live among drug dealers and the dregs of society as a mercenary for hire, so he could focus on the only thing he had left. She knew he hadn't thought about tomorrow because, for him, there wasn't one. Kinkaid hadn't counted on living beyond this mission, but with so much at stake, Alexa knew.

She wouldn't be the one who stood in his way.

"Come on. I'll show you. But not before I bandage that shoulder."

After Alexa had cut up her shirt to use as a bandage to stop Kinkaid's bleeding and give protection to his bare feet, she led him and Estella down the collapsed corridor that she'd seen Guerrero and his boss escaping. It was dark, and the going was slow. They had to be careful they weren't headed into an ambush. She'd followed a heavy blood trail. The big man Guerrero had helped get away was hurt bad.

But with Kinkaid barely able to walk without her and Estella's help, they weren't in much better shape. Jackson's bare feet were holding up, but she knew he was in pain. And as they neared a busted door that looked like it led to the outside, Alexa took the lead and aimed her assault rifle.

"Stay behind me," she said, mainly for Estella's benefit. "And don't move until I say so."

Gripping her MP-5, she found a bloody handprint on the doorjamb and knew Guerrero and Pérez had come that way. She listened through the door before she opened it, but what she heard had disturbed her.

Nothing. She heard absolutely nothing, and the stillness bothered her.

She had expected to hear the UAV making a run overhead or the sounds of Garret's men outside. When that didn't happen, she kicked the door open and squinted into the first rays of sunlight. Brilliant orange painted the top of the ridge where they'd pulled surveillance. Alexa slowly stepped out into the sun and looked around, clearing the way for Kinkaid and Estella.

Inside the perimeter, fires were still burning, and black smoke spiraled into the early-morning sky. The smoke would make them an easy target for the local cops, who would see the attack site from a distance. And wherever Alexa looked, she saw no one to help them.

Pérez and his men were gone, but so were Garrett and his people. They were alone.

"Damn."

"Garrett couldn't take the risk. You know that. He had his men to consider." Kinkaid's low, gritty voice gave her comfort. "I'm sorry, Alexa. If you want to beat it, I'll understand. I can stall 'em until you and Estella get out of here."

"Stall who?" she asked.

Kinkaid answered by pointing, and saying, "The Federales. And unless you want to see a remake of Butch and Sundance, you better take me up on my offer."

On the horizon, Alexa saw a cloud of dust on the dirt road heading toward the hacienda. Several vehicles with flashing lights were barreling toward them. She didn't need binoculars to know that the Mexican Federal Police were only minutes away. Their time had run out.

"No way, Kinkaid. No man left behind, remember? Come on. We gotta go. Now."

When Alexa turned, she came face-to-face with Estella. The girl looked scared. And she didn't have to open her mouth. Alexa knew what was on her mind.

"You can't come with us," she told her. "It'll be too dangerous."

"But please, don't leave me here. They will put me in prison."

"You didn't do anything. Just tell them that. I'm sure after they question you, they'll let you go."

The girl grabbed her hand and begged.

"No . . . please. You don't understand. I was Ramon's whore, not by choice, but the police won't care about that. I don't trust them. They will lock me away to punish me."

Kinkaid could barely stand, but he gave her the eye again.

"Don't look at me like that. You know how this is going to play out. She's better off without us."

Alexa had hoped the girl would be questioned and released, like they would have done in the States.

"With the drug wars they've got down here, she could be right," Kinkaid said. "There's too much corruption and not enough good cops to cover the territory. They're overworked and underpaid. She could fall through the cracks, easy."

Kinkaid made good sense. It was possible Estella could pay a price no one would intend her to pay. They couldn't leave her behind and only hope she'd be okay. Without knowing for sure, they couldn't take that chance. The girl needed a break, and they owed her.

"Okay, you can come with us"—Alexa nearly got bowled over by a squealing Estella, who hit her with open arms—"but only until we find a safe place to drop you off. Understood? Did you hear me, Estella?"

The girl grinned and nodded. And without saying another word, she hugged Alexa again. With Estella wrapped around her, Alexa noticed the faint smile on Kinkaid's face, busted lip and all. He knew she wouldn't leave the girl behind.

He'd counted on it.

"I saw that, Kinkaid." She shook her head. "Now make yourself useful. We need a way out of here, *pronto.*"

She followed Kinkaid's gaze across the compound as they looked for a way out. Pérez's helicopter was nothing more than a fireball, completely blown apart. If Guerrero had escaped with the drug-cartel leader, they hadn't flown out. The UAV drone had taken care of that. And Pérez wouldn't get far bleeding the way he was. They had to have wheels to get to Guadalajara and the nearest doctor.

"How else would Guerrero make his escape?" she asked Estella. "Do you know where they kept their vehicles?"

"Ramon had a van and another car. Over there." The girl pointed to an outbuilding that looked intact.

By the time Alexa got there, she found more blood and knew they were on the right track in trailing Pérez. She saw the building had been used as a garage, but the vehicles were missing. Without a car, they'd be on foot, with the Mexican police having every advantage.

Their odds of getting away clean sucked.

"Damn it. I can't catch a break. We could sure use some good luck about now."

"Will I do?" A man's voice came from behind them.

Alexa spun and aimed her weapon at the silhouette of a guy bracing an assault rifle on his hip. He wasn't threatening them with his weapon. His body eclipsed the sunrise behind him, making it hard to see his face until he leaned against the open garage door. Alexa hadn't heard him walk up on them, and Kinkaid hadn't either.

She only knew one man who could do that.

"Garrett? I thought you left."

Garrett Wheeler's face lit up with a grin that put the sunrise to shame. Alexa hadn't seen him smile like that for a very long time, but she knew exactly how he felt.

"And miss a good ass kicking? Never," he said

as he walked up to them with his usual swagger. "But I did send the team home."

"In case you haven't taken a head count lately, if there's an ass kicking, it's gonna be ours," she said. "And Kinkaid has a jump on us in that department."

"Everyone's a critic." Jackson gave her a sideways glare that softened into a smile.

Alexa knew they were in plenty of trouble, with more on the way, but she couldn't help it. Having Garrett and Jackson with her, alive and well, made her feel damned lucky. And being on the right side of the dirt was always a good thing.

"Then we better get a head start. I've got a car and a GPS signal to follow." Garrett's expression became more somber as he turned to leave. "Come on. We've got ground to cover."

CHAPTER 16

La Pointe, Wisconsin
Morning

"You want me to do what?" Seth asked. His sleepy voice told her that he was still in bed. "Sorry, I'm not awake yet. Worked late last night."

"Your assignment with Tanya?"

"Yeah."

Jessie was already working on her third cup of motel-room coffee. Dressed in jeans and a T-shirt, she'd been up for hours looking through the local phone directory, trying to locate the witness names she'd remembered from Chief Cook's murder book.

She heard Seth yawn, but he didn't say anything more about what he was working on for his direct-report boss at the Sentinels. And she knew better than to press him for details. They both would have secrets when it came to their mutual employer.

"What's this about my dad's old case file?" he asked.

Jessie knew Seth had kept a copy of his father's biggest case with the Chicago Police Department. Harper's dad, Max, had rescued her and the other kids that Danny Ray Millstone had kidnapped and tortured at his sprawling old Chicago home.

"You still have it, right?"

"Well, yeah. Sure. What's this about, Jessie?"

Seth's father had killed Millstone. He shot the man dead in front of her when the bastard had come to kill her. She was only a kid at the time, but she never forgot what it felt like to be carried out of that hellhole—from the darkness into the light—by a man she always had remembered as a hero. But the price Max had paid, when he became obsessed with the serial pedophile, had been the estrangement of his son, Seth. And that case had cost Max his marriage, too.

"I need to know if there were any boys held at Millstone's house?" She cleared her throat, having a hard time talking about her ordeal again. "And I guess that would include the bodies the police found buried on his property."

Harper had dealt with his rift from his dad by taking Max's casebook and had attempted to make contact with every survivor of Millstone's. Seth had needed to see with his own eyes that his father's obsession had been worth the sacrifice his family had made. At least, that was what Harper had thought when he first started his own fixation. Jessie had a suspicion that he saw things differently now, and that difference had brought him closer to his father, but if anyone knew about the victims of Danny Ray Millstone—then and now—it was Seth Harper.

"Wait a minute, Jess. Take pity on me. I haven't had my coffee yet. You better start from the beginning."

Jessie told him about Chief Cook's misleading her with his lie of omission, that there had been two DNA samples found at the old DeSalvo crime scene. Cook had gotten a hit on her DNA and made contact through the Chicago PD, a call fielded by her friend, Sam Cooper. Once she'd gotten Harper up to speed, she got around to telling him what she'd been thinking and asking her favor.

"So you think Millstone was your . . . father? Oh, Jessie. I'm so sorry you're going through this alone. I can drive and be there in nine hours. Just let me find a place for Floyd."

"No, Seth. Thanks for the offer, but I need you to help me another way. And no one can do this but you."

"I'd do anything for you, Jess. What do you need?"

She heard sympathy and commiseration in his voice. The old Jessie would have heard only pity and resented him for it. She would have sabotaged any relationship they had and dealt with her pain by pushing him away, but it felt good to have someone to talk to about the worst days of her life. Harper was her sounding board, a guy she could trust with her worst suspicions.

"Look into Millstone's list of victims. I need every boy's name—alive or dead—and their ages when they were found. And it would be great to have photos of the boys. Can you do that for me?"

"Yeah, will do. I only remember girls' names, but I could be wrong. And I haven't looked at the names of the dead kids in a while. I was more after the ones still breathing, but there could've been boys on that list. I'll let you know what I find out."

"Thanks. That'll help."

Once she narrowed down the kids' ages, she could show the photo of any boy who matched the description the witnesses in La Pointe had reported. From what she remembered of Cook's interview records, the witnesses were consistent in reporting a boy and a girl. And the descriptions had been similar enough to sound like the same kids had been seen by more than one witness.

"And what have you got Sam looking into?" he asked.

"Sam's checking out the evidence archives, trying to find any record of Millstone's DNA that might have been missed when they digitized the old cases. If we can connect that second DNA sample to Millstone as a direct match, then we can link him to the murder and ID who killed Angela DeSalvo."

"Wait a minute," Harper interrupted. "Didn't Chief Cook tell you he'd looked into the Millstone case? Millstone would've been a likely candidate for the La Pointe murder. Cook would've connected the dots to him if he could. And as a cop, he would've had access to the same information that Sam is looking for. Don't you think he would have noticed if Millstone's DNA matched anything he'd found at the DeSalvo crime scene? I mean, he'd say something to you, right?"

"Yeah, like I'd believe anything coming out of his mouth? He's already lied to me about finding more than one DNA sample at the scene."

"Yeah, but why? That makes no sense."

"I know. The more I look into this, the more questions I have."

"Maybe this'll turn out to be a good thing."

"Oh? Enlighten me."

"Cook found you when that DNA sample scored a hit on you as a missing person. Well, barring any fat-finger data entry, if that second DNA sample didn't come up on the hit parade, I'd prefer to focus on the positive."

"Yeah, what's that?" she said.

"That the DNA is from your brother. And that he's alive and had never been a missing kid. You've got a 95 percent probability match to family, Jessie. And if we can rule out Millstone as daddy dearest, then that could mean you have a brother who might've had a normal life, whatever that is."

Harper was right. Thinking positively gave her a warm feeling when she thought about having a brother, especially one who had a better life. But her cynicism didn't let her enjoy that moment long.

"Even if we don't match that second sample to Millstone's DNA, that doesn't necessarily mean that bastard didn't kill Angela DeSalvo. It just means we'd be back to square one without any evidence for our theory," she said. "And like you say, that DNA could belong to a brother I may never find. This could all turn out to be one big dead end. And I may never know how or why I ended up with Millstone in Chicago after being in Wisconsin."

Pessimism was an acquaintance she'd grown up with. After barely surviving her encounter with Danny Ray Millstone, she'd learned to deal with her peculiar emotional balancing game. On the one hand, she'd been fortunate to have survived him, but she had a hard time reconciling her bad luck in crossing his path in the first place.

"I'll do some digging into the case," Seth said. "You've given me plenty of food for thought. I'll let you know what I come up with . . . after I feed my java addiction, and Floyd gets his breakfast, and not in that order."

"Thanks, Seth." She smiled. "I love you."

"I love you, too, Jessica Beckett. Don't ever forget that."

Outside Guadalajara, Mexico

With Garrett driving a rented SUV, they had taken advantage of the vehicle and gone off road for the first hour. Once they got to a road, they took the long way around Leguna de Chapala and stayed off the main highways until they had ditched the local cops. Garrett kept driving northwest until he saw more traffic, a sign they were nearing Guadalajara.

"They've got to be heading for medical attention if Pérez is still alive," Alexa speculated, when they were twenty miles out. "From what I saw of the blood trail we followed, Kinkaid got his licks in."

"I'll check on that," Garrett said as he locked his gaze on hers in the rearview mirror.

Alexa had sat in the backseat with Kinkaid, taking care of his shoulder. She'd managed to stop the bleeding, and the wound looked shallow. Despite the pain he was in, Kinkaid was nodding off from sheer exhaustion and blood loss. The steady rock of the vehicle and the drone of the engine had lulled him to sleep.

The days of torture had finally caught up to him. When he didn't have to play the tough guy, he'd let his guard down and dared to shut his eyes as long as he was with friends who had his back. Alexa felt tired, too, but she couldn't take her eyes off the road. She was too wired and hyped on adrenaline.

"I think we're clear of the local LEOs," Garrett said into his cell phone after he'd called the handler for the mission. "If you still have that GPS signal, give me the coordinates when they stop. They're probably looking for a doctor."

Kinkaid opened an eye to listen, but that didn't last long. Sleeping was as good as any weapon, and Jackson took advantage of the downtime. Estella was sitting in the front seat next to Garrett.

The girl looked carsick. She probably hadn't eaten either. None of them had.

"Here." Alexa nudged Estella's shoulder with one of the bottles of water she had found stashed in the seat pocket behind Garrett. The girl savored each sip before she tried to give the bottle back.

"No, you keep it. That's yours." She waved her off, whispering in a low voice while Garrett talked on his cell, "And here's an energy bar. Even if you don't feel like it now, eat it."

The girl did as she was told. Garrett's backseat gear was a treasure trove. Alexa forced herself to eat and sipped on another bottle of water that she'd found. And she'd saved some for Kinkaid when he woke up and for Garrett once he got off the phone. They all needed to refuel.

Once they got to Guadalajara, they'd drop off Estella wherever she wanted to go before they would start their hunt for Pérez. They'd have to play it smart. The Mexican police would be on the alert, looking for them. And when they found Guerrero and his boss, they'd have to hit them fast and hard.

With her mind on the fight to come, she was surprised when Kinkaid laid his head on her shoulder to sleep. She held her breath, not wanting to wake him and spoil the moment, but eventually she cupped her hand to his cheek and nuzzled her chin against him. She was about to close her eyes, when something stopped her.

She saw Garrett staring at her from the rear-view mirror. He didn't say anything, and neither of them looked away. It was as if he was telling her it was okay or that he'd moved on, and so should she. And maybe his basic respect for Kinkaid had something to do with it.

Alexa had had a hard time reading Garrett lately, but she didn't look away. That wasn't her style. Of all people, Garrett understood what it meant to live on the edge, not knowing if there would ever be a tomorrow. So Alexa held Kinkaid as he slept, and she shut her eyes, sending Garrett a clear message of her own.

She wasn't ashamed for having feelings for Kinkaid even if Jackson didn't feel the same.

Downtown Chicago
Two hours later

Seth spent time digging through his father's old murder book and case notes, with Floyd's chin on his thigh. His new roommate didn't say much, but his company was appreciated, especially today.

When Seth's father had retired, he'd made copies of the case he would never forget. The pages had yellowed and smelled stale, but there was a familiarity to them that comforted Seth as he looked at his dad's notes and recognized Max's handwriting. It was as if he got a glimpse into how his dad's mind worked. And on more than one occasion, he had imagined Max writing in the margins of the investigative journal.

He thought he'd practically memorized the contents of the files, but each time he looked at them, he saw something new or read his father's notes differently. Jessie wasn't the only one who had mixed feelings about rehashing a past they both would have preferred to forget.

His part of that equation wasn't nearly as bad as what Jessie had been through—and was still going through. But he'd learned long ago that if a wound didn't heal, ignoring it wasn't an answer. Jessie's instincts were solid to deal with the darkness that haunted her, head-on. He admired her strength and courage, respected her tenacity, but he loved her for the vulnerability she had trusted him enough to show.

When he got to the list of Millstone's victims, the missing and the dead, he scanned every name three times. He didn't want to make a mistake. Boys' names didn't stand out. Only a few had first names that could go either way. After he made a note of them, he compared the gender-neutral names to the photos taken of the children who had survived and the ones who hadn't.

"Sick bastard."

Millstone had ruined so many lives. Even beyond the immediate names, Seth knew that being a victim of violence radiated out to affect the families, friends, and the community, which had suffered, too.

By the end of his search, he had trouble confirming the gender of two names—Jamie Littlefield and Cameron Harte. Both kids were dead, and their decomposed bodies had been discovered in shallow graves behind the old Millstone family home. He'd have to dig for photos or autopsy reports to confirm the gender or find any photos of those kids before they had died. But since the rest of Millstone's victims had been little girls, the odds were that the bastard wasn't into boys, too.

"This is good news, isn't it, Jess?" he muttered as he looked over the list one more time.

Seth wanted to give Jessie a lead to follow, but he had mixed feelings about that lead coming from the Millstone case. Would Jessie be better off not finding her brother at all if it meant the kid hadn't been taken by that sick pervert? He had a strong feeling Jessie would agree. Ruling out Millstone had its own merits, even if it didn't give Jessie something more to go on.

But before he pushed too hard on coming up with more from the Millstone files, he decided to talk to Sam Cooper. They both loved Jessie. And he knew Jess had asked them to work different angles of the case.

"Maybe face time wouldn't hurt," he muttered as he pulled out his cell phone.

Seth hit his speed dial for Sam. Flying solo had gotten him nowhere. It was time to join resources and make a better run at helping Jessie. Maybe kicking around ideas—with the only other person who knew Jessie's story better than he did—would make a difference.

Guadalajara, Mexico

Jackson had asked Garrett to drop Estella off at a local church. On the drive over, the girl had argued that the Church would not want her once they knew what she'd done. The girl was obviously embarrassed and had censored what she told Jackson in English, until he spoke to her in Spanish. Whatever Kinkaid said, he must have convinced her to keep an open mind about the Church. Alexa got the sense that he was telling her something private between them, and it must have worked.

When they got to the church, Alexa spoke to a priest and made a donation to care for the girl, at least until she got on her feet. When she headed for the car, Alexa saw Jackson with Estella near the front entrance. She didn't mean to eavesdrop, but their voices carried like an echo through the chapel.

Estella hugged him, crying. "I can't believe I am free of Ramon . . . because of you. God answered my prayers when he sent you to help me."

"Believe me, I'm not anyone's answer to a prayer. And God and me parted ways for good reason, but if it makes you feel better, put in a good word for me." He turned to go, but stopped and looked over his shoulder. "You have a chance to reinvent yourself and start over. Not everyone is capable of that, but you're a survivor, Estella. I think if anyone can do it, you can."

Alexa wasn't sure he was talking about the girl's future anymore, but he'd made starting over sound easy, for her sake.

"Put what Ramon did behind you, if you can," he told her. "He committed an act of violence against you. His sin is not yours."

Fresh tears ran down Estella's face. And when it took her a long, awkward moment to find the courage to speak again, she avoided looking at him.

"But what man will . . . have me now?"

Jackson didn't hesitate. He stepped closer, reached for her chin, and made her look him in the eye when he said, "A damned lucky one."

Kinkaid never said much. He was a man of few words, but Alexa knew he'd said enough to make the girl a believer in second chances. And he darned near convinced her, too.

An hour later

They had followed the GPS signal of Guerrero's cell phone until the signal had stopped in one location. Garrett had parked down the street from the home of a local doctor and was setting up his thermal imager. According to his handler, the home was the personal address of Dr. Carlos Hernandez, a physician who got paid on the side by the drug cartels.

Alexa liked the setup. The doctor's modest ranch-style home was at the end of a long block, with most of the surrounding land belonging to him. The grounds were gated, but no guards stood watch. With the house relatively isolated from any neighboring residence, the situation was perfect for minimal collateral damage. If they executed their plan with precision, they had a good chance of not firing a shot.

"Don't see a car or that van Estella told us about," she said.

"With Pérez wounded, they wouldn't have parked on another street and walked over," Jackson said. "They probably have their vehicle in that garage."

"Yeah, I agree." Garrett looked up from his surveillance gear. Even if he didn't have his high-tech thermal imager, Alexa would still know someone was inside. Drapes near the front door moved with regularity—a dead giveaway that someone was home . . . and downright nervous.

"Curtain moved again." Sitting in the front seat, Alexa had binoculars and got a closer look. "I can't be sure. That could be the guy I saw in the hall, the one who helped Pérez escape."

"Let me see." Kinkaid poked her shoulder from the backseat, where he had changed into BDUs Garrett had given him. She handed him her binoculars, and it didn't take long for Jackson to catch a glimpse of a face at the window. "Yeah, that's Guerrero. Looks like he's waiting for someone. How many are inside?"

Garrett had the thermal imager working in the front seat.

"Two in that front room. And someone is in back," Garrett said, not taking his eyes off the imager's display. "One in the front is stationary and hasn't moved much. He's alive, and that could be Pérez."

The thermal imager picked up on the heat signatures of people in the house, but it didn't give a layout of the rooms except for ghost images of walls that gave off heat. Although the imager gave them good information, without a schematic of the house, they'd be at a disadvantage.

"And I'd bet money the person in the back is a housekeeper or the doc's wife or kid. I can't tell, but that looks like an odd-shaped room, too. No telling where they're at until we get in there." Kinkaid had handed back her binoculars and was looking over Garrett's shoulder at the thermal screen. "Someone had to let them in. Guerrero probably has them locked up until the doc arrives. Where's Hernandez?"

"My guy tells me he works at a local clinic, but he's not there now. The receptionist didn't know where he went. He got a call and headed out. If that's true, he should be here soon."

"Got a car at six o'clock, moving fast." Garrett had his eyes on the rearview mirror. "Get down."

They all ducked and waited for the car to pass before Garrett slowly raised his head.

"If that's the doc, we give him twenty minutes inside before we move in. You gonna hold up your end?" Garrett looked over his shoulder at Kinkaid. When Alexa saw that, she turned and waited for Jackson to answer.

"I've waited years for this, Garrett. And I let those bastards beat the crap out of me to get

Pérez to think he had the upper hand." Kinkaid rummaged through weapons and gear that Garrett had stowed in the back, but he stopped long enough to say, "You're damned straight I'm gonna hold up my end."

Kinkaid looked like a different man than he had a few hours ago. Despite his shoulder wound, he had a new spark in his eyes that almost scared her until he caught her still looking at him. Kinkaid ran a hand through her hair and trailed a finger down her cheek. And he stopped long enough to smile.

"And thanks to both of you, I get the chance to keep a promise I made a long time ago."

Alexa had never known Kinkaid had a wife and child until their recent hostage-rescue mission in Cuba. Hearing about them had shocked her, mostly because he'd been so willing to entrust her with his life on any mission, but he hadn't trusted her enough to share his family. With something so important, Kinkaid didn't have faith in *anyone,* except Garrett, when he had no choice. And considering how *that* had turned out, she could understand how withdrawn he'd become.

The whole point to keeping his personal life secret was to keep his family safe. And when that didn't happen, he had lashed out at Garrett and anyone he thought had been responsible—but no one had taken the heat more than what he'd heaped on himself.

Finally, his vendetta would be over, one way or another. His act of revenge wouldn't bring back his wife and child, and she had no doubt that he knew that. He could kill Pérez a thousand times over and even the score, but that wouldn't fill the void in his life where his beloved wife and child used to be. And living with that cruel reality had to leave him feeling damned empty inside, no matter what happened in the next few minutes.

Her gut instinct told her Kinkaid might think that dying there would be easier than living with the aftermath of what had happened, when he had no one else left to blame.

She prayed she was wrong.

CHAPTER 17

Garrett had tried to assign Kinkaid the back of the house since he was wounded and not in the best of shape, but Jackson refused. He wanted to be first one through the door and nearest Pérez.

With Dr. Hernandez inside, Garrett had monitored his thermal imager to check his movements within the walls of his residence. The person in the back of the house had moved but was still there. Whoever was there was either hiding or had been confined to a room. Either way, no one could be ignored. And after the doctor entered the house, he went straight for the front room. The movements on the imager gave them more intel to plan their strategy.

"You cover the back. When you're in place, we'll make our move," Garrett told her. "With the doctor working on Pérez, Guerrero will be distracted. Since we don't know the layout, picking the lock might buy us time to get in tight and take them by surprise."

"When you get inside, let me know," Alexa said as she put on her com unit. "I'll secure the rear of the house after I hear from you."

"Kinkaid and I will focus on the three in the front. Guerrero is the one to watch. He'll be armed and nervous. If we hit them hard, this could be over fast."

"Guerrero doesn't strike me as someone who'd risk his life for Pérez," Kinkaid said. "If it comes down to him or his boss, I'd bet money he'd give Pérez up once he knows they're not getting out of this. We just have to convince him that he's not important to us. We're not cops. We won't arrest him or turn him over."

"Yeah, good point. Talking him down will be your job," Garrett said. "Anything else?"

Kinkaid and Garrett looked ready to go, but Alexa had something on her mind and she had to bring it up now, for Kinkaid's sake.

"Once we get Pérez, what then?" she asked. She shifted her gaze between the two men, but when neither of them said anything, she pressed. "I mean, if he doesn't put up a fight, is this an execution . . . or do we have another plan?"

Given what she did for a living, Alexa found it more than a little ironic that she'd suddenly become the voice of reason when it came to morality. The Sentinels were a covert vigilante organization. Their operations were about doling out justice without the red tape of the court system and jurisdictions. When they went after a target, they had proof of the crime to justify their actions, and they usually confronted criminal organizations who were clearly in the wrong, but working for the Sentinels required her to have an adaptable moral code.

She believed in what they did, or she never would have joined the group and sacrificed having a normal life for one mired in secrecy. But this operation had been Kinkaid's vendetta. And even though she completely understood Jackson's motivation, if he murdered Pérez in cold blood, would that trigger an even deeper slide into desolation for Kinkaid?

She didn't care about a man like Pérez. The man was a total waste of skin. He was a known drug dealer and head of a brutal cartel. Assaulting his hacienda outside Guadalajara had been easier because they knew the man had Kinkaid as a hostage, and they had proof of that. And Pérez's men had fought back, but here, that might not be the case. If the cartel boss gave himself up, would they still execute him?

When Kinkaid was the first to speak, she thought she knew what he would say, but she would've been wrong. Jackson surprised her.

"I have to see this through, but I can take it from here if you can't stomach what'll happen in there." Kinkaid gave them a way out if they wanted it.

"And as far as I'm concerned, Garrett, the slate is clean," Jackson said. "You don't owe me anything anymore . . . if you ever did. What happened wasn't your fault. It's taken me years to see that. And killing Pérez won't bring my wife and little girl back, but I have to see this through. I destroyed Pérez's cartel before, and he only rebuilt it. He'll do it again, and I can't let that happen. I can't stomach the thought of that man thriving from all this, but I won't blame either of you if you decide this isn't for you."

"If Pérez gives himself up, what do you see happening?" This time Garrett asked the question. And only Kinkaid could answer it.

It took Jackson a long moment to think about what he would say, but eventually he did. And he did it as he looked Garrett square in the eye.

"I trust you. Both of you. I just want Pérez brought to justice. Whatever happens, you make the call, Garrett. I can live with that."

Kinkaid sounded as if he wanted to play nice. And Alexa hoped he meant it. If he did, there was hope for him yet. He might have a future if he lived through this. But a part of her remembered the ruthlessness in his beautiful fierce eyes that she'd seen in Cuba and how haunted he'd been when he finally told her about his wife and baby girl. Pain like that didn't just fade away. It lasted a lifetime.

People change. And she wanted to believe Jackson had, too, but the paranoid part of her wasn't so sure.

She could also see why Kinkaid would trust Garrett to finish this. Leaving the decision up to him didn't mean Pérez would walk. Garrett was the head of the Sentinels for a reason. He knew how to make the tough calls, and he'd killed plenty in the name of justice, but maybe Kinkaid would say anything to stay on the team and face Pérez one last time to play judge, jury, and executioner.

Without knowing what was in Kinkaid's head, Alexa had to make one last-ditch effort to reach him.

"I hear what you're saying," she told Jackson, looking him in the eye. "And I want to believe you can put this behind you when this is all over, Jackson. But revenge never lives up to its hype. Obsessing over it like you've been doing can make you an addict who never knows when to quit."

When he had a hard time meeting her gaze, she reached for his arm. "Will you know when it's time to let go?"

Jackson never answered her. He stared back with his battered face, a reminder how much he'd already been through, but he never said another word. She tried reading something into his silence but came up empty. It was time to go. And whatever would happen between Kinkaid and Pérez lay ahead of them.

Alexa wasn't sure why Jackson had handed Pérez's fate over to Garrett and had used the word "trust" to do it, but given the expression on her boss's face, he hadn't missed that point either.

Garrett only nodded, and said, "Let's move out."

In the study near the front door, Ramon Guerrero looked out the front curtain one last time as he aimed his weapon at Dr. Hernandez. The neighborhood was quiet this time of day, but Ramon knew the importance of being careful. He'd picked the doctor's library to hide his boss because it had two entrances. One door was off the foyer, and the other led to a vacant guest bedroom in another wing of the house. The study was a pass-through. After the doctor had come into the house, he'd accosted him in the foyer and escorted him to where Pérez was. He'd locked both doors and secured the room.

Now Ramon had his weapon pointed at the doctor's head as he told him what would happen.

"We have your wife locked in a room. If this man lives, you'll see her again. You understand?"

"Yes. Just don't hurt her. I'm here. I'll do what I can." The doctor reached for the leather bag he'd brought with him before Ramon stopped him.

"Hold it."

Guerrero grabbed the bag while he kept his gun on the man. He searched the contents to make sure the doctor didn't have a weapon hidden in his medical supplies. When he didn't find anything suspicious, he threw the leather case onto a coffee table.

"Get to work. He's lost a lot of blood."

"He needs a hospital. I brought a couple of bags of O-negative, but he'll need more."

"Just shut up and do what you can. We'll talk about that later."

His boss had collapsed on a sofa in the doctor's library and was bleeding all over the man's expensive furniture. His chest was heaving, and he had panic in his eyes.

"Ramon, don't let me die. When this is over, I promise you. Anything you want."

Pérez was making promises out of his delirium and fear. Earlier today, the man had accused him of betrayal when he brought the American to his hacienda. Now that his life was in Ramon's hands, the man promised him anything he wanted.

He'd helped Pérez escape his fate once today. A second time might ensure him a higher rank within the cartel. As he saw it, Ramon had nothing to lose by letting the doctor do his job, no matter which way things turned out.

"Get to work. And he'd better live, Doctor, for your wife's sake."

Pérez heaved a sigh and shut his eyes as the doctor hovered over him, checking his condition and preparing to remove the bullet from his chest. Ramon knew the doctor had been right about his boss needing a hospital, but they couldn't afford to take the chance. If the police got word he was wounded, they would arrest him while he was vulnerable.

But while the doctor was filling a syringe with medicine, Ramon thought he heard something.

"Shush." He aimed his weapon at the doctor and whispered, "Don't make a sound."

"What's happening?" Pérez lifted his head and shifted his gaze around the room.

Guerrero handed his boss a weapon and forced the doctor to his feet, putting a gun to his head. He moved toward the door near the foyer, clenching his hostage by his collar.

Was he being paranoid, or had he heard something? Guerrero held his breath and tensed his body as the hair on his neck stood on end. Instinct had sent him a message.

Someone was in the house, and he was no longer in control.

Garrett had used shrubs and hedges in the front of the private residence to get closer to the front door, with Kinkaid close on his heels. Without a nearby neighbor, they had a good shot at not being seen.

Once they got to the front entry, he'd picked the lock in seconds. Before he went inside, he whispered into his com unit to Alexa.

"We're going inside . . . now. When you hear us, make your move."

"Copy that," she said.

Garrett used a hand signal to give the order to Kinkaid to enter the premises of Dr. Hernandez and follow his lead. The front door was the closest point to where the thermal imager had shown activity. And when Garrett found double doors to the right of the foyer, he knew Guerrero and Pérez were only steps away.

He put his back to the nearest wall—with Kinkaid taking the other side—and listened at the door. When he heard nothing, he gave a nod. No words were necessary. Jackson reached a hand across and tested the lock.

When Kinkaid shook his head, Garrett knew the door was locked. This time stealth wouldn't do it. They'd have to break through clean in order to get the drop on Guerrero and his boss. Garrett gripped his assault rifle, the muscles in his body growing taut as he stared at Kinkaid.

In seconds, this would all be over, one way or another.

CHAPTER 18

Guerrero didn't wait for what he knew would come.

"Keep your mouth shut," he whispered into Dr. Hernandez's ear. "And do as I say."

"What's happening?" Pérez kept his voice low. But when he tried to sit up, he couldn't. The man even had trouble holding the gun he'd been given.

If they were about to be attacked, his boss would be of no use to him. Ramon was on his own. He put his arm around the doctor's neck and squeezed, pulling him back. He kept the man's body in front of him as he moved deeper into the room and away from the foyer door.

"Unlock this door," he hissed into the doctor's ear, only loud enough for him to hear, and pointed at the door behind him. When the man did as he was told, Pérez spoke louder.

"Something's going on. What is it? Talk to me."

The bastard was talking too loud now. If someone was outside the study door, Pérez was making it easy for them to locate where they were. Ramon moved back to the center of the room, closer to his boss. His mind reeled with the scenarios racing through his head. And when he saw a dim shadow move under the threshold of the library door, he knew he'd been right.

Someone had come in through the front and was outside the study. In seconds, he would know who they were, but that would be far too late.

Garrett gestured to Kinkaid. On the count of three, he'd kick the door in. Jackson would cover him with his assault rifle and be first through the door, with Garrett close on his heels. They'd done the maneuver countless times, but everything hinged on how clean he hit the door and busted it open. And with the doctor inside, they had to be careful. Opening fire without a clear target might get the man killed.

When Garrett moved into position to kick the door in, he heard gunfire.

One shot. Two.

He lunged for the wall and ducked for cover, talking fast into his earbud to Alexa. "Shots fired. Not us."

"Copy. You okay?"

"Yeah," Garrett whispered. "Secure your target before you assist, is that clear?"

"I copy."

When Garrett was done talking to Alexa, Kinkaid nudged his head toward the door. He'd heard a noise coming from inside, and so had Garrett. He gave him the signal. They'd go on three . . . again.

This time when Garrett kicked the door, it crashed open, and both he and Kinkaid rushed into a library with assault rifles tight at their shoulders. They aimed at the man on the sofa, and another man screamed and held up his hands. He was cowering on the floor near Pérez.

Dr. Hernandez had been gagged. And blood ran down his cheek from his temple. Another door across the room gaped open. It led into a bedroom. Garrett kept his rifle on the doctor and the big man on the sofa while Kinkaid got a look into the bedroom. When he didn't see anything, Jackson shrugged, and said, "Clear."

Garrett stepped closer to Pérez and stared down at the man. The cartel boss had his mouth open, with his dead eyes glazed over. Two bloody holes had dented his skull, and bigger exit wounds spilled brains onto the couch cushions.

Pérez was dead.

When Kinkaid stepped back into the room, he helped Dr. Hernandez with the gag as he stared down at Pérez.

"Please . . . don't shoot me. They have my wife. I only did as I was told . . . so they wouldn't kill her. You have to believe me."

The doctor had stayed on his knees to beg for his life. He had no idea who they were. All he saw were their guns.

"Where's Ramon Guerrero . . . the other man who was here?" Garrett asked.

Before the doctor answered, Alexa came into the room, escorting a frantic woman in a house-dress and apron, who was crying.

"Carlos, thank God you are safe." The woman rushed to her husband's side and fell to her knees, hugging the man who had nearly gotten her killed, all because he wanted to earn extra money working for the cartels.

But Garrett got his answer on where Guerrero had gone when an engine started. And after they heard a loud crash of grinding metal, Kinkaid rushed to the window.

An SUV burst through the garage door and ripped it apart, with Ramon Guerrero at the wheel. It didn't take a genius to figure out that Ramon had given himself an edge—at the expense of his boss, Pérez. And if he was going to run, he didn't want Pérez coming after him for his betrayal. That was why he'd killed the man.

"That's my wife's car. He's stealing my car." The doctor stared at them, like they should care. He actually looked as if he expected them to give pursuit.

"You've got a dead cartel boss on your sofa. A stolen car is the least of your worries, man."

Garrett shook his head and fought a smile as he gave Kinkaid a sideways glance.

"But I had nothing to do with that," the doctor argued. "That man killed him, not me. He shot him in the head twice, in cold blood. You have to believe me."

"Oh, I do. But I don't think you've fully grasped the situation."

"What do you mean?"

"That"—he pointed to the dead man on the couch—"that could've been you and your wife."

The doctor looked stunned as he clung to his sobbing wife, but not half as stunned as when Garrett, Kinkaid, and Alexa turned to go.

"Wait a minute. Are you leaving? The police . . . what do I tell the police?"

"I'm sure you'll think of something. Doing what you do for the cartels, I'm sure you're good at lying to cops," Garrett said as he walked through the foyer on his way out, with Kinkaid and Alexa beside him.

"We've done as much as we can do here," Garrett said.

And as they left out the back of the house, he stopped before they made their exit. He grabbed Kinkaid by his good shoulder.

"It's over, Jackson. Pérez is dead. I know it's not the way you wanted it to end, but there's nothing more for us to do here."

It took Kinkaid a while to respond, but eventually he nodded, and Alexa did the same without saying another word. They had no choice. After Guerrero's gunshots, any neighbors within earshot would have heard the noise and reported it. The police would be coming soon.

Ramon Guerrero hadn't been their target. Like the other men who had dropped their guns and run from the hacienda—not wanting to die for Pérez—Guerrero was no different. They hadn't come for him.

Kinkaid's vendetta was over, and he'd done what he came to Mexico to do. He'd brought down the Pérez cartel, and their actions had cut off the head of the snake. They'd all have to settle for that, but Garrett could tell by the empty look on Kinkaid's face that it hadn't been enough.

From experience, Garrett knew that revenge

didn't always come delivered with a nice tidy bow, just as Alexa had tried to tell him. And no matter how justified, vengeance wouldn't bring the only thing that Kinkaid would've wanted in return—his wife and child back. Their memory would always be tainted by the violence that had ended their lives, and Jackson would have to live with that.

Of all people, he understood Kinkaid's pain and his sacrifice. And Garrett knew the burden of guilt. He had more than his share of ghosts who would haunt him until the day he died. He only hoped that Kinkaid would eventually find peace and learn how to live with an ache that would never go away.

Jackson Kinkaid deserved better.

La Pointe, Wisconsin

Jessie had spent the rest of the morning into the late afternoon locating the few people who had actually reported seeing kids at the DeSalvo place during the week of Angela's murder. And after she'd exhausted those leads, she hit the ones she'd found in the newspaper archives—the colorful rumormongers of the town.

While Chief Cook and Sophia Tanner had been reluctant to talk about the old murder case, the people she'd tracked down were just the opposite. They all wanted to rehash it again, and they even embellished their original stories, probably fueled by the rumors they'd helped spread after things had died down. It was human nature. Everybody wanted their fifteen minutes of fame. And it had been in her best interests to keep them talking.

The few who had officially reported seeing the children to the police were consistent in their descriptions of a dark-haired little girl and a sandy-haired younger boy, while other townspeople ranted about DeSalvo running something illegal at her place. None of what they'd said ended up in Chief Cook's evidence box, and she could see why. It didn't take someone living in La Pointe to realize some folks loved having an audience. And a newcomer to town was gullible enough to listen to whatever they had to say without calling them on their bull.

So what had turned out to be a promising start to her day had ended in frustration by late afternoon. With food to go from Lotta's Lakeside Café on Main Street, near the ferry dock, she unlocked her motel-room door, and after she tossed stuff onto the table, she collapsed on her bed to stare at the ceiling.

She'd hit a dead end, but she still had Sophia Tanner in her sights. And the bastard who had tailed her the other day had gotten better. Earlier, she'd felt him but never actually seen him. If she was going to catch him in the act, she had to get cagey.

But just as she was figuring out how to do that, she got a call on her cell. She got up and grabbed her phone off the table and answered on the third ring.

"Hey there, Harper. What's going on? Great timing, by the way." She ran a hand through her dark hair and paced the room.

"Hey, Jessie. I've got you on speaker because I'm here with Sam," Seth said. "Say hi, Sam."

"Hey, Jess."

"Sam has something you need to hear," he said.

"Shoot, Sammie."

Jessie chewed a hangnail on her thumb. She was so wired, waiting to hear what they had to say, that she stared down at the carpet as she paced, unable to look in any of the mirrors. She was afraid what she might see in her eyes.

"Millstone isn't your father, Jessie. You hear me? I got my lab guys to confirm that. We had to search through evidence, but we found what we needed to make sure. It just never got digitized for the database, but that's fixed now."

Sam's voice got muddled in her head. After her friend had said that the son of a bitch who had tortured her wasn't her father, tears filled her eyes, and she had a hard time breathing. She sank onto her mattress when her legs felt wobbly.

"Oh, my God. Just give me a minute." She sucked air into her lungs like a drowning woman. And when she could finally speak, she said, "Thank you, guys. Not knowing has been killing me. That's good news."

"Yeah, it is. Ruling that bastard out means the odds of your having a brother are pretty good, Jessie." Seth came onto the line and told her what he'd found out. "You'd asked me to look for names and pictures of any boys Millstone might have abducted or killed. Well, I didn't find any. There were names like Cameron and Jamie that I had to chase down, but those were girls."

"Guess that's another good thing," Jessie said. "It means that my brother didn't end up with that scumbag."

"Yeah. I thought that was good news, too, but after I went over my dad's file for the third time, it got me thinking that the copy I had was something Dad had made when he left the force. Whatever I had wasn't what Sam would have if anything got updated after Max retired."

"Oh, my God. I never thought of that, Seth. I just figured after Millstone was killed, the case was done."

"And that would've been possible if the case had been a single homicide, Jessie." This time, it was Sam's voice that broke in. "But with the Millstone case being high-profile, other investigators contributed to the evidence after Seth's father quit the force. And, of course, the news media chased down leads on who Millstone was."

"So the two of you decided to compare notes and look through the updated evidence Sam had? Is that what I'm hearing?"

"Yeah," they said in unison.

"Gosh, I love you guys." Jessie couldn't help it. Even with all the runaround she'd gotten in La Pointe, it was nice to know she had real friends watching her back. "So talk to me. What'd you find out? I'm assuming you didn't call just to say hello."

When she only heard silence on the phone, Jessie couldn't sit anymore. She got off the mattress and paced the floor again. If they were both stalling, she figured it was for good reason.

"Spill it, guys. You're making me nervous."

"Someone had done a more thorough background check on Millstone after he'd been killed. I got this from other detectives who were around back then, working the case. They told me that folks came forward after the news broke. A lot of the calls were phony leads CPD had to chase. It took time to wade through it all, but in the evidence downtown at headquarters, we found a reference to Millstone that we thought you should know. You ready to hear it?"

Jessie didn't answer at first. She took in a deep breath and felt a wave of nausea. She had blocked out so much of that time period from her mind. As a kid, all she wanted to do was be left alone. And for her own sake, the foster-care folks had purposefully kept her isolated from the headline news during that time.

And after she'd gotten older, she had deliberately avoided anything having to do with Millstone, as if it had never happened. She still felt that way, but now she had to know how all this connected to any link she might still have to family.

"Go ahead. I'm ready. Tell me what you found out."

An hour later

After the lengthy call from Sam and Harper, Jessie had a hard time controlling her anger. She tossed her dinner without eating it. And her mind wrestled with the idea of what her next move should be, but all she had on her mind was confronting Chief Cook once and for all.

How much of what Sam and Seth had told her did Cook already know? And why had he made contact with her, only to stonewall her once she got to La Pointe? She knew he'd deliberately lied about there being two DNA samples tested by his state crime lab. Sam had discovered that. Had he also lied about the Tanner interview? She still had missing pieces to the puzzle, but she had one last shot at finding out the truth.

Jessie grabbed her rental-car keys, checked her Colt Python, and put it back in the holster she carried at her waist under her windbreaker. By the time she got outside, the sun had just drifted below the horizon. It would be dark soon.

When she pulled out of the motel parking lot, she might've missed the headlights coming on as she turned toward the police station, but with her hinky radar switched to hyperdrive, she hadn't missed those headlights at all. She'd picked up a tail again. Someone had been following her since she got to the island, and that old hinky vibe had jump-started a whole new surge of adrenaline. With all that was going on, she'd had enough.

As she drove the speed limit, careful not to spook the sneaky bastard, she made a call on her cell.

"This is Jessie Beckett," she said as she looked in her rearview mirror. It was too dark to see a face, but a man was driving the truck that followed her.

"Where are you, Chief Cook?"

"None of your business. You still in town, Ms. Beckett?"

"I thought you'd know that . . . since this is your town, Tobias." Before he found a new way to insult her, she didn't give him a chance. "I have a pretty good idea who killed Angela DeSalvo. And if you have any curiosity at all, you'll meet me in thirty minutes."

She eyed the mirror one more time as she made a turn, with the truck still with her and not far behind.

"Where?"

When she told him, the chief schooled her in how to cuss, but he didn't say no.

"I'll be there in thirty. And you better be on the level, or I'm locking you up and throwing away the key."

With a smile on her face, Jessie ended the call without saying anything more. And when she shifted her gaze to the rearview mirror, the truck was still with her.

If she was going to meet the chief in thirty minutes, she had to move quick.

Thirty minutes later

Right on time, Chief Cook pulled his squad car into Sophia Tanner's driveway. Jessie had parked on the road, not wanting to frighten the woman. Living alone on the island couldn't be easy for a woman. When the chief saw Jessie, he shut his patrol-car door and walked over to where she stood.

"Thought you'd be inside, scaring that poor woman. Are you blowing smoke . . . or do you really know who killed Angela DeSalvo?"

"I have a pretty good idea, but before we go inside, I've got a question for you."

The chief didn't bother to give her the go-ahead. He crossed his arms and cocked his head, waiting for the bullshit to flow, like he was expecting it to. And Jessie sure hoped she wouldn't disappoint him.

She stepped back toward her sedan, twirling her car keys on her finger. "Why did you have someone following me ever since I got to the island? What was *that* about?"

"Following you? What are you talking about?"

When Jessie popped her trunk, she and Chief Cook stared down at a man, tied up hands and feet in Flexicuffs with a gag in his mouth. He was bawling like a baby and was red-faced as a beet. And he didn't have a stitch of clothes on, except for some seriously neon red plaid boxers.

"Now you see, I would've figured this guy for briefs. He one of yours?"

"Jesus, Tyrell, what the hell are you doin' in

there?" Chief Cook glared at the man once his initial shock wore off.

"Yeah, that's his name. Tyrell Hinman. You see? I knew you could help me with this." Jessie fished the man's ID out of her windbreaker pocket. "He's one of your deputies, isn't he? I saw him the day I was at your station. He got me coffee, the sneaky, arrogant, son of a bitch."

"Is that so, Tyrell? Were you following her?" Cook leaned into the trunk and asked the man directly. When the guy only shrugged and had a hard time staring him in the eye, the chief turned to her. "I swear, Jessie. I have no idea why Tyrell would do such a thing, but I'm getting to the bottom of this, so help me God."

Jessie wanted to believe him, but there was still so much more he needed to explain.

"Until you find out what's going on, Tobias, I think I'd leave God out of this."

Once Jessie had gotten a good look at who'd been following her, she recognized him. But the night she'd chased him on foot, he was in civilian clothes, and she hadn't seen his face. Nothing fit until she saw him tonight, after she'd pulled a fast one on him.

She'd run a red light and left Tyrell pinned between two cars. And after she turned a corner and flipped off her headlights, she played cat and mouse with him in the dark. It didn't take much for her to lose him and flip the tables, tailing *him* for a change. After he gave up, he pulled into a parking lot to use his cell phone. That was when she walked up to his car and showed him the business end of her Colt Python.

When she aimed the muzzle square between his eyes, she had one question.

"What are you . . . a boxers or briefs kind of guy?"

Now she had Chief Cook's full attention, even with one of his deputies half-naked in the trunk of her car, all bug-eyed and whining.

"Like I said, I have a pretty good idea who killed Angela, but you and me gotta talk before we go inside. I figure if I give you what you want, maybe you'll give me what I need."

After the chief nodded, she asked, "What do we do with him?"

Chief Cook grimaced and looked down at his deputy, saying, "Tyrell? You're an idiot."

He slammed the trunk closed, with Tyrell yelling and pounding his fists as they talked.

"Why did you lie about there being two DNA samples? Mine wasn't the only one."

The chief's face was dimly lit from Sophia Tanner's porch light, but even in the dark, she saw that she'd surprised him.

"And that other sample had a 95 percent probability of matching mine. Do you have any idea how scared I was that the sample belonged to Danny Ray Millstone? After all he did to me, the idea that he could have been my father tore me up. And you kept your mouth shut even after you admitted checking into the Millstone investigation. Why did you lie about all that?"

"Look . . . you don't understand."

"Apparently, I don't. Explain it to me."

Tyrell had been banging on the trunk until they started talking. When he got quiet, Jessie knew he was listening, too. *The jerk!*

"I *did* look into the Millstone case. And when I made the connection to you, I wanted . . ." Cook stalled and avoided her eyes.

"Wanted what, Tobias?"

"I wanted to be sure before I said anything. I knew that wasn't something you'd want to hear. And speculating about something like that would give you some sleepless nights. I didn't want that for you, but I guess that happened anyway." Cook heaved a sigh. "I reran that unidentified sample through CODIS and NCIC again, but came up dry. That's when I went back to the source. The Chicago PD had the case files, so I put in a request to search for Millstone's DNA the day you got here. I haven't heard back yet, but wait a minute." Cook narrowed his eyes. "You used the word 'scared,' as in past tense. You said you were scared that DNA belonged to Millstone. Do you know something about that DNA I don't?"

"Well, yeah. When I had the same hunch you did, I had Detective Cooper pull the records and check Millstone's DNA, compare it to mine. I found out about that today."

"Guess I don't have your clout with the Chicago PD. I'm still waiting for word." Cook shook his head. "I knew that detective was a friend of yours."

"Okay, I pushed to get that done. And I may have some influence with CPD, but why did you lie about that interview being missing from your murder book? What were you covering up? And why are you protecting that woman in there?"

Jessie pointed toward the Tanner house. With their voices carrying in the night, she saw Sophia Tanner at her window, peeking through the drapes. And when Chief Cook saw her, too, he raised his hands and tried to calm Jessie down.

"Keep your voice down. Please." He shook his head and glanced back at the Tanner house. "I don't know how that interview got misplaced, I swear. I didn't lie when I said I'd seen it. And I wouldn't have marked it on my case map unless we had that interview in hand."

"You'll forgive me if I don't believe you. You

don't exactly have the best track record when it comes to telling me the truth."

"Guess I can understand why you'd think that, but what I've told you is the honest-to-God truth," he said. "And if that unidentified DNA wasn't a match to Millstone, then you've got a brother to find."

"Yeah, I guess I do, but where do I start looking?"

"Let's see if Sophia can help us with that. Maybe all she needs is the right motivation."

When Cook turned toward the house, Jessie stopped him. "Aren't you forgetting something?"

She nudged her head toward the trunk of her car and dangled her keys in front of him. Without a word to her, he grabbed them and liberated Tyrell Hinman. He pulled his half-naked deputy from the trunk and cut him loose with a pocket-knife.

"Get in my squad car and stay there until we're done with Sophia."

"Yes, sir." Tyrell had his head down and didn't look up at either of them. He headed for the passenger seat in the front.

"Oh, hell no. You're ridin' in the back. That's where criminals go, Tyrell."

Jessie couldn't help it. A smile tugged at her lips when she got a glimpse of Tyrell tiptoeing toward the chief's patrol car in his bare feet, but Tobias didn't see any humor in it. He walked with her in silence to the front door of Sophia Tanner's place.

She had a pretty good notion that Chief Cook would finally be honest with her. And if he did that, she might clue him in on who killed Angela DeSalvo.

CHAPTER 19

"What's this about, Tobias? It's kinda late. Can we do this tomorrow at a more civilized hour? I'm having my dinner."

Sophia Tanner stood in her front door, blocking the way into her home. And she was hurling every reason she could think of to avoid what was coming. Tomorrow morning might be more civil, Jessie thought, but nothing about this case would even remotely resemble civilized.

"Sorry, Sophia. This can't wait. May we come in?" Chief Cook didn't wait for her answer but took a step into her home, and she backed away.

"But I . . . I'd really rather not . . ."

When Cook didn't take no for an answer, Jessie was close on his heels and stood by him in the living room as the police chief took charge.

"Do you know any reason why Tyrell Hinman was following Ms. Beckett?"

"Tyrell? I don't know. Why would he? And why are you asking me?" The woman's face looked all pious and indignant, but she had a nervous twitch to her eyes that contradicted everything out of her mouth.

"I'm just gonna say this, so we can cut to the chase." Cook pointed Sophia Tanner to a chair, and said, "You better sit."

"Tobias, you're scaring me. What's this about?" Her voice cracked, and she fanned her face like she was about to faint.

"I asked you this before, but now I've got to know the truth."

"Are you insinuating that I . . ."

"Stop this, Sophia." Cook raised his voice and glared at her. When her eyes grew wide, Jessie knew the chief had her attention. "Just so you know, Tyrell has told me everything. But I told him I wanted to hear your side of it before I pressed charges against the two of you."

Jessie had to admit that Cook had a real folksy way of interrogating that reminded her of old *Columbo* reruns. He laid on a liberal dose of small-town cop and mixed it with street smarts that came from years of experience. He pretended that he knew more than he did to get her to open up. And from what she saw on Sophia Tanner's face, his tactic was working.

"Charges? What charges?" Mrs. Tanner slumped back in her chair and heaved a sigh. "Please don't arrest Tyrell. He only did what I asked him to do."

"I'm listening," Cook said.

"I only wanted to know what she was up to, that's all." Mrs. Tanner finally turned her attention on Jessie. "You're not an investigator helping with an old case. You've got a personal stake in this, don't you?" Mrs. Tanner raised her chin in defiance. "I asked Tyrell to do me a favor. He really didn't do any harm."

"But how did you know I was coming to La Pointe?" Before the woman answered, Jessie cocked her head. "Maybe I should rephrase that. The fact that I was coming here wasn't the important thing. You knew *why* I was coming, didn't you? Tyrell told you about the DNA report from the crime lab. That's what triggered all this, but why was I such a threat to you?"

Jessie had made a leap in logic about the DNA analysis, but it made sense. And when Sophia Tanner didn't correct her, she knew she'd guessed right about how she'd found out about the lab results. But the woman was hiding something more than getting a deputy and former coworker to do her a favor.

"Threat? You're no threat to me. I was just curious, that's all," the woman protested, but Jessie had a hard time believing her. And so did Chief Cook.

"Tyrell tampered with evidence when he took that interview of yours," the chief said, making a leap of his own that surprised Jessie. "I'd seen that original report years ago, but it's gone now. Why did you have him take it from evidence, Sophia?"

"Tyrell had nothing to do with that. I'd taken it years ago, when I worked at the station. I don't want him charged for something I did."

"But why? I mean, you gave that interview. Why hide it now? What was in it that you were so afraid of?" Jessie had to ask the question, but after thinking about Sophia's part in all this, she played a hunch. "You saw the kids at the DeSalvo place. You saw me, didn't you? You were the closest neighbor. What did you see, Mrs. Tanner?"

"My interview didn't have anything in it. I only said what everyone else did. With me living so close, I figured that's what folks would expect. And not saying anything about the children would've raised suspicion."

"I don't believe you. You're hiding something." Jessie had to work hard at keeping her voice calm and steady. All she really wanted to do was yell.

When the woman couldn't look her in the eye and kept her mouth shut, Jessie took a deep breath and tried talking to her another way. She knelt at the woman's feet and touched her hand.

"I had my childhood taken from me . . . by a man who tortured and abused helpless little girls." Jessie's voice cracked. "That man took me from my family, a family I've never known. And all I have left is proof that I have a brother. And I think you know something about what happened to us. Why won't you help me?"

Sophia Tanner put a trembling hand to her lips. And tears rolled down her cheeks.

"I want to help. Believe me, I do. But I just can't."

"You're protecting someone. Why?" Jessie pressed her for more. "You know something about what happened to Angela, don't you?"

"No"—the woman shook her head—"not really."

She'd pushed Sophia Tanner as far as she would go. Jessie saw it in her eyes. The woman was protecting someone very important to her. And no matter what happened because of her meddling, she didn't look as if she'd say anything more unless she was given no choice.

Chief Cook must have realized that, too.

"I know what you're hiding, Sophia." His expression softened, and so did his voice. "You may as well tell us what you know. All I need is a court order, compelling you to provide me a DNA sample. Is that how you want him to find out?"

Sophia Tanner's eyes watered as she gasped. She crossed her arms and rocked where she sat, muttering things Jessie didn't understand.

"Him? Can someone clue me in?" Jessie asked.

Cook didn't answer her. He stared at Sophia, waiting for her to break the strained silence. It didn't take long for that to happen.

"You were right about Tyrell telling me about that DNA. He was just passing the time, thought I'd be interested since I used to be Angela's neighbor. But when he told me, I lost it. I just knew someone would put two and two together. And I couldn't let that happen. I told him what . . . what I did. He was only trying to help me . . . protect someone. It wasn't his fault."

Sophia grasped Jessie's hand and squeezed it. "I'm just so tired. This has been such a burden. I was only trying to . . . do the right thing."

"I can see that, but please . . ." Jessie begged. "I have to know what happened."

"You have to promise me that you'll listen to everything I have to say. Please."

"I promise."

Jessie could've backed off and sat on the sofa, but she didn't want to sever the tie she had to the only woman who might know anything about her brother. She was so close to knowing something real that she felt a mounting ache in her belly when Mrs. Tanner opened her mouth to speak again.

"Angela had always been a little standoffish. Like I'd said before, we were never close. I'd talk to her, but she hardly ever offered anything personal back. It was like she was hiding from something . . . or someone," Mrs. Tanner began. "But one day, a man showed up. I saw him from my bedroom window. He had two children with him. And when he showed, Angela argued with him. They yelled so loud that I almost heard what they said, but they were too far away."

Jessie could have accused her of not reporting vital evidence, but instead of pointing the finger, she focused on the one thing she thought Mrs. Tanner would respond to.

"I bet those kids were scared, seeing them argue like that." Jessie tightened her grip on the woman's hand. "Was I scared, Mrs. Tanner? Was my little brother scared, too?"

"Yes, you were, at first. But when Angela let him into her house, I figured it was a lovers' quarrel, and everything had blown over. She took you kids in, and everything seemed all right."

"But it wasn't all right, was it?"

"No, it wasn't. And I was afraid for you kids. I began to watch that house. Angela's visitor scared me. He never acted like any father I ever saw. He ignored the little boy, but he never let you out of his sight. I thought that was strange."

Jessie shut her eyes, blocking out the images that were flooding her mind, dark memories of Millstone. She had to strain to hear Mrs. Tanner go on.

"Then one day that man's car was gone. I watched and waited to see Angela, but when I saw that precious boy wandering in the field between our two houses without Angela or that man around, I rushed to get him." When she shook her head and dropped her chin, a tear made a glistening trail down her face. "His little pajamas were covered in blood . . . so much blood. And he was hysterical, crying real hard. I knew something terrible had happened."

"Did you call the police?" Jessie turned to Chief Cook. "I thought a yardman had found her and called it in."

Before the chief could speak, Mrs. Tanner broke in.

"I grabbed that boy and held him in my arms until he calmed down. All I could think about was you. I had to know you were all right." She clenched her jaw and took a deep breath before she went on. "But by the time I got to Angela's property, the police were already there, and it looked real bad. I don't know why I did it, but I clung to that little boy. We hid in the bushes, with me rocking him to sleep in my arms. I hid and watched what the police were doing. I swear, I figured you were all right . . . that they had you, but when I read about the murder in the papers, they never mentioned finding a little girl."

"The police were right there. You could've told them what you saw." Although questions flooded Jessie's head, one weighed heavier on her mind. "What happened to the boy?"

It took Mrs. Tanner a long time to answer. She sobbed and looked at Chief Cook, who looked miserable with sympathy for her. Cook knew something about what she was about to say. That was why he'd bluffed her into talking.

"That boy is grown up now. His name is Ethan and he lives in Alaska. He's got a good job, and he's happy." Sophia Tanner's eyes watered again. "I never told him what happened. I just couldn't."

"Why? He had a right to know."

"That boy had a right to a normal life." The woman raised her voice and glared with a newfound fire in her eyes.

When Jessie glanced at Chief Cook with a puzzled look on her face, he obliged her with an answer.

"Ethan Tanner. He's her son," he said.

Jessie collapsed back on her haunches and

pulled her hand from Sophia Tanner's. And without thinking, she stood and looked at every photo the woman had displayed in her living room—seeing her brother's face for the first time.

In one, he had a white communion suit on. In another, he had cap and gown. Every photo told the story of his life as he grew up. He looked happy, and healthy, and whole. Jessie grabbed the most recent photo and held it in her hands. Her tears splashed onto the glass as she memorized his face and traced a finger down his cheek. He did look happy, and normal, and he was everything a little brother should be in a perfect world.

She clutched the framed photo to her chest and shut her eyes, feeling the sting of tears. If Sophia Tanner had gone to the police right away, Jessie might not have become one of Millstone's victims. The police could've followed his trail sooner, but that would have meant Ethan would have grown up in the foster-care system like she had. And he would've suffered through years of therapy like she did, trying to erase the nightmare of witnessing a brutal murder. Sophia Tanner had done the wrong thing, but Ethan looked happy and normal—and loved.

Deep regrets found a dark corner in Jessie's

heart and made the tears come faster, but she had a hard time blaming someone who had raised her brother as if he were her own.

"I'm so sorry, honey. I wish I could have found you, too." Mrs. Tanner's voice broke through Jessie's profound sense of grief.

"I couldn't have children of my own. My husband had left me for someone who could. I felt like such a failure as a woman, but that day I had a little boy in my arms. A beautiful little boy. And it felt so good to hold him and smell his hair and feel his warm skin as he slept. I couldn't give him up. I just couldn't."

"I knew Ethan wasn't your son, Sophia," Chief Cook said. "But you told everyone that a sister you had out of state had died and left him with you. Guess that was a lie."

"I made up a story about having to leave town quickly. One of my sisters had been in a car accident. I told everyone that I stayed to get her affairs in order. So when I came back with Ethan, no one questioned that. And when I adopted him, no one questioned that either."

Jessie kept her back to the woman, holding on to the photo of Ethan as Mrs. Tanner told the rest of her story. When the woman was done, Jessie turned to face her.

"I'd like his address."

This time Sophia stood and shook her head.

"No. That's not a good idea. I don't want him to know who you are."

"What?" Jessie wiped the tears off her face, glaring at the woman who had stolen her family. "He's my brother. I have a right to see him."

"You have to understand. It took years for his nightmares to stop. He'd cry himself to sleep and didn't know why, but he was so little, I figured he'd forget. And eventually he did."

"Trust me, he didn't forget," Jessie argued. "You can't forget something like that. When I went into that house, I knew I'd been there before because I remembered. Flashes hit me, and I knew I'd been there. You don't forget."

"But don't you see, you wouldn't have known that if you hadn't stepped foot into that house again. All that nasty business can become so . . . fresh, like an open sore that won't heal. I'm asking you . . . no, I'm begging you. Forget you ever had a brother. I've been a good mother to him. I'm all the family he needs. He needs to forget more than he needs a sister like . . . you."

Her words hung between them like a toxic cloud. By Sophia Tanner's admission and a 95 percent DNA match, Jessie had a brother. She had finally found her family, but if she showed up on his doorstep, she could ruin his life. That was what it came down to.

Making any attempt to see Ethan Tanner would be a purely self-serving act. Sophia was right. Ethan didn't need to find out he'd witnessed a murder and dredge up the nightmares she knew were only lying beneath the surface.

And he sure didn't need a sister as messed up as she was.

Jessie left Sophia Tanner's house feeling lower and in more emotional turmoil than when she'd walked in. And Chief Cook kept quiet, sensing her frustration. The only concession Mrs. Tanner made was letting Jessie keep the photo of Ethan. She carried it in her hands, held tight to her chest.

"If you want to talk to that boy, you let me know. He's a grown man, old enough to make up his mind if he wants to see his own sister. Just say the word."

Jessie hadn't thought of Ethan's being old enough, but Mrs. Tanner had made a good point. If Jessie cared what happened to her brother, making the decision to see him would take a lot more thought—and a damned good reason.

"Thanks, Tobias. I really appreciate your offer. And what you did in there, I'm grateful for that, too." She sighed and stared up at the night sky. "But if I need to track down my brother, I can do that on my own. That's what I do for a living, remember?"

"You promised to let me know who killed Angela, but I have a pretty good idea."

"Yeah, thought you would." Jessie forced a smile and turned toward him when she got to her car. "When Sophia talked about a man coming to see Angela, I figured you'd do the math. My friend Sam Cooper told me that she dug through the case. And in the updated records, they'd found that Millstone had a sister. And her first name was Angela."

"Well, I'll be."

"They found that out sometime after the case went national, but it never made headline news. Danny Ray stole every bit of limelight the media had. His atrocities were more important than any convoluted family tree with no follow-up interviews when she couldn't be found. Angela had run from her family, but she didn't get away, apparently."

"But if you weren't related to him, how did you and your brother wind up in his car?"

"Sam has a lead on something that happened in Detroit a few days before Angela was murdered, but I don't have my hopes up. She said that when a vagrant woman was arrested for drug possession, she made a claim that someone took her kids. CPD thought she was blowing smoke to distract from her possession charge, but she described the kids. And what she said matched our descriptions, but nothing ever came of it. She never pressed charges, which says it all."

"And since I never got a missing-persons hit on Ethan's DNA through NCIC, I doubt you'll find anything now," Cook said. "But you don't remember anything about where you came from? I can see Ethan not remembering, but you were older."

"No. The only way I survived Millstone was to zone out. It took me years to remember things. And I get flashes from time to time, nightmares mostly."

"I hate to say this, but maybe Ethan can recall something you can't."

"Yeah, maybe. But I can't see using him to find my answers. If there's a chance I could trigger a lifetime of bad memories for him, that would kill me."

"I'm sorry, Jessie. Wish things had turned out better for you, but I appreciate your help on my case. And at least now you know you *have* a brother. That's got to count in the win column."

"Yeah, it does." She nodded and filled her lungs with cool night air. "You're a good man, Tobias, but I've gotta tell ya. I'd never play poker with you." She forced a smile. "See you around."

Jessie got in her car, knowing Chief Cook was right. Finding out she now had a brother living in Alaska counted for a lot. She had ties to the Alaska State Troopers, through retired trooper, Joe Tanu. If she wanted to locate her brother, she could call Joe and find Ethan in a New York minute, but would that be the right thing to do?

Nothing in Jessie's life had *ever* been easy. Easy was for sissies.

Next day

The drive back from Wisconsin would have dragged on forever except that she filled her thoughts with the images of Ethan growing up. She pictured herself at his graduation and imagined whole scenarios in her head where she played the part of his big sister, giving him advice that he'd roll his eyes at.

Filling her mind with those kinds of memories were better than the ones she had—the gaps, the nightmares, and the flashes of new horrors that she knew were coming from Angela DeSalvo's house. Angela had been the only memory she had of a mother, but after she'd learned the truth, those memories would be tainted. The woman had tried to take care of them, but she never got the chance. And Jessie had to remind herself that Angela hadn't done the one thing she should have.

She should have called the police.

By the time Jessie got to Chicago and pulled into the underground parking of Seth's building, she couldn't wait to see Harper. She found her heart racing, just thinking about him. And when she got out of her rental car, she didn't even take her bag. She left it in the car and ran to Seth.

When he answered the door, with Floyd grinning at his feet, she flung herself into his arms and breathed him in.

"Ah, Jessie, I missed you, too. I'm glad you're home." He nuzzled her neck, and she felt his sweet breath on her skin. In his arms, she felt warm and safe—and loved.

"Home." She said the word, getting used to it. "Yeah, I'm home."

When Seth said the word "home," it sounded damned good coming from his lips. It gave her the courage to say what she'd come to tell him.

"I'm moving back to Chicago. And if the offer is still good, I want to make a home . . . with you. I love you, Seth."

He grinned and wrapped her in his arms. "Yeah, the offer's good. Are you kidding? I love you, too, Jess."

Jessie hadn't grasped before how much it meant for her to have a family, but on her drive down to Chicago, she realized she already had one.

"You're all the family I need, Harper."

Flashes of her brother's face melded into the many memories she'd already built with Harper, with more to come. And for the first time in a long while, Jessie was truly happy.

CHAPTER 20

New York City
11:00 P.M.

Garrett had taken his time getting back to New York. He had justified the time by thinking he needed to clear his head, but in truth, he wasn't sure how to do that. Getting over a woman like Alexa Marlowe wasn't intended to be easy.

Riding in the back of a cab, he watched the blur of neon pass his window and barely paid attention to the streets as they went by. Seeing her as a brunette had surprised him. And she'd been fearless going in for Kinkaid, risking her life to save his. Garrett still hadn't gotten used to wrapping up a mission and having her walk out of his life until the next time. Coming back to New York wasn't the same, especially knowing she had taken a few days off to help Kinkaid heal.

The taxi pulled to the curb at the private entrance to his building. With a travel bag over his shoulder, Garrett paid the driver and headed inside. Before he got out his keycard to unlock the door, two men stopped him on the street as the cab pulled away.

"Donovan Cross wants to see you." The man nudged his head toward the curb as a black sedan pulled up. "Now."

One man stood in front of him, the other was at his back. And a third man emerged from the shadows to join them. From what he could tell, all of the men had weapons. And he knew the look. They were ex-military or covert ops. Cross had sent an invitation he wouldn't be able to refuse.

"Lead the way, gentlemen."

Before he got into the vehicle, they searched him for weapons and confiscated a Beretta that he carried in a holster under his suit jacket and the .380 Walther PPK/S that he had strapped to his ankle. Cross's men were quick and efficient. After they'd tossed his bag in the trunk, they opened the back door of the sedan and got in both sides, leaving him in the middle.

Garrett had let his guard down. Alexa had warned him about Cross. He knew something was off, yet he did nothing about it. He thought he'd have time once he got back to home turf, but that wasn't going to happen. For Cross to get this aggressive, he had to have a lot of confidence someone was backing his play. Whatever Donovan Cross was up to, Garrett was about to find out—and no one would have his back.

Forty minutes later

Garrett sat on a wooden chair under a harsh light. He hadn't been blindfolded, and his hands hadn't been tied. He was merely . . . waiting. He sat center stage in an empty warehouse that must have been near the docks. He smelled the faint odor of fuel that mixed with a heady stench coming off the East River.

The men who had taken him stood in the shadows beyond the light, making it hard for him to see them. Only the echo of their footsteps gave them away. And being good operatives, they hadn't talked to him.

"I thought you said Cross would be here," he called out.

When no one answered him, he squinted into the dark, looking for any means of escape, but before he found one, a door creaked open. He saw the shadow of a man in an overcoat eclipse a security light near a side entrance. And he heard the low murmurs of two men talking before one of them walked toward him. When the man came into the light, Garrett recognized him.

"Donovan Cross. I hear you've got ambitions and a touch of job envy," he said.

When he tried to stand, Cross shook his head, and said, "Please . . . sit down." And to the rest of his men, he yelled an order. "Give us privacy, gentlemen. I can take it from here."

Without a word, the three men left them alone in the warehouse. The move for privacy really stumped Garrett. He had no idea what Donovan Cross was up to.

"Why all the secrecy? A little melodramatic, even for you. What do you want, Cross?"

"I don't want anything from you, but I can't speak for everyone. You've made enemies, Garrett. And unfortunately, I'm the messenger."

"Ever hear of e-mail?"

Cross smiled. "You can't walk away from this, I'm afraid."

He looked at his watch and held it up to the light.

"It's almost time." Cross looked at Garrett. "For the record, I didn't want it to come to this, but I don't see any other way. I'm sorry."

Minutes later

Donovan Cross walked out of the warehouse just in time. The blast nearly knocked him off his feet. He'd cut it close. A fireball mushroomed into the night sky, and a series of explosions rumbled through the old warehouse, grinding metal and toppling steel as it went.

Garrett Wheeler hadn't been ready for his exit, but for the sake of the Sentinels, Cross had no other choice. While the building burned and sirens of emergency crews coming to the scene blared in the distance, Cross made a phone call.

"It's done. You see it?"

He knew the man was watching from a safe distance, a bird's-eye view.

"Yes, I do. And after you take over Wheeler's job permanently, you can thank me later."

The man ended the call, leaving Cross to watch the aftermath of what he had done. Now it was his turn to make his own enemies. And he had no doubt that Alexa Marlowe would top that list.

Somewhere in the Caribbean

Instead of going back to New York after Mexico, Alexa traveled with Jackson to the place he called home. Years ago, he'd bought a small private island in the Caribbean, using the money he had stolen from the cartels over the years. Most of his cash had wound up in the hands of charities, like the missionary school in Haiti run by his good friend, Sister Kate, the woman he'd rescued in Cuba. Kate hadn't known about his Robin Hood gig either. And as far as Alexa knew, the nun *still* didn't.

Drug cartels made for dangerous victims, but they never reported Kinkaid's outlandish and resourceful thefts because he was too good to get caught. And Kinkaid definitely knew how to keep a secret.

That's what he'd been doing before she hooked up with him in Cuba. Back then, Alexa had thought he was only a mercenary who sold his services to the highest bidder, and he'd never told her the truth until he'd brought her to his home and shared his life with her for the first time.

Maybe Kinkaid's coming clean meant he cared what she thought of him. She hoped she was right about that.

Jackson lived modestly. He had a dock with a boat to get around. And his home was a small place on the beach. He had all the basic amenities, but he didn't live in a lavish style, considering what he did for a living. But as simple and beautiful as his home was, Kinkaid had secret storage under his floorboards and in walls where he kept his stash of weapons, money, fake IDs, and anything else he'd need to disappear in a hurry.

Some things never changed.

"We should change your dressing and check out your shoulder. How does it feel?" she asked. When he gestured for her to sit next to him in the sand, she did.

"I'm good." He nodded. "It feels better."

Kinkaid had been sitting alone on the beach in cutoff jeans, staring out toward the ocean. His long dark hair looked finger combed by the warm sea breeze. And even though his face was still bruised, the sun had colored his skin to a rich brown, masking the torture he had endured in Mexico. When Jackson had gotten up that morning, he had gone off alone without saying a word. After Alexa had awakened to an empty bed, she'd gone searching for him, to find out why.

"You're awfully quiet this morning," she said. Forcing a faint smile, she braced for the worst. "You want to talk about anything?"

When he didn't answer right away, she replayed every moment she'd spent with him, alone on his island. The days they'd spent together, while he healed, had been quiet, peaceful ones, filled with the sounds of lapping waves, exotic birds flitting from branch to branch in the lush green canopy overhead, and moonlit walks on the beach.

The first time they'd made love, it had been filled with urgent need that they both shared. Flashes of that memory would always be with her. And she remembered crying when it was over. The rush of emotion had overwhelmed her. Her being together with him, finally and completely, had been the culmination of years of her intense, one-sided attraction.

And last night they had made love on a blanket under the stars. Even though a bottle of chilled white wine had played a part in their loss of inhibition, the moon shining down on their bare skin had been magic. Jackson had undressed her. And his strong hands and warm mouth had stirred a passion she'd never felt before.

She never felt closer to him than she had last night, and she'd been certain that he felt the same, until this morning, after she'd awakened alone.

"There's something I want you to do with me," he told her. "You may not want to. And I'll understand if you can't . . ."

Before he finished, she let him off the hook and stroked his windswept hair. He'd become her addiction, and she couldn't resist touching him.

"What is it?" she asked.

He swallowed hard as he stared at the ocean,

but eventually he turned toward her, giving her his full attention with his intense green eyes.

"I have the ashes of my wife and child here on the island with me. I've kept them here. And I haven't been able to let them go." When his words caught in his throat, and his eyes filled with tears, he reached for her hands and held them in his. "But I think with you here, I can do that now. Will you . . . help me?"

Alexa had no words. She pulled him into her arms with tears of her own rolling down her cheeks. She knew how hard it would be for him to finally let go. And since she'd never been the type who wore rose-colored glasses, she also knew Jackson Kinkaid was far from whole.

But he'd asked her to help him deal with his grief. And that had to count for something.

Alexa woke up the next morning, listening to the sounds of Kinkaid's heart beating in the quiet. It was a sound she could get used to. Feeling his warm bare skin next to hers was addictive.

She ran a finger through the curly hairs of his chest. And when she saw his strong hands lying across his stomach, she remembered how gentle they had been when he spread the ashes of his wife and child in the ocean at dusk last night. The ebb and flow of the salt water at their bare feet had reflected the brilliant orange of the sunset. That memory would stay with her forever. He said his good-byes, as he spoke aloud to them, making her a part of his ceremony. And when it was over, she felt as if she'd lost her family, too.

They didn't make love last night. Without saying a word, they held each other and listened to the waves edging the shore until it lulled them both to sleep.

By morning, she could have stayed in bed forever, but when her cell phone rang, she felt compelled to answer it. Being with Kinkaid felt like she'd dropped off the planet. That was a good thing. She'd never felt so relaxed, but when her phone rang, she had to answer it.

"Hello."

"Alexa, it's me."

She recognized Jessie's voice. She wasn't used to having a partner as aloof as Jessie was. So for her to call out of the blue, it took Alexa by surprise.

"You still on your trip?" Alexa kept her voice low as she left the bedroom, trying not to wake Jackson. She slipped into a light robe and went outside to walk the beach.

"No, I'm heading back now. Harper says hello."

Alexa grinned. "I knew he had something to do with your great escape. You get things taken care of? Is everything okay?"

With a strange silence on the phone, Alexa waited for Jessie to answer.

"Yeah, I guess. But I've got something to tell you."

"Oh?"

"I made a decision, and it feels right."

"What did you decide, Jess?"

Alexa braced herself. She had no idea what Jessie would say.

"I decided to move back to Chicago. Seth asked me to move in with him, and I'm gonna do it."

"That's . . . great, I think. You still gonna be my partner?"

"Yeah, sure. Of course." Jessie cleared her throat. "Who's gonna watch your ass if it's not me?"

"Good point." Alexa grinned. "Well, I'm happy for you."

"What do you think Garrett will say? Both of you recruited me. And I think he wanted me to like New York more than I did. What can I say? I'm a Midwest girl."

Alexa hated to think about Jessie moving back to Chicago just as they were becoming closer as partners, but she heard the joy in her voice and knew she was doing the right thing.

"You leave Garrett to me. I got you into this. And I'm glad you're still my partner. When will you get back to New York?"

"Tomorrow. I'll call you. We've got catching up to do."

"Uh, I won't be there. I took a personal trip of my own, but I'll see you soon, okay?"

"Yeah, sure." Before Jessie ended the call, she said, "Hey, Alexa? I just wanted you to know that I'm happy you recruited me. Working a real job for Garrett and having Seth in my life, I feel like I've turned a corner, you know?"

Alexa knew about turning corners. "Yeah, I do. And I'm glad you're happy, Jessie. See you soon."

As she walked along the shore, Alexa turned toward Jackson's house, feeling the ocean breeze on her face. Hearing Jessie sounding so happy had been contagious. When her phone rang again, so soon after her partner's call, she had a grin on her face when she answered.

"What did you forget now, partner?"

She heard a soft sniffle on the phone, and a woman came on the line, "Honey, is that you, Alexa?"

She recognized the voice of Tanya Spencer.

"Yeah, Tanya, it's me. What's up?"

"I've got some bad news, baby girl. And this time, it's for real." From the sounds of it, Tanya was crying. And it took a lot to make that woman break down. "You've got to come home, honey. I can't do this without you."

"Talk to me, Tanya. Tell me what happened."

New York City
Upper East Side
The next night

Garrett's memorial service was in three days, but Alexa had come back early to help Tanya with the arrangements. Because of the severity of the explosion, his body had never been found. They'd only found enough DNA to make ID, but that was all they had.

Alexa thought about the lie Donovan Cross had once told her about Garrett being dead. Had Donovan Cross been predicting an outcome he would have something to do with, or had his lie been a coincidental guess? In the covert world she lived in, coincidences were always suspicious. And that left her raging against the man who had taken Garrett's job—and most probably, his life.

Jackson had come back to New York with her. He was sleeping in her bed, still weak from his ordeal. But when she couldn't sleep, she got up and slipped on a robe before she crept into her living room to pour a shot of single-malt scotch. Sitting in the dark, she drank and lost count of how many she'd had as she stared out her window to the park across the street.

She couldn't get her head wrapped around Garrett being dead. His smile, his face, his eyes were still fresh in her memory. How could his death be real? And yet this time she felt it was.

When her glass was empty, she went to refill it, but a shadow under her threshold caught her eye. And when she heard a soft swish and saw something slide under her front door, she went for her gun.

Armed, she kept the light off and reached for the door handle. Before she opened it, she listened for any sounds coming from the hallway. When she didn't hear anything, she flung open the door and aimed her weapon.

No one was in the hall, but someone had definitely been there.

She stepped back inside to find an envelope on her floor. After she flipped the dead bolt, she picked up the note, using her robe to hold it, not wanting to contaminate any evidence if it came to that. She dropped the note on her kitchen counter and used the end of a pencil to open it.

When she recognized the handwriting, she gasped and stared at the message, having trouble breathing. When she finally collapsed onto her sofa, she held the note in trembling fingers, careful to preserve the paper as much as she could.

From what she saw, the message was from Garrett.

Alexa—

I couldn't leave without telling you what happened. I'm alive, Alexa. I didn't die in that blast, no matter what proof they come up with.

I don't know what role Cross played in this but know that he had a choice. He could've killed me, the way he was probably ordered to do. But if you say anything about getting this letter from me, or that I'm still alive, they will hunt me down and go after Cross, too.

There's still a lot I don't understand. And I don't fully appreciate what Cross did, but maybe that will come in time. Thanks to Donovan Cross, I have a chance to make a new life for myself if I want it.

Don't make the same mistake Jackson did, by clinging to the past. Make a future that's worth holding on to. You always deserved better than I could ever give you.

    Know that I will always love you,
    Alexa. Always.

       Garrett

When she'd finished reading, she felt the cool trail of tears on her cheeks. She hadn't realized she'd been crying. Garrett was alive? How was that possible? Her emotions ran the gamut from intense anger to relief that he might be all right— "might" being the operative word. She had no way to be sure.

It was comforting to believe Garrett had actually written the message, but she didn't trust Donovan Cross. The personal script in Garrett's handwriting, and delivered to her door in cryptic fashion, had been a nice touch. The words sounded like him, especially the personal part about Kinkaid, but she had no way of knowing for sure. Paranoia was a hazard of the job.

And not knowing the truth, one way or the other, hurt just as much as thinking he was dead.

Given the covert life she had made with the Sentinels—recruited by Garrett Wheeler himself— the truth was hard to recognize, even when it came in the form of a handwritten note from a man she would never forget.

Sentinels' Headquarters
Next morning

Alexa held her head high as she walked down the corridor to Garrett's . . . to Donovan Cross's office. She braced for the flood of emotion she knew she'd feel. Imagining someone else behind Garrett's desk would be a shock, especially now that she'd have to accept that Garrett was really gone from her life.

She'd wanted to believe that he hadn't died in that dock explosion. And the pain of her grief had been tempered by the hope that the message from him had been real, but she didn't want to play the part of a fool—*Donovan Cross's fool*.

If Garrett had a second chance at a normal life—knowing that returning to his covert world would be dangerous for him and the people he loved—would he take it? If he was alive, would he want his old life back, the one that had been stolen from him? Garrett had always been a fighter. She couldn't see him severing ties to a life he'd worked hard to build, not willingly.

The way she saw it, Donovan Cross and the men behind him had orchestrated a clever coup to eliminate Garrett. And the coup de grâce to put her out of her misery over his sudden departure had been that message. Maybe they thought it would shut her up and quell any curiosity she would have over what had happened to Garrett.

Alexa knew she had a choice to walk away and give up the life or stay put and keep an eye on Cross. With her partner Jessie so happy, the decision she'd made to stick hadn't been difficult. Someone had to watch Jessie's back, especially with the double-dealing Donovan Cross at the helm. If Alexa believed what was in Garrett's note, Cross might have saved his life, but the man was also working for the faction within the Sentinels that had ordered a hit on him.

How could she trust someone who played both ends to his advantage without a semblance of guilt or bad conscience?

She barged into his office to see Cross was on the phone, dressed in a sharp pin-striped navy suit with red power tie, looking impressively dapper. When he saw her, he ended the call in a hurry.

From the look on his face, Donovan Cross had been waiting for her.

"Ah, Marlowe. It's good to see you. How was Mexico?" The man didn't smile. He wanted her to know that nothing had escaped him. "Please . . . sit."

"Aren't you going to tell me how sorry you are about Garrett?" Alexa ignored his invitation to make herself comfortable. She'd never feel comfortable with this man.

"Yes, of course. That goes without saying," Cross said. A corner of his lip curved into a faint show of smugness. "Sorry for your loss."

"I'm having a serious déjà vu moment, hearing you say that. If this whole spy game thing falls through, you could always make a living as a gypsy, telling fortunes." She crossed her arms and glared at him. "Your ability is uncanny. When you first told me about Garrett dying, had that been a prediction . . . or a promise?"

"Neither, but I doubt you'll believe me."

"Now you're a mind reader. Truly amazing." She raised her chin and locked her gaze on the man behind the desk, Garrett's desk. "If I find out you had anything to do with what happened to him, there won't be a place you can hide."

Alexa didn't wait for his clever comeback. She wouldn't give him the satisfaction. She'd delivered the message she'd come to say. And she'd had her fill of smug.

"Are you quitting, Marlowe?" he asked, calling after her. "Because if you are, that would be a pity. I was really hoping we could work together."

"Quitting? Not hardly." She glared at him over her shoulder as she left. "Over your dead body. And I mean that."

Walking out of Cross's office, Alexa had a sly smile on her face. The word "quit" wasn't in her vocabulary—not today. She had no idea what Cross's agenda was, but she had every intention of finding out.

She'd do it for Garrett.

MASTERWORKS OF
GRIPPING SUSPENSE FROM

JORDAN DANE

NO ONE HEARD HER SCREAM
978-0-06-125278-5

They never found her sister's body, but Detective Rebecca Montgomery knows her murderer is still out there. In the five months since Danielle went missing, there have been two more brutal abductions.

NO ONE LEFT TO TELL
978-0-06-125375-1

The body of a brutally slain man is found on the holy grounds of a chapel. Detective Raven Mackenzie and her partner uncover the dead man's connections to a powerful female crime boss, and her mysterious head of security who is the prime suspect.

NO ONE LIVES FOREVER
978-0-06-125376-8

Jasmine Lee needs Christian Delacorte's help freeing her kidnapped lover, a powerful mogul linked to Chicago's underworld. Christian doesn't trust her, but Jasmine entices him to leave behind the woman he loves, Detective Raven Mackenzie, to help her.

And don't miss

EVIL WITHOUT A FACE
978-0-06-147412-5

THE WRONG SIDE OF DEAD
978-0-06-147413-2

THE ECHO OF VIOLENCE
978-0-06-147414-9

RECKONING FOR THE DEAD
978-0-06-196969-0

Visit www.AuthorTracker.com for exclusive
information on your favorite HarperCollins authors.

Available wherever books are sold or please call 1-800-331-3761 to order.

DAN 0611

New York Times Bestselling Author

FAYE KELLERMAN

FALSE PROPHET

978-0-06-199933-8

When Lilah Brecht is beaten, robbed, and raped in her own home, L.A.P.D. Detective Peter Decker finds it hard to put too much credence into the victim's claims that she has psychic powers that enable her to see the future. But when Lilah's dark visions turn frighteningly real, Decker's world is severely rocked.

THE BURNT HOUSE

978-0-06-122736-3

A small commuter plane crashes into an apartment building. Among the dead inside the plane's charred wreckage are the unidentified bodies of four extra travelers. And there's no sign of an airline employee whose name was on the passengers list.

THE MERCEDES COFFIN

978-0-06-122737-0

Lieutenant Peter Decker resents having to commit valuable manpower to a cold case, but when the retired detective who originally investigated the murder case commits suicide, Decker realizes something evil has returned.

BLINDMAN'S BLUFF

978-0-06-170241-9

Peter Decker is summoned to investigate the brutal murders of a billionaire philanthropist, his wife, and four employees. At the same time a chance meeting puts Decker's wife, Rina Lazarus, directly into the path of the relentless killers.

Visit www.AuthorTracker.com for exclusive
information on your favorite HarperCollins authors.

Available wherever books are sold or please call 1-800-331-3761 to order.

FK1 0411

PASSION
Intrigue
ADVENTURE
and
Suspense

from *New York Times* bestselling author

ELIZABETH LOWELL

DEATH ECHO
978-0-06-166442-7

Emma Cross abandoned the tribal wars of CIA life for a position with an elite security firm. Now she's tracking a yacht with a lethal cargo that can destroy a major American city.

BLUE SMOKE AND MURDER
978-0-06-082986-5

When a string of ominous events culminates in a threat to her life, Jill Breck turns to security consultant Zach Balfour to help her unmask a ruthless killer.

INNOCENT AS SIN
978-0-06-082984-1

Although suspicious of each other, private banker Kayla Shaw and landscape painter Rand McCree realize they need each other as the violence of the past erupts in the present. And now innocence alone will not be enough to keep Kayla Shaw alive . . .

THE WRONG HOSTAGE
978-0-06-082983-4

Grace Silva clawed her way out of poverty to become one of the most respected judges on the federal bench. Now her teenage son is in the hands of a desperate and bloodthirsty criminal—and Grace is forced into a shadow world where laws don't exist.

Visit www.AuthorTracker.com for exclusive
information on your favorite HarperCollins authors.

Available wherever books are sold or please call 1-800-331-3761 to order.

LOW1 1110

Masterworks of crime fiction from
New York Times bestselling author

LAURA LIPPMAN

EVERY SECRET THING

978-0-06-050668-1

Two little girls are about to make a disastrous decision that will change their lives—and end another's. Seven years later, another child goes missing in a disturbingly familiar scenario.

THE LAST PLACE

978-0-380-81024-6

A single common thread to five senseless, unsolved murders is beginning to emerge and leads a disgraced p.i. to the remote corners of Maryland in search of a psychopath.

IN A STRANGE CITY

978-0-380-81023-9

On the night of the anniversary of Edgar Allan Poe's birthday, a mysterious caped figure visiting his grave is felled by an assassin's bullet.

THE SUGAR HOUSE

978-0-380-81022-2

A year-old supposedly solved murder case is turning up newer, fresher corpses and newer, scarier versions of Baltimore's abandoned Sugar House Factory.

Visit www.AuthorTracker.com for exclusive information on your favorite HarperCollins authors.

Available wherever books are sold or please call 1-800-331-3761 to order.
LL2 1207